THE
RUSSIAN

THE
RUSSIAN

BEN COES

ST. MARTIN'S
PRESS
New York

First published in the United States by St. Martin's Press, an imprint of St. Martin's Publishing Group

THE RUSSIAN. Copyright © 2019 by Ben Coes. All rights reserved. Printed in the United States of America. For information, address St. Martin's Publishing Group, 120 Broadway, New York, NY 10271.

www.stmartins.com

Designed by Steven Seighman

The Library of Congress Cataloging-in-Publication Data is available upon request.

ISBN 978-1-250-14079-1 (hardcover)
ISBN 978-1-250-14081-4 (ebook)

Our books may be purchased in bulk for promotional, educational, or business use. Please contact your local bookseller or the Macmillan Corporate and Premium Sales Department at 1-800-221-7945, extension 5442, or by email at MacmillanSpecialMarkets@macmillan.com.

First Edition: July 2019

10 9 8 7 6 5 4 3 2 1

For James Gregory Smith

It was a mistake in the system; perhaps it lay in the precept which until now he had held to be uncontestable, in whose name he had sacrificed others and was himself being sacrificed: in the precept, that the end justifies the means.

—Arthur Koestler, *Darkness at Noon*

PROLOGUE

118 Partridge Lane, N.W.
Palisades
Washington, D.C.

Rob Tacoma sped the Italian sports car across downtown Washington, D.C. It was a balmy evening in early spring, cooler than usual, and the sky was filled with stars and the occasional roar of a jet overhead, descending into Reagan National Airport. The lights of the capital city this Friday evening were like diamonds, glittering from every direction. Tacoma had the roof of the Huracan Spyder down and the wind blew his long dirty-blond hair back and tousled it. The engine revved loud enough for pedestrians along Wisconsin Avenue to turn their heads, though it was a tempered, frustrated growl by the 630-horsepower engine, for Tacoma stayed within ten miles per hour of the speed limit. He crossed through the campus of Georgetown University, where students watched the sleek vehicle, and its driver, as it purred down one of the cobblestone alleys on campus. He took a side route down to Canal Road, along the Potomac, and opened it up a little, finding 100 mph while at the same time keeping in check and not creating any risk for the cars he was weaving by on the busy road. He took a right on Arizona and found his way to a residential street, an address north of Georgetown, a neighborhood of simple, Colonial-style homes, in a part of Washington called Palisades.

The director of the Central Intelligence Agency, Hector Calibrisi, had given Tacoma the address. He was to meet a man named Billy Cosgrove—an operator just back from the Middle East. Like Tacoma, he was an ex–Navy SEAL, but Cosgrove had stayed in government, and was now the Pentagon's top exfoliation man in the thousand-square-mile territory bordering the Khyber Pass, where Pakistan met Afghanistan. He ran all kill teams in-theater. He liked two-man teams. Occasionally, if the target required an extra layer of manpower, Cosgrove went along.

Or at least he used to. The CIA had recruited Cosgrove for a different job. Tacoma too. They would be working together. A two-man team. It would be their first meeting.

Tacoma parked the car in the driveway, next to a maroon Chevy Silverado pickup. He walked to the front door and rang the doorbell. Tacoma waited, listening for footsteps, but he heard nothing. After a few moments, he rang it again.

Tacoma reached for the doorbell a third time, then stopped before pressing the button. He remained silent and still for a dozen seconds. He smelled the faintest trace of chemicals, a smoky aroma of petrolate. He glanced at Cosgrove's pickup. Tacoma removed a pick-gun from his pocket and put it against the lock and pressed the button. A small alloy pin extended from the device and found its way into the keyhole. A few seconds later, the lock clicked open. Tacoma opened the door and slowly pushed the door in.

He said nothing as he stepped inside the house.

The entrance hallway was empty except for a few cardboard boxes stacked against a bare wall. He walked into Cosgrove's home.

He shut the door gently and looked around. The entrance hallway was dark and it was hard to see anything. He looked into a room off the hallway. There was enough light from outside to illuminate the room. He saw several large cardboard boxes stacked up, a leather chair, and a rolled-up carpet. Cosgrove was a man who had never unpacked.

The house was a picture of divorce, the result of trying to build a family inside the life of an operator. The fruits of Cosgrove's sacrifice to his country.

Though all was still, the scene had the sense of prior chaos.

After a few moments, Tacoma became aware of a light flickering at the end of the hallway. He walked toward it and came to a set of stairs. But what he thought was the flickering of a light was something altogether different.

There were lights on upstairs. The flickering was caused by something twirling slowly in the air at the bottom of the stairs, causing the light to undulate, light then dark, as it spun slowly around in a makeshift hanging ground.

He looked up. Strung up from the ceiling, by a rope around the neck, was Cosgrove.

Cosgrove's face was beet red, his eyes were shut and badly bruised, his face caked in dried blood. A long iron railroad spike was nailed completely through his chest. His shirt and everything below were drenched in red.

Tacoma looked up at Cosgrove with a feeling of utter horror, a feeling, even, of fear. He had killed many men and he'd seen many men die, but he felt, in that moment, as if he was looking into the eyes of the devil himself.

Tacoma removed his cell and dialed Hector Calibrisi. As he pressed the button for speed dial, he forced himself to look up at Cosgrove's face. It was badly beaten. There had been a fight.

The floor felt sticky beneath his shoes. He looked down and registered a wet, glassy sheen of liquid. A pool of blood covered the floor, and Tacoma suddenly realized he was standing in the middle of it.

He studied the growing pool of crimson. He felt paralyzed. For several seconds, he had a hard time breathing. He remained still and, as he waited for Calibrisi to answer, checked his weapons.

Tacoma knew Cosgrove's wife was remarried and lived with their two young children in Atlanta. Tacoma would never wish divorce on anyone, but as he looked up at Cosgrove's swollen face, he was glad he was the one—and not Cosgrove's wife or children—who had found him.

"What is it?" said Calibrisi.

"Cosgrove is dead," said Tacoma as he stared at the steel spike that was stabbed into the center of Cosgrove's chest.

"*What?*"

"Billy Cosgrove, the guy you sent me to meet. I'm at his house."

There was a long pause. Through the phone, Tacoma could hear the din of conversation at a restaurant in the background.

"Say that again, Rob," Calibrisi whispered.

"He's hanging by a rope," said Tacoma. "They hung him by the rafters and stabbed him with a spike."

"Don't touch him," said Calibrisi. "*And for chrissakes, get out of the goddam house right now!*"

Tacoma saw movement. He looked up past Cosgrove's dangling corpse to the stairwell that ran up straight to the second floor. He hung up the cell and pocketed it, then stepped behind Cosgrove to the base of the stairs. It was just a patch of light—or darkness—a flutter in his peripheral vision.

Tacoma knelt. He removed a gun from beneath his armpit, a P226R, with a custom-made, snub-nose alloy suppressor screwed into the muzzle. Tacoma moved to the stairs, stepping around the dangling corpse, which continued to slowly turn and create a prism of patterns across the wall, and across Tacoma's face as he moved up the dark stairwell.

THE
RUSSIAN

CHAPTER 1

Saint-Tropez
France
Three Days Ago

Tacoma took the RISCON Gulfstream G150 across the ocean and landed in Nice at 4 P.M. local time. He rented, with an anonymous Mastercard, a Ducati 1199 Panigale and took it at a furious clip down the coast of France to Saint-Tropez, along the D559, which zigged and zagged above the rocky Mediterranean coastline, like a rattlesnake on the side of a steep cliff. It was a sun-filled day and the waning bright light wreaked havoc on the roadway, blinding Tacoma for moments at a time as the light hit the tinted visor of the helmet, a black and silver Reevu MSX1, yet he pushed the Ducati to 156.7 mph, screaming into turns no sane man would take at 80. He slowed as he saw the outline of Saint-Tropez in the distance, cutting right onto a road called Boulevard des Sommets, which led through a pretty golf course. After a few winding country roads into the hills, Tacoma saw guards at the end of a driveway. He didn't acknowledge them, as if he belonged, and they did nothing. He pulsed the bright yellow Ducati past the guards and up a steep hill, then pulled up in front of the crowded, brightly lit château, uninvited. He climbed off the bike and removed the helmet.

Tacoma was in a blue blazer with white piping along the edges. Beneath he wore a red T-shirt and white jeans. He had on a pair of Adidas running shoes.

He cut around into the backyard of the beautifully kept, sprawling limestone mansion built in the 1700s. Down a gravel walkway that led from the terrace, he walked through a sweeping garden of perfectly manicured boxwoods and wild bluffs of lavender, now at the seasonal apex of their purple-colored beauty. Ahead stood a large white tent, filled with people.

Music could be heard from inside the tent along with the sound of conversation, laughter, and celebration. Somewhere there was a band—and Tacoma entered the tent with his eyes scanning.

Tomorrow, the vows would be taken in the chapel, a small, pretty stone and brick structure, built by hand along with the villa, which loomed now behind Tacoma, back behind the geometric green gardens lit by lanterns in the dusk.

This was a celebration. A rehearsal dinner for the daughter of a billionaire, a man, in fact, worth more than $10 billion. It was one of the man's many properties. She was his only daughter—the man had three sons—and her rehearsal dinner would cost him more than $2 million.

Much less than RISCON's fee, a charge being footed by the father of one of the bridesmaids.

The temperature was in the seventies and there were no clouds in the sky. In the distance, the dark blue waters of the Mediterranean glimmered beneath an early evening that was painted tangerine, black, silver, and blue. Yachts were visible as small white appurtenances and appeared as if they weren't moving, as if placed there by a small paintbrush in the hands of a master in an Impressionist painting of striking beauty.

Beneath the large white canvas tent, the rehearsal dinner was well under way. Several hundred people were there, spread out at big tables, men, women, and children, all dressed in stylish clothing, casual but neat. This was the highest echelon of society.

Tacoma knew no one at the rehearsal dinner, yet he soon blended into the alcohol-infused anarchy of the party.

He found a seat at a long, fancifully accoutered dining table, with a white tablecloth, crystal stemware, and beautiful women in low-cut dresses. The men were in button-downs and casual linen and khaki pants, and were, like the women, tan and good-looking.

According to the report, all the bridesmaids were from England. One was royalty, and all but one were the daughters of privilege, including the daughter of his client, who was seated next to the bride-to-be.

The table was packed. The lighting was low. The sound of music from another part of the estate whistled above conversation and laughter.

The château was located in the hills above Saint-Tropez. The meal was prepared by Yves Soucant, considered the best chef in France.

Tacoma's dirty-blond hair was brushed back over a thick cowlick that jutted up slightly at his forehead, parted to the left, dangling Down to the lower ends of his ears. His face was tan. He was clean-shaven, with a sharp nose and big lips. Tacoma was thick and athletic, all muscle. The blazer pressed out, a little tight, accentuating Tacoma's body.

RISCON had been approached through MI6 about the project.

This individual—the client—had received a call from a high-level SAP executive whose daughter had been pawned—that is, conned and robbed by a very adept thief who'd already stolen millions from women across Europe and the United States.

RISCON had been hired to penetrate the wedding and take action on a charming twenty-five-year old Dubliner with dashing Irish looks and swagger. He was at the wedding with one of the bridesmaids, the client's daughter. His name was Jonathan Greene, but Greene was a fraud, a serial scam artist who'd run through Vienna, Amsterdam, Paris, San Francisco, and Dallas, and was now preying upon London. His methods were textbook and well executed. Get women to fall in love, propose marriage, then, in the interim period between engagement and wedding, steal millions.

According to the report RISCON had done upon being hired, the man, Jonathan Greene, was engaged to two different women in London, and had already pilfered more than nine hundred thousand dollars from the client's daughter. His basic strategy was simple. Can I borrow a hundred dollars? Write me a check. Greene would then write "thousand dollars" after the "one hundred" and add a few zeros.

Nobody seemed to notice until after Greene had moved on to another city, another country, another woman. He left little trace.

RISCON took on the job based on its standard fee structure. A $10 million monthly retainer was required for a minimum of four months; oftentimes RISCON's actions would lead to counteractions and their continued involvement would be necessary. After the retainer, RISCON proposed fees and such things as per diem, based upon the feasibility of the mission. The harder the objective, the higher the fee. Hiring RISCON wasn't cheap.

In this case, if RISCON succeeded in removing the con artist, an $8 million bonus was to be wired immediately. It wasn't the highest of RISCON's success fees, but it wasn't the lowest either.

The client, a New York City–based oil trader, had agreed to it immediately. He didn't care what it cost to save his daughter from a scoundrel.

Tacoma ate ravenously but didn't drink anything except water. He made small talk with a middle-aged couple from London.

The wedding party took limousines to a nightclub in downtown Saint-Tropez, Les Caves.

At Les Caves, Tacoma found himself seated in a big leather booth. He started talking to a girl in the wedding party near the bar. She was black and beautiful, had straight jet-black hair, and wore a sheer pink dress. Tacoma and the woman talked for almost an hour, and normally he would've been interested in her except he was working. However, he used her interest in him and soon he was in the same booth as the target, Greene.

Someone made a toast and pretty soon everyone was taking turns.

"To Thomas and Lizzy," said one of the bridesmaids in a clipped English accent. "This rehearsal dinner is just so superb and you two are the most beautiful couple ever. *Hear hear!*"

In the leather booth, Tacoma was seated beside a young blonde in a white dress. Her hair was curly and she had a British accent. Their legs were pressed against each other and she kept looking over at Tacoma, though she never introduced herself. Her dress was short, at the top of her thighs, and her legs were tan. Tacoma knew many models, and she was as perfect as any he'd seen. He saw a man across the table, a Brazilian whom he recognized, a soccer player.

The toasts went on forever. Eventually, Tacoma watched as Greene stood up at the far side of the table.

The lights were dim.

At some point her hand went down, beneath the table, to Tacoma's knee.

She rubbed his thigh softly for several minutes, then turned, speaking to him for the first time.

"My yacht is down the street," she said in a pretty British accent. "But we'll have to be careful. I don't want my husband to find out."

Tacoma tracked Greene's movement, a weaving, drunken gait toward the restrooms. After Greene went out of view, Tacoma stood up and moved along the same path Greene had just taken. He moved slowly, stopping near the bar and glancing about, buying time. By the time Tacoma reached the restroom, Greene was drying his hands at the sink on the far side of the dimly lit, marble-walled bathroom. They were alone.

As Tacoma shut the door behind him, he flipped the lock, then stepped toward the sink, meeting Greene as he was leaving.

"Excuse me," said Tacoma.

"Perfectly all right," Greene said in an aristocratic British accent.

"Jonathan, right?" said Tacoma enthusiastically.

Greene's face took on a horrified look, but he hid it well, and extended his hand.

"Good to see you again," said Greene, smiling. He reached out to shake Tacoma's hand. "And you are?"

"Rob," he said.

"That's right. Good to see you again, Rob."

As Greene extended his hand to shake Tacoma's, Tacoma seized Greene's middle finger and bent it sharply back, nearly snapping it. He pushed Greene's arm down to his side, next to his torso, twisting brutally.

Greene winced and yelped.

"*What the*—" Greene shouted, then he tried to lunge his knee at Tacoma. But Tacoma held the finger tight, the bone at the breaking point. Tacoma suddenly lurched with his other hand as Greene tried to hit him and kick at him. Tacoma snapped Greene's middle finger mid-bone as his other hand grabbed Greene at the nape of the neck, near the carotid artery, and locked his fingers around a small confluence of bone and nerve, gripping it tightly. Greene abruptly dropped to the floor, letting out a pained moan as he clutched at his neck. Tacoma calmly removed the P226R from beneath his armpit. He threaded a thin but long silencer, designed for maximum noise suppression, as Greene sought to breathe again. Tacoma finished preparing the sidearm just as Greene was able to finally get air into his lungs.

"There's a car waiting outside for you, Jonathan," said Tacoma quietly, in an even voice, aiming the gun at Greene's head. "You'll be driven to Nice, then flown to London. You'll pack up your shit and leave London—permanently—by tomorrow night. You will never have contact with her or any of her friends ever again. If you *ever* contact her or anyone she knows again, I'll come and find you," said Tacoma, the silver spheroid cap end of the suppressor less than a foot from the center of Greene's forehead. "And next time, *Jonathan*, I pull the trigger. Understood? Tell me you understand what I'm saying, Jon?"

From the ground, his face still contorted and beet red, Greene looked up.

"Yes, I understand."

"Good. Now get the fuck out of here."

CHAPTER 2

Aboard the Maxi Yacht Constellation
264 Miles North of Bermuda
Atlantic Ocean

A tall man with almost white-blond hair stood at the helm of an eighty-seven-foot-long offshore racing sailboat, a Maxi boat, as the sailing world referred to the sleek, speedy yacht, which was capable of racing around the world in the roughest of sailing conditions. The hull was obsidian black with red stripes below the gunwales. She was a "maxZ87," the first of the new series by Reichel/Pugh and built by McConaghy Boats out of Sydney, Australia. She wasn't a boat built for comfort. Belowdecks there was a large storage area that held eight separate sets of sails, along with a galley kitchen, two bathrooms, and a room stacked with bunks—and that was all.

Bruno Darré had another yacht, which he kept in Palm Beach, designed for comfort and luxury. The *Constellation* was designed to win.

The crew consisted mostly of Kiwis and Aussies, all young and extremely fit, all world-class sailors, with at least a dozen Olympic gold medals between them, and even more America's Cups.

It was late summer and the occasion was the annual Newport-to-Bermuda race. It was a sailboat race waged by billionaires. Within that small group of type A overachievers, there existed certain annual rituals that showcased, outside the business world, the meaningless but cutthroat level of competition that had fueled their achievements, but also laid bare the odd, sometimes pointless rivalries that existed between very rich men.

In the case of sailboats, there was offshore racing. Egos and aspirations were expressed in one's boat and one's crew, including how well one's crew was taken care of. The competition to be the best at offshore ocean sailboat racing was hypercompetitive and expensive. The fact that a man occasionally died, washed overboard in a gale, for example, his body never to be found again, made the competition all that more real.

Darré looked at a small, iridescent waterproof digital clock on the helm.

00:06:19:39

The clock, though simple looking, was tied in to a $14 million drone now in the sky at four thousand feet. Like the sailboat, the drone, too, was Darré's. At the race's start in Newport, Rhode Island, the cameras on the custom-built drone had snapped photos of each sailboat, a fleet of sixty-seven Maxi boats, and logged them in to a custom-built software program designed to track each boat as it moved south toward Bermuda. From that point on, Darré and his crew were watching the progress of his competitors and charting it against the *Constellation*.

According to the clock, the *Constellation* was more than two and a half hours ahead of her closest competitor.

Which was probably why Darré was being allowed to steer, at this ideal time; with a big lead and a purple sky even now, past nine o'clock, and a calm wind and placid, current-crossed black ocean beckoning them toward the finish line. It was exactly what his racing team had in mind when they crossed the starting line in Newport. They wanted to win yet another race for him. To a man, they all loved Bruno Darré. He paid them better than anyone on the racing circuit, gave them great benefits, and, when mistakes were made, as they always were, he never showed even a moment of anger or regret. He treated them like family.

They built the two-and-a-half-hour lead not just to win the race, but for Darré.

Pinckney, the captain, emerged from below deck with a tray. On it were several dozen shots of tequila, poured into small plastic cups. Pinckney was a handsome twenty-six-year-old from Christchurch, New Zealand. He was tan, like all the crew.

"Mr. Darré," he said with a thick Kiwi accent.

Darré looked up and smiled.

Behind Pinckney came the rest of the crew. Sails had been tied off and secured. The yacht would sail itself for a few minutes.

As Pinckney and the others approached, Darré heard the sat phone chime twice. He looked at the screen.

Assets in place
Awaiting your final approval

Darré registered the words as he lifted a shot of tequila into the air.

"To the best boat in the fucking water!" yelled Darré. A chorus of yells and hear-hears echoed across the sleek deck. He put the shot to his mouth, threw it back, and slammed it down. He grabbed another and slugged it quickly, then looked at Pinckney.

"Thank you," said Darré. "I need to make a call. Can you take the helm?"

Darré walked to the front of the yacht and pressed a speed dial. He listened from the bow of the sailboat as the sat phone rang.

"It's about fucking time," came a gruff male voice. He had a thick Russian accent. "We're minutes away from losing the window."

"You're sure the exit strategy is bulletproof?" Darré said.

"Nothing is bulletproof," said the man. "But yes, everything is in place. There should be little to no trace. Now make a fucking decision, Bruno."

Darré paused and looked up at the mainsail against a crimson sky.

"Do it," said Darré.

CHAPTER 3

Marriott Hotel
Des Moines, Iowa

The crowd was growing restless, though not irritated. They were excited and upbeat. More than two thousand Iowans milled about the windowless ballroom. The event should've been over hours ago. Instead, it had yet to begin.

The hotel was a typical Marriott, with clean, patterned carpets, large, comfortable leather sofas and chairs for guests, gaudy chandeliers, mirrors on most of the walls. All anyone on this night cared about was trying to get closer to the stage.

Most people were standing. Immediately in front of the stage were several dozen seats reserved for senior citizens. The dais was empty. On the front of the dais was a slick-looking rectangular sign.

NICK BLAKE FOR PRESIDENT
TOUGH LEADERSHIP FOR A BETTER AMERICA

An abstract, bright, red, white, and blue flag covered the wall behind the stage. The only word: BLAKE. It looked as if made by a professional advertising agency and popped, even to those at the back of the room. A low din of conversation permeated the room, along with occasional laughter.

The speaker everyone was waiting on was Governor Nick Blake of Florida. Blake was supposed to start speaking at 6 P.M., just in time to hit the evening news cycle back on the East Coast. But a large round clock above the entrance to the ballroom now showed 8:28 P.M.

The people in the room who were not journalists or political operatives were Iowans. Like the citizens of New Hampshire, they were spoiled when it came to presidential politics. In order to run for president, a candidate not only had to come to Iowa, he or she had to practically move into the state. The path to the Oval Office ran right through the dust-covered country roads, the simple kitchens, the hay-filled red clapboard barns, the motels, hotels, diners, and town halls of the small, flat, land-bound state. The Iowa Caucuses were the first real contest in the race for the presidency. It was a cliché to say it, but it was true: every vote in Iowa counted, and if you wanted to be president, you had to earn every vote.

What happened in Iowa would reverberate across the country. Like a thunderclap, the winners of the Iowa Caucuses on both sides of the political aisle would be shot out of Iowa like cannonballs. And while people in other places might respond irrationally to this disproportionate influence and power over the election, Iowans didn't. They listened and debated. They took their responsibility seriously.

That being said, two and a half hours was a long time for anyone to stand around in a windowless ballroom. Des Moines sweltered in a rare Iowa summer heat wave, and it was above eighty even in the air-conditioned ballroom. The hotel manager had cranked up the air-conditioning, but the room remained hot and unpleasant.

At the back of the room, a cordoned-off area held a raised rectangular wooden platform, twelve feet long, six feet wide, elevated on steel supports three feet up, on top of which crowded a half dozen cameramen and on-air reporters. The reporters milled about, speaking mostly into cell phones, the disdain of having to be there in the first place now topped with an incremental sheen of annoyance at the fact that, in addition to having to be in Iowa, they had to wait for a candidate who was nearly two and a half hours late.

A pretty blond-haired woman on the left side of the platform sat nonchalantly in a hotel chair. Her name was Bianca de la Garza. She wore a navy-blue blouse with short sleeves, a red skirt, and high heels. A silver pin with the letters CBS was attached to her blouse above her heart. Her hair was parted in the middle, combed back down to her shoulders. She was pretty, and did not wear much makeup. She didn't have to, which was rare for an on-air reporter. She sat back in the chair, slouched, her legs crossed in front of her. A cell phone was pressed to her ear.

"They're not saying," she said lazily into the phone as she scanned the room warily.

"I want you to stay," said the voice on the other end of the phone, her producer back in New York City, Vance Aloupis.

"The last flight to New York leaves in an hour," she said, not pushing too hard. "We can rip some footage from the pool. Besides, it's one fucking event, Vance. It's nine thirty East Coast time. Who's going to be watching? He might not get on until ten. If I miss the flight, I miss my daughter's recital tomorrow morning."

"I want you there," said Aloupis. "You can catch the first flight in the morning."

"No one is going to beat J. P. Dellenbaugh," she said, her hand in her hair, twisting a clutch of strands.

"You haven't seen this guy live, Bianca," said Aloupis. "I have. It's two and a half hours after he was supposed to take the stage. How many people have left?"

She scanned the packed room with her eyes, barely moving.

"Almost everyone."

"Yeah, my ass. I'm in the control room. I'm looking at a packed ballroom. By the way, that large black thing to your right? It's called a camera."

"Oh, you're so fucking smart, Vance," she whispered, hanging up.

Behind the news platform, across a packed crowd of people, to the side of the door, a small coterie of men stood, calmly surveying the scene. There were four of them. They leaned against the wall. They didn't look like they belonged, not at this event, not in Des Moines, not even in Iowa.

One of the men wore a dark suit and tie. He was clean cut, with neatly combed brown hair and glasses. This was Dean Dakolias, director of communications for the Blake campaign. A second man was short and bald, with thick glasses. This was Justin O'Grady, the campaign pollster. He was poring through a sheaf of papers in his hands, trying to read numbers, cross-tabs on a poll. A third man was tall, with longish black hair, which was slicked back. He had a mustache and a tan face. This was Edward Stackler, Governor Blake's campaign manager. He looked down at his BlackBerry, reading emails. A fourth man had a shaggy aspect to him, his hair long and tousled, an overgrown beard. He was overweight by at least a hundred pounds. This was Brad Williams. He was the one in charge.

"I'm getting too old for this," said Williams.

Williams was the chief strategist and ad maker for the yet-to-be-announced presidential campaign of Governor Nick Blake, Democrat of Florida, a forty-four-year old populist with a fiery, charismatic speaking style whose tough-on-crime policies had made him a hero in Florida and across the country. He was positioned as the savior of the Democratic Party, a party that hadn't won the White House in more than a decade. There were already seven announced candidates for the Democratic nomination, but it was Nick Blake who the White House feared, and who—despite not having formally announced his candidacy yet—was destroying the field in every poll.

"You're getting too old for this?" responded Stackler. "I'm the one who just turned fifty, Brad. You're forty."

"I'm actually thirty-seven," said Williams, laughing.

"Going on sixty," said O'Grady, without looking up from the cross-tabs.

"That's what two divorces will do to you," said Stackler.

"Three," said Williams. "Shelby wants a divorce."

O'Grady looked up from his papers.

"Sorry to hear that . . ."

Just behind the four Blake campaign officials stood another man who was also from Washington, D.C. The four Blake operatives knew full well who he was, though he pretended he didn't know who the Blake people were. This man's presence was indeed significant. It was the first prima facie evidence of how seriously the White House was taking Nick Blake's candidacy for president.

His name was Mike Murphy, and he looked like he'd been up all night. He had hair down to his shoulders and several days' worth of stubble. He wore a wrinkled blue button-down, sleeves rolled up, and jeans. He had on a pair of beat-up cowboy boots. He was a disheveled mess. He stared out from behind round, gold-rimmed glasses, a blank look on his face. He'd been in this situation before, far too many times in far too many ballrooms. In fact, he'd waited precisely like this in precisely this very same

ballroom too many times to count, though this was the first time he could recall nobody leaving.

Mike Murphy was the top political adviser to the president of the United States.

Murphy took a few steps toward the Blake officials.

"Evening, gentlemen," said Murphy. "When's your guy getting here? I need to get my beauty sleep."

Williams laughed as Murphy introduced himself to him, Stackler, Dakolias, and O'Grady.

"Should be soon," said Dakolias. "They had to run around some storms on the flight in."

"Ah, Iowa," said Murphy, shaking his head. "It's not enough that it's in the middle of nowhere. God also thought it'd be fun to have a tornado send a cow flying through the air every few days. I've been lobbying the president to move the Iowa Caucuses to Hawaii."

All four of the Blake men were laughing.

"I must say, your guy looks good," said Murphy sincerely. "I just read a poll from California. Surprisingly strong there despite the fact that the governor of California is also running. Not to mention, look around here. People don't usually stick around like this."

"Thanks," said Williams. "But it's a long campaign, you know that. Anyone could emerge."

"Yeah, but if they're going to, it's gotta happen in Iowa," said Murphy, "and judging from the crowd, your guy's the one emerging."

"Well, thanks again."

"Don't thank me," said Murphy. "This time next year you're going to hate my guts."

"I doubt that," said Williams, laughing.

Just then, Dakolias's phone beeped. He looked down at the screen.

"The governor's plane just landed," said Dakolias. "ETA ten minutes. He wants to go right on."

"Give the pool a warning," said Williams to Dakolias. "Actually, don't. We might get some good footage. When he walks through the door, people are going to go fucking crazy. No warning."

Murphy grinned.

"I like it," he said. "Don't tell anyone I said that."

Dakolias smiled.

"Got it."

Fifteen minutes later, the doors at the back of the ballroom suddenly opened. A swarm of uniformed police officers entered the ballroom. They scanned the room briefly as the crowd became louder and a sense of excitement took over.

Bright halogen lights suddenly burst on atop the elevated TV platform. All news cameras swiveled toward the back of the room, aiming their cameras at Blake. The on-air reporters jolted to life. Bianca de la Garza, like the other half dozen, quickly stood up, popped a communications bud in her ear, then waited for her cameraman to move away from the crowd to her. The press platform became abruptly frenetic, as reporters stood before cameras that started rolling, each reporter speaking directly to the camera, telling viewers that it looked like Nick Blake had finally arrived.

A moment later, behind the swarm of policemen, a tall, brown-haired man stepped into the ballroom. He looked over at Williams, Stackler, O'Grady, and Dakolias, barely nodding. The crowd at the back of the room seemed to all move their heads at approximately the same moment, as if on cue. It was a ripple effect as the first few people saw the governor, then those beside them felt it, then the reaction to Blake arriving seemed to catch wind and move across the crowd. Someone in the crowd began to clap and

soon the room responded. Flashbulbs popped as people snapped photographs of Blake—and then the big ballroom erupted in wild cheers, clapping, and shouts.

Nick Blake's black hair was slightly long and parted in the middle. A smile crossed his face. He was handsome, boyish-looking at forty-four. He wore dark pants and a blue button-down shirt, the sleeves of which were rolled up to his elbows. His tie was gone. Blake was a big man. He towered within the backlit frame of the door as he looked calmly around the room. He stepped forward into the crowd, hands out, and began shaking hands as he made his way toward the front of the ballroom. Blake moved slowly through the crowd, which was now pushing toward him, seeking to touch him, get a closer view of him, meet the man every political pundit in America was talking about.

The reaction to Governor Nick Blake's entrance was astounding. It didn't seem to matter that he hadn't thrown his hat in the ring. He was rapidly becoming the Democrats' great hope for taking back 1600 Pennsylvania Avenue. His policies as governor of Florida showed an independent streak and willingness to break party orthodoxy in order to accomplish his goals. For the Republican White House, Blake was scary because he was outflanking the president on issues usually considered weaknesses for Democrats. He was tough on immigration, a military and foreign policy hawk, and a fierce believer in less government and fewer taxes. What he was most known for, however, was what he'd done in Florida about crime in the state's cities. Blake was at the forefront of the battle against organized crime, which, as a former prosecutor, he knew was the gasoline behind the engine of urban decay, violence, drugs, and poverty. In Miami, Tallahassee, Fort Lauderdale, Jacksonville, Daytona, Tampa, and every other major Florida city, Blake had pushed state and local law enforcement to go hard against the organizations responsible for most of the violence, drugs, and other illicit activities in the cities. Blake had taken on the Russian mob in the streets and alleys that were the group's home base.

The result was a candidate who could not only hold the Democratic base, but who could outflank President Dellenbaugh on the sort of red-meat domestic security issues that Republicans traditionally owned. He was, at least according to some, tougher on crime than the president. In a general election, it meant Blake would strip Dellenbaugh of millions of votes from blue-collar Republicans and conservative independents.

Even more dangerous for the White House, Blake was young and charismatic. And while no one could ever rival J. P. Dellenbaugh's populist political skills, Blake was a blazing character who was setting the political world on fire.

The din in the ballroom was at a crescendo as the clapping and cheers continued.

"On in three, two, one," said the voice in her ear from a studio back in New York City. "You're live."

"This is Bianca de la Garza with *CBS Evening News.* We are live in Des Moines, Iowa, where in just five short months the people of this state will hold the first-in-the-nation caucuses that will play a big part in determining who the Democratic Party will nominate to face a very popular J. P. Dellenbaugh. What you're watching is the arrival of Florida governor Nick Blake, a forty-four-year-old graduate of Ohio State, University of Chicago Law School, a former U.S. Army Ranger, and federal prosecutor. You are watching the arrival live, in Iowa tonight, of the man who some say could be the dark horse candidate to beat President Dellenbaugh. This standing-room-only crowd of Iowans has been waiting nearly three hours to get a glimpse of a man credited with decimating the Russian mafia in Florida, a tough-on-crime chief executive with a fiery speaking style."

Away from the TV riser, across the now excited crowd, bright spotlights suddenly lit up the stage. A short, roundish man in an ill-fitting brown suit moved behind the dais and took the microphone.

"Ladies and gentlemen, my name is Mark Helmke and I'm the Polk County chairman of the Iowa Democratic Party. Thank you all for being so gosh darn patient tonight. I know you all have jobs to get up for in the morning, so let me get tonight's main event up here, how's that? Without further ado, it is my pleasure to intro-duce tonight's guest speaker."

Helmke, short, bald, glistening in sweat, looked up at the crowd, trying to pinpoint his guest, who was still pushing his way through the crowd toward the stage.

"Our guest tonight is a graduate of Ohio State University, where he was a wide receiver for the Buckeyes. After graduation, he joined the army and served as a U.S. Ranger. He did four tours of duty in Afghanistan and earned a Purple Heart when an IED blew up next to the vehicle he was traveling in. He nearly lost his life. After his recovery, he went to law school at the Univer-sity of Chicago, then went to work as a federal prosecutor for the Southern District of Florida, becoming U.S. attorney when he was thirty-six."

Blake made his way to the front of the crowd, then ascended the stairs to the stage, waving to the crowd. A huge roar came from the crowd as he walked across the stage to the dais, where Bolduc continued to speak.

"Three years ago, our guest was elected governor of the state of Florida, where he's built a reputation as a problem solver, an in-dependent thinker, but mostly, as a tough son of a bitch on crime."

The crowd let out another crescendo of cheers.

"Ladies and gentlemen, please join me in welcoming an Amer-ican patriot, a good Democrat, a friend of Iowa, Governor Nick Blake!"

Blake shook Helmke's hand as cheering and clapping continued to drown out everything else. He stood behind the dais, smiling and waving to the crowd. He didn't wait for the crowd to stop.

"Thank you, Mark," said Blake, his voice gravelly and confident. "And thank you, Iowa."

At the word *Iowa*, the cheering started again.

"Thank you, everyone, for coming out tonight. I know you all waited almost three hours. I'm not sure I would've."

Laughter burst from the crowd.

Blake paused. He lifted the microphone and moved out from behind the dais.

"I'm going to tell you something you should probably know about me," said Blake, combing his free hand back through his thick brown hair. "I voted for J. P. Dellenbaugh."

The crowd grew silent. There were even a few low groans of disapproval.

"I'm not a politician," said Blake. "I'm a leader, and if I agree with you, if I think you're doing a good job, I'll praise you, vote for you, ask you for advice. Leaders don't find solutions based on which political party came up with the idea. Yeah, I voted for J. P. Dellenbaugh because I thought he was doing a good job, plain and simple. But somewhere along the line, J. P. Dellenbaugh went soft on crime, soft on urban violence, soft on organized crime!"

Wild cheers and applause spontaneously erupted. It exploded across the room and lasted for more than half a minute.

"Drugs. Murder. Violence. Brought to you by the Russian mafia. I've seen it firsthand and I fight it every day. Russian organized crime is the plague of our American cities. You know why I worry less about the Mexican cartels and the Italian mafia? Because the Russians are taking care of them for us. Heroin, fentanyl, human trafficking, murder, and mayhem. It's the greatest threat America faces, because it's here. It's right down the street, in Miami, in Des Moines, or it's coming. Without peace in our cities, there can never be opportunity for our children, for our future, for the pursuit of happiness that is the birthright of every American!"

From the front of the room, a pair of high schoolers suddenly began a low, steady chant.

"Nick Blake! Nick Blake! Nick Blake!"

Cheering grew louder, the chant reached a rowdy crescendo, and Blake acknowledged it by pausing and moving across the stage, waving to each part of the room.

Near the back of the ballroom, a man with short gray hair turned and pushed his way slowly and politely through the crowd. No one noticed him. When he reached the back of the ballroom, he went to one of the large double doors that were now closed. He pushed the door slowly and quietly until it was open, then, with his foot, put the doorstop down so that it would remain open. He looked through the lobby of the hotel and out one of the large windows near the entrance. A white Chevy Suburban was parked across the street, its windows tinted black.

CHAPTER 4

Sparks Steak House
New York City

There were fancier steak houses in Manhattan, and certainly trendier ones, but few could match Sparks's storied ambience. Behind the large glass windows, through the wide, lightly creaking mahogany entrance, the restaurant was alive with movement. Red-and-white-checkered wallpaper looked as if it had been there for a century. A coffered ceiling dangled with crystal chandeliers. Semicircular booths of high-backed green leather were packed with people around tables covered in steaks, wineglasses, plates of au gratin potatoes, wedges of iceberg lettuce the size of footballs, drizzled in bleu cheese dressing and bacon, and half-empty wine bottles, each booth meticulously serviced by an all-male waitstaff dressed in white uniforms, men in their fifties, all of whom had been at Sparks for decades.

Sparks Steak House was crowded. Sparks was always crowded.

Between the walls of booths were dozens of tables in the center of the brightly lit main room. Every table, like every booth, was filled with customers.

It was raucous, with hearty conversation, bursts of laughter, the occasional shout, the clinking of glasses, and the scraping of knives against plates, all churning in a medley of noise and celebration.

In the farthest corner of the restaurant, a man sat alone in one of the booths, the so-called chef's table, within eyesight of the dozen chefs and sous chefs scrambling to prepare the meals. By design, the table was always reserved and kept vacant by the restaurant's manager, available when certain people called or walked in at the last minute. The list of people who had the ability to make that call and garner the table was short. Several celebrities were on the list, actors such as Al Pacino, Robert De Niro, Tom Hardy, and Russell Crowe. There were a few athletes, including Zdeno Chara of the Boston Bruins, and Rafael Nadal, the tennis player. There were even a few superstars. Mick Jagger usually came in once or twice a year. There were prominent businesspeople on the list, such as Brian Moynihan, the CEO of Bank of America, Martha Stewart, and Rupert Murdoch. Several politicians also enjoyed the privilege. The mayor of New York City liked to eat at Sparks every few months. The governor of New York State came more often than that, always taking the time to go into the kitchen and talk with the chefs and waiters.

Tonight, a tall, older, silver-haired man in a gray, pin-striped, three-piece suit sat in the booth. He had a prominent, sharp nose and cheeks that were bright pink, due mainly to his nightly ritual of three or four gin and tonics followed by a bottle of red wine. The man wore thick, square glasses. His hair was parted on the right side, combed back and slightly messy. He appeared a little disheveled but in a professorial sort of way. His only company, beyond a bottle of Chianti, was a book on the table in front of him. It was a hardcover edition of *Anna Karenina* by the great Russian novelist Leo Tolstoy, its blue leather cover worn and cracked from use.

John Patrick O'Flaherty, the senior United States senator from the state of New York, read *Anna Karenina* every decade or so. O'Flaherty, a former professor at Columbia University School of Law, found the book to be like a compass, not only providing lessons and moral truths that helped remind him of his place on earth, but also enabling him to look back at himself in relation to where he was, as an individual, only ten years before. Had he remained true to his purpose? Had he made the right choices and not simply the popular ones? Had he above all else remained humble in the face of the great gifts and opportunities he'd been given? Had he fought against those dark forces that less powerful people—his constituents especially—were powerless in the face of? Had he done enough as, at age seventy-six, he began to contemplate retiring from the U.S. Senate?

Only O'Flaherty understood that this was why he read the book.

A decade ago, the answer to the question, have you done enough, was no.

He read quickly, holding a wineglass in his left hand and sipping as he read and flipped pages. When he reached the end of a chapter, he leaned back. He didn't smile. Instead, he realized that the answer to the question this time around was maybe, or quite possibly even yes. For Senator John Patrick O'Flaherty had spent the decade risking every ounce of political and intellectual capital he had fighting for what was right. Fighting against a dark force that had been born and raised in his own state, even while he was a junior senator.

The Russian mob.

When the Soviet Union broke up in 1991, a system of oppressive government was abruptly gone. For all the rhetoric about how terrible the Soviet Union had been, the fact is, the very oppression and brutality that the government was criticized for also served a vital purpose: it kept the animals at bay.

Be careful what you wish for.

That was the lesson O'Flaherty now understood about the breakup of the Soviet Union, for once the system of government control was gone in the Soviet Union, the criminals and thugs were unleashed. The most aggressive, greedy, and talented of the animals went immediately to the place where the rewards for brutality and hard work were highest: the United States.

To Brighton Beach, not far from where O'Flaherty had grown up. Ten years ago, O'Flaherty realized that he bore some culpability in the rise of the largest and most dangerous criminal enterprise in the U.S. He'd done little to stop it. That was what he realized a decade ago.

Now, most Americans understood that O'Flaherty was the charismatic, brilliant, charming, and eloquent face of the fight against the Russian mafia.

O'Flaherty had authored two landmark pieces of legislation, using his deep understanding of the law, to expand RICO and effectively target the Russian mafia. He'd pushed them past two presidents—Rob Allaire and J. P Dellenbaugh—to ramp up Justice Department efforts to go after the Russians. O'Flaherty had been a vocal critic of the FBI, arguing publicly and privately that the Russians posed a darker and deeper threat to America than La Cosa Nostra ever had.

He was one of a handful of U.S. senators at the forefront of the fight against Russian organized crime. When Yuri Malnikov, one of the godfathers of the Russian mafia, was arrested by the FBI off the coast of Florida, O'Flaherty had gone to Administrative Maximum Facility Colorado, aka Supermax, or ADX, the most secure prison in the world. Senator O'Flaherty—whose laws had taken Yuri Malnikov down—had flown to Colorado to visit him, bringing with him a bottle of raspberry liqueur and, for hours on end, had asked Malnikov questions, though Malnikov didn't answer any of them. O'Flaherty wanted to understand how it worked, how it grew, how the young animals of the Russian mob were able to so quickly and so effectively take over a town or city and destroy it. O'Flaherty knew that drugs would always exist. He believed an accommodation could be made on some level with those who brought the drugs in and sold them. Not leniency, but rather, understanding. The lesser of many evils. But the Russians were not the lesser. Their tactics were without moral consideration. Their brutality was unrivaled, disproportionate, and random. La Cosa Nostra, for all of its killing and violence, was more humane than the Russians. El Chapo and the Mexican cartels could be almost as brutal as the Russians, yet in every city controlled by the cartels that the Russian mafia entered, they destroyed their competition, leaving piles of corpses in their wake. Yuri Malnikov did not speak for the entire visit, choosing instead to stare at O'Flaherty.

Malnikov was released a year later under a secret arrangement between his son, Alexei, and the U.S government—quid pro quo for helping America avert the detonation of a nuclear bomb in New York City. O'Flaherty had flown to Denver again to see Yuri Malnikov before he got on the plane. Malnikov had shaken O'Flaherty's hand, but even then he didn't say a word to his nemesis.

O'Flaherty was an American institution, popular across the country, a gentleman who still had a head of hair and a charismatic way about him.

Across the restaurant, a dark-haired woman was seated at the bar, enjoying a glass of white wine. Without looking directly at him, she was tracking O'Flaherty out of the side of her field of vision.

She wore stylish, light navy-blue slacks that came down in a slight flare, like bell bottoms: Saint Laurent. She had on a pair of Prada leather high-heeled sandals that showed off her pretty feet, and toenails painted a shiny white. A white, sheer blouse was opened up enough to display her chest. A necklace of gold with a sapphire shamrock was around her neck. Her hair was cut in a sixties-like bangs—sharp, mysterious, and utterly mesmerizing.

She sat with her right leg over her left, casually sipping her wine and staring off into oblivion, not a care in the world, un-approachable. She felt her cell phone vibrate and looked around, preparing to move, her time at the restaurant now operational in nature.

The bar was crowded. Most were men, there for a business dinner and waiting for their table. Four different males had come to her side and attempted to engage her in conversation. With each one, the look was the same, total detachment, as if she wasn't listening, not a smile or an attempt to get to know them.

She knew the rhythm of the waitstaff by now. There were three men covering the table. The waiter, who spoke to the sena-tor like an old friend, and two others who rushed wine, or bread, or swept up bread crumbs, right behind. She saw one of the men emerge from the kitchen with a plate. She picked up her wineglass and took a sip, put it down, then put her hand in her clutch. Her fingers found a small object, the girth of a ballpoint pen, but short, the length of a child's pinky. She removed it from the clutch and pulled a small silver cap, being careful not to touch what was be-neath it, a tiny needle that jutted out less than a quarter inch. She clasped it in her hand—between her ring and middle fingers—as she watched the senator's table. She knew the rhythm now. The first server would bring out the plate and the headwaiter would follow him and be the one to lay it down on the table.

She stood and cut through the small enclave of people at the bar. She walked down the aisle between the booths on the left and the tables in the middle of the restaurant. She felt the small vial in her hand as she moved calmly toward the back of the restaurant.

As she came toward the waiter, who was now placing the plate in front of Senator O'Flaherty, the woman slipped. The heel on her sandal turned awkwardly over. She went tumbling, helpless, toward the back of the waiter now serving O'Flaherty. The weight and velocity of her forward motion caused her to slam into his back. The waiter was pushed forward, out of control. The plate turned over—the food was suddenly thrown—as the waiter tried in that split second to not land on O'Flaherty, who attempted to duck to his right. The woman cried out in pain as she fell forward, into the booth, holding the back of the waiter so as not to go crashing to the floor. The waiter was partially successful; the food went sprawling across the table, the book, and O'Flaherty's lap, though the waiter tumbled awkwardly—with the woman behind him—into the booth just next to O'Flaherty.

It all appeared to be an accident.

But the woman's arm found its way surgically down between the waiter and O'Flaherty. In the scrum, she found O'Flaherty's elbow and jammed the needle hard, for a brief moment, then removed it, all as the scene devolved into the three of them, food all over the place, and the realization by everyone that the beautiful woman had slipped and caused it all.

Silent shock cut across the restaurant. All eyes were on O'Flaherty, a moment in which the establishment was looking to him for a reaction. He suddenly lifted his wineglass and smiled.

"Cheers!" he said loudly.

As laughter and clapping came from patrons seated at the surrounding tables, several Sparks staff members and even a few customers came rushing over to help the woman and the waiter back up.

She apologized profusely as she climbed back to her feet. The senator was a gentleman throughout, telling her that it was the most excitement he'd had in months, even as he unconsciously rubbed his elbow.

She walked slowly back through the restaurant as people looked at her sympathetically, a few saying things like, "Are you all right?"

She held her head down and a hand across her face, masking it from view.

She exited through the front door of the restaurant. To her left, at the curb, sat an idling black Ferrari 458. The throaty growl of the Michael Schumacher–designed engine mingled with taxis rushing down the street and a sidewalk dotted with people. She walked to the vehicle and opened the door, then climbed in. She looked at the driver. He returned her glance and then hit the paddle, putting the car in gear and cutting into a break in traffic. The roar of the Ferrari momentarily ripped above all other noise, across the Manhattan evening.

Inside Sparks, Senator O'Flaherty was several bites into his steak, which the manager of the restaurant told him was on the house because of the accident a few minutes before, an offer O'Flaherty told him was appreciated but that he would not accept. O'Flaherty began to feel warmth growing from somewhere inside his chest, and then it was as if his whole body was hot, even feverish.

A memory flashed. It was the face of the woman who'd slipped and pushed the waiter, and herself, into the booth on top of him.

The memory was from a moment earlier in the night, as he'd been reading, when he had inadvertently looked across the restaurant to the bar and caught her looking back at him.

O'Flaherty reached for his water glass, but his hand stopped in midair. O'Flaherty caught sight of his fingers as he felt a strange rubbery sensation in his knees. His fingers had become, in just minutes, thick and bloated, too thick to pick up the glass of water. A sharp jolt of pain stabbed him in the stomach, then in his head, as the poison took permanent hold of his seventy-six-year-old frame. His heart stopped beating in the same instant his eyes rolled up back into his head. He slumped listlessly to the side as his body slackened. His last breath occurred as he slithered limply from the leather booth down, knocking over glasses, his chin slamming into the side of the table, then sliding to the floor, where his lifeless corpse crumpled beneath the table.

CHAPTER 5

Marriott Hotel
Des Moines, Iowa

The white Chevy Suburban looked just like every other vehicle parked on the street—dark and lifeless, its owners inside the hotel, at the political rally.

The windows of the white Suburban were tinted dark.

Inside, a man sat in the back seat, passenger side. He wore a plain, light-green T-shirt and a pair of black jeans. His hair was dirty blond, close-cropped. He was a big man with an odd face, ugly and hard to look at; his eyes somehow not aligned, almost like a monster. In front of him, stabilized by a complex series of braces, was a weapon: a CheyTac M200 Intervention, a long-range, high-powered sniper rifle; this one dark green, with a Picatinny rail and thermal laser optic. Bought less than an hour ago. Screwed into the gun's muzzle was a long, cylindrical, black alloy flash suppressor. The somewhat heavy weapon was trained across the seat in a diagonal direction and was aimed at the driver's window.

The man wore black, tight-fitting cashmere gloves.

Beyond the window was the Marriott Hotel.

In the man's ear was a communications device. He was absent-mindedly listening to Governor Nick Blake of Florida as he stared through the firearm's advanced thermal sight. At this moment, the weapon was aimed through the lobby window and at the entrance doors to the ballroom. All he could see was the steel of the door.

Then, the door opened and the sniper was suddenly looking through the scope at Governor Nick Blake, at least two thousand feet away.

The sniper didn't move. Instead, he studied a complex array of indices in the optic, checking and rechecking his calibrations, making sure he'd properly accounted for distance, temperature, wind, and for the thick—though not bulletproof—panel of glass at the Marriott that the cartridge would have to travel through on its way to its destination.

"*So let me ask you, my friends from Iowa,*" came the words in his ear. "*Do you believe there's room for a new way to govern our country? Where we can take care of those less fortunate by cracking down on those who are destroying our cities, our towns, and our neighborhoods?*"

The gunman lowered the front window, just a few inches. The entire weapon and the suppressor remained inside the Suburban, but he didn't want to break the glass, which would only draw attention.

"*Being tough on crime isn't about punishment. It's about compassion. In Miami, we targeted the Russian mafia and we have virtually dismembered it.*"

He felt his finger on the steel trigger. He waited an extra moment, then pulled back on the trigger. A low, metallic *thwack* was followed by momentary silence as the bullet ripped through the large plate-glass window of the Marriott, then came the sound of shattering glass and the bullet found Blake's forehead, kicking Blake backward in a horrible wash of blood and brains.

Then came the screams.

CHAPTER 6

Private Terminal
Dulles International Airport
Dulles, Virginia

Tacoma watched through the window as the Gulfstream made its final blistering push toward Dulles Airport. In the main part of the sprawling airport he could see dozens of flashing blue and red lights.

As the jet taxied to the private terminal, Tacoma got up, walked to the cockpit, and leaned in.

"I'll get the door," said Tacoma. "Can you shut everything down?"

"Yeah, I've got a few hours of after-flight shit I need to do," said RISCON's executive pilot, Stephen Owen. "I'll turn out the lights."

"You think you can handle that?" said Tacoma, smiling.

"Possibly," said Owen.

"Try not to wrap this thing around a tree," said Tacoma.

"I'll try but you know how much I like trees."

They both started laughing.

Tacoma climbed down to the tarmac, still dressed in the same

T-shirt and blazer. He walked across a wide, empty tarmac reserved for certain entities, of which the firm Tacoma worked for and owned half of, RISCON, was one. The hangar was large, angular, black, sleek, and dark. This was RISCON's hangar, large enough to hold two airplanes and a variety of other things such as automobiles, motorcycles, weapons, gold, golf clubs, a pool table, a waterbed, cash, and years' worth of food. There was enough ammo inside the hangar to fight a war, or at least start one. Beneath the concrete floor, sixty-seven feet down a winding stairwell, was a nuclear bomb shelter. When RISCON bought the hangar, the bomb shelter was already there. Rather than get rid of it, Tacoma and Katie Foxx, Tacoma's partner, decided to modernize it, a small expense compared to the actual construction cost; why not, they thought? There probably wouldn't ever be a nuclear war, and if there were they would most likely be blown up, but what if they knew it was coming and could get to the shelter in time? The new shelter had the capability of sustaining four lives for a decade, and included black-band access to a piece of the military power grid beneath Dulles that would survive any nuclear blast and keep the shelter online to any parts of the internet still intact after a catastrophic war.

The hangar was one of four such buildings across the globe that RISCON owned. The others were in Amsterdam, Tokyo, and Johannesburg. They looked like any other hangar, but they were not like other hangars. Each was a veritable fortress. They were high tech, highly weaponized, a sanctum, designed for the ultimate crisis, designed to sustain an EMP or other sort of combat scenario, above all else, survival.

RISCON was the last resort for billionaires and governments throughout the West. RISCON's fees were exorbitant. Retainers started at $10 million a month and actions were billed per diem: $2 million a day. But the results were indisputable.

Tacoma came to the door of the hangar as, in the near distance, Owen taxied the shiny black jet. Tacoma put his thumb against a small glass aperture next to the door, then looked straight ahead as a camera the size of a pinhead scanned the irises of his eyes. A moment later, the lock clicked and Tacoma turned the knob.

Inside, it was dark. Tacoma went to his left, not even attempting to see. Rather, he shut his eyes and walked gingerly, feeling with all four limbs as he crossed a section of the pitch-black hangar. His left foot hit wall first, then his hands found the board. He flipped a row of switches and the hangar was abruptly illuminated in bright yellow. He found a red plastic cover and lifted it. Beneath was a switch. Tacoma flipped it and the gargantuan door to the hangar began a loud, hydraulic whistle as it lifted into the air.

Tacoma reached into his pocket and took out a phone. He opened the camera and moved beneath another plane, a King Air 6500, a pressurized turboprop designed to withstand the harshest of elements. After the lights came fully on, he looked up at the shiny, green-winged, yellow-fuselaged King Air. He loved the plane, if only for its toughness under pressure. Tacoma took a pic. He looked back as Owen steered the Gulfstream into the hangar and the $35 million jet purred its final throaty meow of the night.

He exited at the far end of the hangar, stepping into the parking lot, which was half-filled. He came to a red McLaren 600LT, approaching from the rear, leaning down and feeling along the top of the back left tire, where, less than twenty-four hours before, he'd left the key. But there was nothing there. Tacoma felt again and then got down on his hands and knees and felt all along the ground near the tire, where perhaps it had fallen in a strong wind. But there was nothing.

He stood and scanned the parking lot. He swept his eyes twice and in the second pass saw movement. He focused in on a minivan three rows away. It was dark and still, yet he found the light again, just a glimmer. There was someone there, and whoever it was had established strategic advantage before Tacoma had even landed.

You fucked up—but if they wanted you dead, you'd be dead.

Tacoma moved away from the McLaren and crossed several rows of cars, stepping toward the dark minivan. He looked in through the windshield as he approached, recognizing the outline of the face of the individual seated in the driver's seat. He came to the window and looked in at a gorgeous blond-haired woman in a white tank top. She sat in the driver's seat with a blank stare, looking straight ahead. Tacoma knocked on the window. A few seconds later, the woman inside reached her hand up and lowered the window.

"Can I have my key?" said Tacoma.

Katie Foxx turned her head in a precise, sharp way.

"Took you a while," she said.

"Not that long."

"I could've killed you," said Katie.

"Okay, tough guy," said Tacoma, smiling.

"How'd it go?" said Katie.

"Good. I think the boyfriend is going to be leaving England soon, just my gut. By the way, what's with the minivan?" said Tacoma. "You getting married? Who's the lucky fella?"

Katie opened the door and climbed out.

"I just wanted to remind you that if someone wanted to kill you, you'd be *dead*," said Katie. "You walked out here like a deer in the headlights."

Tacoma stared at Katie.

"I'm tired," said Tacoma.

"We need to debrief."

Tacoma's face was expressionless.

"Can it wait?" he said. "I just want to go to bed, Kate."

Katie Foxx was like the sister he'd never had, and when he called her Kate, it meant he was tired.

Katie put her hand up to Tacoma's cheek.

"I'm sorry," she said. "I thought I was being helpful by making you aware of a vulnerability in your routine."

"You did," said Tacoma. "I'd be dead. But I admit I lost and now I'm just plain tired."

Katie grinned and handed Tacoma a small envelope.

"Payday."

"Thanks."

"Can you give me a ride?" she said.

"Yeah, sure. By the way, what's with all the police cars?"

Katie looked at him with disbelief.

"You didn't hear?"

"No, what?"

"All outbound flights in the country are temporarily grounded," she said. "Remember John Patrick O'Flaherty?"

"Senator O'Flaherty?"

"He and Nick Blake, the governor of Florida, were assassinated tonight."

"How?"

"O'Flaherty was poisoned, Blake got shot in the forehead by a sniper."

"Who did it?" said Tacoma.

"It seems obvious," said Katie. "It was the Russian mob."

CHAPTER 7

Oval Office
The White House
Washington, D.C.

President J. P. Dellenbaugh still had his coat and tie on, despite the fact that it was 10:46 P.M. He was seated behind the big desk with a phone against his ear. When he did speak during the call, it was in a soft, hushed tone. Mostly he was listening. A solemn expression was on his face.

A set of bookshelves along the wall was opened up and pulled back, like a secret door. Behind the bookshelves were TV screens: Fox News, ABC, and CNN were all on, the volume low. All three channels showed different variations of the same story, the deaths of Senator John Patrick O'Flaherty, Republican of New York State, and Governor Nick Blake, Democrat of Florida. A fourth screen was a web page. The Drudge Report had two photos, O'Flaherty on the left, Blake on the right, with the letters R.I.P. emblazoned in red between them.

Below were the headlines with links to stories:

SPECIAL REPORT: FL GOV. NICK BLAKE SHOT DEAD IN DES MOINES;
SEN. JOHN PATRICK O'FLAHERTY, "LION" OF THE SENATE, COLLAPSES
AND DIES IN NEW YORK CITY

TIME OF DEATH: SEN. O'FLAHERTY 9:56 P.M. EST
TIME OF DEATH: GOV. BLAKE 9:58 P.M. EST

"Yes, I know," said the president into the phone. "It's times like these that make us question everything. Please know that Amy and I are here for you, Charlotte. If there is anything we can do, call me."

Dellenbaugh finally hung up the phone. He shut his eyes and reached to the bridge of his nose, rubbing it for a time.

Standing before the wall of TVs were Adrian King, the White House chief of staff; Bo Lovvorn, the new FBI director; Hector Calibrisi, the director of the Central Intelligence Agency; Josh Brubaker, the president's national security adviser; and a half dozen other senior staff members.

When Dellenbaugh stood up from the desk, all eyes cut to him. He walked to the screens and stood with the others.

"Who was that, Mr. President?" said King.

"That was Senator O'Flaherty's daughter," said Dellenbaugh quietly.

"How's she doing?"

Dellenbaugh didn't answer. Instead he stared at the screens for a few moments, focusing in on Drudge.

BOTH DEATHS OCCUR WITHIN MINUTES OF EACH OTHER;
ONE DEMOCRAT, ONE REPUBLICAN: BOTH RESPECTED;
LEADING ARCHITECTS OF WAR ON RUSSIAN MAFIA

"They're implying the deaths are connected," said Dellenbaugh.

"And they aren't?" said King sarcastically.

"I'm just surprised they went there this quickly. Where's John?" said the president, referring to his Press Secretary, John Schmidt. "I need to make a statement tonight."

"It's the optics," said Calibrisi. "Two minutes apart? Even an idiot would suspect something. And as we know, the media by and large are a bunch of idiots. This was a military-style operation. The killers wanted what's about to happen to happen, namely chaos. Now that the media believes there's smoke, they're going to start looking for fire. That complicates our efforts to get to the bottom of it."

"Get to the bottom of it?" said King incredulously. "Isn't it obvious? The Russian mob killed these guys! Wake the fuck up! O'Flaherty was the architect of every piece of anti–Russian mafia legislation in the last twenty years. Blake? It's his main issue. How he cleaned up fucking Florida and now is gonna 'clean up America.' Let's call a spade a spade. Be honest with the American people. The Russian mafia killed two American heroes."

"It's a lot more complicated than that," said Calibrisi. "Yes, it seems clear the Russians did it, but there are several families who control the Russian mafia. Who do we accuse? The Malnikovs? The Odessa Mob? And which family in the Odessa mafia? The Bergens? The Rostivs? One of the others? They hate each other and compete against each other and try to kill each other. Sure, one of them probably did it, but they could be framing one of the other families. Don't forget it was the Bergens who tipped off the FBI about Yuri Malnikov being in that boat off the coast of Florida. He spent a year inside Supermax."

"What's your point, Hector?" said Dellenbaugh. "This doesn't look like someone was setting someone else up. It looks like they were removing their two biggest enemies in the United States government."

"Mr. President, my point is, we don't know who did it," said

Calibrisi. "We don't know which family is behind it. Who do we accuse? Even if we did know, what would we do? Until we know, we can't go out there and start pointing fingers."

"All I know is, we have to go out and find these motherfuckers," said King. "Then we need to kill them all."

"Are you kidding?" said Lovvorn, the FBI director. "I agree with you. But I didn't know if I should speak up."

"I'm not kidding," said King, anger in his voice. "*This is fucking war!* They killed a guy who might've become the next president—sorry, sir," he said to Dellenbaugh. "They also killed a major figure in the U.S. Senate, arguably one of the greatest senators of the past century. I was a lawyer on the Foreign Relations Committee for three years when he was chairman. He was a brilliant man."

"Adrian is right," said Brubaker. "This *is* war. Unfortunately, we're not allowed to fight wars on U.S. soil. We're not allowed to use the military or the CIA."

"Well, it's a stupid goddam law if you ask me," said King. "What if China invaded? We couldn't fight back just because we're on U.S. soil?"

"You know the answer to that," said Dellenbaugh, shaking his head.

"Actually, Mr. President, with all due deference, I don't know the answer to that. We were just attacked," said King. "Invaded. It's time to change the rules."

Dellenbaugh didn't say anything, but stared at his hotheaded chief of staff, deep in thought. In his typically bare-knuckled, blunt way, King had made a point. A good point.

There were several laws that prohibited the president from using military and intelligence assets on American soil. The purpose was to ensure no president or politician could ever order the military and CIA to attack U.S. citizens, political opponents, and most important, that no president could execute a military take-over of the United States.

The CIA, National Security Agency, and other agencies were also banned from intelligence gathering and all other covert operations on U.S. soil.

A knock came at the door to the Oval Office and John Schmidt, the White House director of communications, stepped inside. His brown and gray hair was slightly messed up and his face was red. He was also breathing heavily.

"Sorry I'm late," said Schmidt. "*The New York Times* is writing a story for tomorrow's newspaper. They have someone inside the Blake campaign who's going to speculate that the administration was somehow involved."

Dellenbaugh, King, Calibrisi, Brubaker, and Lovvorn all looked shocked, shaking their heads.

"Call Sulzberger right now," said King, seething. "Tell that miserable fucking bastard if he prints something like that, the next time a *New York Times* reporter sets foot in the White House there'll be flying cars and vacation houses on the fucking moon."

"You need to hold a press conference tonight, sir," said Schmidt calmly, ignoring King.

"We don't know what happened yet," said Calibrisi.

"You can keep it vague," said Schmidt. "Threatening the *Times* isn't going to kill the story. What will kill it is you going out there and talking about Nick Blake and John O'Flaherty. I also think it's the right thing to do, Mr. President. You need to calm a nation, sir."

Dellenbaugh looked at Calibrisi.

"Don't do it to kill the story," said Calibrisi. "Who cares about some stupid story that's going to be laughed at and disproven? But I agree with John. You do need to say something. It's the right thing to do."

Dellenbaugh remained silent. He turned and walked to a thin

door near the entrance to the Oval Office, pulling it open. Inside was a small bar. Dellenbaugh poured himself a glass of bourbon, moved to one of the two large, tan Chesterfield sofas at the center of the Oval Office, and sat down.

"Help yourselves," said the president, taking a sip.

When everyone had gotten a drink and was seated, Dellenbaugh looked at Lovvorn, the new FBI director, who was reading his phone.

"What do we have so far?" said the president.

"Let's start with New York," said Lovvorn. "According to witnesses at the restaurant, a waiter fell onto Senator O'Flaherty as he was bringing the senator his dinner. Several people, including the waiter, say the waiter was pushed from behind by a woman. She apparently broke the heel of her shoe and fell into the waiter by accident. Ten minutes later, he was dead. One of our coroners already made a first pass at the corpse. He found a fresh puncture wound in O'Flaherty's left elbow. We'll know more when the lab tests are done, but it looks like he was poisoned. Needless to say, the woman disappeared."

Dellenbaugh shook his head.

"As for Governor Blake, well, the situation is a mess out there," said Lovvorn. "Obviously, he was assassinated, but by whom? From where? The slug was a 6.5 mm Creedmoor. The front window of the hotel shattered at the same time Blake was shot. Both the slug and the window indicate he was killed by a sniper positioned somewhere outside the building. We have no witnesses, other than someone who saw a man open one of the doors to the ballroom immediately before he was shot. Based on a rough approximation of the trajectory of the bullet, the shooter was at ground level, probably in a vehicle across the street. The vehicle is gone. There was a security camera but it was spray-painted black. There's no footage to look at."

Dellenbaugh sipped his drink, shaking his head, frustrated, upset, and angry.

"The Secret Service was supposed to protect Nick Blake," said Dellenbaugh. "As for Senator O'Flaherty, who can you blame? NYPD? The FBI? The truth is, nobody is to blame. Nobody except the people who did this. At some point, the U.S. government realized that La Cosa Nostra posed an existential threat. It took decades, but we decimated the Italians. This is a hundred times worse than anything La Cosa Nostra ever did. Yet, we're nowhere with the Russians. They control organized crime in America."

"Mr. President," said Schmidt, "I'm just a little old press secretary, so at the risk of speaking above my pay grade, you need to get out there. Who did it, what we're going to do, all of that stuff needs to be put on hold. You have a room full of reporters, sir."

Dellenbaugh finished his drink and stood.

"Good ideas have nothing to do with how much you make, John," said Dellenbaugh. "Okay, fine. Go tell the press corps I'll be out in five. We'll do it in the briefing room."

"Yes, sir."

King, Lovvorn, Brubaker, and Calibrisi stood up.

"Hector, stay for a minute, will you?" said the president as the others moved to the door.

When they were alone, Dellenbaugh shut the door.

"Hector, we need to figure out who did this," said Dellenbaugh.

"You have the FBI running hard at it, President Dellenbaugh."

"I don't trust the FBI to do it," said Dellenbaugh.

"If you're talking about running an off-balance-sheet investigation, I have to warn you, Mr. President, it would look bad and it might be against the law. You heard John. The *Times* is going to print a story accusing you, accusing us, of complicity in the crime."

"Which is why we need something better than the FBI," said Dellenbaugh, his voice rising.

"There are no options other than the FBI," said Calibrisi. "It's that simple. We can't do anything on U.S. soil."

"What about private contractors?"

"To do what? Fight the Russians? First of all, you'd need an army, and a very good one. There are no private security companies with the kind of scale you would need to be effective. But even if there were, if we hired private contractors to go after Russians on American soil we'd probably end up in jail. It's against the law."

"I know," said Dellenbaugh quietly. "I'm not suggesting we subvert any laws. But I'm angry as hell."

"You're frustrated, sir," said Calibrisi. "I don't blame you. I am, too."

Dellenbaugh stared at Calibrisi an extra moment.

"Can I trust you?" said the president.

"What the hell does that mean? Of course you can trust me. Why?"

"Follow me."

Dellenbaugh walked behind his elegant cherrywood desk and continued to the back corner of the carpet. As Calibrisi watched, the president knelt and pulled back the carpet. Beneath it was a hidden panel. It was black, made of steel, a few feet in length and a few inches wide.

A small digital screen on the panel was illuminated with the letters NIO/ADF.

Dellenbaugh placed his thumb against the screen. After two or three seconds, the secret compartment made a nearly silent click. Two small steel rods moved up from the ground. Dellenbaugh grabbed them and lifted the steel plate, putting it down on the rug.

It was some sort of safe, though hidden in the floor and not the wall. Calibrisi watched as Dellenbaugh reached in and removed a manila folder. He handed it to Calibrisi.

"Read it," he said.

Calibrisi opened the folder. Inside was a single piece of thin parchment laminated atop a thick piece of paper. It was a document, old and yellowed along the edges. It had, at one point, been folded. Most remarkable of all, it was handwritten.

> *September 10, 1787*
>
> *We, the undersigned, make known by these presents the following:*
>
> *That there may arise times of such crisis in the Republic wherein it becomes necessary to enact temporary laws outside the charter and process of the U.S. Congress. The following codicil memorializes and creates the ability for the president, in ahistorical times, to create law in secret, as long as such law benefits America and mankind.*
>
> *That the President of the United States shall be able to call upon a committee of Senate Members cast equally from temporal partisan cloth, upon whose jurisdiction and expertise it shall arise so as to be therefor unimpeachable, unbiased by issues of the day, said committee thus enabled to create law in secret. The insurance is thus that the senators shall be required to vote unanimously on the proposed action therein, without opportunity for misconstruction, so as to ensure equality of representation as well as be done in such a way as to be considered fairest opinion in the land. In order for such law to be legal, such amendment may last but one year, and if re-enacted must be done by the same manner as hereto described, with sincerity and duty,*
>
> *In which the first was done.*
>
> *So be it, this day . . .*

Beneath were dozens of signatures, which Calibrisi stared at in disbelief. Adams, Jefferson, Madison, Hamilton, and other Founding Fathers.

Calibrisi held the document for a few more moments, rereading it. He looked at Dellenbaugh.

"Has it ever been used before?" said Calibrisi.

"It's been called four times," said Dellenbaugh. "The last time was by Franklin Roosevelt in 1941. Of the four times, only once has there been a unanimous vote, and that was in 1941. Roosevelt asked for permission to start helping Churchill."

Calibrisi handed the folder back to President Dellenbaugh, who replaced it in the safe, shut the panel, and put the carpet back.

Dellenbaugh stood up and straightened his tie.

"I need to get to the briefing," said Dellenbaugh.

"Mr. President, you obviously have something in mind," said Calibrisi.

"I'm going to ask a committee of senators—the Senate Select Committee on Intelligence—to give the Central Intelligence Agency an exemption from various posse comitatus laws allowing it to operate on U.S. soil."

"In my world, the word 'operate' has a fairly specific meaning, sir," said Calibrisi.

"I know," said Dellenbaugh. "This would not be an investigative unit."

"You're talking about a kill team."

Dellenbaugh nodded as he pointed to the screens on the far wall.

"That's exactly what I'm talking about," said Dellenbaugh. "Whatever we're doing isn't working. The enemy has invaded our country and we're fighting back with our best soldiers on the sidelines."

"Why not JSOC?" said Calibrisi, referring to Joint Special Operations Command, a component of the Pentagon responsible for running covert operations throughout the world.

"JSOC? No way," said Dellenbaugh. "The CIA is one thing. The Pentagon is another. There's no way the SSCI would allow the Pentagon to operate on U.S. soil. My guess is, they won't even allow the CIA, but they trust you, Hector. You're not political. You've been transparent with both parties. You've stopped attacks on this country."

"Thanks, Mr. President, but I haven't," said Calibrisi. "The people who work for me have."

"You get the point."

"So what do you want from me?" said Calibrisi.

"After the press conference, I'll have Adrian draft the action," said Dellenbaugh. "I'll submit it under an *emergency priority* classification. I want a meeting immediately with SSCI. I need the design from you."

Calibrisi nodded.

"Mr. President, it's one thing to be killing people in some dark alley in Paris or Tokyo," said Calibrisi. "If my people are allowed to operate on U.S. soil, it will be in secret. There won't be any legislative record of it. They could be charged with murder."

Dellenbaugh grabbed his suit jacket from the back of his chair and put it on. He started walking toward the door, deep in thought.

"What do you have in mind?" said the president.

"We'll need to give anyone involved a preemptive presidential pardon," said Calibrisi.

Dellenbaugh had his hand on the doorknob to the Oval Office. Slowly, he started shaking his head.

"A preemptive pardon would mean they could do anything on

U.S. soil," said Dellenbaugh. "For the rest of their lives. I'm not comfortable with that."

"You're the one who said it, sir," said Calibrisi. "It's about trust. But trust needs to run in both directions. I'm not going to put people in-theater if they could be incarcerated for actions we ask them to take."

Dellenbaugh nodded. He smiled at his CIA director.

"You're absolutely right," said President Dellenbaugh. "Fine. I'll have Adrian take care of that, too. I want a plan we can take to the fifteen members of SSCI tomorrow at the crack of dawn."

Dellenbaugh walked alone through the dimly lit halls of the West Wing, which was mostly empty until the part of the building that housed the offices of the communications staff as well as the press briefing room. This part of the West Wing was abuzz.

Dellenbaugh stepped into John Schmidt's office. Schmidt was sitting down. Two members of the communications staff were standing near him. They were watching a special report from ABC about the assassinations of Blake and O'Flaherty. A reporter was standing on the klieg-lighted steps of the Capitol Building interviewing a high-ranking U.S. senator—a Democrat—who appeared truly sorrowful at the loss of John Patrick O'Flaherty, despite their philosophical differences.

Schmidt and his colleagues were mesmerized, to the point that they didn't notice the president's entrance. But Dellenbaugh didn't say anything. Instead, he watched, too, listening as O'Flaherty's political opponent talked about going sailing with O'Flaherty, drinking great wines with O'Flaherty, and being not just colleagues, but friends. When the interview ended, Schmidt shook his head, signaling his disbelief and sadness. He finally turned and found himself looking at J. P. Dellenbaugh.

"Sorry, sir," said Schmidt, standing up. "I didn't know you were here."

"No need to apologize. But let's get this rolling."

Schmidt looked at the two younger staffers and nodded them out of the room.

"Get Cory," he whispered to one of them.

He shut the door after they left.

"Let's talk about ground rules," said Schmidt. "Do you want to take questions?"

"Not particularly. But I'll do whatever you think is best."

"I wouldn't take 'em. But I suggest you see how you're feeling, sir. You're excellent at it. Now, what are you thinking about what you'll actually say?"

A knock came at the door, then it opened. A tall, bespectacled bald man stepped into the office. This was Cory Tilley, the president's twenty-six-year-old head of speechwriting. He was holding a piece of paper.

"Hi," said Tilley. He handed the paper to Dellenbaugh. "John and I thought I should put something down on paper, just in case you wanted it. We know you probably don't want it and would prefer to talk from the heart, so to speak, sir. I actually support that and think whatever you would say would be a heck of a lot better than this. We wanted you to have it just in case."

Dellenbaugh smiled and patted Tilley on the back.

"You're right," said the president. "I don't need it, but I appreciate you two making sure."

"Let me cue it up," said Schmidt.

"It's eleven at night," said Dellenbaugh. "People want to get home. I'll be fine."

"Roger that," said Schmidt. He reached for the doorknob, opening the door for the president, who walked out of Schmidt's office, took a left, and entered the White House briefing room.

There was a low-decibel hum of conversation in the room as Dellenbaugh entered.

At the back wall, a line of cameramen stood on a slightly raised platform. Most of the room was occupied by reporters, an even mix of female and male, all dressed in business attire, eight rows by twelve across, reporters from every major news outlet across the media complex—TV, cable, internet, newspaper, foreign correspondents—all credentialed and there doing what was considered the most prestigious job in journalism: covering the president of the United States of America.

At the front of the room was a slightly raised stage, upon which was a dais emblazoned with the presidential seal. Dellenbaugh moved to the dais and looked out on the roomful of reporters.

"President Dellenbaugh, is it true—"

"Hannah, please stop," said Dellenbaugh, staring at the reporter. "This is my press conference, not yours."

The roomful of reporters, who, other than the CBS correspondent, Hannah Blazer, had already gone quiet, all eyes on the president as he established a semblance of order in the room.

Dellenbaugh paused and scanned the room of reporters with his eyes, a cold, emotionless look on his face. Finally, after nearly a minute, he spoke.

"They killed a man I served in the United States Senate with," said President Dellenbaugh. "He was my mentor. I was a thirty-six-year-old former professional hockey player who didn't know anything. John Patrick showed me what to do, mostly out of pity, I think."

Dellenbaugh paused, gripping the sides of the dais as he fought to hold back emotion.

"I had dinner with Nick Blake three nights ago," said Dellenbaugh. "He flew to Washington on my invitation. We ate hamburgers upstairs, sitting on the terrace of the White House, looking at the sky. Nick might have been trying to beat me, but I wanted to understand what he'd done in Florida when it came to organized crime. Russian organized crime. Did he have ideas we could use in other parts of the country? That's what I wanted to know. We had a wonderful time. He was a truly special person."

Dellenbaugh paused, and his face took on a sincere and fierce demeanor.

"They killed a young, bright, up-and-coming governor who was doing a tremendous job," said Dellenbaugh. "Even I can say that. You know what? He might've beaten me, and that would've been all right. That's what democracies are about. Nick and I even talked about it. We laughed about it. We promised each other that above all else, we would try and have fun. It would've been a challenging, hard-fought, inspiring campaign, a real battle about how best to protect our country and our children. Imagine how great the debates would've been?" said Dellenbaugh, shaking his head remorsefully. "A world-class prosecutor against a former hockey player. Gee. I wonder who would've won?" Then Dellenbaugh stopped, reaching for his eyes. "But it was not meant to be," he said softly. "A lion of the Senate was murdered tonight, as was a future president—two great men, cut down for no reason."

Dellenbaugh paused. At this point, his eyes went from empathetic to stone as he found the live cameras at the back of the briefing room.

"Tonight will be scarred into the United States of America forever," said Dellenbaugh. "The Russian mafia declared war on our country tonight."

Dellenbaugh stared into the cameras that took his message

across the globe. His voice was rising in anger and his hand flew into the air, as if pointing at the perpetrators.

"By its actions, the Russian mafia declared *war* this night on America. Our way of life. Two great sons. Well, know this," said President Dellenbaugh to the cameras. "We will not rest until the people behind these crimes are discovered and brought to justice, and you better believe that American justice is coming. Put your insurance carriers on notice. America is coming and we *will* destroy you."

CHAPTER 8

Moscow

Yuri Malnikov was sleeping when the light in his bedroom went on. He looked up. His only child, his son, Alexei, was standing in the doorway, wearing only a pair of boxers, his hair tousled.

Alexei Malnikov was a big man, with broad shoulders and a muscled frame. He had dark hair and a sharp, aquiline nose.

"We have a problem," said Alexei.

Yuri reached over and turned on a bedside lamp.

"What is it?"

"The United States. John Patrick O'Flaherty and Nick Blake, the governor of Florida. They were both assassinated earlier tonight," said Alexei.

Yuri Malnikov climbed out of bed and walked to the wall, flipping on a light. Next to the light was a bar. He poured two vodkas, handing one to his son. They clinked glasses.

"The Americans will blame all of us," said Yuri.

Alexei nodded, putting the glass to his mouth and gulping it down.

"They'll come after all of us," said Alexei. "Whoever did this knows that."

"I spent a year in a Colorado prison," said the elder Malnikov. "You worked with the Americans to win my freedom. I think you should reestablish contact. In this matter, our interests are aligned with America's."

Alexei poured himself another half glass and unceremoniously downed it.

"I'll reach out if you want me to," said Alexei. "But we both know this was the work of the Odessa Mafia. I'd rather take our revenge directly. It was that fuck, Andrei Volkov, down in Miami. He runs everything."

"Do that too," said Yuri Malnikov, sipping a large gulp of vodka from his glass. "But make no mistake, the Americans will be looking for blood. I will not go back to prison, Alexei. I would rather die. You need to call Hector Calibrisi and explain. We have to educate them, otherwise we'll both find ourselves at Supermax. I am under three separate indictments and you're under two," said Yuri. "This has to be a face-to-face meeting, and I don't think you can set foot on U.S. soil."

"I understand," said Alexei Malnikov.

CHAPTER 9

22 West
1177 22nd Street, N.W.
Washington, D.C.

Tacoma dropped Katie off in Middleburg and drove to down-town Washington, D.C. He parked outside the front entrance of a high-rise apartment building. It was 5:15 A.M.

Near a bank of elevators, he put both thumbs against a pair of scanners and stared into an iris reader. After a second or two, and a series of electronic beeps, one of the elevators opened.

The elevator took him to the top floor, opening directly into it. The apartment was vast, the walls a shock of glass. The space was high-ceilinged, like a loft, and stretched in each direction. Though the floor was carpeted, there was no furniture. Instead, the sweeping space appeared empty, except for a mattress some-where in the distance, near one of the corners of the $18 million condo. Tacoma came to the king-sized mattress, with a neon green sleeping bag on top of it.

Surrounding the general area of the mattress were piles of clothing, at least a dozen of them, some dirty, some freshly out of the dryer, though nobody—certainly not Tacoma—knew for sure.

Tacoma simply removed all his clothing and dived toward the middle, his eyes shut before he hit the mattress. He was quickly sound asleep.

CHAPTER 10

Office of Chief Justice Mark Hastings
U.S. Supreme Court
Second Street, N.E.
Washington, D.C.

The presidential motorcade departed from the White House at
5:45 A.M. Dellenbaugh had contemplated bringing the Senate Select Committee on Intelligence to the White House, but Adrian
King, his chief of staff, talked him out of it. The bipartisan group
of fifteen senators needed to be assembled on neutral ground, in
a setting that would make every senator willing to put aside party
loyalty. Because President Dellenbaugh was asking each senator
to do something that had never been done before, namely, allow
the CIA to operate on U.S. soil, there could be no hint of partisan
advantage or political intrigue.

Mark Hastings, Chief Justice of the U.S. Supreme Court, had
agreed to host the secret meeting of the SSCI.

In the presidential limousine sat Dellenbaugh, Calibrisi, and
King. King, a lawyer by trade, had worked alone through the
night drawing up a series of documents built off the original addendum to the Constitution regarding emergency actions.

The first was a sworn affidavit attesting to the provenance of the original document, which the president had already signed. Another affidavit would memorialize the fact that Dellenbaugh was hereby calling for the committee to abide by its constitutional duties in hearing the proposed emergency action. A third document outlined a process for the voting by the senators on the merits of the proposed emergency action. The process had to adhere to and meet the guidelines of the original documents, that is, unanimity by a court "unbiased by opinion or resolve."

In addition, there were two more documents. Preemptive presidential pardons.

The motorcade moved into the heavily fortified entrance tunnel off Second Street and thundered into the underground parking garage.

Dellenbaugh and King took the elevator to the second floor, where the chief justice was waiting.

"Mr. President," said Hastings enthusiastically, extending his hand, "great to see you, sir."

"You too, Your Honor," said Dellenbaugh, shaking his hand.

"Hector," said Hastings. "Good to see you, chief."

"You too, Mark," said Calibrisi.

Hastings gave King a once-over.

"Uh-oh," said Hastings, smiling. "You brought the goon squad, Mr. President?"

King smiled as Dellenbaugh, Calibrisi, and Hastings broke into quiet laughter.

King had clerked for Hastings after he graduated from Yale. Hastings knew him like a son.

"Just kidding, Mr. Chief of Staff," said Hastings, giving King a hug. "Great to see you. Follow me, you guys. Everyone is in my office."

Hastings's office was entered through a large antechamber,

where several desks, belonging to various assistants and clerks, sat empty at this early hour. They followed the chief justice through a large doorway, entering his corner office. The ceiling was fifteen feet high, the windows massive, with views of the Capitol Building. Hastings's massive desk was in the corner, piled neatly with several stacks of files and papers. A credenza behind the desk was filled with various framed photos of Hastings with his family, as well as a few of him with past presidents and other dignitaries. One of the photos showed Hastings with Dellenbaugh's arm around him. Both men were dressed in hockey gear and their hair was wet with perspiration. Dellenbaugh wore an old University of Michigan jersey, Hastings had on an even older jersey from Harvard, where, as an undergraduate several decades before, he'd played goaltender. Large, modern paintings hung on one wall while the other was occupied by bookshelves containing leather-bound legal volumes. At the center of the office was a square of four leather Chesterfield sofas, all surrounding a glass coffee table, atop which sat a silver coffee service, cups, and saucers.

Already seated on three of the four the sofas were the fifteen members of the Senate Select Committee on Intelligence. They were dressed in business attire. There were eight Republicans and seven Democrats. Dellenbaugh, Calibrisi, and King went around the room shaking hands, then sat down on the unoccupied couch. It was Dellenbaugh who began.

"First of all, thank you for coming," said Dellenbaugh.

A gray-haired, regal-looking woman, Senator Tracy Wadmore-Smith, a Republican from South Dakota, spoke first.

"Why are we here, Mr. President?" she asked.

Dellenbaugh looked at the gathered group of senators.

"There exists a codicil to the original U.S. Constitution," said Dellenbaugh. "Under a strict set of conditions, the United States

Senate may allow the president to seek permission in order to enact temporary law in emergency situations."

"Why at the Supreme Court?" said a large, gray-haired, distinguished-looking man who was very thin, Peter Lehigh, the senior senator from California, a Democrat from San Francisco.

"A level playing field," said Hastings. "I'm a witness, but I've also read the original document. This codicil to the Constitution was last used in 1941 by Franklin Roosevelt. He was seeking permission to send arms to the British in order to help stop Hitler."

Dellenbaugh looked slightly surprised at Hastings. He was supposed to be neutral, but he was using the prestige of his office to reinforce the importance of the occasion, thus elevating the vote above partisanship. But the underlying effect was unmistakable. He glanced at King, whose face was emotionless.

"So it's for emergency measures," said Lehigh. "You want to take an emergency measure. Is that correct, Mr. President?"

Dellenbaugh nodded. "That's right." He looked at King.

"Mr. President," said one of the senators, Carly Bowman, a Republican from Arizona. "If you don't mind my asking, why are you exercising this provision? We're all shocked by what happened last night, but is it a national crisis?"

"That's up to you to determine, Senator Bowman," said Dellenbaugh. "I believe the Russian mafia has left us no other options. Law enforcement is failing in its battle. Last night the nation saw firsthand how badly we're losing."

"John Patrick O'Flaherty was a groomsman in my wedding, Mr. President," said a large black man, Senator Henry Cadomyer of Alabama, a Republican, his accent southern and warm, his words flowing slowly from a chiseled, ancient face. "My guess is, you intend to ask us for permission to do things—whether it's the NSA, the CIA, or some other thing I haven't even heard of yet. You're going to ask us for permission to do whatever it is you do—but on domestic soil. I know what I think of that, and I sure as hell know what George Washington would've thought of that."

"The codicil is clear, Henry," said a middle-aged woman with long black hair, Senator Danica Wade, a Democrat from Massachusetts. "Our role is to see that the emergency declaration is done according to the codicil and then to vote yes or no. Your opinion as to the proposed action is rhetoric. The fact that we're in the most hallowed ground of our country's legal system means we have to put our partisan feelings aside."

"Senator Wade is correct," said Hastings. "In fact, my read of the codicil is that the senators now assembled are being asked to cede power on behalf of a larger cause, meaning national security. That is what the codicil is about."

"That's right," said King, the White House chief of staff. "The codicil has strict requirements. Initiation by the president, an adjudication process that is witnessed as being fair, which we have endeavored to achieve by virtue of having the chief justice host and witness the event, an automatic sunset after one year's time, and most importantly, a unanimous vote by you, the members of the committee. We're here to seek your opinion up or down, with all due respect. Understand that a vote against means that anyone who opposes the Russian mafia not only is a target, but has nobody defending them."

"Is that a threat?" said Eric Ramirez, a Democratic senator from Florida.

"Not from me," said King, his voice rising. He took a step toward Ramirez. "They killed one of your colleagues last night, Senator. Who's to say you're not next?"

"*Adrian*," snapped Dellenbaugh.

"It's okay," said Ramirez, grinning. "Adrian is right, but it doesn't mean I have to like it."

"No, sir, it doesn't, but you do have to participate one way or another in fighting against it," said King.

Another senator, John Wetherbee, a Republican from Connecticut, pointed at Calibrisi.

"Is Hector involved?" asked Wetherbee.

"Yes," said the president.

"Then whatever you're asking for has my vote," said Wetherbee. "That's a man I trust right there."

"Thank you, Senator, but don't base your vote on me," said Calibrisi.

"Oh, I won't," said Wetherbee, winking at one of the other members of the committee.

Over the next hour, the fifteen members of the Senate Select Committee on Intelligence voted. Hastings compiled three piles of paper, sending each pile consecutively around to either be signed or left blank by each senator. One was a yes sheet, one a no, and one an abstain. The idea was to keep the votes private, though confidentiality—at least inside the chamber—was not required.

Several senators announced their support, while others, such as Carlo Von Schroeter, the senior senator from Texas, kept their cards close to the vest.

With the three piles arrayed facedown on the table, Hastings leaned forward and grabbed the first pile, which was the "Abstain" pile. He flipped through and didn't find a single signature. He put the pile on the floor, next to the wheels of his large leather desk chair. He then went to the "No" pile. It would only take one no vote—one signature—to stop the proposed CIA unit. Hastings had his own beliefs, which he attempted to hide, but when he didn't find a single no vote—and he knew the fifteen members of SSCI had given Dellenbaugh and Calibrisi what they wanted—he let out a slight "yes" as if quietly celebrating a touchdown.

Hastings nodded to King.

"One more thing," said King. He reached into another manila folder and removed fifteen sheets of paper. He handed one out to each of the senators, who read the paper over in silence.

The President shall have Power to grant Reprieves and Pardons for Offences against the United States, except in Cases of Impeachment.

U.S. Constitution, Article II, Section 2, Clause 1

In 1927, the U.S. Supreme Court stated, "[a] pardon in our days is not a private act of grace from an individual happening to possess power. It is a part of the Constitutional scheme. When granted it is the determination of the ultimate authority that the public welfare will be better served by inflicting less than what the judgment fixed.

It was another senator, a black woman, Rashawna Ungerer, a Republican from Michigan, who spoke first.

"What are you asking us to consider, Mr. King?"

"Preemptive presidential pardons," said King.

"Why are you asking?" she said. "Or should I not want to know the answer to that question?"

King smirked.

"Senator Ungerer," said King, "without getting into the details of what we're going to do, suffice it to say we're going to be asking certain individuals to do things on U.S. soil that are not legal, but they may become legal should you have deemed them to be so."

"In other words," said Ungerer, "if you get permission for the CIA to operate on U.S. soil in secret, and someone gets caught killing someone, say, for example, a Russian mobster, you don't want them to go to jail?"

"Something like that."

"I taught constitutional law," said Ungerer. "Article Two is clear. As long as it's not impeachment, it's part of the presidential power to pardon. I would add that if the codicil is part of the Constitution, the intent can be construed as to further exist by which unforeseen legal consequences such as the one you're talking about should be deemed to have been constructed at the time of the passage of the original codicil."

"Thank you, Senator Ungerer," said King. He looked around the room. "Does anyone disagree?"

"Even though I probably disagree with whatever scheme you boys are dreaming up," said Cadomyer, "I also know that Rashawna is right. It's clearly vested within Article Two. Plus, on a practical level, what kind of government is going to punish someone for doing something we ask them to do?"

"Good luck, Hector," said Wetherbee, standing up. "We'll be rooting for you."

"Who are the individuals you've selected, Hector?" said Senator Danica Wade.

"I haven't selected anyone yet," said Calibrisi. "I'll be reviewing files after we're done."

"The committee is entitled to know who the men we're setting loose on the United States are," said Wade.

"The Russian mob," said King, interrupting. "We're setting them loose on a bunch of killers and thugs."

"I stand corrected," said Wade. "My point is, we have a right to know the people we're authorizing preemptive presidential pardons for."

"I agree," said Senator Wadmore-Smith.

Several other senators nodded.

"The knowledge of who these men are must be extremely guarded," said Calibrisi. "I'm not sure I'm comfortable sharing their identities."

"I'll speak for myself," said Wade. "I took an oath to protect any and all information shared with the committee by the Central Intelligence Agency. I intend to honor that oath. But as long as I have a constitutional oversight role over the CIA, I expect to receive information that could effect my constitutionally mandated responsibility. Either I know the names of the CIA agents or I rescind my vote."

"Hear, hear," said several senators.

Calibrisi looked at Dellenbaugh. Dellenbaugh was blank and emotionless. He was telling Calibrisi that it was Calibrisi's decision.

Calibrisi glanced at Adrian King, the White House chief of staff. King, an experienced federal prosecutor, was shaking his head back and forth, saying to Calibrisi, don't do it.

Calibrisi walked over to King.

"Please excuse us," said Calibrisi.

They stepped to the corner of Hastings's large office.

When they were out of earshot, Calibrisi spoke.

"Are you thinking what I'm thinking?" said Calibrisi.

"What? That I don't trust half of these mother*fuckers* as far as I can throw them?" said King, nodding politely and smiling at the group of senators out of earshot.

"Something like that," said Calibrisi, grinning. "Maybe not quite as harsh."

"Oh, hell, chief," conceded King. "You have to tell them. Senator Wade is actually right. Besides, she's got us over a barrel—and she's not alone."

Calibrisi walked back to the conclave.

"Fine," said Calibrisi. "It's eyes only and no staff members. As I said, I haven't selected the members of the unit. When I do, I'll apprise you of their identities."

CHAPTER 11

CIA Headquarters
Langley, Virginia

By the time Calibrisi arrived back at CIA headquarters, Bill Polk, the bespectacled, balding head of the agency's Directorate of Operations—Langley's secretive, clandestine, highly trained crew of spies and assassins—was waiting.

Calibrisi's instructions to Polk had been simple. They needed to find two individuals for a deep-cover, possibly long-term mission. Calibrisi wanted three things: fluency in Russian, tenure inside the Eastern Bloc, and a "quadrant-level kill ratio," an internal measure of an operator's killing ability inside complex, lethal situations, especially in dead zones.

Calibrisi entered his office and immediately removed his coat and tie. Polk was seated in one of two chairs in front of Calibrisi's desk. With his brown corduroy suit, bow tie, and horn-rimmed glasses, Polk looked more like an English professor at a small, New England liberal arts college than the man responsible for directing Langley's paramilitary projects across the globe.

"You got me some names?" said Calibrisi, reaching for the manila folder Polk was holding.

Polk pulled it back before Calibrisi could grab it.

"What's it for?" said Polk, a cagey look in his eyes.

Calibrisi stared at him.

"Like most of the world, I'm vaguely aware of what just happened," said Polk warily. "You know and I know we are not allowed to operate on American soil. I'm not going to jail because someone higher up than me is pissed off at the Russians."

Calibrisi nodded, then grinned.

"I knew you'd say that," said Calibrisi, chuckling. "I'm going to tell you about something. It stays between us, Bill."

"Got it."

Calibrisi sat down and walked Polk through his conversation with Dellenbaugh and the codicil. He walked Polk through the process for voting. Polk listened without asking questions.

When Calibrisi was finished, Polk handed him the folder.

"So SSCI voted unanimously?" said Polk.

"That's right."

"We're speaking the same language here, right, chief?"

"Kill team," said Calibrisi. "A domestic exfoliation crew. Preemptive presidential pardons for any and all acts on U.S. soil. In-theater command control. No leashes, no oversight. Expires a year following creation of the unit. Must be reinstituted."

"And the president got seven Democrats and eight Republicans to agree on something?"

"Yes," said Calibrisi.

Polk nodded.

"What are you contemplating?" said Polk. "How many? Obviously, I know the background you're looking for."

"Two to begin with. We'll be designing it on the fly, and I don't want more variables than we can manage."

"*We* can manage?" said Polk. "Hector, unless you and I are also getting pardons, we ain't managing shit."

"Understood. I didn't mean we. I meant they."

"Well, I brought you three names," said Polk.

Calibrisi opened the folder. There were three pages. Each was a "spec sheet"—a summary page—on the individuals Polk had selected. Each sheet was stamped EYES ONLY—DCIA in red. At the top of each sheet was a black-and-white face shot. All three were male.

The first sheet showed a young, dark-haired, thick-necked Hispanic man with a mustache and a blank, deathly stare.

"Friendly-looking fellow," said Calibrisi.

VAZQUEZ, PABLO MARTINE

NOC 3320P-8   CAREER HIGHLIGHT(S):
ITC: RUS/UKR   Tenerife (Exxon/SINOPEC) Massacre
                      Lexan (Sevastopol) affair
                      Polikhaz Assassination

Fmr.
SPECIAL OPERATIONS GROUP
Eastern Sector
Active assignments:
Sevastopol
Kiev
Siberia

COMBAT APPLICATIONS GROUP (dis. Langley)
U.S. MARINE CORPS

LANGUAGE(S):
ENG
SPA

RUS
ARA
UKR

#K.R. 57.2%   (NOTE: Tier 1/Rank 7)

Action(s):

Madagascar, 2018	2
Cairo, 2018	1
London, 2018	4
Sau Paolo, 2018	1
BVI, 2017	2
Reykjavik, 2017	1
Paris, 2017	3
Verbier FR, 2014	5
Paris, 2014	1
Moscow, 2013	2

University of Southern California Dec 2012
Intl Relations B.A. 3.97 GPA
Varsity Swimming
Varsity Soccer (Captain 11–12)

Calibrisi moved to the next sheet. A pale-skinned man with a slightly crooked nose, as if it had been broken a few times. His eyes were hollow-looking, with dark bags around them. He had longish dark hair, down to his shoulders. He looked almost like a hippie, but another photo showed him in a wet suit, emerging from a swamp, a rifle in his arms, trained forward. It was a photo found on the man he'd been sent to kill, who accidentally took it with his cell just before the pale-skinned man gunned him down. Like Vazquez's, the look was emotionless, unless one knew his background, and then the look made sense: operational; a killer of the highest caliber.

"This guy actually makes the first guy look friendly," said Calibrisi.

"We're not running a preschool," said Polk.

"Yeah, I picked up on that."

SMITH, JAMES GREGORY

NOC 65T-55	CAREER HIGHLIGHT(S):
Special Assignment: Moscow	Assassination Binkerton (MI6 loan)
OP: "Exfoliate"	Assassination Polykov (GRU)
Per DDCIA	Assassination Verner (Freytag)

Fmr.
SPECIAL OPERATIONS GROUP
Eastern Sector
Active assignments:
Moscow
Greenland (Arctic Mining Recon)

NOTE: Proficiency in extreme climatic conditions, subterranean explosive design, and hand-to-hand combat.

COMBAT APPLICATIONS GROUP (dis. Langley)
U.S. ARMY RANGERS

LANGUAGE(S):
ENG

RUS
ARA
FR
#K.R. 60.9%   (NOTE: Tier 1/Rank 3)

Columbia College, Columbia Univ. May 2009
History B.A. 3.47 GPA
Theater
Varsity Fencing (NCAA championship 06, 08, 09)

Calibrisi flipped to the third sheet. It showed a bald man with a muscular forehead and eyes set a bit wide. The man's neck was thick and appeared to be about the same width as his head. He had an overgrown beard and mustache. Like the others, the stare was like a statue, stone cold, alert, fearsome.

"Well, at least one of these guys has your hairdo, Bill," said Calibrisi.

"A plethora of testosterone," agreed Polk. "Thought we should have at least one good-looking guy."

COSGROVE, WILLIAM JOSLIN

NOC X5-994	CAREER HIGHLIGHT(S):
Special Assignment: Venezuela	"Savage Night" (GRU
	trap) Caracas 2
Caracas (active)	Exfiltration
	Markov, P.
OP: "Clear Cut"	Assassination
	Zimmer, D.
	(Freytag)
Per DDCIA	Assassination
	Sanchez, N. (CIA)

Fmr.
SPECIAL OPERATIONS GROUP
South America Sector
Active assignments:
Rio
Karachi
Caracas
Buenos Aires
Greenland (Arctic Mining Recon)

U.S. Navy SEALs (dis. Langley)

ACTIVE: Tier 7a (JSOC) command, Section 4
Pakistan border/Afghanistan border
EXF 22
Direction of all units within 100 square mile quadrant along
the Khyber Pass.
Government ID# 227Y
Provisional authority under SECDEF 1.B

LANGUAGE(S):
ENG
RUS
URD
SPA
FAR

#K.R. 49.0%   (NOTE: Tier 1/Rank 18)

Duke University May 2008
Film Studies B.A. 3.22 GPA
Varsity Football (captain 08)

Calibrisi put the folder down and looked at Polk.

"Cosgrove is the only one who doesn't meet the criteria," said Calibrisi. "Kill ratio is below fifty-five. I assume you have a reason, beyond his good looks?"

"Actually two," said Polk. "First, he's highly organized. That's why he's in Peshawar. He's running wipeout teams up the Khyber Pass. You need someone organized to run this. Also, he's a great guy. I recruited him myself."

"Two?"

"He's good-looking," said Polk. "Look at that kid's hairdo."

Calibrisi laughed.

"What's two?"

"Vazquez and Smith are deeply embedded in dark zones," said Polk seriously. "It's taken us years to build out."

"Got it," said Calibrisi.

"There's another thing, and it doesn't feed into the decision, but it's real," said Polk. "Cosgrove has a family. His wife divorced him while he was in Karachi. He has two young children. If this is inside the United States, it would give him a chance to see them every once in a while. She took the kids to Atlanta. Broke his heart. She's remarried. If he could be more of a father it would be the least we could do for being the cause of it."

"How soon can you get him here?" said Calibrisi.

"He's in Peshawar," said Polk. "Assuming I can find him, tomorrow."

"Do it," said Calibrisi.

"I thought we wanted two guys," said Polk. "It sounds like we only have one."

Calibrisi stood up and picked up the folder. He looked at Polk.

"You know and I know who the other one is," said Calibrisi.

Polk said nothing.

"He has the highest kill ratio in the history of the Agency," said Calibrisi. "He's fluent in Russian and Ukrainian."

"He's in the private sector," said Polk.

"It's because you know him too well," said Calibrisi. "He's not just a name. You know how dangerous this fucking thing is going to be. He's the best choice and you know it."

"He's never spent material time inside a deep cover," snapped Polk. "He's an assassin. You know it and I know it."

"Which is precisely why he's the person we want for this," said Calibrisi.

"If we place him inside any sort of Russian paradigm, we might get him killed," said Polk. "You asked me for my advice and I'm giving it to you."

"We're fighting a war on American soil," said Calibrisi. "If you don't believe it, just ask Nick Blake. We need Rob Tacoma right now."

"Fine," said Polk. "I'll call Billy Cosgrove and get him on a plane. Do you want me to call Tacoma?"

"No, I'll talk to Rob myself."

CHAPTER 12

Torkham
Near Peshawar, Pakistan

Billy Cosgrove skulked silently down the alley and then down
a crumbling flight of stairs. He quickly picked the lock and entered the basement through an old wooden door, removing a suppressed Glock 19 from a concealed holster at his waist.

Cosgrove stood at six foot four and weighed in at 260 pounds,
most of it muscle. His face was painted a patchwork of dark green
and black, the whites of his eyes the only detail visible in the
darkness.

The room reeked of stale garbage. It was dark, and blisteringly
hot.

If his source was right, the door at the far side of the basement
would lead to another room. Above that room was an apartment
inside which the man was staying.

Cosgrove pulled night optics down over his eyes and flipped
them on, scanning quickly in a bright green hue. He looked silently across piles of garbage and cardboard, stacks of paint cans,
and then it all went white as someone flipped a light switch and
the room was illuminated in bright, blinding yellow.

"*Marhabaan, ya sadiqi,*" came a voice.

Hello, friend.

Cosgrove turned and looked toward the door. Three men were standing in a loose row. The two men in back had guns out. Their spokesman stood with his arms crossed, a look of confidence and anger on his face. He was young and bearded, dressed in tribal clothes.

Cosgrove acquired him in the site line of the suppressor.

"*Ma aldhy tafealuh huna?*" the man said.

What are you doing here?

"*Thlatht 'iilaa wahid,*" said Cosgrove as he squared off, moving backward, buying time. "*Tahtaj thlatht rajal?*"

Three to one. You need three men?

"I don't need three men. But it makes it more fun."

Break the team into parts. Start with the strongest. Kill quickly.

The lead man moved forward and began to slowly circle in an arc as the other two flanked him at either side, guns raised and trained on Cosgrove. Cosgrove again inched backward, creating distance, gun still raised and moving quickly now, across the three gunmen; he had little time.

The goal was to fire three consecutive shots, in three linear targets, either right-left or left-right, prior to the sound of your first shot causing the third man to fire, as he has been trained to do. In other words, take down all three before they kill you.

It's the only way. Imagine an eye chart. Measure and sweep in a line.

"Who told you?" said the guard.

"I have no argument with you," Cosgrove said. "If you want to live, I suggest you get out of my way."

"Are you going to take him?"

"No."

"Who is he?"

"None of your fucking business."

CHAPTER 13

Office of the Director
CIA Headquarters
Langley, Virginia

Calibrisi was on the phone, seated at his desk, when Lindsay, his assistant, stuck her head inside the door.

"He's here," said Lindsay.

"Let me call you back," said Calibrisi, hanging up the phone.

The glass door to Calibrisi's office opened. Cosgrove stepped in.

"Hector?" he said.

"Hi, Billy," said Calibrisi, standing up and walking around the corner of his desk. "Thanks for coming."

Billy Cosgrove's shaved head showed the dark outlines of what would have normally been a thick head of black hair. He was clean-shaven; rugged looking, like a football player. He wasn't handsome. His face looked as if it had been pummeled a few times. But he was big, with a muscular frame.

Cosgrove stepped into Calibrisi's office and shut the door. Calibrisi pointed to the seating area, a large rectangle of long leather sofas around a big glass coffee table. They sat down across from

Cosgrove swept the gun a few inches left and fired. The bullet struck one of the men in the eye, kicking him back, just as Cosgrove fired again, this time hitting the other backup thug in the throat, dropping him.

He trained the Glock on the remaining man, the young leader. "I gave you a chance."

The man's eyes were wide and dark, fear and panic glistening in them. Cosgrove fired, striking the man in the forehead.

Cosgrove found the man upstairs, asleep. He was an old man, in his seventies. He was alone. Cosgrove placed the end of the suppressor a half-inch from his chest and fired. A dull, metallic *thwack* echoed from the damp walls, floor, and ceiling. The bullet ripped through the target's heart.

He snapped a few photos and then saw the red flashing light of an incoming call. He put the phone to his ear.

"Identify," came a soft female voice.

"NOC X five dash nine nine four."

"NOC X five dash nine nine four." A two-second pause. "Identified. Please hold for DDCIA Polk. Confirm."

"Confirmed," said Cosgrove.

each other in the center of Calibrisi's large, glass-walled, sound-proof corner office.

"How's Peshawar?" said Calibrisi.

"I think you know the answer," said Cosgrove.

Calibrisi paused. "I lived there for two years. It was my second station. I kind of liked it."

"It's changed," said Cosgrove. "In nine months, I've lost thirteen men. You guys need to understand. It's not al-Qaeda. It's Hezbollah. It's the Iranians. Every gunfight we're involved in there always seem to be Iranians. We've killed a number of them. All Quds or Hezbollah."

"I read the reports," said Calibrisi. "I know it's a tough spot."

"Why am I here?" said Cosgrove.

"I assume Bill briefed you."

"He told me to get on a plane. I don't know shit."

"Tell me what you do, Billy," said Calibrisi.

"You know what I do."

"In your own words."

Cosgrove leaned back, crossing his legs.

"I run exfoliation crews," said Cosgrove. "We get intelligence, environment's too populated for a Hellfire, they call me."

"How many people have you killed since you got to Pakistan?"

"Me personally—or my guys?"

"You personally."

"Twenty or so."

"How about your teams?"

"Fifty-seven," said Cosgrove. "Actually, sixty-one, if you include tonight."

"Where are you getting your men?" said Calibrisi.

"Delta."

"You were a SEAL."

"Yeah, I know the kind of guy I need and I know how to pick them out. I spend a week every two or three months at Bragg looking at guys, same with Coronado."

"Are you saying Deltas are better than SEALs?"

"No," said Cosgrove. "I'm saying they're trained for different purposes. I'm running men into villages with precise information. I don't need a team. If I did, I'd be running DEVGRU. These are tight-seam, volatile-kill missions. In-theater stuff, instinct. Deltas are crazy, but they're the perfect sort of crazy for kill teams in Pakistan and Afghanistan."

Calibrisi leaned forward. After a few moments, he stood and walked to the far wall, pushing against a shelf. A door opened and a bar was hidden behind it.

"I'm having a bourbon," said Calibrisi. "Would you like one?"

"Sure," said Cosgrove.

Calibrisi opened a bottle of Buffalo Trace and poured two glasses. He returned to the seating area and handed Cosgrove a glass. Cosgrove took a sip as Calibrisi sat down.

"We're creating a unit and I want you to run it," said Calibrisi. "Obviously, it's top secret. You don't talk about it with anyone but me or who I tell you you can talk about it with. Don't trust anyone. Do you understand?"

"Yeah," said Cosgrove. "But I have a question: Are you guys asking me to do it or telling me?"

"Asking," said Calibrisi.

Cosgrove took another sip of bourbon.

"I'm all ears. Where's the job? To be honest, the last thing I feel like doing is heading back to a dead zone."

"The job is domestic," said Calibrisi. "While you might have to do some foreign travel, I expect it'll be rare."

Cosgrove nodded, a hint of interest for the first time flashing on his face.

"The Senate Select Committee on Intelligence met in secret session," said Calibrisi. "They can sometimes be called upon by the president on security issues the president believes pose significant enough threat to warrant sub rosa temporary amendment to U.S. laws."

"Like a star chamber," said Cosgrove.

"I suppose."

"Why were they meeting?"

"After the assassinations of Nick Blake and John Patrick O'Flaherty, the president sought permission to allow the agency to operate on American soil under a very tight focus: hunt down Russian mob and exfoliate. The vote was unanimous."

Calibrisi let the words sink in. Cosgrove remained still, with a blank expression on his face.

"A kill team? Won't I be breaking the law?"

"You and one other individual received authorization," said Calibrisi. "Each of you will be granted a preemptive and official pardon by the president for all actions on U.S. soil, even actions unrelated to the core mission. Technically, you can go rob banks if you want, but we hope you won't."

"I wouldn't be so sure," said Cosgrove, pointing at the bar. "You mind if I get another?"

"Not at all," said Calibrisi. "I'll take one too."

Cosgrove walked to the small liquor cabinet nestled in the bookshelves at the far side of Calibrisi's office. He poured two glasses and returned to the seating area. He handed one to Calibrisi.

"Russian mob, huh?" said Cosgrove. "So they're the ones behind what happened?"

"The Russian mafia now runs organized crime in every major city in America," said Calibrisi. "The U.S. government systematically destroyed the Italian mafia, but in its place came the Russians. They're a quantum level more brutal and violent."

"I'll become a target."

"Not if you do it correctly."

Cosgrove sat back down across from Calibrisi.

"You mentioned another member of the team. Do you have someone in mind?"

"Yes."

"Do I have any say in that?"

"No, you don't," said Calibrisi, shaking his head. "I'm the one who was given authority in terms of team selection. I picked you because you understand how to organize and run kill teams. The second individual is a guy named Rob Tacoma. I picked him because he knows how to kill. He's also fluent in Russian. By the way, he hasn't agreed to it yet. If he doesn't, I am considering sending you back to Pakistan and unwinding the operation."

"He's good?"

"Yes," said Calibrisi. "Very."

Calibrisi reached to a manila folder on the glass coffee table. He handed it to Cosgrove.

Cosgrove flipped it open and downed the rest of the bourbon. It was a few sheets of paper. At the top of the first sheet was a headshot. It showed a man with medium-length dirty-blond hair, parted in the middle. He had a layer of stubble, blue eyes, stripes of black beneath each eye, and was handsome, disarmingly so.

TACOMA, ROBERT THIERIAULT

Citizenship: USA
DOB: 4/12/90
Home:
New York City, NY
Middleburg, VA

Milan, Italy
Washington, D.C.

University of Virginia May 2010   Russian Studies B.A. 2.77
GPA
Varsity Lacrosse [Captain 08–09, 09–10] All-American 06, 07,
08, 09
U.S. Navy: enlistment Jun 09 [Charlottesville, VA]
U.S. Navy SEALs—training Coronado, CA
Rank: 4 in class of 232
U.S. Navy SEAL Team 6 DEVGRU: Virginia Beach, VA [Mar
10-Dec 12]
CIA Special Operations Group [Dec 12-Jul 15]
RISCON LLC, Middleburg, VA [Jul 15-present]: private security
firm founded with Katherine "Katie" Foxx, ex-director, Special
Operations Group

CAREER:

U.S. Navy SEALs/SOG:

- Stockholm: Jan-Mar 12: Reclamation of intellectual property
from traveling Facebook executive, Garin (mission success)
(Note: Garin terminated under in-theater provision 4)

- Panama City—COS: Apr-May 12: DOT Task Assignment,
removal of Jaidi, Ambassador PAN to Russia NUY, TPL, VEN
(mission success)

- London, ENG: Jun 12: Assassination P.D. Zarls, banker,
Goldman Sachs/special money laundering provision 77.b
(mission success)

- Munich, GER: Jun 12-Jan 13: Destabilization of German government, aka, Project Cold Rider, assassination of Adolf Kairnax, known uranium vendor (mission success)

- Berlin, GER: Jan 13–Mar 13: Assassination of Fields Bohring, German secretary of defense and intelligence (mission success)

- Rio de Janeiro, BRZ: Mar 13-Oct 13: Anti-narcotic: ARG, COL, CHI, and BOL: Total kills: 117 confirmed. Kill metric 76.7%.

- Paris, FR: Dec 13: Assassination Pierre Scott, Canadian businessman attempting to sell Canadian passports to El-Shaimeen, QUDS executive colonel. (mission success)

RISCON:

Enterprise retainer: $10000000/mo

Iran May 17: Theft of Iranian nuclear device

NYC July 17: Stop Pyotr "Cloud" Vargarin

Paris, FR, Aug 16: Project Eye for an Eye; removal of Fao Bhang

MISC:

- Raised in NYC. Youngest of two brothers [Bo born Sep 89]

- Bo Tacoma Lt. Cmdr, U.S. Navy SEAL Team 4 [Mar 09-Oct 14]: Bronze Star [Oct 09], Navy Cross [Oct 09]: Both awarded for actions resulting in the rescue and exfiltration of U.S. diplomat and family captured in Sri Lanka and subsequent firefight in which 4 members of SEAL Team 4 were KIA.

- Father, Blake Tacoma [b. Oct 58-d. May 12] U.S. Attorney for Southern District of Manhattan [Jan 07-May 09]

- Attorney General US (Jun 09-May 12)

- Portland, ME [May 12]: AG Blake Tacoma assassinated at public restaurant while on vacation with wife (Susan). Murder remains unsolved though FBI believes killing was reprisal for actions taken as DA and AG against factions of Russian mafia.

- Severomorsk, RUS (Murmansk Oblast region) [Oct 14]: Bo Tacoma, while on Observation + Assessment operation in the waters near the Port of Severomorsk, headquarters of Russia's Northern Fleet, is lost in early winter storm. After two days of reconnaissance efforts, he is declared Missing In Action and presumed drowned. All other members of unit survive.

Behind Tacoma's CV was a small stack of after-action reports. Over the next twenty minutes, Cosgrove read through all of them as Calibrisi watched.

"I've heard of him," said Cosgrove, putting the folder down on the table. "After that whole bomb incident near the Statue of Liberty, I read the stories. He's obviously talented, as you said. Probably a lot more talented than me. But . . ."

Calibrisi took a sip of bourbon.

"But what?"

"They killed his father?" said Cosgrove.

"He'll be motivated."

"Yeah, no shit he'll be motivated. And, he'll have a license to kill."

"Exactly," said Calibrisi.

Cosgrove shook his head.

"I don't like emotion in my teams," said Cosgrove. "Anger, revenge, sympathy, whatever—it alters things. You're setting in motion something that could become very unpredictable."

"I'm not sure I follow."

"If the Russians killed my dad, and I was allowed to go after them, I would kill as many as I could. And in a week or two, I'd be dead. That's what I'm saying. You're talking about putting nitroglycerine in a Ferrari. Don't be surprised if the Ferrari wraps itself around a tree going three hundred miles an hour."

"Point taken," said Calibrisi. "Your job will be to make sure that doesn't happen."

Cosgrove leaned back.

"Where do we work out of? Here?"

"Arlington," said Calibrisi. "We're setting up a Tier One secure site inside an anonymous-looking office building, heavy-duty security."

"What's the budget?"

"It's an off-balance-sheet appropriation," said Calibrisi. "A black budget. Technically, the money will come out of a long-forgotten national emergency fund that was originally set up by Ulysses Grant within the Treasury Department. Bottom line, you spend whatever you want."

Cosgrove took a sip of bourbon and looked at Calibrisi.

"I'm in," said Cosgrove, leaning back with a small smile. "When are you going to tell Tacoma about it?"

"I thought I'd brief him before you two meet, see if he's willing."

"When will I know?"

"He's on his way," said Calibrisi. "If he agrees, I think you two should get together, sooner rather than later. I'll handle the Pentagon and your various reassignments and commendations. We'll lock up your pension. Just so you know, you set your own salary. It's a black budget. I'm not telling you to be greedy, but we should be paying guys like you the way we pay major league baseball players."

"Understood."

Cosgrove stood up and reached his hand out, shaking Calibrisi's.

"I'm honored you guys thought of me," said Cosgrove. "I'm going to go home. I haven't been there in four months. Pay some bills, feed the cat, that sort of thing."

Calibrisi grinned.

"Have Rob come to my house for a beer tonight," said Cosgrove, "assuming you can convince him."

"Done."

"By the way, when do we start?"

"You just did."

CHAPTER 14

22 West
1177 22nd Street, N.W.
Washington, D.C.

Several hours later, Tacoma awoke to the low hum of his cell, vibrating next to his head on the hardwood floor. He saw the screen:

CALIBRISI, HECTOR

The cell phone was off except for three numbers, one of which made the phone vibrate like a fish on a dock.

"Yeah," said Tacoma, sitting up on the side of the bed. "What is it, Hector?"

"Hi, Rob," said Calibrisi.

"What time is it?"

"I need to talk to you."

There was a long pause as Tacoma ran his hand back through his mop of dirty-blond hair and stood up, naked. He was ripped, with the only mark on him being a tattoo on his right shoulder—a lightning bolt, cut in blue ink. Unlike most operators of his ilk, meaning DEVGRU, Tacoma had no bullet wounds or knife scars.

"I was going to take a few days off," said Tacoma, walking toward his jeans, in a pile on the floor. "What is it?"

"I'll tell you when you get here."

"Fine," said Tacoma. "I just have a quick errand to run."

"Okay, see you when you get here," said Calibrisi.

Tacoma hung up. He rubbed his eyes and looked at his watch. It was eleven in the morning. He pulled on his jeans, then found his red T-shirt and put it on. He stepped into his flip-flops.

Tacoma reached into his pocket and found the check Katie had handed him. It was his quarterly distribution check from RIS-CON. On some days, he was in disbelief at how much money he earned. In truth, most of the time it gave him an uneasy feeling. It reminded him of his father. His father had worked as a prosecutor most of his professional career and they didn't have a lot of money; what they did have put him and Bo through boarding school and college. His father used to talk about how they were going to go on a safari in Africa and then to the Great Wall of China, as soon as they had the time; as soon as they had the money. Every time his father was about to accept a lucrative job at a big law firm he was asked to do something more in government, usually by the attorney general. It was President Allaire who offered him his last job, the job during which he was killed, the job that got him killed, U.S. attorney general.

The check from Katie, instead of making Tacoma happy or proud, only reminded him of the man who had raised him and who died before they could see the lions he used to dream of.

Tacoma walked from the building east, toward the White House, crossing through George Washington University. He weaved down a series of roads and came to a majestic building with white columns and pretty red crosses on the portico peak and above the main door. It was the headquarters of the American Red Cross.

He entered the building. It was slightly chaotic. There were dozens of people sitting in every available seat. Tacoma came to a sign that said:

THANK YOU FOR VISITING THE AMERICAN RED CROSS.
WE ASK THAT YOU PLEASE WAIT FOR YOUR TURN IN LINE.

After almost an hour, Tacoma finally got to the front of the line. A black woman was seated behind a cluttered desk. She waved Tacoma over.

"How can I help you?"

"I'd like to make a donation," said Tacoma, reaching for his pocket. He put the check down.

She read the check and leaned back.

"Wait. Is your name Robert Tacoma?"

"Yeah," said Tacoma. "Do you have a pen?"

She leaned forward and handed him a pen.

"Some people want to talk to you," she said.

"Can you see to it that it goes to veterans?" said Tacoma, taking the pen and slashing his signature across the back of the check.

$16,455,900.92

"We always do, Mr. Tacoma."

"Rob," he said, standing up. "Mr. Tacoma was my dad."

Each time he gave it away it was like a warmth that consumed him in a perfect moment. He didn't need the money. He wanted it, but there was something more powerful that occurred when he gave it all away.

"*Rob!*" came a female voice. A voice not used to yelling. "*Rob Tacoma!*"

He was several blocks away, and the persistent voice continued to call out his name. Tacoma turned. A woman with shoulder-length brown hair was following him. She wore a dark business suit and a white blouse.

She was attractive, smart looking with curious eyes. Her chestnut bangs were wet with perspiration. Tacoma stood still, waiting for her on the sidewalk.

She approached and looked up into his eyes, breathing heavily.

"Rob Tacoma?" she said.

He paused.

"Yeah."

"I'm Elizabeth Penniman," she said, reaching her hand out. "I've been trying to meet you for two years now."

Tacoma shook her hand, then she held it a few seconds longer as she stared into his eyes.

"What do you want?" he said.

She took a final step, as if folding into him, her body coming close to him.

"You've given more than a hundred million dollars," she said, clutching his hand. "I want to know why."

Tacoma stared down into her eyes. They were framed by neatly cut locks of autumn brown.

"I don't need it," said Tacoma, shrugging his shoulders.

"Maybe someday you will?"

"Maybe," he said. "But I have enough already."

Tacoma started to walk away.

"May I ask you a personal question?" she said.

Tacoma stopped and looked back at her.

"Sure."

"How do you make so much money?" said Elizabeth. "We're taking it and giving it away. Do you do something bad and this is how you pay off your guilt?"

"It's all legal, if that's what you're asking," said Tacoma. "I give it away because I feel like it."

Elizabeth put her hands in her pockets, trying to think of something to say, but all that came out was a whisper. She looked down at her shoes, kicking the toes softly against the sidewalk.

"I don't understand," she said. "But I'm very grateful. We're very grateful. Thank you."

Tacoma smiled.

"You're welcome," he said.

"Would you like to get a cup of coffee?" she asked. "My treat."

"I can't," said Tacoma. "Rain check?"

"Sure. You know where to find me. But you didn't answer my question," said Elizabeth insistently. "Why do you give all your money away?"

"When you have nothing, you aren't afraid to lose it all."

CHAPTER 15

Greenwich, Connecticut

The mansion was visible from the road, though it was behind steel gates that ran around the ten-acre estate. It was far away, down a long gravel driveway, through overhanging trees and past lawns of manicured green. It was a veritable palace, three stories tall, its stucco façade painted in pale yellow.

The road itself was lightly traveled, a country road that wound north from downtown Greenwich toward the Merritt Parkway.

When Darré bought the estate three years before, he'd written a check for $100 million. There were twenty bedrooms spread across the top two floors. The first floor of the mansion looked like a modern art museum married to a George Smith showroom. Darré's wife, Nikki, had hired Manhattan's most esteemed interior designer to furnish it at a cost that was more than that of the mansion itself.

Darré knew the killing of Blake and O'Flaherty—a pair of seminal figures in American politics, executed at the same moment—would send the United States into a sense of chaos and anger the likes of which had never seen before. It was Volkov who designed the actual operation; the poisoning of the senator at the steak house, the shooting of the popular governor at the hotel. The bold killings had sparked a crisis at the highest levels of American government. As expected—as Darré had hoped— the crisis was leading the U.S. government directly into the trap Darré had hoped to set, a trap that would ensnare the entire Russian mafia, not just his organization, in the crosshairs of J. P. Dellenbaugh's administration, and thus cause the internecine war that Darré wanted.

Darré believed the ensuing chaos was the only way for his crime empire to climb to number one in the largest and most profitable market in the world.

That Darré was not Russian was a strange irony.

Without the Russian mafia, Darré would not be a billionaire. Yet, because of them he was now worth nearly ten. His hedge fund, the Darré Group, managed $45 billion. His public face was that of a brilliant stock picker, a value-oriented investor who saw disparities between the stock-market-defined value of a company and its real value.

That world was legitimate. It was a world he kept separate from the darker world that now took center stage.

It was 6:15 A.M. Darré stepped out the front entrance of the house and walked to a waiting silver Mercedes limousine.

An hour later, Darré walked off the elevator at the sixty-ninth floor and into the glass-walled canyons of his investment firm.

He'd founded the Darré Group twenty-one years ago. Then, it was him and a young associate named Connolly he brought with him from Paulson. Darré started with $100 million of his own money. At age twenty-seven, it was all the money he had. By the end of the Darré Group's first year he'd raised another $4 billion. A large pool of capital for him to simply invest and make money. In some ways easy, but in the end, not so easy. Hard. Yet Darré had a theory on value in relation to energy price trends, distilled into a set of proprietary algorithms that had caused the Darré Group's assets under management to go from $4 billion to $30 billion without new capital investment, over a period of two years. The firm had never had a down year, continuing to grow.

But now all Darré saw was the black sky beyond the glass. He'd amassed a fortune, but at what price?

A bitter memory flashed into his mind as he entered his office and shut the door.

He thought back to a dinner long ago. It had been more than a decade now. A dinner that the Darré Group was hosting for limited partners, that is, those institutions and individuals who'd invested money into the Darré Group. The dinner was held on a private floor at the Langham Hotel in Chicago, a sprawling, modern, glass-walled suite that took up half a floor of the Mies van der Rohe–designed building.

A man Darré didn't know approached.

"Congratulations, Mr. Darré," the man said. He was a very tall man, with a block of black hair, dressed in an ill-fitting suit. Darré was six foot two, yet the stranger hulked over him.

"Thank you," said Darré, smiling widely, his charm perhaps his most valuable asset. "I hope you're having a good time. Have we met before?"

"No," he said. "My name is Kaiser. I need you to listen to me."

Great wines had been consumed already and ties were off. Everyone had a good buzz on. Every person at the dinner was male, but soon the room became more filled as female attendants came to take drink orders.

Darré looked at the man, a pale-skinned, abnormally tall

individual. He had a slight stoop, perhaps from so many years of having to look down at people. His hair was neatly combed but oddly parted. If he announced he was from Transylvania, Darré wouldn't have been surprised.

"What's on your mind, my friend?" said Darré, glancing back at the reception.

When Darré looked back at the man, Darré's eyes were face-to-face with a knife edge, less than an inch from a steel blade, which the man was holding a few inches from Darré's neck, clutched by one of his large hands, out of view of anyone who might be observing, including, because of the man's stoop, security cameras.

"I'm not here to hurt you," said Kaiser in a baritone voice with an eastern European accent. "The knife is simply meant to make you listen."

One of Darré's assistants walked toward him—from behind Kaiser—with a glass of champagne. Darré held up his hand, telling her to turn around.

"What do you want?"

"When you raised the original amount of money for your firm," said the large, hulking Kaiser, "do you remember a certain investor, a group called PVX?"

"What do you mean, do I remember them?" said Darré. "PVX is my largest limited partner. They put in a billion dollars when I was just getting started."

"I'm PVX," said Kaiser. "You work for me, Mr. Darré. Or may I call you Bruno?"

"I'll redeem your money tomorrow," said Darré. "I don't work for you."

"You do," said Kaiser, moving the tip of the blade closer to Darré's neck, pressing lightly against Darré's carotid artery. "Bruno, you're a smart man. You've made yourself billions with our money. I want you to make more. I don't care about the money. But you need to understand something. You now work for us."

"Who is us?"

"The Odessa Mafia."

Darré washed the memory from his mind as his cell phone started to chime. He looked at the screen.

UNKNOWN

Darré answered.

"Who is this?"

"Mr. Darré, we need to talk. It's Senator Lehigh."

CHAPTER 16

The Hay-Adams Hotel
Washington, D.C.

A man entered the hotel lobby wearing a baseball hat and sunglasses. He was trying to hide his identity, though the last place a United States senator should've been, were he or she trying to remain unseen, was at the Hay-Adams hotel.

It wasn't the most luxurious hotel in Washington, D.C., though it was quite luxurious. At one point, it had been the city's most splendid hotel, a place where diplomats and world leaders stayed. Slowly, over time, the Hay-Adams had evolved. It was now the epicenter of a certain kind of activity that had always and would always take place in the nation's capital. The Hay-Adams was the crossroads where foreigners sought to intersect with U.S. politics, a place where espionage occurred, where classified information was leaked, bureaucrats, reporters, and politicians recruited, all under the fanciful canopy of gilded limestone and crystal chandeliers, in dimly lit corners filled with worn, red leather chairs, but mostly in suites on the floors above.

The man, Senator Peter Lehigh, crossed the grand lobby of the Hay-Adams and went to the front desk.

"I reserved a suite," said Lehigh.

"Your name, sir?"

"Richards. Harry Richards."

"I'll need a credit card, Mr. Richards."

He looked nervously about, then reached for his wallet. He removed a credit card and handed it to her.

"This is an AMEX gift card, sir," said the woman. "I need to see a license, sir."

"I don't drive," he said. "I reserved the room and prepaid for it."

She looked at him with a suspicious look.

"Okay, yes, that's fine. Hold on, please, Mr. Richards."

Ten minutes later, Senator Peter Lehigh, the senior U.S. senator from the state of California, entered the suite and locked the door, bolting and chaining it.

He removed a disposable cell phone from his trench coat pocket and dialed. After several moments of clicks and beeps, the phone started ringing.

"Who is this?"

"Mr. Darré, we need to talk. It's Senator Lehigh."

Lehigh went to the minibar and opened the door, searching for a bottle of something to drink.

"I have information, but it's highly confidential. I want to re-negotiate our deal. I am going through considerable risk if I tell you."

Darré stopped thinking about Kaiser. He needed to focus. Darré pictured Lehigh, all 130 pounds of him, a slouching, balding, white-haired hypocrite, a former Berkeley professor whose main skill was getting poor people to hate rich people, and manipulating that hatred into votes. He was yet another one of the freeloaders. Darré knew he needed to pay freeloaders like Lehigh in order to have the sort of information that would enable him to do things, such as kill Nick Blake and John Patrick O'Flaherty.

Lehigh was an old annoyance. Yet, it wasn't every day that the ranking minority member of the Senate Select Committee on Intelligence called.

"Senator," said Darré. "I appreciate the call. What is the information?"

"I want to discuss the deal first."

Darré heard his office door open. It was Alison, one of his assistants. She was carrying a cup of coffee. Darré waited until she was gone to speak.

"We don't renegotiate. I'm the one that sets the terms of our deal," said Darré. "I'm sick and tired of you. We've paid you more than five million dollars, and for what?"

"I helped you enter Los Angeles," said Lehigh. "Do you not remember? The unions?"

"That was then, this is now," said Darré. "What the fuck have you done for me lately?"

"I have something for you that is worth much more than five million dollars," said Lehigh. "And I'm not asking for more money."

"What are you asking for?"

"For you to leave me alone," said Lehigh. "Our deal is done and you never call me again. I'm telling you something that is top secret. I could get hung for telling you."

"What is it, Senator?" said Darré evenly.

"It has to do with what happened last night," said Lehigh. "In Iowa. In New York City."

Darré's head jerked right, as if struck by a fist.

"What makes you think I had anything to do with what happened last night?" said Darré.

"I . . . I don't," stammered Lehigh.

Darré knew he had a situation on his hands, a perilous one or perhaps a very lucky one. He had an insider's view into the workings of SSCI, and Lehigh wanted to not owe him anymore.

"Go on," Darré said.

"This morning, the Central Intelligence Agency received authorization to operate on U.S. soil," said Lehigh. "SSCI voted unanimously to let the Agency have a secret team on U.S. soil whose sole mission is killing members of the Russian mafia."

Darré was silent as he considered the senator's words. His first thought was that, yes, indeed, Senator Lehigh was telling him something worth much more than $5 million. The reaction showed where America was going with what happened to Blake and O'Flaherty. *A kill team*. It caused a slight chill to run up Darré's spine.

Darré's second thought was that, if it was true, it represented a historic opportunity. The opportunity to take control of organized crime in the United States.

"They have a so-called black budget," said Lehigh. "It means they can spend as much money as they want, with no supervision. Also, the team they've selected has been given preemptive pardons by the president."

Darré was quiet for a few moments.

"How can they do this?" said Darré. "It's against the law. I don't practice law, but I did go to Yale Law School."

"They received permission," said Senator Lehigh. "In secret, a unanimous vote by SSCI."

"You voted for it?" shouted Darré.

"What should I have done, been the lone holdout?" said Lehigh. "It would look pretty suspicious."

"What would?"

"If I voted against it," said Lehigh, "and if they start examining my bank accounts, there will be questions."

"I understand," said Darré. "You made the right decision. Tell me more."

"The CIA team will have two individuals, highly trained operators," said Lehigh. "I only know one of the names. I will tell you this man's name on one condition. This erases all my debts."

"Mr. Lehigh," said Darré. "You will always be in debt to us. You lost your ability to negotiate a long time ago. Tell me the name. In exchange I won't have one of my people in Washington come over and rip your fucking throat out."

There was a long, uncomfortable pause. Darré could hear Lehigh clearing his throat.

"As I said, I only know one of the men. His name is William Cosgrove. But you should beware. I wouldn't touch this if I were you, Mr. Darré."

"What are you suggesting?" said Darré.

"The CIA will go to places the FBI doesn't know even exist," said Lehigh. "They will come after *everything*. If they find me, they find you. You need to get to this man, buy him off. I don't pretend to know what you folks do, but it would seem to me to be prudent to stop this team before it even begins, starting with Cosgrove."

Darré hung up and dialed. He stared out the glass outer wall of a large office; the other walls, in bird's-eye-maple brown, displayed paintings by Ellsworth Kelly, Benjamin Foster, and Damien Hirst. The outer wall was glass from floor to ceiling, the corner suite. The interior was walled like a library. It was meticulously clean and large.

Darré stood at the glass, staring into the distance at Central Park. He remembered the first time he came to New York City. He had a little more than one hundred thousand dollars, lent to him by his father-in-law. Darré's wealth had exploded. By forty he was a billionaire, but he wasn't happy. He didn't regret the fact that he'd sold his soul. He regretted that he didn't know for ten years. That he'd never gotten the chance to make the choice between good and evil. It had been made for him.

Darré had been introduced to a young Russian goon from Miami named Andrei Volkov. He was now Darré's right-hand man. Volkov ran the criminal enterprise from a cargo terminal at the Port of Miami. Volkov was Darré's only connection to the illegal activities the enterprise conducted on a day-to-day basis. He oversaw the import of drugs and human beings, but mostly Volkov was his enforcer, a brutally violent killer who perfectly executed Darré's strategies and ideas.

Darré knew that the only way to do it was to be the most cunning and ruthless of them all, even as he hid in plain sight. The government would eventually find almost anyone, but not him. That would be his ultimate accomplishment.

Also, he couldn't complain. The year before, he had earned $477 million from the Darré Group. But as astonishing as that was, he'd made more than a billion dollars from the Odessa Mafia. On one day the year before, he had received notice from one of his banks in Switzerland that, that day, fully $815 million had been wired into his bank account. As much as he hated it, as much as he didn't need the money anymore, Darré couldn't help but be astonished at the size of the empire he controlled. That it was but a fraction of the Odessa Mafia was an ineluctable fact he found hard to fathom. He wasn't even Russian. Yet his own empire was immensely interwoven with the Russians', as he could only now see. It was hard, as an American, to watch. The fact that he was helping make it happen only made his guilt feel worse. He needed to hide it.

He lifted his phone and dialed. Soon, he heard Volkov's gruff voice.

"Bruno," said Volkov.

"Andrei," said Darré, staring out at the Manhattan skyline.

"Did you see the news? The team succeeded," said Volkov.

"Yes, I saw it," said Darré. "But we have a more pressing issue, and I need you to focus."

"What is it?" said Volkov.

"The CIA was given permission to operate on U.S. soil," said Darré. "The sole mission is to kill members of the Russian mafia. That includes you."

"And you, too," said Volkov.

"Yes," said Darré. "I know. We're in this together. Don't ever forget that. But now is the time when your value takes center stage."

"What do you need from me?"

"I have the name of the first man on the CIA unit. Presumably, he lives in the Washington, D.C., area. I'll find out the address and text it to you. When you get it, send one of your D.C. thugs over and kill him. Okay? I have to go."

"Hold on," said Volkov. "This is a guy the CIA just recruited?"

"Apparently."

"I can't just send anyone in, Bruno," said Volkov. "These guys don't go down easy."

"You can do it."

"Listen to me," said Volkov calmly. "We can go and try and kill him right now with a couple minor-league pieces of shit, but if one of them gets caught, they find me, and then they find you. Get it? Stay in your fucking lane."

"However you do it, just get it done," said Darré. "I didn't ask you how to make a watch, Andrei; I asked you what time it was."

"Understood," said Volkov, his Russian accent thick. "We're on the same page, Bruno. I'll get it done."

CHAPTER 17

APQA Cargo Terminal
Miami, Florida

Volkov tried to understand what he had begun, but he was lost in a prism of paranoia and weariness.

He dialed his cell.

"Where are you?" he demanded.

"I'll be there soon," said a female voice.

Outside, in the canyons of warehouses, a high-pitched whistle screamed as the clock hit 5 P.M.

Volkov stood up from his desk.

The whistle—signifying the end of the shift—roared for another few moments, then stopped.

Volkov's office was in a large warehouse, one of literally hundreds in the labyrinthine metropolis that was the Port of Miami. He moved to the door and opened it. Outside, a walkway, a parapet, clutched to the outside of the steel gray warehouse. Volkov stepped out onto the steel grate.

Below, the men had already started to gather.

At shift's end, the ritual was always the same.

The workers would gather around, in a large circle. There were more than four hundred workers at APQA Cargo Terminal, and others from neighboring terminals would come over to watch.

Hundreds of men gathered in concentric circles in between the warehouses.

Volkov stared at the tarmac crucible below, where four or five hundred men had gathered, pushing toward the front of the human scrum, to get a better view, to throw more money down.

The ritual was simple.

Each night, there would be a fight. People threw money in. How much they threw was based on the anticipated quality of the fight. The reigning fighter had to pick someone to try and beat the shit out of in a bare-knuckled fight with no rules other than weapons were not allowed. If the reigning champion chose a small, unworthy man, only a few bills would pile up. But when the reigning fighter chose a worthy adversary, the money always tumbled in as the two men squared off against each other in the human square.

This night was the seventeenth night in a row for Tikkar, the six-foot-seven giant from Kiev. He was the first man in more than a year to get into double digits.

All of the men were drenched in sweat and grime after a twelve-hour shift on the docks.

A tall man with a beard emerged.

"*Serdityy Medved!*" someone shouted.

Angry Bear.

The man entered the center of the human ring as the chanting from the four-hundred-plus gathered men grew louder. He was tall, thickly built, with a broad, dark face that sent shivers through many of the men. Tikkar stalked into the human circle. He pointed at a stocky bald man and they entered the human scrum, as workers threw money down and men started howling and screaming.

It would be a nasty fight. Tikkar had chosen an animal, one of the freight managers, a fierce Serbian named Egorov, whom everyone feared. Egorov was much shorter than Tikkar, but he was built like a tank and he was perpetually red-faced, looking for a fight.

Egorov entered the ring and tried to rile up the crowd, lifting his arms up triumphantly. Egorov swooped closer to Tikkar without looking at him, smiling at the crowd, and then abruptly lunged. But Egorov's arm was met with Tikkar's fist. The giant grabbed Egorov's arm at the elbow as it swung. The crack of Egorov's elbow was low but loud enough for everyone to hear. Egorov screamed in pain. As Egorov reached for his broken arm, Tikkar sent a crushing fist into Egorov's chin, knocking him back and down, his head falling hard against the tar, totally unconscious.

Shouting and clapping erupted as Tikkar moved to the ring of bills that awaited him.

A few men moved to Egorov, whose broken arm was bent unnaturally sideways.

Volkov took the steel fire escape down to the ground and found Tikkar.

"Not bad, Tikkar," said Volkov.

"I am honored that you watched, Mr. Volkov."

"You have a fearsome style," said Volkov. "But always beware. You grow arrogant, Tikkar. You want to beat my record? A little humility."

Tikkar's eyes cut hard, fueled in anger, staring daggers at Volkov, then he fought to control it.

"I am always trying to learn," said Tikkar.

"Good," said Volkov.

* * *

CHAPTER 18

Director's Office
CIA Headquarters
Langley, Virginia

Calibrisi stared out the glass-walled office, looking at the trees in the distance, lost in thought. A knock on the door startled him from his reverie. Tacoma stepped inside.

"Hey," said Tacoma, smiling.

"Rob," said Calibrisi. He stood and walked round the desk. He shook Tacoma's hand and they sat down across from each other on the leather sofas in the middle of the office.

"What's up?" said Tacoma.

"I want you to come back into the Agency."

Tacoma had a look of disbelief on his face. He started laughing.

"No way," said Tacoma finally, shaking his head. "I'm not dealing with the bureaucracy over here."

"It's a self-directed unit. You'll have in-theater command control and autonomy. Obviously, Bill and I will be involved."

"Hector, I'm trying to save up," said Tacoma. "I can't exactly do that on a government salary."

Volkov climbed back up the steel stairs and entered his office. When he did, he found himself looking at a young brown-haired woman with an elegant, sculpted face.

She was dressed in a knee-length tweed skirt and a red blouse, and had on a pair of shiny white Gucci boots.

"Hello, Audra," said Volkov.

"Andrei," she said emotionlessly.

"I need you to do something," said Volkov. "I don't trust anyone else. It's a two-person job."

"So killing John Patrick O'Flaherty wasn't enough?"

"The CIA is coming after us. We need to kill someone, one of the men."

"Why?"

"Because, otherwise, in six months or a year, we will both be dead," said Volkov. "Get the sniper you hired."

"I want a million dollars, Andrei, otherwise I'm not interested."

"You'll do it, Audra, or else I'll drive to your house—"

"And do what?" said Audra. "Kill me? We both know what would happen if you tried to kill me. So do we agree?"

"Yes. A million."

"Wire it and I'll leave. By the way, where is it?"

"Washington, D.C. I'm texting you his address."

"Yes, I'm aware of how much you and Katie make," said Calibrisi. "And I know you give every nickel of it away, so don't try and bullshit me."

Tacoma leaned back.

"At least let me tell you about it," said Calibrisi.

"That's fine," said Tacoma, "but nothing you say is going to get me to change my mind."

"This morning, SSCI authorized the CIA to create a unit that will have full lethal protocol on U.S. soil," said Calibrisi.

"'Lethal protocol'? What the hell does that mean?"

"A kill team."

"How big is the team?"

"Two people, with some support."

"Who's the other guy?"

"His name is Billy Cosgrove. SEAL Team 4, a little older than you."

"What if we get caught?"

"You don't," said Calibrisi.

Tacoma shook his head.

"What if we do?"

"You have a preemptive presidential pardon," said Calibrisi. "For anything you do on U.S. soil. It can't be taken away."

"So I can do whatever I want?" said Tacoma.

"Yes," said Calibrisi, shaking his head, "but it's based on trust."

Tacoma laughed, then nodded, surprised, even a little impressed. Then he remembered.

You don't want to do it.

"No, thank you," said Tacoma. He stood up. "I like my life the way it is. I like traveling, Hector. Also, I like giving it away. There are people out there I served with who now have nothing. Maybe some of it's getting to them, know what I mean?"

"Think of the people you'll be helping by getting rid of this scourge."

"Look, I'm flattered and all that," said Tacoma, turning. "There are other guys out there who can do what I do."

"We both know that's not true."

Tacoma was at the door. He turned to Calibrisi as he pulled the door open.

"What about Dewey Andreas?" offered Tacoma. "You know he's the best, and he's certainly a hell of a lot better at this shit than I am."

"This requires the kind of subtlety I'm not sure Dewey is capable of," said Calibrisi. "Not to mention, Dewey doesn't speak Russian."

Tacoma turned. His eyes cut into Calibrisi's, a hint of emotion behind them, curiosity mixed with anger. A single moment of seriousness.

"Rob, we're going after the Russian mafia."

"I get it," said Tacoma. "The bastards who killed my dad have now just shot Blake in the head and poisoned O'Flaherty. It's very tempting, but no thanks."

"I wouldn't have asked you if I didn't need you," said Calibrisi.

He wrote out Cosgrove's address on a slip of paper and handed it to Tacoma.

"Go meet with Cosgrove," said Calibrisi. "He's a good guy. If you still feel like you don't want to do it, you don't have to. I'm just asking you to have an open mind."

Tacoma nodded as he took the paper.

"I can do that, I guess," said Tacoma. "But the answer is still going to be no."

CHAPTER 19

118 Partridge Lane, N.W.
Palisades
Washington, D.C.

As Cosgrove pulled his pickup truck into the driveway, Slokavich was already inside the garage, Audra in the house. Both were waiting as Cosgrove lifted the garage door from the outside. Slokavich was stashed to the left, down in a crouch, a suppressed handgun targeted on the door as Cosgrove lifted it up.

Audra was in the living room. She, too, was gun ready, ostensibly as backup, but she doubted Slokavich would need it; Slokavich had Cosgrove at the crossroads of the garage door and the driveway, like a sitting duck.

As Cosgrove lifted the door, Slokavich waited, hoping that Cosgrove would pull the door back down after he went inside. It would be much cleaner that way, with no chance of a neighbor accidentally seeing something suspicious.

When the door was all the way up, Cosgrove stepped inside and reached for the inside handle to pull it back down. Slokavich aimed and—

In that moment, there was a pause in the door's downward

track, as if it was stuck. For Slokavich, it was a moment of confusion, and light from outside masked Cosgrove's shadow inside the garage. Then it happened. Cosgrove ducked and—in the same fluid motion—flicked his hand from ten feet away. Slokavich caught a glint of reflected steel and then felt the ripping shock of a knife blade stabbing deep into his stomach. Slokavich fired, but the abrupt trauma from the blade—the horrible pain, the sight of crimson spilling like water—interrupted his actions. The Russian's arm moved ever so slightly as he fought for breath. The suppressed pistol spat a bullet—a low metallic *thwap*—but the bullet hit the wall behind Cosgrove, who was gone, charging for the door into the house at the far side of the garage.

Slokavich tried to stand and felt the sharp, searing burn of the blade in his torso. He reached down. It was a small, tactical neck knife, sheep's-foot-shaped, two finger holes, short and stubby, sharpened to a lethal edge. He yanked it out of his stomach, moaning in agony, then ran for the door to the house.

In stride, Cosgrove pulled a Glock 19 from the holster beneath his left armpit. He reached the door just as Slokavich fired again. This time, the bullets struck the door just as Cosgrove opened it and ducked inside, gun drawn.

Cosgrove swept the interior of the kitchen for others. Seeing no one, he moved into his living room. As he turned to take aim at the door to the garage, he saw a woman in black clothing. Their eyes met. Cosgrove pivoted in a fraction of a second. But by the time the Glock's muzzle was on the woman, she had leapt, sending her foot in a vicious bend that caught Cosgrove in the chin, a hard blow that snapped his jaw immediately. As he fell backward, before he could catch himself against a counter, the woman tracked him and stormed forward, punching Cosgrove with both fists, a flurry of fists, pounding Cosgrove's nose, breaking it, as Cosgrove attempted to get his hands in the way. He struggled to remain lucid, then saw her leg cock back again. He ducked left. Her foot went inches above his head. Cosgrove slammed the gun wildly, swinging for dear life, and struck the killer's neck. She went backward.

Slokavich arrived, the blood now flowing from his stomach.

As Cosgrove went to kill the woman, Slokavich lunged, tackling Cosgrove to the ground, pulling his gun from his hand just as Audra got back to her feet and converged on the two men. Cosgrove punched fiercely, elbowing, trying to knee at Slokavich's bloody torso, but Audra came to Cosgrove's side and kicked him in the head. She kicked him another time, a violent kick to the eye which caused Cosgrove to moan. She kicked him again, and again, until he was unconscious.

Slokavich looked up from the ground at Audra. He was out of breath and bleeding badly. The ground was spattered with blood.

"I'll find a rope," she coughed.

Slokavich found a steel railroad spike, and by the time Audra returned with a rope, he'd stabbed it through Cosgrove's chest. They hung Cosgrove from a stairwell rafter, using a rope she found in the garage. Audra took several photos and texted them to Volkov.

As they prepared to leave, it was Audra who heard the low grumble of the approaching vehicle as it came closer. She went to the window and looked out.

"What is it?" said Slokavich.

"Someone is here," she said. Her cheek was covered in blood. "Lamborghini."

"How many people?"

"A driver, that's all. He's getting out of the car."

"Upstairs," Slokavich said, holding his stomach. "Whoever it is, we kill him then get the fuck out of here. I need a doctor."

CHAPTER 20

118 Partridge Lane, N.W.
Palisades
Washington, D.C.

Tacoma knelt on the stair landing on the first floor, next to Cosgrove's dangling body. The people who'd just stabbed and hung Cosgrove were upstairs.

Tacoma glanced one more time up the stairs, then removed a blade from a sheath at his torso. He reached up and cut the rope above Cosgrove's head and caught Cosgrove, setting him down on the landing. He cut the noose off his neck, then pocketed the blade and reestablished his focus on the upstairs.

From the first stair beyond the landing, Tacoma glanced back and scanned the only windows that brought light to that section of the house, a line of vertical windows in the large kitchen. He looked for a vehicle, seeing nothing.

Tacoma was now operational. There was only his environment, and that was all—and that was all he had at that moment.

There had been no external environmental factor to cause the shadow.

Someone was upstairs.

Tacoma moved up the stairs, clutching the P226R.

The upstairs was dark. Whatever light there was came through the windows. The day was slipping into evening, and a bluish, dusky light filled the upstairs. Doorways, a painting, an Oriental runner—and then another flicker of shadow.

The movement had come from the last doorway, at the end of the hallway.

Tacoma moved down the hallway, aware of the fact that whoever it was knew he was coming.

And yet the killer had moved. It was the only way to explain the shadow.

Tacoma swiveled his head, looking back at the stairs, pausing. A seemingly endless moment of utter silence, darkness, and lack of movement inhabited the hallway and stairs. Then, Tacoma saw another undulation in the light.

There was another person. He or she was now at the end of the hallway, coming toward him.

Tacoma looked back to the bedroom doorway where he'd seen the flicker of shadow, just as he heard the tuft of rug being slid on one of the stairs.

Tacoma's nostrils flared slightly as he recognized that he was hemmed in, one man left, one right.

He heard a footstep and then, down the hallway, heard the sound of metal scratching against clothing. Tacoma ducked left, into a room, shutting the door behind him. He searched the wall for a light switch, then turned on the lights. It was a bedroom, neat and tidy, a guest room that probably hadn't been used in years.

The footsteps were louder now.

As Tacoma turned, he felt dull steel at the back of his neck.

"Plokhoy vybor," came a low voice, in a thick Russian accent.

Bad choice.

Someone came through the door. Tacoma swiveled the P226R at the door. A woman entered, clad in black, training a gun on Tacoma, even as he acquired her in the crosshairs.

He felt the muzzle of the rifle against his neck. He craned his head and took in the sight of a tall man with a strange, monstrous face. The man was pale, with a long nose. In his hands was an AR-15 rifle, which he kept pressed hard at Tacoma's neck.

Tacoma noticed that the man's clothing was drenched in blood from the stomach down.

Tacoma was in the crosshairs of both weapons, but he held the woman in his own and a tense silence loomed in the bedroom.

The room was small and tight, the lights bright and unpleasant.

The woman was tall, thin, and gorgeous, with short-cropped brown hair and bangs, and a very pretty face. Tacoma had seen her kind before. Her gun was a Stechkin, a silencer jutting from the muzzle. She had a cut beneath one of her eyes, and a wash of red dripped down her cheek.

"*Ty srazhalsyas nim,*" said Tacoma in flawless Russian, taunting them. "*Vy ne budete srazhat'sya so mnoy?*"

You fought him. Why won't you fight me?

Tacoma moved his gun slowly away from the woman, so as not to scare them with sudden movement. He lowered the pistol and tossed it to the floor.

Out of the corner of Tacoma's eyes he watched as the female agent kept her gun trained on him. She reached to a sheath at the base of her back and removed a large knife—a KA-BAR, black steel, extended version, military issue.

Tacoma made eye contact with her.

Timing is everything is a myth perpetuated by the weak. The time is now. There is no other time unless you confront the task at hand.

With the steel of the rifle muzzle at the back of his neck, Tacoma lunged his elbow back in the same moment he ducked left and grabbed the muzzle, fighting against the gunman, yanking the muzzle, and aiming it in the direction of the woman. The gunman behind him panicked and pulled the trigger. The bullet shot past Tacoma's ear and barely missed the woman, who stepped toward him. He lashed a foot wildly at her arm, kicking the Stechkin from her hand. Tacoma gripped the muzzle tight as the man behind him kicked at the back of his legs, then tried to wrap his arms around Tacoma's neck, just as the woman lunged, blade out. Tacoma launched a fierce elbow behind him, into the man's collarbone. A dull snap was followed by a groan and the big man crumpled to the ground, gasping for air.

Tacoma registered the oncoming knife blade as the woman slashed the black knife at him, cutting the air, grunting a high-pitched yelp as she thrust the sharp steel. Tacoma caught her with his fist, meeting her strike, blocking her at the wrist. His other hand reached for her shoulder, clawing at her upper arm. Suddenly, Tacoma thrust forward and kicked the woman's knee. She let out a pained groan, then teetered sideways, off balance. As she fell, Tacoma held his entire arm in a viselike grip beneath her armpit. The woman's own weight and momentum did the rest of the work. She tumbled sideways, down to the floor, screaming, as every tendon, nerve, muscle, and ligament in her shoulder ripped so loudly it could be heard, followed by the dull twang of her elbow snapping.

Then Tacoma let go.

As the woman fell, Tacoma grabbed the KA-BAR from her weakened clutch, then turned, instinctively ducking just as the tall killer stood back up, took aim, and fired, missing Tacoma. Tacoma dived at him before he could get off another round. Tacoma stabbed the blade into the gunman's thigh as hard as he could. The blade cut through skin and muscle until it found bone deep inside the thigh. Tacoma ripped up, gutting even more tissue. The man screamed as he dropped to the floor. Both of his hands found the blade, now embedded deep in his thigh, and he tried to pry it out as blood flooded down and he let out a horrible groan.

The smash of breaking glass was sudden. Tacoma pivoted, watching as the female assassin crashed through the window, letting out a low scream as she broke through the panes of glass and went flying out, falling to the ground outside the home, a floor below.

Tacoma got to his feet, grabbed the AR-15 from the ground, then started firing at the black shadow of the woman as she ran into the woods and disappeared.

Tacoma turned to the lone remaining killer. He was a mess, drenched in blood, pulling weakly at the KA-BAR sticking out from his thigh. He was too weak to pull the knife out—or else the serrated top edge of the blade was caught on something, a tendon or bone perhaps. He was moaning something in Russian, something even Tacoma couldn't understand, as blood coursed from his stomach and leg, creating a puddle on the hardwood floor.

In Russian, Tacoma spoke to the killer.

"You try anything, I shoot," said Tacoma, pointing the gun. "You move, I shoot. I won't kill you, but I'll blow a hole in you, understand? If I were you I would stay still and shut the hell up."

"No. Please don't. Just shoot me," he moaned as he pulled at the long blade embedded in his thigh.

Tacoma spoke quietly to the man as he stepped forward:

"Hold still," said Tacoma.

"Fuck you," the man muttered.

Aiming the gun at the man's head, Tacoma reached down and grabbed the KA-BAR. He stepped on the man's knee, then pulled up, fighting the blade out as the Russian yelped a low, horrible scream and blood spilled down on the carpet of the bedroom.

Tacoma went to the doorway and stepped out into the hallway. He dropped the bloody knife on the carpet outside the door, then put the AR-15 next to it. He went back in the room, picked up his shoulder holster, and pulled it on, then picked up the silenced P226R and aimed it at the man. The Russian said nothing. Instead, he just stared at Tacoma, in agony at first, and then with a resigned stare, the look of the prisoner, close to death; a cold, blank stare. The stare of an operator, a good one, the moment in time when, in order to survive, one swallows the pain in order to live to fight again.

What have you gotten into?

The man spoke in Russian.

"Mne nuzhen vrach," he said. *"Ya sobirayus istech krov'yu."*

I need a doctor. I'm going to bleed to death.

"Vy dolzhny byli podumat' ob etom, prezhde chem ubit' yego," snapped Tacoma.

You should've thought about that before you killed him.

"You won't be able to interrogate me if I die," the Russian coughed.

"Good point," said Tacoma.

"I want a lawyer," he whispered.

"I'll get right on it," said Tacoma.

"It's my right," he said.

"Why'd you kill him?" said Tacoma.

The man said nothing. His face was contorted, anguished with pain, but he said nothing.

"Why?" Tacoma repeated softly. "Who sent you?"

Tacoma looked carefully at the man. He knew he was a professional. It would take a team from Langley and some electricity to find out who he was and how in the hell he found out about Cosgrove.

But one thing was clear: someone in a very small, very tight pocket of American government had leaked Cosgrove's identity to someone.

Tacoma's eyes caught the man's abrupt movement, but a second too late. The killer's wrist shot out and a small silver-sheen blade was suddenly in the air. The killer hurled the blade at Tacoma. The knife swiveled across the room, reflecting the chandelier as the blade edge pivoted. It had torque but missed, though not because Tacoma avoided it. The killer had timed it perfectly. But he threw wide. The blade cut into the wall behind Tacoma, stabbing deep into the wood.

Tacoma aimed the gun at the man's hand—the hand that had thrown the blade—and fired a single blast. A dull metallic *thwap* hit the air as a bullet ripped into the goon's thumb. Blood, skin, and bone spat across the wall behind him.

He screamed in pain and agony as blood coursed from his hand.

"That's about as close as you're going to get to a lawyer," said Tacoma. "A lot less expensive, too."

Tacoma stepped back into the hallway, at all times keeping the gun trained in the direction of the bedroom. He stood in the hallway for several minutes. He heard the sound of the door opening downstairs, then felt his cell vibrate. He picked it up and looked at the text. It was from Calibrisi. He heard the heavy baritone of Calibrisi's voice from downstairs.

"Goddammit," he heard him say in a low voice that seemed to echo up the stairs.

Tacoma—the gun trained through the doorway—stepped to the banister and looked down at Calibrisi. Calibrisi was kneeling beside Cosgrove. He looked up and caught Tacoma.

"I told you not to touch him," said Calibrisi. "There's important evidence that you may or may not have compromised."

Tacoma looked quickly back at the injured Russian, holding him in the crosshairs. He stared into the thug's eyes as he responded to Calibrisi.

"I think I got some even better evidence, chief."

When Calibrisi arrived at the second floor, he registered the silenced P226R in Tacoma's hand and followed the trajectory of where it was aimed. He walked past Tacoma into the room, assaying the bloody scene.

Just behind Calibrisi were three men in suits from the Agency, one of the forensics units. Another was on its way, along with a cleanup crew.

"Stop the bleeding," said Calibrisi to a medic. "Nothing too fancy. Put him in a van and get him out to West Virginia."

CHAPTER 21

Bal Bay Drive
Bal Harbour, Florida

Volkov felt the outline of his cell phone in his pocket as he looked across the dining room table at a crowd of people, six couples in all. Across from him was his wife. She was voluptuous, with bottle-blond hair and fake breasts, and wore a mesh tank top to accentuate her figure. She was also beautiful.

The mood was boisterous, fueled by alcohol and THC. Despite the fact that Volkov's workers at the Port of Miami oversaw the import of cocaine by the kilo, often in forty-foot containers, there were no drugs at the party harder than a few pens filled with sativa oil. Volkov didn't let harder drugs enter his body or his inner sanctum.

A wineglass and place setting filled with food in front of him sat undisturbed. Without saying anything, amid the din of laughter and raucous conversation, Volkov stood up.

Outside, he lit a cigarette as he opened a text from Audra with photos. They showed the American, Cosgrove, badly beaten, hanging by a rope, a railroad spike driven through his chest. One of the photos showed the mercenary Audra had hired, Slokavich, in the corner of the frame, his beard visible. He appeared to have a smile on his face.

But there had been no communication since the photos.

"Why hasn't she fucking called?" whispered Volkov aloud, to himself.

Volkov had responsibility for all operations in the U.S. for the entity he worked for. They were, genealogically, a bastard splinter child of the Odessa Mafia. They had set themselves apart, and the group was new and mysterious. Darré, Volkov knew, was a mastermind of the highest order. This meant Volkov needed to run the most brutal, savage, and profitable crime enterprise possible—or else Darré would simply replace him, or someone would replace Darré.

Darré owned large companies in almost every state in the U.S. Their intersection was the conduit between Darré's legitimate business and crime, and Volkov was the other side of the crossroads. Volkov had absolute freedom as to how he ran the affairs of the entity, that is, that part of it that broke laws. Volkov worked out of one of the companies that the entity owned, a large cargo terminal at the Port of Miami, through which flowed all drugs the entity brought into the U.S.: cocaine, heroin, fentanyl, meth.

Neither Darré or Volkov worried about law enforcement. The FBI was an agency of, for the most part, bumbling idiots. The smart ones were corrupt.

Volkov was six feet tall and packed with muscles. He shaved his head and had a rough demeanor, pale skin, and a wide nose that had been broken before. His arms, chest, torso, and legs were jacked, like a running back's.

His Bal Harbour mansion was in a gated community on a cul-de-sac of large homes, all built recently, all enjoying two-acre lots and privacy. It was meant to look like a French château. It had a pool, a three-car garage, a wine cellar, and eight bedrooms.

A dinner party was going on inside.

Volkov stood in the driveway, a gravel showpiece where Volkov and his friends all had parked their Ferraris and Lamborghinis. He was smoking a cigarette.

Volkov was twenty-seven years old.

Now, he waited for the call. It had been hours, and he sensed that something was wrong.

He'd sent Audra to kill the CIA agent, Cosgrove. As he smoked his third cigarette in less than a half hour, he realized how vulnerable he was. If they had her, he could be in imminent danger.

From the driveway, he looked down across the lawn to the ocean. The waiting was like a ticking time bomb.

He felt the vibration of his phone.

Finally!

It was Audra.

"What," said Volkov, putting the cell to his ear. "*What happened?*"

"I'm hurt," she breathed. "There was another man who came in. He has Slokavich."

"Where are you?"

"On a bus," she said. "I'm going to Philadelphia. I'll fly back to Miami."

"What does Slokavich know?" said Volkov, his voice inflected with anger.

"He knows me, that's all."

The dinner party was breaking up. An older man, Volkov's mentor in the Russian mob, Dmitri, approached. He was with a much younger woman. He brushed his hand toward one of the Ferraris, telling her to get into the car. He approached Volkov.

"What's wrong, Andrei?" Dmitri whispered.

Volkov looked at the old man with a scornful air. He covered the phone.

"Nothing," said Volkov. "I hope you enjoyed dinner."

"You look like someone urinated on your cornflakes," said the old man with a thick Russian accent, smiling.

Volkov managed a polite grin, then cupped the phone.

"Fuck off, asshole," said Volkov smiling. A fake smile.

"Andrei," came a female voice. It was his wife. Volkov took another puff of his cigarette, then flicked it down.

"I have to go," he said to Audra.

He hung up the phone.

"Be right there," he said.

His wife was standing in the front entrance. In the light, her tank top looked sheer. She was standing and holding a glass of red wine.

"What are you doing?" she said.

"Nothing," said Volkov.

She walked down the front steps to her husband, who was leaning against a bright yellow Lamborghini.

"Did you just talk to her?"

"Who?" said Volkov.

"You know who. *Audra, the whore you fuck!*"

Volkov swung his arm and struck his wife with the back of his hand, hitting her cheek with a brutal slap. She screamed and nearly fell over, but then lurched at him with both fists flailing. He caught her arms and overpowered her with ease, then threw her down onto her back, onto the ground.

He walked to the Lamborghini and opened the door. It scissored up. Before he climbed inside, he looked at his wife.

"Watch your tongue," he said calmly, "or next time I'll cut it out with a dull butter knife."

CHAPTER 22

118 Partridge Lane, N.W.
Palisades
Washington, D.C.

Tacoma and Calibrisi remained at Cosgrove's house as two teams of CIA forensics experts and a six-person sanitization crew made it look as if nothing had happened at the house. The plaster wall where the bullet that had passed through the Russian's thumb was embedded had been sanitized and patched up. All traces of blood upstairs and down were gone. Even an experienced investigator would have found nothing more than some molecular-level DNA. The cleaning process had included a thorough cataloging of all fingerprints in the house, followed by a methodical washing of every surface, followed by a radiological burst, in which every room in the house was exposed for a brief time.

Cosgrove's home had a two-car garage, and this was where Calibrisi decided to fix the surviving Russian up before his short trip to the mountains of West Virginia, where there was a CIA property down a long, country road. This property looked, from the outside, like a large, brick homestead on a hill, surrounded by more than a thousand acres of land. Calibrisi made the decision to not take the Russian to a medical facility, even though there was a CIA clinic within a half mile of Cosgrove's home. The more people who knew what had happened, the greater the odds that they would never figure out who had sent the killers—and how they found out. Calibrisi already knew why they'd come for Cosgrove. It was obvious. A warning to Langley and, by extension, the U.S. government:

Stay the hell away.

The injured Russian was drugged and carried downstairs to the garage, where he was strapped to a movable gurney. Doctors sewed up his stomach, hand, and thigh and gave him several pints of blood to stabilize him. When he was done being fixed up, the gurney was carried by four agents.

Calibrisi walked alongside the Russian. He stared into his eyes as they put him in the back of a white truck. Without looking away, Calibrisi spoke:

"Take him to the cabin," said Calibrisi. "Get one of our doctors out there and keep him alive, then start a pharma program. We'll start interrogating him tomorrow."

They shut the back of the truck. It left the house immediately, a few minutes after midnight.

Inside the garage, Cosgrove's body was placed in a large ceramic box that looked like a coffin, then carried to another van, which departed for Langley. There was probably nothing to be found, but Calibrisi wanted the forensics team to thoroughly examine him. More important, he wanted Cosgrove cleaned up as best as was possible. It's not that anyone would ever see his body, but Calibrisi wouldn't have it any other way. It was the least he could do.

"How will it be explained?" said Tacoma.

The two men climbed into the back of a black sedan.

"What do you mean?"

"To his children. His ex-wife. His friends. People at the CIA."

"He died in the line of duty," said Calibrisi. He looked at the driver. "White House," he said, then returned his attention to Tacoma. "He'll get a hero's burial, a memorial service, I'll nominate him for the Agency Cross."

The sedan started moving back down into Georgetown.

"What about his pension?" asked Tacoma. "It didn't look like he exactly had a ton of money."

"His wife will receive the pension."

Tacoma stared out at the passing lights of Washington, D.C. The streets were mostly empty, though a few clusters of students from Georgetown and young Capitol Hill staffers were still out, wandering between bars on a Friday night.

"What about the interrogation?" said Tacoma. "Who does it?"

"You do," said Calibrisi. "Unless you don't want to."

"Of course I want to," said Tacoma. "What just happened is fucked up."

"I know."

"The vote was today and tonight the head of the unit is murdered," said Tacoma.

"I'm aware of that. What's your point?"

"*They knew who Cosgrove was, where he lived, and they knew about the whole goddam thing!*" yelled Tacoma. "I mean, it's almost a suicide mission, only it's not a mission. It's permanent. They're going to try and kill me and anyone else associated with this! What the hell are you going to do about it?"

"What are *we* going to do about it?" said Calibrisi. "*We're* going to find out who sent them and go get that son of a bitch and then find out who told him. Rob, you're in charge now."

"I'm in charge?" said Tacoma, shaking his head, a dumbfounded look on his face. "Me? I'm twenty-nine, Hector. Trust me, you don't want me in charge."

"Yeah, you."

"No. Ask someone else."

"We need you."

"No, thanks."

Calibrisi looked at the ground, pausing a few moments.

"Rob," said Calibrisi quietly. "The truth is there's no one else who'd do it after what just happened, certainly no one in their right mind."

Tacoma laughed.

"Oh, that's great!" he yelled. "Thanks. Way to get me to want to do it."

Calibrisi pointed his finger at him.

"You need to do it, Rob. You're one of the best operators who's ever come through DEVGRU. You're fluent in Russian. We're fighting a war here. Tonight, you saw what the Russian mafia is capable of."

Tacoma shook his head in frustration.

"I want to do it my way," he whispered.

"I know," said Calibrisi. "I want you to do it your way."

"I'm going out to the Cabin," said Tacoma. "There was a woman who got away. He'll know who she is. I'm going to find her and kill her."

"It's your operation," said Calibrisi. "Do whatever the hell you want. But you were right about one thing: they're going to be looking for you. If they knew Cosgrove's identity, they know yours, or they will soon. They know their guy has gone missing. They'll assume we have him. You want to go hunt her down? Fine. Go out to West Virginia and get her identity out of the prisoner."

CHAPTER 23

Private Living Quarters
The White House

Calibrisi had insisted on meeting with the president—just he, Tacoma, and the president.

When Calibrisi and Tacoma entered the presidential living quarters, Dellenbaugh was already seated on a chair in the large living room directly off the elevator.

Calibrisi looked at his watch as he shook Dellenbaugh's hand.

"I apologize, Mr. President," said Calibrisi.

"Don't," said Dellenbaugh. "Hi, Rob."

"Mr. President," said Tacoma.

"What's going on?"

Calibrisi pulled out a cell. He handed it to Dellenbaugh. The president scrolled across dozens of photos showing Cosgrove, his face red and badly beaten, rope wrapped around his neck.

Dellenbaugh winced.

"Who is it?"

"Billy Cosgrove," said Calibrisi.

Dellenbaugh stared a few extra moments, then put the cell down.

"We captured one of the killers, Mr. President," said Calibrisi. "We're working on a plan. But that's not why I'm here."

"We have a leak somewhere," said Dellenbaugh angrily.

"Precisely. It had to have come from one of the fifteen senators on the Senate Intelligence Committee. Or from someone at the White House."

Dellenbaugh nodded, agreeing.

"How do we find out who?" said Dellenbaugh.

"I need Jim Bruckheimer at NSA to run some analysis on the senators as well as anyone at the White House who knew about the unit," said Calibrisi. "We need to run this ex post facto. I'm going to do some fairly advanced diagnostic work on people here predating creation of the unit. Including you, sir. It doesn't mean I think you—or they—did something wrong. It could be a bug on a phone, a relative, or it could be a traitor. But I need your permission, Mr. President."

Dellenbaugh handed the cell phone back to Calibrisi.

"You got it. Find out whoever the hell did this," said Dellenbaugh. "Find him and put him in the deepest pit of hell we have."

CHAPTER 24

Director's Office
CIA Headquarters
Langley, Virginia

It was a little after 2 A.M. when Calibrisi pushed open the glass door to his office and went behind the desk, removing his coat and tie and hitting a speed dial on his landline phone console. He threw the coat and tie down on the floor.

"Hector," said Bruckheimer. "It's the middle of the night."

"Yeah, I'm sorry to wake you, Jim, but it's important."

"You didn't wake me," said Bruckheimer. "I'm still at the office."

Jim Bruckheimer ran Signals Intelligence Directorate, or SID. SID was a branch of the National Security Agency, the group charged with running all NSA cryptographic systems and directing agency strategy as it related to surveillance.

Bruckheimer ran SID from behind a cluttered desk on the fifth floor of a glass-walled office building in Maryland, one of two such buildings that constituted Fort Meade. He was a burly man, fifty-six, who had played linebacker at the University of Oklahoma, though he didn't look like he could do it again.

"To what do I owe the pleasure of your communication?" said Bruckheimer. "Let me guess: you want me to break the law."

"I thought you did that for a living," said Calibrisi.

"It depends on what the definition of the word 'law' is, chief," said Bruckheimer.

"We need to run some trace protocols on American citizens. Some fairly well-known people, including the president. He's aware of it and approves. I'll paper it tomorrow."

"What are we talking about here?" said Bruckheimer.

"SSCI voted in secret to allow the CIA to run a two-man kill team inside the U.S. Five hours later, one of the guys was found hanging from a rope."

"So you got some leakage," said Bruckheimer. "You think it was one of the senators?"

"Most likely," said Calibrisi, "but it could be a White House staffer."

There was a long silence as Bruckheimer exhaled.

"So what's the ask?" said Bruckheimer.

"You tell me."

"Let me start with PRISM and Pinwale," said Bruckheimer, referring to two NSA surveillance programs.

"How long will it take?"

"A few days."

"I need it sooner, Jim."

CHAPTER 25

CIA Headquarters
Langley, Virginia

When Calibrisi and Tacoma walked into the seventh-floor director's suite, Bill Polk met them just inside the glass entry doors.

"Hector, I need to speak to Rob for a sec."

"It'll have to wait," said Calibrisi.

"It can't," said Polk. He looked at Tacoma. "Can you give us a minute?"

"Sure," said Calibrisi. "I'll be in my office."

When Polk and Tacoma were alone, Polk looked at Tacoma with a serious expression.

"There's a leak," said Polk.

"No shit."

"Which means they know about you, Rob, or they will soon."

"What are you saying?" said Tacoma.

"We need to stand down on this thing before you get killed," said Polk. "It's too dangerous. We lost a tier-one operator. I'll be damned if we're going to lose another one, especially you."

Tacoma ran his hand back through his thick mop of dirty-blond hair.

"I appreciate your concern," said Tacoma, "but it's my decision and I'm going after the killers. Besides, the toothpaste is out of the tube. They're going to try and kill me no matter what."

"This isn't a game," said Polk.

"What's the alternative?" said Tacoma. "I go into hiding the rest of my life?"

"Just for a little while, long enough for us to track the leak. We'll find out who did it, interrogate the shit out of them, find out who's behind it, and bring them all to justice."

"No, thanks," said Tacoma. He paused. "You trained me. This is the best intelligence agency in the world. Trust what you taught me."

Polk nodded and a smile crossed his lips. He removed his glasses.

"I trust you," said Polk. "I just think you're making a mistake, and I don't feel like burying another operator I helped train, especially one I happen to care about."

Tacoma smiled. He reached out and put his arm around Polk's shoulder. Tacoma was half a foot taller than Polk and a brick of muscles compared to the professorial Polk.

"Hey, don't worry so much, Bill," said Tacoma. "I'll be fine. Come on, let's see what they found out."

CHAPTER 26

EPPS Aviation Terminal
Dekalb-Peachtree Airport
Chamblee, Georgia

Volkov instructed the pilot to head north, to Atlanta. When the Gulfstream landed at the private terminal, a black Suburban was waiting. Volkov climbed in, glancing briefly at the brown-haired woman who was driving.

He said nothing as the vehicle moved out of the airport, toward a building in the center of downtown Atlanta.

It was a steel and glass skyscraper. At the security desk, Volkov approached the two black-suited guards who stood behind a long marble entrance desk. Rather than pull out his wallet, Volkov removed a suppressed HK45 ACP, suppressor at the muzzle. He pumped a slug in the first man's throat then another in the other one's left eye, dropping both men.

Volkov didn't need to be here. The man he was going to see, Baldessari, owed him $15 million, but it wasn't the most owed Volkov by far. Truth be told, he was in a violent, murderous mood and Atlanta was a quick plane flight.

He'd loaned the gentleman, a highly leveraged professional

sports team owner from Atlanta, $15 million to buy a racehorse and field a team to go after the Triple Crown.

Interest was 25 percent, compounded daily.

When the $15 million filly broke her leg on a rainy-day training run in a Kentucky stable, the man's fortunes had changed rather dramatically. He hadn't paid back a cent and wouldn't return Volkov's phone calls. Yet Volkov cared less about the offense or amount than the opportunity to quickly vent some anger.

They had Slokavich. They were working him over.

Volkov didn't want to think about all that.

Grabbing a badge from one of the dead gunmen, Volkov moved to the wall of elevators, entered an empty one, and punched the number for Baldessari's floor. The elevator climbed. When the doors opened on his floor, he waited, watching, tucked in, from the corner of the elevator cab. At the last moment, Volkov emerged from the elevator and into the hallway. He saw movement to his right and pumped a slug into a shadow, then moved closer. It was a gunman, now groaning on the ground. Volkov had struck his torso. He finished the man with a slug to the chest.

As he looked down at the dead man, Volkov became angry; rather than pay him back a little bit at a time, the sports team owner was employing a small army of security guards, all trained up; an expensive crew. It made Volkov—for the first time—hate Baldessari.

He went down the hallway and came to the corner. He tucked the gun back in his coat and then rounded the corner. Midway down the hallway, two men stood. Each man was armed with an assault rifle, and as Volkov approached they swung them up, aiming at Volkov.

Volkov held up his hands, innocently, as he walked toward them.

"I'm here to see Mr. Baldessari," said Volkov.

"Identification."

Volkov reached into his coat and pulled out the .45. He fired before either gunman even had time to react. The dull, metallic *thwack thwack* echoed in the corridor as slugs ripped from Volkov's gun into the men, the first into the man on the left's chest, into his heart, the other into the neck of the second guard.

Volkov kicked the door in behind the dead gunmen. He moved through an empty office suite and came to the outer glass of the skyscraper. He pumped the trigger and the bullet struck in the center of the massive pane, shattering it like snowflakes, which rained down fifty-six stories to the street below.

Volkov reached the broken window and clutched the steel frame, then leaned out and targeted his pistol at the floor above. He fired once, then ducked in for several moments as glass rained down from above. He heard screams as he reached up to the edge of the steel casement of the floor above. Volkov pulled himself up to the next floor. A small party was going on in the suite of rooms.

People had already scattered, and those that remained watched in fear as Volkov moved into the room.

He came inside and went left, down a hallway, where a blond-haired man with thick muscles was standing. Volkov nodded at him as he walked past, coming into a palatial living room, with music playing, low lights, glass everywhere—views in every direction of the city—cocaine on trays, bottles of champagne.

In a chair, a dark-haired man sat, smoking a cigar. Volkov saw him and drew his suppressed .45 ACP. Volkov moved the gun line in a straight trajectory toward his skull.

"Alexei," said the man, coughing as he pulled the cigar from his mouth. "What brings you to Atlanta?"

"I wanted to deliver a message," said Volkov.

He swung the gun right. He triggered the .45 and a bullet smashed into the woman seated next to the sports team owner, striking her eye and blowing her brains across the wall. "With interest, you owe me twenty-two million dollars," said Volkov.

The other people in the room fled. Volkov held only the one man in the crosshairs.

"And you will be paid!" yelled Baldessari, who stood up and lurched at Volkov.

Volkov met the man's lunge with a brutal kick to his stomach. As he fell to the ground, Volkov moved over him, training the end of the suppressor at his eye and then jamming it down into the socket, hard, until the eye almost ruptured.

"You can either wire the money right now or I can kill you," said Volkov.

"You're just going to kill me anyway," he groaned.

"Probably," said Volkov. He moved the gun away from the man's eye and stood up, then fired into the man's thigh.

The man screamed in agony.

"But you're worth more to me alive than dead."

The man awkwardly stood up, his face creased in pain. Volkov kept the pistol trained, though it was unnecessary. The man's leg was drenched in blood and he sweated profusely. He was nearly incapacitated. He hobbled to a desk and removed a small laptop computer. Soon, he was typing on the keyboard.

"Twenty-two million dollars?" the man said. "I'm wiring it right now."

"Make it an even twenty-five," said Volkov. "Your fee for making me come to this shithole of a city to get *my* fucking money back."

CHAPTER 27

Moncrief County Road
Waterford, West Virginia

Tacoma cut off the main road in Waterford and onto Moncrief County Road. The road was hilly and winding, surrounded on both sides by large trees that canopied a chute of tar, cracked from age, the occasional faded yellow line, and potholes. It was in the proverbial middle of nowhere.

Tacoma had the 670 hp Dodge Charger moving at a little over eighty. He wore sunglasses, a white cable-knit fisherman's sweater, and khakis. Behind the glasses, hidden by reflective lenses, his eyes were cold and emotionless, except for the faintest trace of anger, which he worked to quell.

He had stayed up all night. It was 7 A.M. when his eyes recognized the flare in the tar up ahead.

Off to the right, a dirt driveway was cut from a wall of oak trees. A strip of grass ran down the center of the dirt lane, which, after a hundred feet or so, disappeared into the trees. He didn't bother slowing down, instead sliding into a screechy, burning turn toward the opening in the trees, the back tires fishtailing in a controlled spin along the tar, then regripping and shooting the car forward at the driveway and woods.

Tacoma slowed down in the last stretch, which was honeycombed from above with overhanging branches. He felt the engine roar as he throttled the torque, touching the left paddle near the steering wheel. A throaty, angry pitch erupted from the engine, forced to slow just as the tires were becoming like glue to the dirt and the wind was taking hold of the aerodynamics.

The Charger sped into the driveway, Tacoma slamming the gas hard, nearly spinning the car off the road.

A half mile in, a brick house sat behind an oval-shaped gravel area. There was little movement and yet there was activity. Four men in jeans and tactical vests stood around a vague perimeter, out of sight. Each man clutched a high-powered rifle, and all were looped into a central COM block by small earbuds.

The house was big and pretty, with black shutters, a slate roof, and low green boxwoods cut in lines out to fields of tall green grass. The land spread out farther than the eye could see. A thousand-acre piece of land meant there were no other houses for miles.

Five vehicles were parked in the driveway: two black Chevy Suburbans, a shiny dark blue Ford van, a white truck, and a black Cadillac sedan.

Tacoma crested the last hill and caught air, as a smile crossed his face. He'd been here before. It was during training, after he'd been recruited away from DEVGRU by Katie Foxx, who was in charge of Special Operations Group. This wasn't the so-called Farm. This was where they took you after you were selected from everyone at the Farm. This was where they groomed the ones Langley expected to step into the void, in any country, at any time.

This was where Tacoma had showed his true colors.

As much as he hated the memory, Tacoma couldn't help gunning the Charger at a lip in the road, catching a moment of air, slamming down and turning the wheel at ninety miles an hour, fishtailing in a loud, squeaky turn, barely avoiding a tree. Moncrief Road—aka "The Cabin"—was where Tacoma had been taught about interrogation and survival. It was where the elite of the elite of American operators were schooled in the science of physio-psychographic warfare. First as receivers, then as givers.

Tacoma reached for the radio and turned it off, wanting to hear the roar of the engine.

They only trained one man at a time, staggering the training sequence, never letting more men through than they could properly assess and develop, though by the time they were at the Cabin they no longer needed development. Now it was about inner strength.

For Tacoma, his recruitment started when he was kidnapped in Mosul and drugged. He awoke days later in a fetid room, tied tight, his ankles bound, his elbows pulled behind him and tied together, so tight that he felt as if his arms would rip. A ball gag was in his mouth, a black nylon bag covered his head. At first, he thought he was in a cave in the Kush, or maybe an apartment in Karachi, or Lagos, or anywhere for that matter.

He had been under for three days, he calculated.

The thing is, Tacoma, after three days under, gagged and tied up, assumed he had been captured. In point of fact, he was right here, at the Cabin.

In SEALs, during Hell Week in Coronado, he remained awake for a week straight, less the few precious hours they let them nod off. The Cabin had been designed by the same man who'd come up with the military concept underlying Hell Week. It was a brutal, self-defining, Darwinian challenge that ultimately weeded most operators out.

The CIA was culling the elite from the elite. It wasn't simply about skill. They all had skill. Langley had to find the ones who wouldn't crack under pressure.

Instead of long swims in cold water, lugging telephone poles, running until your feet bled, the Cabin attacked the core of an operator's psyche. The operators selected to go were the best of the best, and they knew it. Most didn't make it through. Every year, Langley selected seven men for Special Operations Group.

For six days, Tacoma was kept in a windowless room. There was nothing in the room, only concrete and a lightbulb. There wasn't even a bucket for going to the bathroom. Loud music, or sometimes just noise, would blare from speakers in the ceiling, for hours on end, and then abruptly stop.

Then there were the beatings. Three or four would come into the concrete space and beat him. On the first night, Tacoma, despite being shackled, had managed to butt his forehead into the nose of one of the men, shattering it. It was his only victory that lonely week. A week in which, by the end, he was curled up in a fetal position in the corner. When they came to pull him out—to give him water, to make sure he was still alive—they removed his shackles. But they didn't try to help him.

By the time they came into Tacoma's cell on that sixth day, he hadn't had water in three days. As for food, nothing.

It was meant to break a man, and most men it did.

Tacoma passed the hours in a half-sleep reverie, singing songs to himself, inside his head. "She's a Rainbow" lasted for hours until he remembered "Idiot Wind," by Dylan. But that was early on. By the time they came to see him he was lost in a state of permanent white, transfixed by a vision of a lightbulb, watching as speckles of dust made the yellow halogen flicker ever so faintly. He was shackled in an unmovable way, hands behind his back, legs wrenched backward and secured tight.

Loud, distorted music was blaring when the guards entered and Tacoma registered them, his throat so dry it hurt to breathe.

"He's gone."

He heard the voice from above him.

Another voice, this one an older man's. He felt a dry, cold hand against his neck.

"Take him to Dr. Basin," he said in a scratchy voice. "Once he's back on planet earth, send him back out to Coronado. This is officially a *no-pass*."

That was when Tacoma felt the tension ease at his wrists. Were he a threat, it would've been at that moment that Tacoma might have lurched for something, for someone, for a lifeline . . .

But he was catatonic. His arms barely moved. He was like a dead fish, lying with two open eyes looking up listlessly. He felt the rope around his ankles as someone loosened it. Then it disappeared.

Tacoma didn't hesitate. By the time the rope was on the ground, he'd slashed his leg beneath the man who'd just released him, kicking the man at the back of his ankles and grabbing his pistol as he tumbled backward. The guard let out a loud yell as he hit the wall behind him. In that moment, Tacoma swept the muzzle of the gun and trained it on the other man. Slowly, he stood up, keeping both CIA interrogators in tight range.

"If you want to live," Tacoma whispered as he held both men in the crosshairs, "don't move. Don't say anything."

A door to the windowless interrogation room suddenly opened. A young, very good-looking woman stepped inside. She had blond hair down to her shoulders, cut in bangs above her green eyes. Tacoma pivoted, acquiring her in the crosshairs. He took a few steps backward. He now held the three individuals in the crosshairs. She stepped toward him and he fired.

Nothing happened and she came closer.

"Blanks," said the woman.

The two men he'd just taken over slowly stood up. One of them nodded to Tacoma. It was a look of praise, as if to say, "Good job."

"My name is Katie Foxx," she said as she stepped into the center of the concrete hole. "Congratulations, Rob. You're now NOC, tier one, Special Operations Group. That is, if you'd like to."

Tacoma turned off the car and grabbed a camouflaged, pump-action 12-gauge Benelli from the back seat. He stuffed shells into it, then climbed from the vehicle.

Standing in the middle of the driveway were two men. Both had on khakis, short-sleeve dark blue polo shirts, sunglasses, flak jackets, and weapons vests. Both men clutched high-powered semiautomatic rifles, with suppressors. They kept them trained at the dirt as Tacoma walked toward them.

"Identification, sir," said one of the men, a tall, stocky bald man with a thick beard. He looked familiar. "SOP."

"No worries. Who are you?" said Tacoma, reaching for his ID.

"Patchford," said one of the men, looking at Tacoma's ID card. "I was DEVGRU, too."

"Congratulations," said Tacoma. "Where is he?"

"In the tank," said Patchford. "They already ran a diopharma on him."

The sound of an engine came from up the driveway. A black sedan came into view, its tires kicking up dust as it moved to the side of the driveway and stopped. Calibrisi climbed from the back of the dark sedan. Calibrisi nodded at the two CIA gunmen. He followed Tacoma as he moved to the front of the house, shotgun in hand, aimed up at the sky.

"Wait up," said Calibrisi.

Tacoma stopped. He turned and waited for Calibrisi to catch up.

"What's the plan?" said Calibrisi.

"Beat some information out of him and then kill him," said Tacoma. "In that order."

"Why?"

"Because if you kill them first, they get very quiet," said Tacoma.

"I mean, why kill *him*?"

"Because he deserves it, Hector."

Calibrisi barely nodded, letting his eyes take in Tacoma, including the pump-action shotgun.

"So that's your big plan?" said Calibrisi.

"Yes," said Tacoma. "You like it? I just thought of it."

"This guy is the only connection we have to Cosgrove's killer, Nick Blake's killer, John Patrick O'Flaherty's killer," said Calibrisi. "The ones who declared war on us. And your solution is to just walk in and kill him?"

"Exactly," said Tacoma. "We're on the same page. Make him suffer a little, blow his kneecaps off, that sort of thing."

A bird somewhere abruptly flushed from the trees behind the house. It was a grouse. Tacoma watched as it took flight.

"We're *not* on the same page," said Calibrisi. "You kill him and we have nothing to go on."

Tacoma nodded, meeting Calibrisi's stare.

For the first time, a more studied, serious, even mature look came to Tacoma's face. Something between anger and recognition.

Another grouse took flight a few moments behind the first.

This time, Tacoma swung the Benelli down toward his left hip so that his left hand grabbed the forearm. He slammed it back, chambering a shell, as he tracked the bird and fired. The sound of the shotgun was like a thunderclap. The grouse dropped from the air.

"Seems to me we already have nothing to go on," said Tacoma quietly, so only Calibrisi could hear, for the first time showing a hint of hard edge and cynicism.

Tacoma walked toward the fallen bird to pick it up.

A guard stopped him politely.

"I'll get it."

Tacoma turned just as Calibrisi grabbed his shirt and stepped closer.

"What does that mean?" said Calibrisi. "'Nothing to go on.'"

"You know what it means," said Tacoma. "We have nothing to go on. We're in over our heads. The Russian mafia knew about Cosgrove. Not only that, they killed a U.S. senator and a governor—two pretty important guys—and we have *fucking* nothing. This whole thing feels bad from the get-go. They're professionals, and we unfortunately look like we're in kindergarten."

Calibrisi listened carefully. It was the first time he'd ever heard Tacoma speak seriously—take something seriously.

Tacoma was an operator, plain and simple, but the sight of Cosgrove strung up by the neck had forced him to face an unpleasant reality. He was now in charge of a secret unit of the Central Intelligence Agency that wasn't so secret after all. That what he'd signed up for was something altogether different than what he expected, than what was originally intended, and yet he couldn't quit. He owed his father that much. He couldn't just walk away and ever live with himself again.

"I agree, Rob," said Calibrisi. "But we have to start somewhere. If you want out, then turn around."

"When did I say I wanted out?"

"I would."

"Would you?" said Tacoma.

"No, but that's me. You haven't agreed yet. I don't want you to do this based on false pretenses."

"I'm not quitting," said Tacoma. "But I'm also not doing it the Agency's way."

Calibrisi nodded.

"If this guy survives," said Tacoma, pointing inside, "some corrupt individual is going to rescue him and sell me out. It's called perimeter security, and we don't have any. None. I read the document. I have total immunity. I'm not leaving until he's dead."

"This guy will never see the light of day again. You have my word."

"I know I have your word," said Tacoma, turning and moving toward the front door of the house, "but that's not enough, is it?"

"If you go in there and kill him we lose whatever information he has inside his head."

Tacoma stopped. He looked at Calibrisi.

"Unlike you, I've been through this place," said Tacoma.

"What does that mean? It's not relevant."

"Yeah, it is," said Tacoma. "The first thing I learned at the Cabin is kill or be killed. I'm running this, which means I'm running this."

Calibrisi grabbed him at the wrist.

"I shouldn't have asked you to do this," said Calibrisi. "You're too immature."

Tacoma let Calibrisi stop him, even though he could have thrown him to the side. He paused for a few seconds, then pushed— politely but firmly—toward the door, even as Calibrisi held his wrist.

"Let go, Hector," said Tacoma evenly. "It's my operation, whether you like it or not."

"You're not going in there with the shotgun," said Calibrisi firmly. "You can kill him in a few days if you want, but not today. You're too pissed off—and he's the only connection we have."

Tacoma nodded, then handed Calibrisi the shotgun.

"Fine," said Tacoma.

"Thank you, Rob."

Tacoma and Calibrisi went inside the house, past another CIA gunman, through the hallway to a doorway. Tacoma opened the door and they went downstairs. It was a typical-looking basement, lights off, dark, a large oil tank to the left. Across the low-ceilinged room was another door. It was steel. Next to the door was a glass panel that looked in on the interrogation room.

Outside the door, a middle-aged black woman with short hair was standing.

"Rob?" she said. "I'm Karen Roberts."

"Hi, Karen," he said, shaking her hand.

"Nice to meet you," she said. "Hi, Hector," added Karen as he trailed Tacoma into the antechamber.

"Hi, Karen, how are you?"

"I'm fine, thanks."

Tacoma felt the hairs on his neck stand up as he smelled the musty basement. His eyes took him to the sliver of light beneath the steel door. He'd spent almost a week behind that door. The light gave him a hard, uneasy feeling. At the Cabin, there wasn't a huge difference between night and day, between light and dark, between good and evil even. But there was another feeling. The feeling of having survived. An unmistakable feeling of triumph.

Karen handed Tacoma a sheet of paper, which he and Calibrisi read together.

"We ran his photo against Rampart, Main Core, Fairview, PRISM, Pinwale, and every other fingerprint, DNA, and facial recognition program we or the NSA has," she said. "It was an FBI database—Gravestone—where we got a facial on him. His name is Boris Slokavich, he's Russian, and he lives in Fort Lauderdale. He's a *bratok* in the Odessa Mafia."

"*'Bratok'*?" said Tacoma.

"Soldier, thug, killer. *Wet squad*. There's no record of him coming into the U.S., so obviously he's here under a false identity. Once I knew his name I ran it back against PRISM. Nothing. No cell tracks, credit cards, emails we've been following. He's a ghost. But these guys are always one step ahead. You're lucky to be alive, Rob."

Tacoma remained emotionless.

She handed him another sheet of paper. It displayed several photos. All except for the last photo were black-and-white. All of the photos had been taken from a distance. They showed an ugly-looking man with thick hair, a long face, and a long, bent nose. Tacoma stepped to the window and eyed the goon who killed Cosgrove, Slokavich, strapped into a chair with a large white bandage wrapped around his chest and torso.

The photos were accurate. They had definitely found Slokavich, whoever he was.

"Did you call anyone at IOC-2?" said Calibrisi, referring to the U.S. government's interagency group created to go after the Russian mafia, the International Organized Crime Intelligence and Operations Center.

"I spoke to Peter Buckey at Quantico and Joon Kim in the D.A.'s Office for the Southern District of New York. Slokavich wasn't even on their radar screen, but neither of them was surprised. The Odessa Mafia and the Malnikovs are the two biggest Eurasian criminal enterprises in the world. They're secretive, they move people around a lot, and there's a high mortality rate. Buckey told me it's like tracking ants."

"Good work," he said and handed her back the paper. He reached for the steel door and stepped inside.

Three walls were covered in bare, old, faded pine board. The fourth wall was glass, behind which was another room filled with electronic equipment, diagnostic hardware, and a small team of doctors and scientists, there to assess and control the condition of the prisoner.

The glass was bulletproof.

The Russian, Slokavich, was seated in a steel chair bolted to the floor. He was bigger than Tacoma remembered. He appeared to be in his mid-twenties, with a lopsided crew cut and scars on his pale face. A stainless-steel helmet was over his head. Wires were bound tightly across his face, clamping down his nose, mouth, and neck. A red rubber ball was strapped tight in Slokavich's mouth, gagging him. He was flex-cuffed to the steel chair. His hand, where Tacoma had shot him, was wrapped in a bandage, as was his leg, where Tacoma had stuck a knife.

Tacoma looked at one of the two men in the room.

"Take everything off. Remove the gag," said Tacoma to one of the men.

"Everything?"

"Everything," said Tacoma. "And tell the guys behind the glass to shut off the cameras."

Tacoma watched, pacing from the other side of the big interrogation chamber as the guards approached the big Russian. Slokavich coughed after the ball gag was out of his mouth and then leaned down pathetically, rubbing his wrists. It took him only a few seconds to acclimate and then become operational. He looked at Tacoma with a savage stare.

"Leave us alone," said Tacoma.

"Yes, sir," said one of the men.

The two CIA agents left the interrogation room.

Tacoma looked at the prisoner.

"Hi," said Tacoma enthusiastically. "I'll be your host for the next few minutes. So just sit back, relax, and enjoy the flight. You might want to buckle up. I hear there might be a little turbulence."

"*Chego ty khochesh?*" said Slokavich in Russian.

What do you want?

"*Kto poslal tebya?*" said Tacoma.

Who sent you?

"You may as well lock me back up," said Slokavich. "Chain me up this time. That was a big mistake. I could've gotten out of here."

"Yeah, right," said Tacoma. "I'm sure you could've. Thanks for not taking advantage of us, Slokavich."

The Russian looked momentarily surprised by the sound of his name.

Tacoma registered Slokavich's reaction to his name being said aloud. Tacoma's hands moved to his side as he stepped into the heart of the room, in front of the Russian. He saw Slokavich's eyes study Tacoma's legs and arms.

"Why'd you unlock me?" said Slokavich.

"I'm establishing trust," said Tacoma. "I need answers. You want to live? Start talking. Who sent you? Who was the woman?"

"What woman?" spat Slokavich as he glanced desperately around the interrogation chamber.

"The woman whose arm I almost tore off when I was beating the shit out of you two," said Tacoma.

Without any sign, the Russian suddenly charged at Tacoma, running at him despite the injured leg, collapsing the space between them. Slokavich raised his good hand and swung for Tacoma's head.

Tacoma looked surprised, then ducked and slashed his foot violently and low, catching the charging Russian in the knee, collapsing it. The Russian tumbled to the ground, headfirst, an awkward tumble, moaning in pain.

"Get up, Slokavich," said Tacoma.

Slowly, the Russian stood, and as he did he swung at Tacoma again, fist cutting the air before Tacoma's face, but Tacoma leaned back. He let Slokavich's fist breeze by his face, then met the Russian's forward momentum with a sharp fist to the chin, breaking his jaw, the *snap* of bone audible. Slokavich fell as blood coursed from his mouth.

Tacoma stood above him.

"I said, who sent you?"

Slokavich was on the ground, his mouth gushing blood.

"It only gets worse," said Tacoma.

"Go ahead and kill me," said Slokavich. "I won't tell you a fucking thing."

"Tough guy," said Tacoma.

He bolted both doors into the interrogation room—the door he'd entered through and the door to the technical lab overseeing it all, behind the glass—so that no one could come in. He saw Calibrisi in the control room and made eye contact just as he removed his P226R from a concealed holster at the front of his waist. He aimed it at Slokavich.

"Did you kill Blake?"

Slowly, Slokavich nodded, yes.

"What about the woman? Was she the one who poisoned Senator O'Flaherty?"

"*Da.*"

"Who sent you?" said Tacoma.

"Fuck off."

Tacoma pumped the trigger. A bullet ripped into the ground an inch from Slokavich's knee.

"Did you hear my question?" said Tacoma. "Or do you want me to install a listening device in your knee?"

Slokavich looked up, saying nothing.

"Who's the woman?"

"I met her on Tinder," said Slokavich, grinning.

Tacoma fired, blasting an oval off Slokavich's knee into the carpet beneath. His scream was terrible, clotted with blood that was already in his throat. The Russian went from pain to an altogether different world. His face became serene, even as it was spattered in blood.

Tacoma stepped above Slokavich, aiming the gun at his head.

"Boris, if you want to live, tell me who sent you," said Tacoma, staring down into the Russian's eyes. "Something tells me you want to live."

"I swear I don't know."

"What do you know?" said Tacoma. "I'm afraid if you don't know anything there's really no compelling reason for me to keep you alive."

"How can I trust you?" Slokavich mumbled.

"You can't," said Tacoma.

Calibrisi rapped on the door. Tacoma glanced at him through the window, then looked quickly back.

"That's my boss. He doesn't want me to kill you."

"You should listen to your boss," said Slokavich, panting.

"Shoulda, coulda, woulda," said Tacoma. "You have exactly four seconds to tell me something or I shoot out your other knee."

Slokavich screamed.

"Well?" said Tacoma as he took aim. "Three, two, one . . ."

"I only know the person who hired me," said Slokavich. "The woman. Her name is Audra."

"Where is she?"

"Florida. Miami."

"What's her last name?"

Slokavich shook his head, as if to say, I don't know.

"What's her last name?" repeated Tacoma.

"Audra," groaned Slokavich. "It's all I know. Audra."

"So someone calls you, you don't even know her last name, and you fly out to Iowa and kill the governor of Florida?" said Tacoma.

"That's how it works, yes. Fifty thousand up front, a hundred on completion."

"And Cosgrove?"

"Another hundred thousand dollars."

"Who does she work for?"

"I swear I don't know. It's all I know."

Tacoma stared down at the Russian, the gun still aimed at the man's head. He looked at the room full of engineers. He went to the door to the control room and flipped the dead bolt. The door to the interrogation room opened up and a woman in a white uniform entered.

Tacoma abruptly turned back to Slokavich and fired a round into his other knee. Slokavich screamed.

"He's told us everything he knows," said Tacoma to the CIA doctor. "Kill him and bury him."

"Yes, sir," she said.

"No, wait," said Slokavich. "I remember her last name."

"What is it?" barked Tacoma, aiming the gun at his head.

"Are you going to kill me?"

"Not if you tell me her last name."

"Buczko. Audra Buczko. She lives on Jupiter Island."

Tacoma holstered the weapon.

"Keep him alive," said Tacoma. "I want a new pharma package run on him, something that cuts through the pain. Find out if he knows anything more."

In the driveway, Tacoma was climbing into the Charger when he heard Calibrisi.

"Rob!"

Tacoma paused and looked back.

"Stop," shouted Calibrisi.

Tacoma shut the door and walked back toward Calibrisi.

"You had to shoot him?" said Calibrisi angrily.

"I told you I was going to kill him," said Tacoma. "The only reason I didn't is because he might know a little more. He's a dead man."

"You can't do this alone."

"So far it's working," said Tacoma.

The CIA director was a large man, a former CIA agent himself, one of the first-ever recruits into Special Operations Group, which, at that point, didn't have a name. Calibrisi was classified as a Bravo 4, a classification having to do with killing ability, i.e., Bravo, and geographic assignment. The "4" referred to Berlin, a hard assignment, crossroads of treachery, where, for various reasons, the fundamental cells of terrorism existed.

Calibrisi was the hunter. He spent two years moving relentlessly across Europe, like a tourist with a Eurail pass. Killing. But he was an older man now. He stumbled as he approached Tacoma. Tacoma stepped toward him and put both hands on him, stabilizing Calibrisi just as it seemed he might stumble and fall.

"You all right?"

"Yes, thank you," said Calibrisi. "Look, Rob, if you want to do it alone, fine, but it means we're out. You're on your own."

Tacoma paused. He looked at Calibrisi, then at the ground.

"I'm sorry," said Tacoma quietly, shaking his head in a moment of regret. "You're right. I'm just really mad. I feel responsible. Maybe if I'd been there on time he wouldn't be dead."

"Leave the car," said Calibrisi. "I just called a chopper. Let's get back to Langley. We need to find Audra Buczko."

Calibrisi called Polk from the back of the helicopter.

"Hi, Bill," said Calibrisi.

"Chief," said Polk. "What do you need?"

"Can you handle everything outside this? I've already papered everything so that anyone with knowledge of the unit, or who performs duties for the unit on an ad hoc basis, is protected by presidential order."

Polk nodded.

"I understand," said Polk. "That wasn't necessary, I'd do it anyway, but thanks. I'll focus on all tier-one projects, you don't need to worry about them."

"What I also need you to focus on, Bill, is a *counterstrike*," said Calibrisi. "We have to be careful what we do on U.S. soil, but anything outside our borders is another matter altogether. This was a terrible failure of intelligence by the FBI. By, frankly, the United States of America. *But we're the goddam CIA!* The Russian mafia is out there, and we can do something legally outside the U.S."

"So to speak," said Polk.

"I want hard target hits and I want them now. Don't involve me, you run it."

"Ten-four, chief, you got it. You want Nagasaki or Pop Warner?"

"Keep it tight," said Calibrisi, "but make it violent. Trusted men, relatives, whatever hurts the most. If we have to burn a few nonofficial covers doing it, so be it. We can reassign them. *Real* wet work, our best effort."

"Got it," said Polk. "You do understand this will create added problems for Rob?"

"Yes, I understand," said Calibrisi.

"What about the Malnikovs?" asked Polk.

"Keep them out of this," said Calibrisi. "We might need them at some point. This was the Odessa Mafia."

"Will do. Safe travels."

CHAPTER 28

Hart Senate Office Building
Washington, D.C.

Senator Peter Lehigh finished shaking hands in the large reception area. He was tired. He wanted to go sit down on the red leather couch in his large office that looked out on the U.S. Capitol.

Carrie, his assistant, signaled to him, touching her phone.

"He says it's important," she said. "A man named Barry."

Lehigh walked slowly, almost like a skeleton, into his office.

"Put him through," he said. "No interruptions."

Lehigh shut the door and locked it. He went behind his desk and picked up the phone.

"Hello, Mr. Darré."

"I'll keep this short and to the point, Senator," came the voice. "Who's the other American assigned to the unit?"

"I don't know. I'm afraid the offer—"

"Shut up," said Darré. "We need the name of the other agent that was assigned to the unit. SSCI has oversight of it. You're a member of SSCI. What's his name?"

"The deal was information on the unit. I never promised you

the names! I gave you Cosgrove's name out of the kindness of my heart, and now he's dead!" snapped Lehigh.

"Give me the name or you'll end up just like Cosgrove. Do you understand?"

"They're looking for where the leak came from," snapped Lehigh. "We haven't been told the other man's name yet. If I ask the CIA for it, and tell you, you'll just kill him. Then I'll be arrested along with every other member of the committee and it'll take the CIA approximately five minutes to trace it all back to me."

"Indeed, that is the situation, you're right," agreed Darré. "I told you to keep everything clean and make sure your affairs are in order."

"*You murdered Cosgrove!*" shouted Lehigh.

"So did you, Senator," said Darré evenly. "Now, get me the name of the other agent. And let me remind you, if you do get caught and you confess, your family will end up in the same place as Cosgrove, hanging from the ceiling. I don't want to do that, Senator, but I will. I'll hang them myself."

There was long pause. Finally, Lehigh spoke.

"They're briefing us later today. I'll find out his name, Mr. Darré," said Lehigh.

"Good. You're contributing greatly to American politics," said Darré. "It would be a shame if you committed suicide, or had a fatal car accident. Your constituents would be very upset."

CHAPTER 29

CIA Headquarters
Langley, Virginia

There were several floors below ground operated by the Directorate of Operations. All were windowless. The lowest floor, called
T2, held mission theaters—large amphitheaters designed for the
live running of missions. There were five theaters, and this one,
Gamma, was sparsely populated but busy.

The room itself was composed of a curvilinear set of rows of
seating on one side and a massive screen on the other.

The amphitheater seated fifty and it was approximately a half
full, with various CIA and White House staff members along
with all fifteen members of SSCI, the Senate Select Committee
on Intelligence.

On the screen were four large photos. The top photos showed
a pair of older men and the lower photos showed younger individuals. The older men, at first glance, looked similar. Each was
in his sixties or seventies, with wrinkled, pale skin and thinning
gray hair. But upon further examination, they were very different.

As for the younger men, the photos were decidedly different.

On the left, the large face shot had writing below.

ODESSA MAFIA
NET WORTH: (Est) $17.9 BILLION
BERGEN FAMILY
NIKOLAI BERGEN 73
NIKITA BERGEN 34
NET WORTH: $7.9 BILLION

Nikolai, the elder Bergen, had a thin face, his eyes calculating and intelligent, like a lawyer's. Nikita Bergen had a shock of black hair, longish, swept from a part on the right over to the left. He had thick eyebrows and an athletic, muscular face, handsome.

There were two dozen individuals seated inside the theater, including Calibrisi, Polk, Katie Foxx, and various specialists from inside Langley who were privy to the covert action.

The door to Gamma opened and Tacoma stepped inside.

Tacoma's hair was wet and combed back, parted in the middle. He wore a short-sleeve white button-down and jeans.

He scanned the room, yet he said nothing. He walked to a chair near the door and sat down, without acknowledging Katie, Calibrisi, or anyone else.

Katie's eyes met Calibrisi's in a silent moment, then Calibrisi stood.

"Let's begin," said Calibrisi, walking and standing in front of the large screen. "Everyone, this is Rudy Laveran from Russia Special Activities Division."

A tall but slouched man with glasses stood up.

"I went to Columbia as an undergrad. When I graduated in 1987, the first stories about the Russian mafia started coming on the news," said Laveran.

He hit a remote and to the right of the photos a map came up and zoomed in.

"Brighton Beach," said Laveran. "That was their official beach-head, but there were others. By then, the writing was on the wall. The Soviet Union was collapsing. The smart ones, the toughest, the real animals from Moscow, then Odessa, then the prisons, they all came to Brighton Beach." Laveran paused. "The Russian mob is a truly American story. It's about opportunity and freedom. Capitalism. The only problem is, the Russians—the real Russians, the descendants of the Cossacks—they obey no rules except live or die. That's it. The Cossacks are the ones who came to Brighton Beach. In 1991, when they broke up the Soviet Union for good, when the central government dissolved, every thug, gangster, and scumbag from anywhere in what had been the USSR came here. Be careful what you wish for. We destroyed the Soviet Union but in so doing we created the Russian mafia, at least the one on American soil."

"Thanks for the history lesson," said Tacoma. "Get on with it."

"Yes," said Laveran, "but it's relevant, and I apologize if it's boring, but it's important."

"We get the point," said Tacoma. "I want to know about what's going on right now."

Tacoma scanned the theater, his eyes catching Katie's but ignoring everyone else's.

Laveran clicked the remote and the photos disappeared, replaced by a map of Russia colored to indicate the range of operations of each individual crime family.

"As you can see, Yuri Malnikov built a truly wide swath of control throughout the Eastern Bloc leading up to the dissolution of the USSR," said Laveran. "By the time the Soviet Union collapsed, the Malnikovs controlled organized crime in Moscow and the most populated and wealthy regions north of Europe. The

Bergens, however, refused to give up St. Petersburg, They allied with a family in Odessa and created the Odessa Mafia," said Laveran, pointing at the map. "The Malnikovs control sixty percent of organized crime, by our estimates, in the former Eastern Bloc, approximately eight billion dollars a year in activity just from the former USSR. The Bergens run nearly three billion in illicit activity inside the region. But we know little about the various factions that have been spawned by the Odessa Mafia. It's rumored they are approaching the Malnikovs in terms of sheer size."

"What about the U.S.?" said a White House staffer.

Laveran clicked the remote. A map of the United States replaced the one of Russia and the USSR. Each city was color-coded.

"Without getting into it city by city," said Laveran, "the numbers inside the U.S. mirror those in Russia."

"Where do they make the money?" said Polk.

"Drug distribution, prostitution, car theft, and hacking, which includes email scams and various forms of data extortion," said Laveran. "Each family brings a ton of product into the United States. The valuable stuff comes in by boat and plane. Boat equals opioids and coke, plane is human traffic, mostly girls. The other stuff is created and harvested all inside the U.S."

"So why kill two important political figures?" said Katie.

"O'Flaherty and Blake have been their biggest thorns," said a White House staffer. "Isn't it obvious? These killings have sent fear through American politics."

"I think the assassinations are a red herring," said Laveran. "Designed to get the American government to go after all of them."

"Why?" said Katie.

"Because the various families will all be pissed off," said Laveran. "All of them will get the blame even though most had nothing to do with it. They'll know who did, and a war—or multiple wars—will be started. This is one of the families trying to start a war with the others."

Laveran pointed the remote and clicked. Photos of crime scenes scrolled across the screen, explosion-torn restaurants and blood-covered corpses, headlines from old newspapers.

Then a photo of Cosgrove.

"That brings us to Cosgrove," said Laveran, zooming in on Cosgrove's badly beaten face.

Tacoma lurched up from his chair.

"Take it off the fucking screen!" barked Tacoma.

The screen went blank as Laveran cowered.

Tacoma walked into the center of the amphitheater, facing all fifteen members of SSCI and various staffers, including Calibrisi and Katie.

Tacoma pointed behind him at the black screen. He had a slightly bemused look on his face.

"So I get it now," he said with mock enthusiasm as he stared out at everyone in the amphitheater. "I'll just go out and kill all these guys! Great idea! Boy, it's real great having you all on my side while I go out and risk my life. Thank you all! Your oversight and contribution are much appreciated. Great idea! I'll kill them and then report back, okay? Does that sound good?"

Tacoma's eyes scanned the amphitheater. His face cut to a brutal, sober, scornful look.

"You created this unit," he said angrily, meeting every eye in the room. "Less than five hours later the guy who's supposed to run it is hanging by a goddam rope!"

"Rob," said Katie, cutting him off. "Okay, everyone, let's take five minutes."

"Fuck you," said Tacoma, looking at Katie. "I'm the one who has to go do this. As far as I'm concerned I'm going to talk all

night and you're going to listen. Tell me again why I should do this? Because this is a death sentence and you can all go fuck off! Understand?"

Katie walked to Tacoma and stood in front of him, putting both hands up, imploring him to stop. He looked slightly crazed, then finally stopped talking. His eyes appeared dazed as he gazed absentmindedly around the room.

Calibrisi stood up and signaled to the room: Get out.

The senators, shocked by how the briefing had unfolded, walked out of the room in silence. After the room emptied, only Calibrisi and Katie remained with Tacoma as they shut the doors to the amphitheater.

There was a long silence as the three stood together, exchanging glances.

"Well," said Tacoma. "How was I?"

"Perfect," Katie said.

"It was fine," said Calibrisi, less impressed. "A little overdone, in my opinion, but the important thing is everyone in that room believes you're quitting, or at least are going to need some time to get your head back in the game."

"'Fine'?" said Tacoma. "That was Shakespeare."

"Whatever," said Calibrisi. He pointed behind Katie. "Let's use the other door. Let's go find Audra Buczko."

In his sedan, on the way back to Capitol Hill, Lehigh breathed a sigh of relief. The other agent, Tacoma, just quit. Soon, the whole thing would disappear.

Bruno Darré didn't need another name. Tacoma quit. It was over now, or at least he hoped it was.

CHAPTER 30

Near Reagan National Airport
Alexandria, Virginia

A black Chevy Suburban, windows tinted dark, pulled into a parking lot behind a grocery store in suburban Virginia, a dozen or so miles from Reagan National Airport. The store was busy and the lot was full, though the Suburban was shielded by a low line of dumpsters. A digital clock on the dashboard of the SUV read 3:36 P.M.

Calibrisi was reading something on his phone. Katie was in the driver's seat.

Tacoma, Katie, and Calibrisi sat in relative silence in the Suburban for almost an hour. Finally, Calibrisi looked at his watch.

"Time to get you to the airport."

Katie handed Tacoma a Russian passport, weathered so as to look used. Inside there was an old photo of Tacoma with his hair cut short.

"Good-looking fella," said Tacoma, winking at Katie.

Katie shook her head.

ORLOV, EVGENY

"Where'd you get it?"

"We altered a photo of you taken back when we were looking at you for SPEC OPS."

"That was six years ago."

"You look about the same," said Katie.

"No, I don't."

"Yeah, you do," said Katie. "Don't let it go to your head. More importantly, it doesn't matter. The date on the passport is one year ago."

"And why can't I just fly down under my own identity?"

"We have to be careful. If they found Cosgrove, they can find you," said Katie.

"Who is it?" said Tacoma, referring to the individual whose identity he would be taking over.

"It's someone who doesn't matter."

Tacoma stared at Katie, then looked at Calibrisi.

"Who is it?" said Tacoma. "If it's not a clean cutout, fine, but I want to know before I use it."

"He's Russian," said Calibrisi. "He's a punk. He got in over his head and we acquired his background in exchange for a new identity inside the U.S. The reason we did that—and he's but one of many—is for this very purpose."

"He won't talk?"

"No," said Calibrisi. "He lives in Phoenix now and works at a company that customizes motorcycles. We have track protocol on him, so we would know if he ever attempted to reengage."

"What did he do?"

"He robbed banks," said Katie.

"Okay, fine," said Tacoma.

"You should assume they know we'll be coming for the

woman, Audra," said Calibrisi. "You need to be prepared the moment you step inside Reagan National all the way through Miami. That's probably where it'll happen. These guys have connections at the airport. If I were them, I'd have connections to TSA agents and cops and airport security, and right now I'd be sending in a team to watch out for you. Even if they don't have your identity, they'll be looking for an operator. We have to assume the worst."

"Why not fly private?" said Tacoma.

Katie paused.

"They'll try to get you at the airport. In fact, hopefully that's where they will focus. You want them to go after you there."

"Bait," said Tacoma.

"Yeah," said Katie, "that and safety in crowds. Rules of warfare."

"And my backup is?"

"No one."

"Rob, this is your operation," said Calibrisi. "Do whatever you need to do. You can get rid of Audra Buczko if you want, but there's someone larger behind this."

"Who?"

"That's the point: we don't know," said Calibrisi. "But I highly doubt whoever has a mole at SSCI, or in the White House, is this woman. She's taking orders. Kill her if you want. If that's your only option, absolutely do it. Take her down. Just keep an open mind. She might've been the one who hung Billy up—she might've organized the whole thing—but she was taking orders. I'd much rather put a slug in that guy's head."

Katie shook her head, slightly upset.

"Just kill her," she said. "Keeping her alive is only going to put you in more danger. If there's someone else, we can find him later. We can send in forensics and sanitize the place by dawn."

"Yeah, got it," said Tacoma, pushing his hand back through his hair. "Get to Miami, find her, then make the call."

"That's part of it," said Calibrisi.

"What's the other?" said Tacoma.

"Survival," he said. "You don't think enough about it. Unlike other deep covers, you're in the U.S. You can simply walk away at any point. If they know you took Slokavich alive, which they do, they'll probably assume we're coming after this Audra woman. We have an advantage right now. I don't believe they'll think we can find her this quickly. But if they're smart, they'll be waiting. It's not going to be a two-man team this time, Rob. You need to live to fight another day."

"Why? So I can get hung up by a rope in a few weeks?"

"Don't get cynical," said Calibrisi.

"You have to admit, the early days of this so-called unit haven't exactly gone according to plan," said Tacoma.

"No, they haven't," said Calibrisi. "The ones that start smoothly get just as fucked up, and you know it. The harder the objective, the uglier it's going to be. Think about it. The unit was created with a goal in mind. It was a tall order then. Kill the Russians who just killed Nick Blake and John Patrick O'Flaherty. Then Cosgrove was killed, and now it's much deeper than that. Someone inside the U.S. government is a traitor, which means they probably know who you are."

"Thanks for the words of encouragement," said Tacoma. "What about firepower?"

"When you get on the plane, an attendant will hand you a coat," said Katie. "It has a pair of P226 SIGs and six extended mags. Both guns are suppressed and hot. There will also be an electric razor. You need to cut your hair before you get to Miami."

Tacoma climbed out of the Suburban. Katie lowered the driver window.

"Thanks for the lift," said Tacoma. "Don't go changin'."

"Rob, please be careful," said Katie, barely above a whisper.

Tacoma reached out. He put his hand affectionately, as a friend would, on her cheek.

"I got it, Katie," he said.

Back in the black CIA Suburban, Calibrisi looked at Katie.

"This is a shitshow," said Katie.

"Yeah, no shit, Sherlock."

"Let's get back to basics," said Katie. "We have a mole and we have no offensive. Audra is a pipe dream."

"Bruckheimer is going to run down the mole, but we need live information for Rob," said Calibrisi.

Katie had the SUV on the highway now, brushing back her blond bangs. She looked like a teenager driving to a friend's house.

"We need an off-balance-sheet hacker and information specialist," said Calibrisi. "There's only one person I know who is capable."

"I know what you're asking and I'm not going to do it, Hector," said Katie.

"He would do anything for you."

"Oh, fuck off, will you?"

"You, in turn, would do anything for Rob," said Calibrisi. "You're a conduit. Igor is going to help Rob survive."

"No," said Katie.

"Oh, come on. What's the big deal?"

"No. Fuck off. Rob can die. I'd rather have Rob die than do it."

"We need him," said Calibrisi. "He helped stop the raid on Columbia University. The fact that he is in love with you is actually your only advantage, Katie. Think of this as an operation. In order to succeed, we need whatever advantages we can get. Rob is right; this *is* fucked up. But it's only the beginning. There's a jet waiting for you. You'll be in Manhattan in an hour. You want Rob to live? I know I do. And I know you do. Get up to New York City and convince Igor to join us."

At the next turnabout on Route 267, Katie took a U-turn and headed back toward Dulles, less than a mile away.

She drove for several minutes, remaining silent.

"Fine, but I should get a bonus for sexual harassment," said Katie as she slammed on the brakes at the base of an idling Gulfstream GV back at Dulles. She opened the door and looked over at Calibrisi. "I want a chopper on the Sheep Meadow at precisely"— she looked at her watch—"ten forty-five P.M.," said Katie. She exited the vehicle. "I want FS Advantage commo. He needs to have access to broadband. You want me to do this? Fine."

She slammed the door shut and walked across the tarmac to the waiting jet. She climbed the stairs and then the door closed; the Gulfstream was quickly airborne. Katie was the lone passenger. She sat down and looked out the window. It was a blue sunset.

As the plane charged down the runway, she whispered aloud, to herself.

"What I wouldn't do for you."

An ECO-Star chopper picked Calibrisi up a few minutes later and ferried him to Andrews, where a jet was waiting. He climbed aboard, and the sleek, silver and red Gulfstream G50 roared down the tarmac and lifted like a bird into the eastern sky, aiming in the direction of the Atlantic Ocean, which soon became the underlying backdrop to the jet's destination as it flew east, and Calibrisi tried to nap, knowing Iceland potentially held the keys to it all.

CHAPTER 31

National Clandestine Service
CIA Headquarters
Langley, Virginia

Polk stood in a large, glass-walled conference room, sealed off from a bullpen of cubicles and bright lights. It felt like a prism, masquerading the fact that they were several stories underground.

It was a mission-planning conference room in the middle of the crowded office space that housed the National Clandestine Service, which included two directorates: a group devoted to political, financial, and technological strategy and manipulation, called Special Activities Division, and its more violent partner in crime, Special Operations Group.

The overhead lights in the room were a little too bright.

The conference table was surrounded by people, twenty in all, and a few more were standing, though whether you got a seat or not had nothing to do with rank.

Polk entered, his sleeves rolled up.

"This is a Russia and Eastern Bloc situation meeting," said Polk, looking around the room. "Assembled are all Langley-based officers inside Special Operations Group and Special Activities

Division." Polk looked around the table. "We are going to be taking lethal action as soon as operationally viable. The targets are organized crime members in your sphere. Briefing sheets were sent around, and I assume you all read them."

There were nods and a few murmurs of "Yes, Bill."

"I want high-quadrant targets anywhere you can find them," said Polk. "Russia, Europe, Ukraine, whatever. I want a manpower plan for how we execute. You move now, and I want to see designs and targets within two hours. I want two-by-two integration of the intelligence with the designs. Angie," said Polk, looking at a pretty red-haired woman, Angie Poole, the head of SAD, "work with Mack. One more thing: don't touch the Malnikovs. They weren't involved and in fact, as with the Statue of Liberty, are helping us."

He looked around for questions.

"What's our free power set, Mack?" said Angie, looking at Mack Perry.

"We have some spare bodies in St. Pete and Moscow," said Perry. "I can turn them on immediately. Moscow'll be a first project, but I'm comfortable with the asset."

"What about Ukraine?" said Polk.

"Warner is down," said Perry. "He's at the hospital in Geneva. He was shot in the leg a week ago."

"I knew that, sorry," said Angie. "How is he?"

"He's fine."

"What about Kiev?" said Polk.

"Kiev—Smith—is in the center of an operation, Bill," Perry said. "An operation you signed off on."

Angie looked at Polk.

"It's no secret, these guys are all over South America," said Angie.

Polk looked at Perry.

"Rio, Montevideo, BA are all in the middle of an OP," he said.

"Call the Activity," said Polk, referring to the U.S. Army Intelligence Support Activity (USAISA), whose job was to gather intelligence in advance of missions by JSOC and SPEC OPS units around the world. "Tell them we might need a Delta for a few days. Meanwhile, figure out the targets. Anything else?"

A large, muscular, bald man, Rick Ahearn, leaned forward.

"Bill, is this really the right way to get back at the ones who assassinated Nick Blake and John Patrick O'Flaherty?" said Ahearn. "We're just creating Beta for our teams, all out of revenge. It doesn't attach for me."

Inside NCS walls, they all knew what he meant by Beta: risk, unpredictability, and increased chances of death.

"When they kill someone on your team, you strike back," said Polk, "even if it involves killing someone who had nothing to do with it. Sometimes it's about the targets and other times its just about saying fuck you. We're going to say fuck you." He scanned the group. "I don't want subtlety."

CHAPTER 32

The Darré Group
New York City

Nathaniel was sitting in Darré's office.

He was Darré's most valuable trader, a thirty-two-year-old Princeton grad with advanced computer skills, and a gifted writer of algorithms. Nathaniel was alone, waiting for Darré to return from a meeting. He had longish black hair parted down the middle. He was dressed in a tan Brunello Cucinelli suit and Louboutin loafers.

When Darré entered, he did a double take, then shut the door behind him. Leaving the real world behind. Or maybe leaving the fake world behind.

"What is it?" said Darré.

"I ran a screen against all flights, public and private, heading to Miami in the next few hours," said Nathaniel.

"Why Miami?"

"Under the presumption they're going after Audra. Assuming Slokavich capitulated."

"Cut to the chase."

Nathaniel hit a button on his cell phone. A large digital screen lowered along one of the walls of Darré's office. A wall of black appeared, then rows of green numbers—then they froze. Within the wall of green numbers was a particular line of numbers that flashed bright orange.

```
985834176-92356
80327502759996799896
88432917507856137529-78
78237598979
23057823857235
```

"What it is, Nate?"

"I expected something not to scan in relation to one of the private flights," said Nathaniel. "That's how I'd send someone in to kill Audra. But I found something else. An extant identity that matched a CIA alias from a few years ago. Someone is flying him to Miami on a commercial flight right now, if I'm right."

"A mistake," said Darré. "I spoke to Lehigh. He said the other member of the unit quit already. He was at the meeting."

"They were fucking with him," said Nathaniel. "They know."

"Perhaps," said Darré. "Or maybe just a subterfuge, or maybe he actually quit."

"I doubt it."

"Is it possible?" said Darré.

"Yes," said Nathaniel. "Not only is it possible, but we should assume it's happening and we should assume Slokavich gave up Audra. That means someone is coming to Miami. We're lucky. We know what flight he's on. It lands in two hours."

Darré went to the window, pondering his next move carefully.

He had planned what he thought would be a pair of surgical hits that would be blamed on the Russian mafia in a vague way. After all, it was a disparate group, with literally hundreds of factions. He thought the blame would be spread out in a wide, media-fueled arc across all of them, without specificity. He certainly didn't think the president would bring in the CIA, nor that he would be allowed to. He knew the law—he'd gone to Yale Law School—but he forgot about the fact that laws could be rewritten, re-created, or, most likely, simply elided. It didn't matter now. Darré had started a war with the U.S. government. He'd succeeded in removing his two biggest enemies, O'Flaherty and Blake, but the news from Senator Lehigh had changed all that. The fact that the Senate would allow the CIA to operate on U.S. soil meant the U.S. government wasn't taking Blake and O'Flaherty's deaths lying down. Now, by murdering Cosgrove, Darré had sent the U.S. an unequivocal response. He wondered if he should have just left well enough alone. His thought process was straightforward. In battle, it was best to strike early and hard. But as bold as the move had been, killing Cosgrove opened up an entirely new and unpredictable front in a war that wasn't going away. For a brief moment, Darré questioned everything.

Darré had believed all of it would somehow remain hidden. He hadn't seen the larger picture: that the U.S. now knew they had a leak. If they were sending someone to kill Audra, which he was still skeptical about, it meant the meeting Lehigh had attended was a fake. If Nathaniel was correct, it could only mean they knew they had a leak.

Darré had gone to Phillips Exeter, Harvard, Yale Law, and Wharton—but it didn't take a genius to understand that an existential threat now existed, not only to him, but to the entire Russian mafia.

Darré phoned Volkov.

"We have a situation," said Darré.

Darré explained Nathaniel's theory, without acknowledging Nathaniel. He didn't want one world, the legitimate world of

Wall Street, to cross into the illegal world. So far, he'd succeeded in keeping the two separate.

"His flight lands in two hours," said Darré.

"I have it," said Volkov. "I'll get my best team. But Bruno, perhaps I should pay a visit to Audra myself, ahead of time?"

"No, absolutely not," said Darré. "Stay away."

"My point is, let's remove her before he gets there."

"No," said Darré, "that's not the way we do things. Audra just pulled off not one but two critical jobs for us. If we start shooting the loyal ones, pretty soon all we'll have left are the rats. Besides, isn't she your, whatever, your girlfriend?"

Volkov was quiet.

"No," said Volkov. "That was a long time ago."

"Look, just kill whoever this agent is they're sending down. The analysis could be wrong. Kill him anyway. Leave the body at the airport. We'll relocate Audra after the dust settles. But make no mistake, if he gets to Audra he gets to you."

"And if he gets to me, then he gets to you?" said Volkov. "Is that your presumption? Because I don't sell out."

"You've never been tortured by the Central Intelligence Agency," said Darré. "If he gets to Audra, he gets to you, he gets to me, he gets to everything. Got it? I know you won't sell out, but the truth is you won't even be aware of what you're saying once they start injecting you with drugs and torturing you. It'll all be a painful blur. I want this man dead, Andrei."

CHAPTER 33

Rose Bar
Gramercy Park Hotel
New York City

Igor was slouched back in a luxurious velvet sofa. Igor was tall, with short blond hair and a thin but handsome face.

The bar was crowded, with a low din of music, talk, and laughter, under faded light from high coffered ceilings and the aroma of marijuana.

Across the bar, he could see a work of art, a large mural of dried butterflies, in the shape of a butterfly. Igor considered the way one could have constructed that same mural on a computer, how could one capture the symmetry of the overall design and yet the randomness inherent in a butterfly itself, not to mention a thousand of them, all perfectly aligned.

A tall, striking black woman was draped over one of Igor's shoulders. On the other side was an auburn-haired beauty. Both were models.

"Say it again," said the auburn-haired woman. "I love it when you talk about math. It's such a turn-on."

"Think of a cube," Igor said to the woman, whose name he couldn't remember.

"Okay, I'm thinking of a cube."

"That cube has a wrapper on it, a wrapper that is composed of numbers and letters, and they are constantly changing," said Igor. "But if we can unwrap it, we can turn it into whatever we want. We can make it tell a printer to make a beautiful poem, or an image of a sunset."

By the time Igor was twenty years old, he had stolen more than $100 million by hacking. At the age of twenty-six, Igor quit hacking and went to work for a large energy company in New York City, where he designed advanced trading algorithms that made the company billions, and himself even more money than he'd made stealing. He gave back all the money he'd stolen.

He'd been brought into the CIA to help stop a Russian terrorist computer hacker named Cloud, ultimately outwitting Cloud and helping prevent a nuclear catastrophe on U.S. soil.

But he'd refused to go work for the CIA, despite being asked by Calibrisi himself. The truth is, deep down, Igor didn't know how long he would have the power he had, the ability to see massive lines of digits and from them capture codes, flaws, butterflies. At least that was what he told himself. He couldn't deny that he enjoyed the freedom he had. Two luxurious apartments in Manhattan and a large château in southern France.

Suddenly, he felt his cell vibrating.

Few people had the number. In fact, no one had the number. It was a burner. Bought for outbound calls, not inbound.

UNKNOWN CALLER

"Hello," said Igor in a thick Russian accent.

"It's Katie."

Igor sat up, becoming alert.

"What is it? Are you okay? Do you still love me? Be honest."

Katie cleared her throat.

"Igor, as I've said before, not only do I not date people I work with, worked with, or will ever work with, but even if I did, I wouldn't date you unless you were the last man on earth, and even then I probably wouldn't date you."

"So what you're saying is, I have a chance?" said Igor.

"Creepy."

"I can practically smell your perfume over the phone," said Igor. "It's driving me wild."

"You see, this is what I'm talking about."

"Well, if this is not a personal call, what is it professionally I can assist you with, my beautiful and very sexy blond American friend?"

"We need your help," said Katie.

"We, or you, Katie?"

"We."

"With what?" said Igor.

"I can't discuss it over the phone."

Igor looked up.

"Fine, but I'm presently indisposed," said Igor. "Let's set something up for next week."

"I'll see you in an hour," said Katie.

One hour later, Igor took a sip of wine and looked toward the bar in the distance. It was packed with people, and yet he couldn't stop staring at someone. She had on high-heel sandals with leather straps that covered her feet, at the base of tanned legs that were perfectly chiseled. She was leaning forward, speaking to the bartender. All that was visible was the back of her head, a shock of blond, straight and sharp.

"Excuse me," said Igor to the two women with whom he'd been conversing. "I'm afraid I have to go."

Igor stood up and moved to the bar. He came up beside the woman and tapped her gently on the elbow.

She turned.

"Hi, Igor," said Katie.

"I knew it," said Igor, in English but with with a deep Russian accent, shaking his head. "Only one human being could have legs that perfect. Katie."

He leaned toward her, wrapping his arms around her, then felt two fingers just beneath his ribs, pressing sharply, hinting of deeper and sharper pain.

"I'm not in the mood," said Katie. "Besides, we need to talk."

"What is it?"

Katie eyed him warily, wondering if somehow he already knew.

"You mean you don't already know?" said Katie.

It was a logical question. Igor had hacked into virtually every intelligence service in the world by the time he was fifteen. He monitored information constantly, unbeknownst to those creating the information.

"How would I know?" said Igor absentmindedly. "What, are you finally coming around to the idea of us as a couple?"

Katie rolled her eyes.

"Is it about Dewey?"

Katie shook her head, no.

"Then what is it?"

Igor pulled a small box from his pocket and opened it. It was a cigarette case, though inside were joints. He lit one and looked at Katie.

"You want a puff, sweetheart? It's a mild sativa, grown outside a small village in northern Spain."

Katie ignored him as he smoked the joint, despite being inside the bar. It was barely noticed amidst the din of conversation and music.

"You really don't know?"

"What? About the top-secret CIA unit?" said Igor. "Cosgrove and whatnot?"

Katie should have been surprised, but instead she became cold, her eyes flashing anger.

"You knew about it and sat on the sidelines?" she seethed. "I knew Hector's idea was a terrible one. You're obviously a selfish bastard who cares more about yourself than about your own country."

"Katie, you're the one who interrupted my evening," said Igor. "Did you fly up here just to insult me?"

"You knew about this and never offered to help?"

"Who do you think is going to save Rob's life in Miami?" said Igor seriously, taking a puff from the joint.

"What are you talking about?" said Katie.

"Rob is about to get attacked in Miami," said Igor. He held up his cell and showed Katie live video footage of a crowded airport terminal. "They picked up whatever alias you purchased the ticket under. Who do you think not only discovered this but is right now hacking into all of the security feeds at Miami International Airport? Rob is about to enter a shitstorm."

"We need to warn him."

"You gave him a communications device?"

"Yes."

"Good," said Igor. "Let's go see what we can do, Katie."

CHAPTER 34

Keflavik International Airport
Reykjavik, Iceland

Alexei Malnikov's Gulfstream G500 landed in the middle of the night, on a restricted tarmac at Keflavik Airport, in Iceland, under a terrible thunderstorm. Iceland represented a sort of halfway point between Moscow and Washington.

Through a porthole window, Malnikov spied another plane on the remote, light-filled, rain-crossed tarmac. It was a red and silver Gulfstream with no markings, and clamped to its fuselage was a row of missiles, small and thin, not meant for war, but valuable in the case of a close-envelope attack. They looked jury-rigged, as if put on the fuselage by someone other than the manufacturer. He hadn't seen this setup before—and he made a mental note to copy the move.

Malnikov hit a button, walked down the jet's air stairs, strolled under the driving rain across fifty feet of tarmac, and climbed inside.

It was a much smaller cabin, not as luxurious as his. But it spoke of utility. This was not a Gulfstream devoted to joy and debauchery, like his was. This was a working jet. Calibrisi was seated in a leather seat facing forward, a table in front of him. Malnikov entered and sat down directly across from Calibrisi. They were both large men and their knees brushed.

Calibrisi reached his arm forward and they shook hands.

"How was your flight?" said Calibrisi.

"Fine, thank you."

"What's so goddam important that you couldn't tell it to me over the phone?"

"I need to know I can trust you," said Malnikov.

"I flew out to Denver and met your father as they opened the door to his cell at Supermax. I drove with him to the airport. I told him what you did to free him. Then I put him on a CIA jet and he went home. Did he not tell you?" said Calibrisi.

"Yes, he did. Thank you."

"I pay my debts."

"I know," said Malnikov. "You are a friend. That's why I called."

Two years before, the United States had needed help from Malnikov. A Russian computer hacker had acquired a dirty bomb and was going to detonate it in New York Harbor. Malnikov was instrumental in helping stop an attack that would have made 9/11 seem small by comparison. More than a million people would have died. Alexei Malnikov was crucial in stopping the attack—in exchange for freedom for his father.

After the attack was thwarted, Calibrisi flew to Colorado. He'd made a deal—and he didn't want politicians or White House staffers to renege. He walked Yuri Malnikov to a white van and drove with him to the airport, to a CIA jet, then climbed aboard with Malnikov. Calibrisi remained on board until they landed in Moscow many hours later.

Alexei Malnikov understood and was grateful. It was the very reason why he was here.

"There is someone above us," said Malnikov. "Someone who

runs the families. He doesn't care about what we do in terms of drugs or whatever. He doesn't even ask for money. But when he tells us to do something, we do it."

Calibrisi's mouth opened.

"The assassinations?"

"Yes," said Malnikov.

"You have proof?"

"No, I don't. But he's there. In terms of actual helpful information, Hector, he's not on the FBI's radar screen. His name is Kaiser. He used to run GRU. He's very tall, has black hair. His skin is pale. He's ugly. He occupies the entire room. I wouldn't want to fight him. I believe I would win, but I could be wrong. He's in his sixties, but I would not want to fight him."

"Why do you listen to him?"

Malnikov stared at Calibrisi, but said nothing.

"Do you know an assassin named Audra?" said Calibrisi.

Malnikov shook his head, no.

"I gave you this," said Malnikov. "I gave you Kaiser. Also, I'm telling you we weren't involved."

"It's not enough."

"I flew here because I want the U.S. government to know the Malnikovs are not involved. That is the extent of what I am here to communicate. I demonstrated it by giving you Kaiser."

"Does he work out of Florida?" said Calibrisi.

"No," said Malnikov, "but let me guess, this Audra does?"

"We think so."

"You're sending in someone to interrogate her and find out who she works for?"

"Yes."

"I'm telling you who she works for," said Malnikov. "Don't waste the bullet. You want to avenge the assassinations of O'Flaherty and Nicholas Blake? Find out who Kaiser is. He's a shadow. Your

incompetent FBI isn't even aware of him, and yet he runs everything. Or at least, he has knowledge of everything and occasionally gives an order."

"Who did he order to do this?" said Calibrisi.

"Odessa Mafia."

"That much we figured out. I need a name."

"It's very big, the Odessa Mafia. I have no idea who carried out
Kaiser's orders. Besides, he's the one you need to find."

"Why do you listen to him?" said Calibrisi.

"That is a question I don't know how to explain," said Malnikov. "We just do. He leaves us alone. We're his frontline soldiers. He wants us to sell things that hurt Americans, like heroin.
Occasionally, we take an order, as some part of the Odessa Mafia
just did."

"But why?"

Malnikov grinned and shook his head, saying nothing.

Calibrisi ran his hand back through his uncombed black hair.

"Why would he want Blake and O'Flaherty dead?" said Calibrisi.

"They're fighting against you every moment of every day," said
Malnikov. "They killed O'Flaherty and Blake because they could.
They knew it would create chaos."

"Do you have a picture of Kaiser?" said Calibrisi.

"No."

"Can you give me a better description of him?"

"No," said Malnikov. "I've given you enough already."

Malnikov abruptly stood up.

"Have a safe flight, Hector," said Malnikov.

CHAPTER 35

In the Air

After a half hour in the air, Tacoma went to the restroom, carrying the electric razor. Looking in the mirror, he shaved his hair down to the scalp, flushing large handfuls of dirty-blond hair down the toilet. He shaved off his mustache and beard, rinsing it down the sink drain. He threw away the electric razor.

When he returned to his seat, he looked at his cell. He saw an attachment to an email. It was from Igor.

TURNKEY FILE
Verit/jeeG—1/2
NOV 6

It was a list of individuals, some sort of file, the writing in Cyrillic. Tacoma scrolled through the list, looking at each agent, each with various photos and a detailed biography. He stopped when he saw the woman from Cosgrove's house. In her file photos, she was much younger and had short, curly blond hair. She'd been sent to Istanbul to seduce an oligarch. It was her fifth assignment, after four successful missions in two years.

BUCZKO, AUDRA

GRU GROUP 54R

T.A.Z. PII-0087

- Insead DCDIA 9

- Language Beta 6.0

- Kinetic SA 4.45

Narrative: Audra Buczko was recruited during her sophomore year at Moscow University. She is Ukrainian by birth but was raised in Moscow. She was identified at a coffeehouse in Moscow by a freelance recruiter for GRU. . . .

She was a trained professional. She had gone from GRU to the Odessa Mafia. Why that happened—how that happened—was irrelevant. She was the individual he was going to find, and he needed to know her background and training.

Tacoma didn't read through the entire biography. Instead, he stared at the photos of her. Some had been taken by satellite, distant blurry images of her.

He put in his earbud.

"Igor," Tacoma whispered, leaning against the cabin window. "To what do I owe the pleasure?"

"Did you get the file?"

"Yes, thank you. Did you show this to Katie and Hector?"

"Not yet."

"So Audra went to work for the Russian mob?" said Tacoma.

"Yes," said Igor.

"Do you have an address?"

"Working on it. By the time you land I'll have it on your screen."

"Thanks, Igor. Nice work."

CHAPTER 36

Private Living Quarters
The White House

A large rectangular maroon phone console next to the sofa was beeping a low but insistent alarm. Dellenbaugh was seated on the sofa, glasses on, reading some papers. Across from him sat Amy Dellenbaugh, who was reading a book.

The president reached over and picked up the phone.

"What's up?" he said to a White House operator inside CEN-COM.

"Mr. President, we have Charlotte O'Flaherty on the line," came a female voice. "It's the fourth time she's called, sir. She's . . . well, she's a little worked up, sir. Buffalo PD wants to know what to do. I know you were close with Senator O'Flaherty."

"Put her through," said Dellenbaugh, meeting eyes with his wife. "And let's get someone from the FBI field office to spend some time with her. I think she just needs someone to talk to."

"Yes, Mr. President."

There were a few clicks.

"Hello, Charlotte," said Dellenbaugh.

He heard the sound of her trying to control her sobs.

"What are you doing about the people who killed my father?" Charlotte O'Flaherty whispered, anger and sorrow in her voice.

Dellenbaugh remained quiet.

"He was my anchor," Charlotte sobbed.

"I know he was, Charlotte," said Dellenbaugh, his eyes on Amy. "We're working on it, trust me. We'll avenge your father's death, don't worry about it. But I need you to relax. I'm as angry as you are, and the people who killed your father are going to pay a very steep price."

He heard Charlotte O'Flaherty struggling to suck in air, as if trying to stop crying.

Amy slowly put her book down and stood up. She came to Dellenbaugh and nodded, asking him, without words, to hand her the phone.

"Charlotte," she said softly, "it's Amy Dellenbaugh."

Amy nodded at J. P. Dellenbaugh, flicking her wrist, telling him to move down and make room for her on the sofa, as only a First Lady could.

Amy Dellenbaugh sat down and leaned back, as if getting ready for a long conversation.

"Hi, Amy," whispered Charlotte, finally.

"Do you have a few minutes?" said Amy. "I lost my father when I was sixteen. I find it helps to talk with others who have experienced the same thing. Even today, it still helps."

"I'd like that."

"Did he have a nickname for you?"

"Yes. Cece."

"My dad used to call me Tinkerbell," said Amy, laughing softly as she reached unconsciously and rubbed her eyes. She heard the sound of Charlotte's gentle laughter on the other end of the phone and put her hand on top of her husband's knee as tears appeared on her cheeks. Amy closed her eyes and listened as Charlotte O'Flaherty talked about the father who would never be coming home again.

CHAPTER 37

St. Petersburg
Russia

A man named Sverdlov stepped outside the front door of his home. It was a respectable block of limestone town houses in central St. Petersburg, near the river. Sverdlov ran St. Petersburg for the Odessa Mafia.

It was nighttime.

Sverdlov lit a cigarette just as two men, who'd been waiting, approached.

Sverdlov was tall, with an ugly face and short blond hair. He was forty years old.

The two men who approached were much younger.

Sverdlov lit the cigarette and walked to the two men.

"What is it?" said Sverdlov.

"You texted us," said one of the two younger men.

"I didn't text you," said Sverdlov.

The air suddenly erupted in a drumbeat of silenced automatic weapon fire as two gunmen emerged from a nearby alleyway, cloaked in black wet suits, faces painted dark, lead spitting from the muzzles of silenced

MP7s. Sverdlov was ripped across the chest and torso; the other men were pulverized in a rip cord of zinc-coated bullets.

The CIA gunmen retreated into the shadows, meeting up a mile down the road, where a chopper picked them up and whisked them away.

CHAPTER 38

Commonwealth Tower
1300 Wilson Boulevard
Arlington, Virginia

Calibrisi took the elevator to the fourteenth floor, which required a passkey to access. He passed a glass door and peered inside. It was dimly lit. The entire room was taken up by high-powered computer servers, 122 in total, enterprise-class, custom made, each in a steel case that could be wheeled and repositioned.

Down the hallway, Calibrisi arrived at another door, put his thumb against a small electronic keypad, and went in. The space was cavernous, open, brightly lit, and immaculate. All interior walls had been removed. At the center of the room, tables were set up in a large X-shaped pattern. On top of the tables sat computer screens, long lines of them. There were eleven separate computer screens in all. One chair was behind the table. It was on wheels.

One section of the floor was taken up by a makeshift seating area. A long, green, leather Chesterfield sofa flanked a low, oval glass table. On the other side were comfortable-looking club chairs, in matching green leather, also Chesterfield, with buttoned tufts and a pretty shine.

A Peloton was in another corner, along with a strange-looking treadmill, modified, controllable not only by the user but, if so selected, by someone on a computer, who could speed it up and slow it down at will. It was a wide machine. Beneath the tread was a complex system of alloy ribs that enabled the machine to go vertical, almost like a Stairmaster, and to introduce a multitude of elevation, pitch, and speed variables into a course, mimicking turbulence or even an explosive going off nearby.

The walls, ceiling, floor, and windows were covered in an almost invisible sheet of copper mesh, laid out meticulously, like Farrow & Ball wallpaper, intended to prevent electronic eavesdropping and other forms of SIGINT capture from outside the building.

The windows were transparent armor—bulletproof, three and a half inches thick, a layer cake of laminates intended to keep bullets out but also to prevent SIGINT capture or eavesdropping.

Katie and Igor did not look up at Calibrisi as he entered the office. Igor was typing into a keyboard and scanning his eyes across several screens. Katie was on the green sofa, glasses on, reading a thick document.

"Where are we?" said Calibrisi.

"I found Audra Buczko," said Igor.

Calibrisi and Katie stepped behind Igor. On one screen, several still photos showed the woman, photos taken from Sparks security cameras. Another screen showed a gridlike frame. At its center was a building, shown from the sky. The outlines of the home were digitally enhanced, bright white lines against darkness. In the middle of the frame, a bright green figure moved about, like a hologram, irradiated in neon against a dark screen.

"Thermal?" said Calibrisi.

"No," said Igor. "Radiological. This algorithm isolates radiation.

Every living thing has radioactivity. The trick is to isolate one source from another."

"Where did you start from?"

Igor pointed to a second screen. It showed nothing but lines of numbers and letters, scrolling fast up the screen. Suddenly, a line of code froze and popped up in red letters. Igor leaned forward, reading the code, then hitting enter; whatever the grid had surfaced wasn't relevant.

"I'll try to explain," said Igor. "I ran the name Audra against every database I could find relating to Florida, then crossed it against other databases, then others, and each time forced the searching algorithm to go back through the other databases, adding certain elements, such as the fact that she was in New York City, that she knew a man named Slokavich, that she understood firearms, that she'd been in Washington, D.C., et cetera and whatnot. A self-eating algorithm. Eventually, the algorithm found its final piece of meat."

"Ewww," said Katie. "Do you have to use such disgusting analogies?"

"I'm sorry," said Igor, apologetically. "Like a starving cannibal eating a corpse? Is that better?"

"Enough," said Calibrisi.

"I ran her against other sources, more real-time sources, Verizon, AT&T, NSA, TSA. She took a bus from New York City to Philadelphia and then flew to Miami."

Calibrisi glanced at Katie.

"Where is she?" said Calibrisi.

"North of Miami," said Igor. "Jupiter Island. I'll give her that, she's a well-compensated assassin." He pointed at three green neon dots near the edge of the frame. "It's gated and electric, high security. See those cameras? Those are Hikvision DS-2s. Thermal, optical, bi-spectrum. Also, I'm seeing guards along the perimeter of her property. Bottom line, Audra Buczko is very well guarded. Now how guarded is she emotionally, I don't know. I haven't had the pleasure of meeting her, though from her photos I would say I wouldn't kick her out of bed if she was eating crackers."

CHAPTER 39

South Beach Road
Jupiter Island, Florida

Audra walked alone out onto the terrace. She held a damp towel against her face. She had several cuts from the glass, from when she leapt through the window. It would cause scars.

She held the towel with her left hand. She couldn't lift her right. It was swollen and painful to the touch. She would need surgery.

But she was alive.

The American, Cosgrove, had nearly killed her. The second man would have killed her.

She remembered the second man, who nearly tore her arm from her socket.

Preserve your life at all costs.

It's what she had been taught.

She'd jumped through the window and landed on her feet, running for the trees at the back of Cosgrove's home.

Audra's mind felt scrambled with a combination of fear and the fog of pain. Her face and shoulder ached.

She stood on the glass terrace, looking to the ocean and speedboats passing by at night. It was an outrageous, modern château of glass and concrete, abutting sand and ocean.

Within the pain, Audra felt adrenaline.

She cast her eyes about, looking for someone. She picked up her phone and called Andrei.

"Are you home?" Volkov said, answering. "Are you okay, my love?"

Audra took a deep breath.

"Yes, I'm okay, but I think I should leave. Slokavich was alive and they're going to come for me, Andrei. Also, I badly need a doctor."

"I've already thought of this," said Volkov. "Someone is indeed coming. In fact, he is going to arrive in Miami soon and be killed. It will happen at the airport."

"But if he—"

"He won't get through," said Volkov.

"If he gets through?"

"I've sent Markus over with four men to guard the perimeter of your property, Audra. They're there right now. But it won't matter. This American will die at the airport."

Audra hung up the cell.

She went to the edge of the back terrace. The house was a sprawling monolith on a four-acre parcel of land just above the ocean. Andrei had bought it for her. The house sat on a bluff above a vast horizon of lawn and a gunite blue-water infinity swimming pool, the ocean just beyond.

She removed her clothing and was naked under a cool wind. She admired the façade of the house, reminding herself of how beautiful it was. Her shoulder hurt and she couldn't move her arm, but she'd endured worse pain.

She walked across the terrace to an in-ground hot tub, shimmering with bubbles caught in the underwater lights.

Audra stared back from the hot tub at the house. She felt the warm, bubbly water as it covered her legs, then moved higher. She shut her eyes beneath the dim, reddish underwater lights, with a glass of vodka in the one hand that still worked. She looked up as one of the guards was walking across the back lawn. She whistled.

The young gunman approached.

"*Snimi odezhdu,*" she ordered in Russian.

Take off your clothing.

She took a sip of vodka and sat back, enveloped in warm water, watching as he removed his shirt and pants, temporarily forgetting about the fear, though the pain would not go away.

CHAPTER 40

Miami International Airport
Miami, Florida

Tacoma's flight landed in Miami at 9:38 P.M. amid a conflux of in-bound flights. The terminals were crowded with people. Beyond security, the central terminal was jammed with waiting families and people getting food before their flights.

Tacoma strolled off the Boeing 737 into the gate and walked into the airport's central terminal. It was an older airport, though retrofitted with bright lights and glass above a large, crowded canopy.

He looked for signs directing people to ground transportation and the garages. There, he would steal a car and head north, toward Audra. Hopefully, Igor would have a hard target by now.

But as he walked through the terminal, looking for signs for the parking garage, Tacoma caught the eyes of a man. In his forties, with salt-and-pepper hair, wearing a leather jacket.

Operational.

Tacoma registered the bulge of the weapon beneath the man's left armpit.

Tacoma kept walking into the crowded terminal, tucking

lower, not looking back, though retaining the precise location of the man in the corner of his eye as he scanned for others. He marked a second man immediately—tall, blond hair, young, in a white Adidas running suit, near the entrance to the moving walkway.

Tacoma thought quickly, trying to understand. He was marked. Best-case scenario, he was wrong. Worst-case scenario, it was a group of them. They'd already figured out he was going after the female assassin, Audra.

At least Slokavich wasn't lying.

He had to figure out what to do, and he didn't have a lot of time. But he thanked God for the phalanx of passengers swarming around him.

Quickly, Tacoma found the P226R beneath his armpit. He removed it. Inside the coat, with his other hand, he threaded the gun with a short, oblong, custom-made, alloy suppressor as he pushed his way through the thick crowd from the gates as hundreds of people poured into the central terminal.

To his right he caught a third man—beneath the shadow of an ATM canopy—bald, ugly, with a mustache. Partially hidden by the ATM canopy, with no one aware of what was transpiring, the man raised a pistol and trained it on Tacoma.

Tacoma took the gun into his left hand and swept it across his torso, tight to his body, concealing it as if adjusting his jacket—then fired, one quick spit across the crowded space.

The bullet struck the killer in the left eye, kicking him sideways just as he himself got off a round that went aimlessly into the ceiling, but it broke glass above.

A young boy screamed as blood from the man's head sprayed him.

Soon, there were several people yelling and shouting.

The fallen corpse was sprawled aimlessly as a pool of crimson formed around him.

The sound of unmuted gunfire was followed by the high pitch of shattering glass, which rained down on the central terminal, causing even more screams, then panic. Everyone within eyesight of the dead man now ran for the airport exits.

Tacoma cut left, away from the fracas, looking for the other killers. He marked the blond one, then the one with salt-and-pepper hair. Each man was scanning for him, not even bothering to go to their fallen comrade, unconcerned by what bystanders thought.

Their mission was absolute, and Tacoma understood the signals.

Kill the target.

He found the earbud and slipped it into his ear.

"Igor," he said, tapping his ear as he sited the two killers, searching for Igor or Katie. "Katie," he said more urgently.

A horrible cry—a woman's high-pitched scream—echoed from near the thug Tacoma had just gunned down.

"Rob," said Katie, finally. "Where are you?"

"Miami, at the airport," said Tacoma as he watched the younger blond man in the tracksuit suddenly find him from across the crowd, maybe forty feet away. He held the man's gaze a second too long, and when he looked up for the other man he was gone.

"Fuck," Tacoma muttered.

"What is it?" said Katie.

"Nothing," said Tacoma.

The man in the tracksuit started pushing through the crowd, his eyes focused on Tacoma. The killer put a hand into his tracksuit, finding his sidearm as he moved.

Tacoma remained placid, stepping casually in a line away from the gunman as he tracked.

A loud, piercing siren abruptly sounded from speakers on the walls of the terminal. Outright panic took hold, a medley of screams and shouts, across an abrupt crosshatch of fleeing passengers, running away from where the dead man lay.

Tacoma cut away from the center of the crowd, out of view of the blond killer, falling in with a line of fear-stricken passengers moving toward the terminal exit. He pushed through, almost at a gallop, knowing the pandemonium was his opportunity to establish some sort of strategic advantage or at the very least get away. He saw a long row of shops and eateries along the side of the terminal as, somewhere behind him, the blond man followed.

"What's happening?" said Katie.

"I was marked after I got off the plane," said Tacoma.

"Whoever it is, blow it off, Rob," said Katie. "You're there to get to Audra."

"I can't blow it off," said Tacoma. "They're hunting me. Are you running the facials?"

"I'm working on it," said Igor. "I'll do a fast cut as soon as I hack into the security feeds."

"How'd they know I was on that plane?" said Tacoma quietly as he glanced left and saw the blond man, eyes locked on him. He clutched the silenced P226R inside his jacket, finger on the trigger, safety off.

"Hector was right," said Katie. "They knew you were coming."

Suddenly, Tacoma watched as the blond put his hand to his ear. Tacoma ducked to his knee as he pulled the sidearm out and swept it ahead of him. He didn't fear the blond man at this point. Instead, he knew they were communicating and, if they were good, were using the blond to drive Tacoma into a target zone.

From the ground he scanned as people rushed by him, then saw a new killer, a black man in a red tracksuit. He was moving directly toward Tacoma, a vicious-looking goon in his early twenties. His eyes scanned desperately; he'd lost sight of Tacoma. From his knee, Tacoma pulsed the trigger once. A metallic *thwack* sounded at the same moment a bullet tore into the killer's forehead. He was kicked backward as a wet cloud of red liquid plumed out behind him, splattering on the terminal floor.

Tacoma rose to his feet as yet more screams burst from terrified passengers and onlookers.

Tacoma scanned for the blond man, studying where he'd just been standing. He pivoted quickly, searching, but the man was gone. He needed more intel. They had men here, and if he just ran to the exit he could end up with a warm bullet in his head, which he knew would mean they'd get away with it all—Blake, O'Flaherty, *Cosgrove*. Tacoma moved back against the rush of the crowd, toward the center of the terminal building, ducking low, sticking his gun back inside the holster beneath his armpit. He removed his combat knife—SEAL Pup—the knife he'd been trained with, black steel, double-serrated, a patina of scratches and wear on each side, plain looking.

Tacoma watched as yet another scrum of passengers ran in terror from the man he'd just gunned down. He aimed for a wall at the corridor entrance, where there were shops and restrooms.

"One of my screens is getting a Code Silver from the airport," said Igor. "The police think there's an active shooter situation."

"I can't imagine why," said Tacoma, tucking into a restroom, sliding along the wall, clutching his P226R as he listened to the screams from the terminal. "I already killed two of them, but they're cutting off the exits. What I need now is eyes in the sky, Igor. Are you into the security feed yet?"

"I'm trying. Hold on."

CHAPTER 41

Club K19
Moscow

A young, tall, slightly bookish-looking blond-haired woman entered K19, an exclusive nightclub in Moscow housed in an industrial ware-house. There were certainly many blondes there, but she stood out. She, too, had blond hair, but she was black.

Ripsulitin saw her from his table and immediately did a double take.

Claire Bayne had been recruited out of Dartmouth, where she was captain of the women's varsity tennis team. She was fluent in six lan-guages, including Russian and Mandarin. Her natural hair color was black, but not tonight.

This was her first assignment. At age twenty-two, she should've felt more nervous, but she didn't. Instead, she enjoyed the loud music as she scanned the club. Ripsulitin moved to the bar and started speaking to a shorter man. Ripsulitin was the target, and she locked him in, per pro-tocol, tapping her right ear.

"Target live and locked in."

"ITCC, affirm that, Claire."

She looked away for more than a minute, then glanced at Ripsulitin and intentionally made eye contact. She moved a few feet closer, inching down the bar, finding a spot at the bar. She made eye contact again, this time holding his gaze, and Ripsulitin took the bait. He came toward her.

Claire should have felt more emotion at that moment, perhaps, but she didn't. She was a grade-blue recruit in Special Operations Group. She didn't know anything about him, other than the fact that he was a top-level general in the Odessa Mafia. As he approached, she stood up and pulled the silenced Beretta 9 mm from her belt, at her spine. She smiled as she moved to meet him, swinging it low then up, placing the end of the suppressor against his chest as he came over to talk. Only the two of them could see what was happening, and they both knew it. He was smiling and excited to say hello, until he felt the hard jab of the tip of the suppressor just below his rib cage.

"Pozhaluysta, nyet," *Ripsulitin whispered as Claire pumped the trigger, sending a muted bullet—*thwap—*through his chest.*

Please, no.

Claire turned and moved to the exit as Ripsulitin dropped in a heap on the floor next to the bar, even as music continued to play loudly across the undulating warehouse filled with drugged-up Muscovites.

A green Audi sedan was waiting outside, and eighteen minutes later Claire was in a Gulfstream G280 at twenty-eight thousand feet headed to Stockholm, almost due west.

CHAPTER 42

The Darré Group
New York City

Nathaniel heard the loud beep and hit a button on his glass keypad. One of the four celluloid screens in front of him flashed. A
map appeared, and when he tapped again the frame zoomed in. It
was live video of the security feed at Miami International Airport.

He zoomed in even more and the camera moved closer to the
feed.

A box on the screen lit up:

IPN ##NON SEQ##
Alert 22.E
KDR 192
IPN 98237592387974192375023765

Nathaniel hit another key and a second screen appeared in digits. He snapped his fingers, alerting Darré, who was at his desk,
reading something.

"What is it?" said Darré.

"The flight landed in Miami," said Nathaniel. "Did you arrange for something?"

"Yes," said Darré. "Volkov has sent men."

"What are they looking for?"

"They know what to look for, Nathaniel," said Darré. "I assume you're recording this?"

"Yes, of course. Whoever it is, we'll have a very clear picture of him."

CHAPTER 43

Miami International Airport
Miami, Florida

Inside the restroom, Tacoma checked the mag, looked in the mirror, then turned back to the door.

Igor's thick Russian accent chimed into his ear as he reentered the chaos-filled terminal.

"I just got the first scan of the facials," said Igor, who was analyzing a facial recognition application he'd just run against the airport security feed. "It flagged someone."

Igor had figured out how to tap into the airport's security system. He went in through an FBI safeguard, a live trunk that existed between all airports and the Bureau. Most of the data being fed was real-time identification information, as people swiped licenses and passports. Igor went back up into the feed and once he established an appliance-level view of Miami Airport, was able to segregate appliances and find the security cameras.

"What does he look like?"

"Black-and-gray hair, good-looking, forties."

"That's one of them," said Tacoma. "Where is he?"

"On the far side of the terminal, behind you," said Igor. "He's in a hold pattern and is scanning."

Igor heard a high-pitched beeping noise. He tapped the keyboard. A three-dimensional digital green grid appeared against a black background. This was a virtual representation Igor had quickly built of the airport, representing all electronic signals—SIGINT—in and out of the grid surrounding the airport. It was a virtual Napoleon cake of layers of SIGINT, from airlines, the control tower, and a hundred other sources, yet the beeping persisted and he isolated it on a trunk coming into the airport. Someone else was watching.

He shut it down immediately, realizing they were looking for Tacoma. They knew he was coming, but they didn't know what he looked like.

It was a significant tell.

Tacoma skulked quickly and low through the massive crowd, stooping forward, tucking in the draft of an older couple who were trying to move to the other side of the terminal. Tacoma kept the blade in his left hand—his strong hand—the sharp steel aimed down at the ground. He registered the blond, looking—searching—near the shops where he'd just come from. He was to the right, near a garbage can, approximately thirty feet away. Tacoma continued forward, searching desperately for the gray-and-black haired man. He had to find the killer before the killer found him.

Tacoma didn't have time to think about why they were hunting him.

"Who does he work for?" whispered Tacoma as he scanned the crowd, searching.

"Who do you think?" said Igor. "This is a Russian mafia situation, Rob. I'm going to try and give you the targets, but understand that you're in danger."

Tacoma listened as screams filled the airport terminal.

"Hurry," he said.

"In front of you, eleven o'clock," said Igor.

Tacoma caught the black-and-gray-haired man seated at a gate not more than fifteen feet away, pretending to be reading a magazine, waiting, but Tacoma knew what was behind the magazine. He could see the man's tensed legs, tactical boots, the bottom part of a leather jacket, and the crest of salt-and-pepper hair.

Tacoma lunged to his right just as a fusillade of bullets blasted from the man's gun, behind the magazine, a silenced weapon whose *thwap thwap thwap* only Tacoma heard. Shreds of paper spat from the magazine just as one of the bullets hit a woman in the back. She screamed a terrible, high-pitched yelp as she dropped to the terminal floor. Tacoma let his momentum take him down to the ground, yanking the P226R from beneath his armpit just as he hit the ground, rolling. The gunman threw the magazine aside and stood up, weapon clutched, unafraid of being seen or caught, yet temporarily unable to find Tacoma behind the scrambling crowd.

Tacoma ripped off two quick blasts as he squirmed across the ground. The first missed, the second hit the goon in the thigh, though the killer continued to move, even as his other hand went to the wound. Tacoma fired again. This time, the slug smashed the man in the mouth, kicking the back of his skull into the seats behind him, dropping him.

"You have another man at six o'clock," said Igor. "He is running directly toward you, Rob."

Tacoma twisted onto his back and aimed up just as the tall blond killer was about to fire. Tacoma pumped the trigger once, twice, three times, hitting the blond in the neck with the last bullet in the mag. The big man dropped in a bloody heap, but it was barely noticed amid the mayhem.

The airport was a crowded, unruly mess of screams and yelling. Sirens, multiple and urgent, wailed from speakers. Hordes of passengers pushed against the small amount of police and security, who were locking down exits, thus keeping the chaos going. They were overwhelmed by the panic and screams, even as they searched for whoever was the cause of the violence.

The mad rush provided Tacoma the opportunity he needed. He crawled to his feet, ejecting the mag, then looked for the second mag, but his hands came away empty. He searched for the mag, patting down the coat as he moved, but couldn't find it. It was at that moment that he eyed another man, with wavy brown hair, watching from in front of a Starbucks.

Tacoma had caught the man from afar, across the gateway.

He was scanning for Tacoma. He was at a key funnel point, backup in case the others didn't kill him.

Tacoma again felt in the jacket for the second mag. Had it fallen out on the plane? It didn't matter now.

He tucked his head even deeper into the jacket and cut into a Hudson News store a few storefronts down from the Starbucks. He found the tourist trinket part of the store and took a pen, then walked to the drinks section at the side of the large store. He opened the refrigerator and looked around behind him, making sure no one was near. He took his knife, prying wide the panel on the right, finding a copper cord, then ripping the blade against the thin cord from behind. After several strokes, the copper tube broke. An aqua green liquid began to spill out and Tacoma took the pen, unscrewed the end, and ripped out the ink cylinder. He carved a sharp cut into the end of the pen, transforming it into a makeshift hypodermic needle. He put the open half under the flowing green liquid, then screwed the cap of the pen back on.

He put it in his hand so that one end was against his wrist and the other was between his right middle and ring fingers, tip of the pen sticking out, nearly invisible, just a fleck of silver in a man's hand in the middle of the chaos of a crowded, panic-stricken airport.

Tacoma registered the man one more time, just to be sure, standing in front of the Starbucks. He appeared agitated. He clutched a phone to his ear as he looked desperately for Tacoma.

Tacoma found a family with a stroller walking near the Hudson News, trying to get out of the airport. He cut to his left, getting behind them, and he saw that their trajectory was established in the general direction of the man, who was scanning for him, but had yet to find him. Tacoma fell into their slipstream, passing in a human tide just inches from the man, seeing the man's hand from the side, gripped on the butt of a handgun. Tacoma abruptly swung his arm and stabbed him in the ribs, pushing in on the end of the pen, punching him deep with the sharp tip. The pen ripped through flesh and muscle. The pain from the strike caused the man to yelp, a sharp cry which few people even noticed. The toxin struck a vein. The Russian suddenly comprehended the fact that the entire operation was not only over, but that he, too, had been undone. His entire body was in some way on fire, poison of some sort, and in a last half second he realized he'd lost. He tumbled to the ground as his throat and face contorted in anguish.

Tacoma grabbed the man's pistol and, with his other hand, flicked the pen into a trash can, moving away just as the man turned with blank eyes, then fell to his left, down in a pile on the airport concrete. Tacoma was several yards past him by then, hidden in a line of passengers, not even bothering to look back; he knew they would be scanning the film.

Tacoma came to the exit at a jog, running in a vast row of humanity desperate to get out of the central terminal. He came to a moving sidewalk crowded with people, stopping and getting to his knees. He waited—pretending to be out of breath—then tucked the spent mag down and to the side of the moving sidewalk, into a space of gears and chains where it likely wouldn't be discovered for months, if ever, and let it go.

He found a bus to the rental car area. When the bus stopped at the Hertz lot, he climbed off with a crowd of people.

Sirens wailed in the distance. Terror clung to the air and everyone looked around suspiciously, but also with empathy. Had they made it through whatever just happened? What *did* just happen?

Tacoma walked past the main Hertz building to the back, a dark lot half-filled with employee vehicles. He went to the back door of the building. The door was unlocked. He opened the door and stepped inside the brightly lit employee area, seeing no one. He went left and held his ear against a closed door, heard nothing, and stepped in.

It was a small employee changing room, and he quickly searched the lockers. He found a set of car keys in the pocket of a pair of jeans hanging in one of the lockers.

In the parking lot behind the office building, Tacoma moved to a beat-up Toyota sedan. He climbed in and started the engine, then moved out of the lot and onto the circuit road that circled the rental company lots.

The red and white flashes and the wailing pitch of sirens clotted the air. They were just now getting control of traffic flow out of the airport, and he knew he needed to move. Soon, the airport would all be shut down. He wouldn't get in trouble, but he would be detained. He was an anonymous soldier now, and that was a gift. If he was detained, he'd be sprung, but that would create an electronic imprint showing various things he didn't want anyone to know. He would lose the edge he had right now; the operational edge, in-theater, when it matters, when knife blades meet on bloody streets.

He saw red flashing lights at the exit.

The Miami police were cutting off the airport exit. They would try to quarantine the facility in order to find those people responsible for the killings. They needed time to scan security footage, arm the officers at the exit, and arrest anyone they believed was involved.

Tacoma couldn't afford to be stuck at the airport. If he was captured, the entire operation would be over.

Perhaps the ones who knew he was coming would be able to get to him before Calibrisi. There was a very real chance that, if caught, he would soon know the feeling of a warm bullet at the back of his head.

He thought of Billy Cosgrove. He didn't know him. He'd never met him, but he was here for him. He was here for a lot of people. Tacoma was here for the country he loved.

Get out of here.

Tacoma took a quick appraisal of the car he was driving, registering mileage and the various lights on the dashboard. He felt the neck of the steering column, reaching down, running his fingers across a mess of steel and wire, hot and cold.

Tacoma gassed the car and moved up through the space between two lines of cars, making it through several rows until he hit the back bumper of a car. He gassed it harder now, banging the Toyota against the other car again as a man shouted. But he was moving faster now, and he hit yet another car on the other side.

People were yelling and screaming as Tacoma pushed the now very dent-covered Toyota up a tight chasm. Tacoma reached to his coat and found the pistol he'd taken off the Russian at the terminal. He steered the Toyota toward the airport exit, driving recklessly. He chambered a round with his teeth.

In the distance, he saw a lone police officer, positioned near the front of the long lines of cars. He was young, in his thirties, and he had traffic at a standstill. The police wanted to scan every driver and car passenger against security video. They hadn't synthesized the video yet, but they wanted to quarantine the area immediately.

Police helicopters appeared in the sky.

Tacoma put the gun in his right hand and out the window, pushing faster and faster as the lanes opened up, and stopped at where the officer had laid down the quarantine line.

The officer saw Tacoma, who was now speeding at sixty toward the airport exit. The officer swung a compact black weapon toward Tacoma and Tacoma recognized it. MP5. Tacoma fired as he pushed the Toyota faster, closer and closer, just as bullets rained across the windshield, turning it into a spider web, even as Tacoma lay tucked to the door, praying the steel of the car would insulate him. Tacoma pumped the trigger. The slug struck the officer in the leg, midthigh, and he dropped.

Tacoma slammed the gas and moved past him—and soon other cars followed. It was a mad rush for the exit. Cars sped past the injured officer, like a piece of carrion, splayed across the tar. Everyone wanted to get away from whatever had just happened at the airport, the chaos of the killing ground they didn't understand.

CHAPTER 44

Tolemaida, Colombia

Cavalieri landed in Tolemaida and climbed out of the helicopter. A white Porsche Targa was idling, lights on, waiting for him. He got in, slammed the gas, and ran for the highway, knowing he was already late.

The kill order was simple. A man on a screen. Dmitri Gonz, eighty-three years old, the man considered the godfather of the Odessa Mafia, now living in exile. It was Polk's ultimate fuck-you to a world he didn't yet know or understand.

For Cavalieri, the name meant nothing as he pushed the Targa harder. Cavalieri didn't think about the reasons why the U.S. government wanted this particular person killed. But they did. It was his job to do it.

Cavalieri unleashed the Porsche Targa on the highway that ran to Bogota. He had the German sports car revving furiously. He scorched across the outskirts of Bogota on the two-lane highway, weaving in and out of traffic and using the shoulder at times when traffic threatened to slow him to under 100 mph.

Cavalieri was late and he knew it. He needed to hit the target at a precise time. At approximately 11:10 P.M., the target would be exposed. The problem was, he wasn't going to make it in time.

He drove with his left hand as, with his right, he looked at his cell. A

CIA app displayed key metrics in print large enough to see, even when driving 100 mph on a crowded road. At the top half of the screen was a map, with a green dot showing Cavalieri's target in relation to the Porsche, displayed on a gridded digital map.

He was getting close. A beeping noise indicated he was less than a mile from the target.

He glanced at the cell.

Two small digitals were in the upper right corner, and Cavalieri knew what they represented. The first was the number of seconds to target—how long until he was close enough to kill him. The second number showed time to abort—the time Langley believed the operation needed to be stopped, most likely for fear of discovery.

00:59   was how long until he was close enough to kill the target.

00:36   was what the application told him was when he had to abort.

He didn't have enough time. The target would be a non-live mission thirteen seconds before Cavalieri could even get in range. He slammed the gas pedal and took the Porsche to 140, staying in the breakdown lane, a maniac driving—any police and the operation would be over— yet Cavalieri played the odds.

The lower half of the cell screen was a series of weapons, represented in green against black, the outlines of the options Cavalieri had to choose from. The first was an AR-15, the figure swiveling around the screen, as if to remind him of all the weapon's assets. He swiped his thumb as he continued to fire up the road, just at the outer envelope of the vehicle's capabilities.

An HK MP7A1 was the next option, and as he kept scrolling the phone while driving, he moved past a silenced pistol, then a compact flamethrower, a pump-action short-barreled shotgun, until he stopped and hit his thumb against the screen.

SASS M-110—*a mobile, compact sniper gun made by Knight Armament.*

Cavalieri hit the screen and a mechanical arm beneath the passenger seat moved in an electric whirr. From the center console, a robotic arm emerged, holding an M-110, loaded, safety off.

He checked the upper part of the screen.

00:13   *distance to target*
00:08   *time to abort*

Cavalieri came onto the road near the park corner at 95 mph, hitting the brakes, grabbing the rifle, and opening the door, all in one motion, lurching from the Porsche even as it fishtailed into a parked minivan. He slammed the tripod down on the ground, then acquired the target 1,806 feet away. As the low, monotone beep sounded from inside the car . . .

ABORT

. . . Cavalieri pumped the trigger. The old man, standing with his dog, was struck an inch above his ear, the bullet shattering his head and spilling him back in an awkward clump to the street corner in front of a coffeehouse, dark for the night.

Cavalieri folded up the weapon and climbed back into the Porsche, accelerating away from the area, mission completed.

CHAPTER 45

Setai Tower
Miami Beach, Florida

Volkov was alone at his condominium, a penthouse in the heart of Miami Beach, atop a recently constructed glass and steel spire called the Setai Tower. The unit had cost Volkov $41 million, $5 million more than the asking price, the premium for being allowed to pay with duffel bags filled with cash. It was certainly an expensive piece of real estate. It was largely unfurnished, glass and concrete, a few walls, two swimming pools, one indoors, the other out, with bold ocean views and a wraparound terrace protected by a glass outer edge, thirty-eight stories up in the turbid, humid, noise-crossed Miami Beach ether.

There was a bed in the master bedroom, and that was all.

He opened a pack of cigarettes, lighting one as he walked across the massive empty space. All he could think was that it was the only thing he had that had never seen death. The walls had never been scrubbed, nor had bodies been carried out, or dissolved in chemicals, or incinerated. In a way, it was sacrosanct, like a church to Volkov.

Marlboro Lights were Volkov's only vice and the most legal thing he did. Everything else couldn't be called vice; Volkov's world was a world of controlled bloodshed and mayhem. Smoking cigarettes was the kindest thing he did.

He wore only a tank top and shorts. His arms, chest, and back were a gallery of tattoos. Wild colors, guns and knives, animals and numbers, weird symbols. One would need to know Cyrillic to truly understand the messages laid out like a triptych across his body. The tattoos hid scars from bullet holes and knife wounds. It was a gallery of violence, all cut into his pale skin before he was twenty.

Volkov was bowlegged and muscular. He was handsome in the way a great prizefighter might be, good-looking and also savage. Even if he wasn't one of the Odessa Mafia's preeminent men in America, his mere presence tended to rattle people.

Still, as luxurious as it all was—for Volkov had similar palaces in Manhattan, London, and Las Vegas—no amount of money could erase the hell he'd endured, having his dignity, family, and hope all taken away at such a young age. It was an ocean away, but it never left Volkov, not for a moment. The anger would never leave. It was why he needed to buy the apartment. He needed to look back across the mighty Atlantic to his homeland, so as to say "fuck you."

He went into the bathroom to brush his teeth. He looked in the mirror. He was twenty-seven years old now and yet when he looked in the mirror he saw the face of an eleven-year-old boy. He stared for an extra moment.

Volkov was a short, scrawny child with a shy demeanor, and he was always picked on, from the earliest age. He was the runt, the unpopular one, but they were all so wrong. It took him a while, but he proved it. For every punch he endured as a child, Volkov had inflicted ten deaths. He saw the same boy every time he looked in the mirror. Not the overseer of a $14 billion empire. He didn't see the organization beneath him, taking down towns in a planned geographic push to the west. No, he saw the other boy, an only child in a Moscow tenement, who just wanted to be with his father and mother.

The memory always started the same way.

It was his first day at St. Agatha's, a Catholic school his father and mother had sent him to in order to get away from the public school at the end of the street, where the older boys were always picking fights with him because of his size. The thing was, Volkov wasn't losing the fights. When the regional principal recommended a different environment, they agreed. St. Agatha's was two and a half hours away from his home in Moscow. He hadn't done anything wrong, other than defend himself, but his mother feared for him. His father had a connection and, as if anticipating Volkov's future behavior, had him committed to a gladiator academy.

Especially at St. Agatha's, he was smaller than the others. He was eleven years old when he got there. On the second night at St. Agatha's, a group of older students came into the bathroom in the dormitory. He tried to hide in one of the stalls, but they saw him and yanked the door open, then pounced on him and beat him. Volkov suffered two broken collarbones, a broken arm, and a severe concussion, not to mention a broken nose and several teeth knocked out. He spent two months in the infirmary. He turned twelve there, at the infirmary; no one said happy birthday, nor were there gifts.

The four students who'd beaten Volkov up were moved to Kolpino Colony, east of St. Petersburg, a Russian penal center where juveniles were mixed in with adults.

After Volkov recovered from his injuries he went back to the dormitory. No one said anything, but everyone knew what had happened. Friends of the four thugs talked trash to Volkov. But they left him alone for the rest of the autumn. After a Christmas spent mostly in angry silence, with his guilt-ridden parents, Volkov was sent back, despite his pleas. On his first night back at St. Agatha's, he was brushing his teeth and was doused from behind by cold water in the same instant he felt a sharp kick at his hip.

That night, Volkov inhabited the fears of his parents in brutal fashion. He started by slashing the toothbrush in his hand into the eyeball of one of them. He was all of twelve and he killed two boys that night, both seventeen-year-olds, and would've killed more, were it not for a pair of proctors who interrupted him, in the bathroom of the dormitory, just after he'd broken his second neck in less than a minute.

When he was sent, at age twelve, to Kolpino Colony, Volkov entered with a severe disposition, a warrior mentality. He hunted down the thugs who'd nearly killed him. He killed each one, all within a few weeks of arriving at Kolpino. Each killing was untraceable. Volkov knew they would know who did it, but by doing it so ruthlessly and without trace, he thought he might be noticed by someone, somewhere. GRU was what he hoped for.

But no one noticed.

Volkov became a leader at Kolpino. By the time he was fourteen he was Kolpino's most feared inhabitant. He'd grown into a six-foot frame of raw muscle and sinew. In fights, even those not involving him, everyone knew that Volkov would adjudicate. When tested, Volkov was consistent. A knockout punch within a minute. He attacked like a hungry grizzly bear. Everyone at Kolpino feared him, even the guards.

Then, one day, Volkov escaped. He walked silently out through the big dormitories as everyone, including the guards, slept. It was easy. He walked to the fence and grabbed a piece of barbed wire and pulled with all his might, creating a gap in the fence. Volkov walked southwest, toward Latvia, over empty farmland and woods, always at night. It was spring when he escaped and he kept moving for several weeks, always looking over his shoulder. The entire way, he hid in bushes and stole food at night. It was the best time of his life, before or since, alone in the wilderness, alone in the world, walking through farmland and small towns, a city or two, miles of forest, with nothing. Volkov crossed the Latvian border at Vecumu Mezi, through a blighted forest.

He lived, homeless, in a small city called Daugavpils, for a year. He settled in with a group of grifters, stealing cars, going for drives, then abandoning the cars. There was little to no profit motive, but they were the first friends he'd ever had. They lived on the outskirts of Daugavpils, squatting in an abandoned rope factory. Sometimes they would go downtown and drink and try and start fights. He was eighteen. Whenever the fights would get out of control, as they often would, and his drunken buddies were outnumbered by a bunch of meth heads, it was Volkov who ultimately stepped in and established the law.

One day, in Daugavpils, Volkov had an idea, and it was a bold idea.

He went to the local high school and spied on the students. He started doing it every day there was school. He watched from different vantage points until he found someone who looked like him, someone athletic and tall. Volkov started tracking the student from the school. He followed him for several days, understanding his pattern. He took a week off, then one spring day he waited in an alley along a street of three-family houses, packed closely together, along the student's route. Volkov came at the student from behind and slashed his neck with a blade, killing him. He dragged the body into the alley and threw it in a dumpster, keeping the boy's wallet.

Volkov knew he didn't have a lot of time, but he needed a little. He went and took photos of himself at the pharmacy, paying with cash from the student's wallet. In a dirty restroom at the train station, he took the boy's driver's license and cut out the dead student's face pic. He inserted his own. He crossed back into Russia the next day.

Volkov stole a car and drove to Moscow. He went to his parents' apartment in the Otradnoye District. He knocked at the door and when his father opened it, he looked at a much older man. When they had sent him off, his father was taller, but now Volkov towered over him. Volkov was only eighteen years old, but he'd been sent away at eleven.

Volkov's father let him in and reached out, tears suddenly coming to his eyes.

"Oh, my son," he sobbed.

Volkov shut the door behind him and embraced his father. As he did, he looked into the small living room, where the television was on, providing the only light in the room. He saw his mother, sitting in one of the two fake leather recliners in front of the TV. He hugged his father and kept hugging him, squeezing him tighter and tighter until his father let out a small groan, unable to breathe. Volkov squeezed harder now, until he felt the weak drumbeat of his father's fists against his back, a low, pathetic yelp coming from him as Volkov broke old, frail bones, then dropped him to the ground and stood on his chest and kicked his father's skull into a bloody swamp.

As he stalked to his mother, she held up the receiver of the phone.

"I've already called the police," she cried.

Volkov grabbed the phone receiver from her and smashed it

into her head at the temple, immediately killing her. He turned just as the police arrived, four officers with guns out. He dropped the phone. This time Volkov was sent to Black Dolphin.

Nathaniel watched his screen as the security feed at the Miami airport went cold. He typed, going back into a source algorithm, then watched as his entire screen went black.

He had heard about these sorts of people. Real hackers. He went to Darré's desk.

"I need to use your computer."

After typing furiously, he came to the central emergency feed for the Miami Police Department.

MDIA
GUNFIRE REPORTED
5 INDIV DEAD

Nathaniel found a central directory in the system and started searching for access to the airport video feed.

Meanwhile, Volkov's cell phone vibrated. He shook his head, pulling himself from the memory of Black Dolphin. He looked at his phone. There were four calls from the same number.

"Bruno," said Volkov.

"Five people are dead at the airport," said Darré.

Volkov was quiet.

"Let me call you right back."

He stepped onto the terrace under a warm wind and looked in the direction of the airport across skyscrapers and lights. He dialed Audra's number and it rang until her voicemail kicked in.

He hung up and tried again. The same. He paused a minute and then called Darré.

"I tried to call her," said Volkov. "She isn't answering. I'll get in touch with the team at the airport."

"Don't bother. You know what those bodies mean," said Darré. "He killed the team you sent and now he's gone. You asked me before if you should kill Audra, and I said no. I think we're beyond that stage. If that CIA agent gets to her, he gets to you. We need to move now. We need our best arsonist, because there can't be any evidence. Do you understand?"

"Yes, I do."

"Either kill her or get her out of the way," said Darré calmly. "Send her to Odessa for a few years. We've paid her enough. But she can't continue to be in the picture or else they'll grab her, and then they will learn about you. If that happens, then you and I are looking at the general philosophical idea of fighting the entire *goddam* Central Intelligence Agency, and I for one don't feel like having that fight. Trust me, we can't afford that fight. Find her, imprison her, or, better yet, kill her. Got it?"

"You started it."

Darré was silent.

"Whoever started it, we need to finish it," said Darré. "There's no looking back."

"I'll go over right now. If I have to, I'll kill her myself."

CHAPTER 46

Allapattah Flats
Florida

Tacoma drove north from the airport, staying within the speed limit, driving for more than ten minutes on the highway. He cut off at an exit for Hobe Sound, geographically north of Audra's house on Jupiter Island.

He passed twice through Hobe Sound, then went west, along a less-traveled road. He drove for precisely five miles into the Allapattah Flats. He found a farm road that cut through a field, finally finding a pond, which he backed the car into until it bubbled and submerged. Tacoma began to run back toward the town. He took the five miles at a fast pace, eyes locked in a brittle gaze ahead, legs moving in a smooth cadence with his arms. Sweat poured down from his face, his hair was soaked. When he finished his run near the outskirts of Jupiter Beach, Tacoma's clothing was drenched in sweat and his face was flushed red. His clothing was wet almost completely through.

Tacoma walked along sidewalks and found a sandy path down to the beach. They knew he had just killed several of their men in an open-air, dynamic situation. They knew he was coming for her.

He started jogging along the beach as an idea coalesced. In stride, jogging down the sandy beach, Tacoma stuck the bud into his ear, tapping three times. He waited for a few seconds, then Calibrisi came on.

"Hi, Rob."

Igor and Katie clicked in.

"Where are you?" said Katie.

"On the beach," he said, in stride.

He finally had a few moments to clear the air.

"They had a whole team waiting for me," said Tacoma. "What kind of fucked-up thing have you gotten me into?"

"Calm down," said Katie. "We warned you. Besides, we needed to understand how sophisticated they are."

"Great," said Tacoma, breathing hard as he ran down the beach at ocean's edge. "How sophisticated are they?"

"They had something before you got off the plane," said Calibrisi. "They're well resourced. Now stop feeling sorry for yourself and focus. They know by now that you're coming for her. You're entering a combat zone and she might not be there any longer. But whoever sent the men to the airport is now aware they have a bunch of dead men."

"What about the security feed?" said Katie.

"I wiped it," said Igor. "As for the house you're going to, I have thermals on it. Looks like four men are guarding the outside and two individuals are inside the house."

Tacoma removed the earbud, placing it back inside his pocket.

Katie looked at Calibrisi.

"The fact they knew he was coming and sent a team after him

says everything," she said, slightly distraught. "They're going to try and kill him."

"They already tried—*and failed*," said Calibrisi. "He's moving inside. Let him do it. No one ever said it was going to be easy."

CHAPTER 47

Jupiter Island, Florida

At the beach, Tacoma walked unseen out into the water. He dived beneath a wave and swam to a point offshore. He swam in a line down the beachfront under a dark sky, letting a weak current move him south. The cold water felt nice after the run.

He remembered the words from training.

If you are at a place in the ocean, it means you got there somehow. Feel the current and think. All you have to do is retrace your steps.

It meant nothing, except it brought him back in.

He emerged along the beach a few houses down from the mansion, stepping from the water with the pistol in hand.

Tacoma approached the border of the property from the high-tide line, along a man-made line of trees and hedges that separated the large mansions from the public beach. He approached under a dimly lit sky. There was no such thing as pitch black in Miami or anywhere along the moneyed South Florida coast, especially here, on Jupiter Island, where billionaires and oligarchs, and various celebrities, including Tiger Woods, lived or owned property. Most kept their property lit, partially for security reasons, partially to show off. Jupiter Beach was a beachfront display of ubiquitous wealth and privacy that ran for miles on end.

Yet that ubiquity also created anonymity, and Tacoma came at Audra's property at the same time a loud party roiled just a couple of mansions away.

Tacoma studied the house where the party was taking place, spying a line of cars out back, limousines and other vehicles, waiting to pick up attendees. Music was playing. Loud toasts were being made. Tacoma cut through the property next door to the party house—between the party house and Audra's. He moved away from the beach, inland, along a fancy iron fence, parallel to the line of cars queued up at the party. He cut into the woods bordering the house in between, heading for Audra's mansion. Tacoma moved quickly, almost at a sprint, blocking branches and swerving. He cut in a diagonal toward the perimeter of Audra's property, under a thicket of trees that concealed a tall steel fence, a mesh of concertina wire laid out in crosshatches, curved ribbons of diamond-edged steel, there to prevent would-be intruders.

Tacoma stopped and knelt next to a tree, studying Audra's security fence. The fence was dimly illuminated by lights from the main gate. He waited and watched. After more than a minute, he saw a gunman, who walked from the beach end of Audra's mansion along the side of the property, moving just a few yards from Tacoma through the trees and fence. Tacoma remained still, watching the man, who clutched a suppressed MP5. A minute after the gunman moved back toward the beach, Tacoma saw another gunman, this one in front of the house, pacing along the driveway, covering road access to the property. He saw a third guard in the distance, walking along the far side of the property, catching him as he met the guard from the driveway and they spoke for a few seconds.

A security camera was mounted on top of one of the main

gateposts near Tacoma. It was on some sort of concrete stanchion, ten feet in the air, and Tacoma moved closer to it. He came from behind the camera. The camera rotated in a slow 180-degree turn, scanning the yard. Tacoma found a small rock and leapt up the back of the concrete post, holding himself in place with one hand as he studied the slow motion of the camera, which made a low electronic whir as it pivoted. When the camera was trained left, toward the road and away from the house, he reached up and jammed the rock at the base of the unit, between the bottom of the camera unit and the fence post. As the camera began to pivot slowly back toward the house, it caught on the rock and, after a few moments of grinding, stopped moving.

Tacoma climbed down and took several steps back, then charged at the fence and leapt, diving at an open space between loops of razor wire. His hands grabbed two vertical iron slats that lay beneath the concertina wire. He had momentum, but he kept his arms straight and pushed backward so that his face, chest, torso, hips, and legs wouldn't hit the long, jagged shards of razor-sharp steel. Before he fell onto the blades, his right foot shot out less than an inch above the curving steel of the concertina wire. Tacoma clung to the fence. He looked at Audra's house beyond, mere yards away, clinging between foot-long blades just inches from penetrating his body. But he'd been trained. Tacoma long ago learned the path up a wall of prison-strength concertina wire. He had a faded scar on his thigh to prove it, a cut that had cost him forty stitches and a decent amount of blood. But now it was like riding a bike. Slowly, Tacoma moved up to the top of the spiraling concertina wire, gingerly coordinating the placement of his hands and feet—controlling noise flow—as he climbed up between blades sharp enough to sever flesh down to the bone. When he got to the top of the fence, he took out his phone and looked around, seeing the two closest guards in the distance, each man looking in the opposite direction. He triggered an app called ISI, then scanned the land below the fence. The phone displayed a green line. It indicated that there was an additional digital perimeter guarding Audra's home.

Tacoma studied the location of the beam. It was below, four feet off the ground, but at least five feet behind the fence. He leapt—grabbing at air and kicking his legs, landing on the ground, pausing, feeling nothing.

He was inside the perimeter.

Tacoma immediately charged to a dark wall, then crawled along the foundation, along the back of the house, across weeds, dirt, and pebbles. He waited, catching his breath, then smelled a faint trace of cigarette smoke. He watched as the guard—a tall man in a black polo shirt—moved methodically across the lawn between the house and the perimeter fence, clutching an MP5. Tacoma raised the suppressed P226R and fired, missing on purpose, and as the gunman turned at the noise, he triggered the pistol a second time. The bullet struck the gunman in the side of his head, next to his ear, and he dropped in a silent pile. Tacoma went and grabbed the dead killer by the collar of his shirt and dragged him into the shadows next to the house.

Tacoma picked up the dead man's MP5 and checked the mag and the suppressor, then set the fire selector to manual. He waited as the gunman along the driveway came to the side of the property, then fired a single blast. A low ringing *thwack* hit the air. The slug found the guard squarely in the center of his neck. He coughed as he fell.

Tacoma moved past him, down the driveway, to the gates. He looked along the ground a few feet inside the gates and saw a long steel box, an inch high, hidden by flowers. He used his pick-gun to open the box. He cut several wires, disabling the electric gate.

Tacoma charged across the driveway, under bright lights,

moving left of the mansion's grandiose entrance. He sprinted to the other side of the property from where he'd entered, rounding the corner and flipping the fire selector on the MP5 to full auto. He came into the side yard just as the third gunman was approaching. The gunman saw Tacoma. He started to swing his firearm toward Tacoma, but Tacoma already held the killer in the crosshairs of the MP5 and pulled the trigger. A brassy staccato of suppressed bullet fire spat furiously from the MP5. A scorch of lead crossed the third gunman across his chest, kicking him down, killing him.

The man, like Tacoma, had a shaved head, and he looked to be about the same size and build as Tacoma.

Tacoma set the fire selector back to manual and moved to the back of the property, walking out in the open. He imitated the pace and manner of the guard, stepping confidently, methodically, and not too fast, until he came to the large green landscaped yard between the back of the mansion and the ocean. He saw the fourth guard as the man walked down near the hedges just above the sand. He came toward the gunman as the gunman walked away from his side of the property. He tracked him and, as he got closer, raised the weapon. By the time the killer turned, Tacoma was less than twenty feet away. The man didn't even attempt to move before Tacoma sent a single bullet into his forehead.

Tacoma went to the side of the mansion and found a door. He placed the MP5 on the ground. He scanned through vertical windows on one side of the doorjamb. He removed his pick-gun, then placed it against the lock and pressed. A thin alloy needle emerged from the piece, lit by flashing digital lights. Tacoma put it in the lock, which, a second later, clicked open. He stepped inside.

He was in a large living room. The far wall was a two-story arc of glass. He saw her across the room, on a leather sofa, curled up with a younger man.

Tacoma entered the living room in silence, still damp from

the ocean. At all times, he kept the SIG trained on Audra. Even as he stepped near to the couple, who were naked and sharing a glass of champagne, neither one noticed until it was too late. The man saw Tacoma first, and his reaction caused Audra to turn. Audra recognized him. Both her and her lover looked at Tacoma in silence. They stared for a few seconds in wariness and disbelief, then Tacoma fired. A suppressed bullet *spat* from the 226—*thwap ching*—and smashed into the young goon's forehead.

He found Audra in the crosshairs, her face sprinkled in blood from the man's head.

"*Privet*, Audra," said Tacoma.

Audra's face was littered with small cuts from the window at Cosgrove's, though she was still beautiful. She met Tacoma's gaze with a knowing look of recognition and fear. He stepped closer, holding the female assassin in a tight range. Her eyes flashed to a window just beyond Tacoma. He pivoted, looking out the window, seeing nothing, and when he swiveled back to Audra she was pulling a gun out from beneath the cushion, her left hand swinging at Tacoma. Tacoma fired, a precise shot from waist high, catching Audra's forearm. The bullet struck just behind the wrist. Her entire arm shot sideways as the gun fell. She screamed as her arm contorted back and blood suddenly spilled from the wound.

Tacoma stepped closer now, even as he looked back to scan the windows. He aimed the muzzle at her naked chest.

"Who ordered you to kill Cosgrove?"

Audra's bloody arm lay quivering. Her other arm was incapacitated. Blood coursed from the bullet wound, spilling out on the leather couch, next to the dead man. She panted, looking up at Tacoma.

"What's in it for me?" Audra asked.

"I'm not negotiating," said Tacoma. "You help me and I'll help you. Who sent you? Who designed it? Who's in charge?"

"I'm a prisoner," she said. "It was all manufactured. They entrapped me."

"Right," said Tacoma. "You were recruited out of GRU. Obviously for a lot of money. Who sent you to kill Cosgrove?"

He stepped closer and grabbed her incapacitated arm at the wrist, twisting. Audra let out a horrible scream.

"Did you poison Senator O'Flaherty?"

From within her agony, she nodded, yes.

"Who ordered it?"

"Who do you think?" She sobbed as she wiped blood and tears from her face.

"This is the last time I'm going to ask."

Audra's bloody hand reached out and grabbed the end of the suppressor, but Tacoma pulled it back. He fired a bullet into her foot, shattering it.

"*Fuck you!*" she cried, tears streaming from her eyes.

"Answer me," said Tacoma calmly.

"Please," she whispered. "I don't want to die."

"Then give me a name."

He waited until she looked up again.

"Do you promise?"

Tacoma nodded.

"Volkov. Andrei Volkov."

Tacoma raised the tip of the suppressor to Audra's forehead.

"But you promised!"

"I promised to kill everyone involved," said Tacoma. He fired. The bullet hit the center of her forehead and sent her head jerking backward, and blood and brains spewed in a gale of red across the leather sofa.

* * *

Tacoma wandered the downstairs of the large house until he found a bathroom. He flipped on the lights and looked at himself in the mirror. He looked very different without hair. His scalp was pale. He looked calm, and yet his eyes stared back in a way he couldn't exactly understand. He felt helpless—yet he also felt alive. He stared for a few extra seconds, then reached for the light switch as his other hand pulled the 226 from the holster. He moved into the corridor, stealing silently against glass, gun raised, silencer jutting forward.

He went back out through the same door and snaked his way through gardens along the border of the property to the beach. He came to the sand, glanced left and right, then started a hard sprint up the beach, back toward where he'd cut in.

Suddenly, he heard the baritone explosion of shotgun fire—three loud blasts. Tacoma turned back. It came from Audra's house. He paused a moment and then ran faster, retracing his route away from the ocean into suburbs and finally countryside.

At some point along the five-mile run, he popped the earbud in.

"Igor," he said, breathing heavily.

"Yes, Rob."

"I have a name: Andrei Volkov."

"I'm on it."

CHAPTER 48

Jupiter Island, Florida

Volkov drove into Audra's neighborhood on Jupiter Island, driving slowly. It was a heavily patrolled area, a quiet, sleepy strip of beachfront mansions and vast wealth. The last thing he needed to do was somehow involve law enforcement. Volkov drove a Toyota Tacoma pickup truck, meandering along South Beach Road at a slow pace. He passed Audra's driveway several times, eyeing Markus, the guard in charge.

Earlier, he had tried to call Audra several times to warn her that someone might be coming, but she hadn't answered. Volkov had sent five men, putting Markus in charge and telling him to guard the perimeter. Markus had told Volkov that Audra was inside the house and safe. Still, despite the security Volkov had sent, he patrolled South Beach Road, on the lookout for the man the CIA had sent to find Audra. Volkov knew that Darré was right; if they got to Audra, they would get to him.

Yet, other than a loud, crowded party a few houses down, South Beach Road was quiet.

Slowly driving back to Audra's house, Volkov called Markus to get a status report. After ringing several times, it went to voicemail. He tried again, and still, no answer. One by one, Volkov called the other men, though after the third guard didn't answer he moved the pickup into the driveway and approached the fancy iron entrance gate. He had purchased the house for Audra. It was a geometric set of glass planes on stilts, $9.5 million.

Volkov had ended their personal relationship once his wife, Leana, found out, though he still dreamed of Audra.

He rolled down the window and entered a code into a small digital pad. The gates, however, wouldn't open. He tried again and still nothing. She'd changed the code. He climbed out and tried a third time. When the gate still wouldn't move, Volkov went up to the gate and looked through. He saw Markus on the ground, facedown, lying in a pool of blood.

Volkov went back to the truck and retrieved his shotgun. He pumped the trigger and fired a round from the sawed-off twelve-gauge, blowing apart the keypad console, then walked to the gate and fired again, this time at the lock interface. A third blast sent the steel gate off its track and he moved in. He saw Leffen, one of his men, sprawled out on the lawn near the side of the home, on his back, gunned down.

Volkov walked around the side of the house, coming at the gigantic living room from the terrace. The floor-to-ceiling glass windows were open to the warm air. Audra was seated on the sofa, naked except for a towel, with another man, Guillaume, one of Volkov's junior lieutenants. They were wrapped around each other, naked. Volkov suddenly registered blood on the floor, beneath the sofa. He came to the sofa as if in slow motion. Audra's beautiful face was destroyed.

Volkov went back outside and down the driveway to the pickup truck. He removed a five-gallon red plastic jug filled with gasoline. He walked along the perimeter of the mansion, pouring gasoline in a stream along the stone foundation. He dragged the four other dead gunman onto the terrace. When he had them all lying in a pile, Volkov poured the last of the gasoline down on them. He tossed the empty canister, then he lit a cigarette and smoked it, trying to think. When he was halfway done with the cigarette, Volkov flicked the burning ember at the front of the house. A moment of silence was followed by an abrupt burst of low, blue flames. Soon, the mansion of glass and steel was engulfed in fire—mad, frenzied, billowing chutes of orange, red, white, and blue flames, though by then Volkov was in the pickup, driving away from Jupiter Island just as the first alarms sounded and the peaceful Florida night dissolved in heat and fire.

CHAPTER 49

The Darré Group
New York City

It was past midnight. Nathaniel was studying what was happening on the other side of the world, specifically the Nikkei 225, where the Darré fund had more than $4 billion invested. He saw a flickering signal on his screen. He went to the icon and tapped it with his finger.

A photo shot up on the screen. It was a black-and-white photo of a man who'd arrived in Miami earlier that day. A single frame he'd managed to capture before someone somewhere wiped the security feed clean. The man was young and had a shaved head. There was a hint of light stubble. It covered a pale scalp. He wore dark sunglasses. Nathaniel stared at the photo for several seconds, then picked up his cell.

"Mr. Nebeker, how may I help you?" came a stern female voice.

"Get me Bruno," said Nathaniel to one of Darré's assistants.

"It's two thirty in the morning, Mr. Nebeker."

"Get him," said Nathaniel coolly.

* * *

Darré was awakened by a high-pitched monotone alarm from his cell.

He looked at the phone console beside the bed.

2:33 A.M.

Darré shook his head and then slapped himself hard on the cheek. He picked up the phone.

"It's Nathaniel."

"What is it?" said Darré.

"I think you need to come down here, Bruno," said Nathaniel.

Darré climbed into a waiting helicopter, whose rotors were already slashing the Connecticut air by the time he stepped through the front door of his mansion.

Once on board and seated in the pressurized cabin, he lifted his cell as he rubbed his eyes, trying to get awake. He phoned Volkov.

"What the hell's going on?" said Darré.

"What do you mean?"

"Did he go to Audra's house?"

"Yes," said Volkov. "I was just there. He killed her."

"Did he find out—"

"I don't know," snapped Volkov. "Obviously, how could I know? Her head was blown off."

"I'm sorry," said Darré. "I don't mean to sound so selfish."

"It's okay," said Volkov. "It's just that I brought her in. I sent her to New York and then to Washington. She was a very kind person."

"I know," said Darré reassuringly, "but if he broke her?"

"He didn't break her."

"*But if he did,*" seethed Darré, "what does she know? She *knows* you, Andrei."

"What are you saying?" said Volkov.

"You need to stay out of sight," said Darré. "Remain at the port. You're well guarded there. Hopefully you're right and she didn't give them your name, but we can't be sure. In the meantime, I'm going to find out who this sonofabitch is."

After hanging up with Volkov, Darré looked up a different number. A number he didn't like to call, a man whose name caused a cold, frightful feeling to grip him from the inside. He found Kaiser's number and dialed.

CHAPTER 50

Eaton Square
Belgravia
London

Kaiser entered his apartment at a little before 9 A.M. He flipped on the lights inside the door, then shut the door. On a gorgeous maple credenza sat a bowl full of golf balls. Surrounding the bowl, the top of the credenza was littered with destroyed golf balls, most crushed in half, plastic shards sticking out, as if the balls had been put in a vise and destroyed.

Kaiser grabbed one of the golf balls from the bowl as he moved into the apartment.

The apartment took up an entire floor, an elegant suite of rooms in one of London's most prestigious buildings. The walls were crowded with windows that looked out on Grosvenor Square.

The apartment was one of London's most valuable. It was a dark, rainy day in the city. The lighting was low and warm, and it cast circles along hallways and rooms of fine furniture and art, like the Presidential Suite at the Hotel George Cinq in Paris.

Hushed music came on, tripped by motion sensor, a Mozart violin concerto.

Kaiser undressed in the master suite, taking off his tie with his left hand as he held the golf ball with his right, rotating it around in the palm of his hand. He had a neatly combed hairdo, a block of short, black hair. He resembled an undertaker. He stood at six foot nine. Though he stooped a little, at age fifty-eight Kaiser retained a fearsome look. He had a hulkish frame, a physicality that, combined with cold, black eyes, made him fearsome to look at. Kaiser unbuttoned his shirt with his left hand.

He stood in front of the mirror as he removed his button-down. He was a large man, not typical looking, but human—at least to his right armpit. From his right armpit down was a prosthetic arm, black alloy to the elbow, then a synthetic-flesh-covered forearm and hand, with a thumb and fingers. He stared at his grotesque arm as he clutched the golf ball. It was thin, the flesh-colored synthetic, and while real-looking to most, it appeared utterly fake to Kaiser.

He clutched the ball and slowly brought his mechanical hand together in a tight fist. The golf ball abruptly cracked into a mess of broken white ceramic plastic, as if it were a hard-boiled egg. Kaiser stared at it, then dropped it on a shelf in the closet.

Back in the living room, Kaiser made himself a vodka martini and put on the television. He found the BBC, which was showing a report on the deaths of Nick Blake and John Patrick O'Flaherty. When he felt his cell phone vibrate, he turned the volume down on the television as he sat down and pulled out his cell.

"What is it?" said Kaiser.

"It's Bruno Darré."

"Where are you?"

"In New York City," said Darré.

"What do you want?" said Kaiser.

"Volkov's people killed the American, Cosgrove, but I'm afraid the matter isn't closed yet," said Darré. "Someone—presumably the Central Intelligence Agency—captured one of his men who revealed the name of Volkov's primary contact."

"The woman?" said Kaiser.

"Yes," said Darré, "Audra Buczko."

"Let me guess," said Kaiser. "You're concerned because she can lead the CIA to Andrei, and Andrei can lead them to you."

"And I can lead them to you," said Darré.

"So kill her," said Kaiser.

"It's too late. Someone got to her first."

Kaiser sipped from his martini and noticed the television, which was now silent. A news report showed some sort of crisis situation at Miami International Airport. The airport was shut down and surrounded by police cars, fire trucks, ambulances, and—behind security cordons—a swarm of journalists.

"What happened at the airport?"

"The man they sent, presumably the other member of the CIA unit, took down five of Andrei's men," said Darré. "He then went to Audra's home and killed another group of Andrei's men before killing Audra."

The phone was silent for several moments.

"I understand," said Kaiser.

"We must cut off the threat," said Darré.

"By threat you mean Andrei?"

"Yes," said Darré. "If they get to him, they'll torture him and use various pharmaceuticals. Ultimately, they'll get to me. I don't blame Andrei. He's been my partner. Without him, the entire Eastern Seaboard will need to be rebuilt. But I would rather do that than spend the rest of my life in prison."

"I understand," said Kaiser calmly.

"I need you to kill him," said Darré. "That's not my area of expertise."

"We're not going to kill Andrei Volkov," said Kaiser.

There was a long pause.

"What?" said Darré. "Did you not hear me?"

"I heard you."

"You started a war," said Darré. "I did what you asked me to do."

"I didn't start a war, Bruno. The war was started long ago, before you or I were even born. We're not killing Andrei Volkov. He's too valuable."

"What the hell am I supposed to do?"

"You must find the other American," said Kaiser in a nonchalant tone. "Stop worrying about Andrei giving you up and start worrying about finding the other man!"

"They're coming after us," said Darré. "The Americans are going fucking apeshit!"

"Yes, they are," said Kaiser. "But we are not going to start killing our most important people, certainly not someone as valuable as Volkov. Get off the phone and find the other agent."

"*You started a war!*" growled Darré.

"*We were already at war!*" shouted Kaiser. "*You're now at the front lines! This isn't a game, Bruno!*"

"You started a war and I'm the one who has to fight it!" yelled Darré.

"You made more than one billion dollars last year," said Kaiser. "Why? Because you're paid to fight wars! If you can't handle it, I'll find someone who can."

"What good is the money if I'm in a jail cell—or dead?"

"If either one occurs, well then, you did not deserve the money, Bruno Darré," said Kaiser calmly. "Do not touch Andrei. Do you understand?"

Darré was quiet.

"Tell me you understand, *you ungrateful fuck.*"

"I understand," said Darré.

CHAPTER 51

Commonwealth Tower
1300 Wilson Boulevard
Arlington, Virginia

"I found something," said Igor.

Calibrisi walked over to Igor as Katie stood up and joined them.

The large screen in front of Igor showed a photo, taken from the sky.

"I hacked into the FBI core," said Igor.

"I would've gotten you provisioned in," said Calibrisi.

"The point of hacking is to find vulnerabilities," said Igor.

The photo showed two men standing on the corner, on the sidewalk of a Manhattan street, surrounded by skyscrapers. They were arguing; it was clear by the anger in each man's face.

"Who is it?" said Calibrisi.

"The big one is Andrei Volkov," said Igor. "This was taken off a surveillance drone feed they had on him."

"Who's the man on the right?" said Katie.

"Exactly the question I asked myself," said Igor. He reached forward and tapped his keyboard. Another screen came to life with a clearer photo, showing the same man, but from street level, HUMINT, a photo taken by an FBI agent during surveillance of Volkov.

The man had thick blond hair that was parted in the middle and a sharp nose, and was dressed in a stylish white button-down. He was smiling. Across from him was the back of a head, a big man with a crew cut, his muscles pushing against the material of his shirt.

"Volkov?" said Calibrisi.

"Yes, the man on the left. That's the back of his head."

"So who is this guy?"

Igor hit the keyboard again and a series of photos appeared in a tile across the next screen. He tapped it again and several news articles appeared: *Wall Street Journal, Financial Times, Bloomberg.* In each article, a name was highlighted by Igor.

"Bruno Darré," said Katie.

"You know him?" said Igor.

"Of course," said Katie.

"Financier," said Calibrisi. "Hedge fund guy. Billionaire. So why is he with Volkov?"

"How the hell should I know?" said Igor.

"Find out," said Calibrisi.

"Katie, can you call Rob and tell him we found Volkov?" said Igor. "He is in charge of a small shipping company at the Port of Miami. He needs to get inside. But it's not going to be easy— their docks look heavily guarded. He's not going to be able to wing it, he's going to need a real plan."

CHAPTER 52

CIA Headquarters
Langley, Virginia

Jenna Hartford was working on a report. She was proposing an operation to take out a high-level British intelligence agent who was selling secrets to the Saudis. It needed to be seamless and clean, an "accident" that would be seen as an accident despite the fact that he was a spy and it wasn't an accident after all. Yet, she couldn't stop analyzing what was happening on U.S. soil; the killing of two politicians, and Cosgrove's brutal murder. While she wasn't supposed to know about Rob Tacoma, she always made it her business to know everything by one means or another. She quietly tracked Tacoma as he moved into Florida and began taking apart the outer circle surrounding whoever did this, the part of the Russian mafia responsible for the acts of war.

Jenna was the CIA's chief mission architect. At age twenty-seven, she designed all tier-one, high-value covert missions for the Agency. Jenna was British, on loan from MI6, the CIA's counterpart in Britain. Jenna was widely considered the preeminent mission architect in Western intelligence, and her opinion was much sought after. As a result, Jenna had full access to all high-priority CIA activities, and she'd used it to surreptitiously monitor the unit from afar.

She went looking for Calibrisi, but his office was empty. When she got back to her office, she called him.

"What is it, Jenna?" said Calibrisi.

"It's this Russian mafia thing," said Jenna in an aristocratic British accent. "There's this rush to judgment just because Blake and O'Flaherty were enemies of the Russian mob, but look at the hits. One is a bullet through the forehead from approximately a third of a mile away and the other is a designer poison, administered with utmost precision. Does that sound like the Russian mafia to you, Hector?"

Jenna was slightly worked up, putting her right hand to her yellow-blond hair and brushing it back, a nervous habit, but when she did it, it looked natural.

"Jenna, I can tell you've been digging into things that are above even your clearance. But as you obviously already know, we're going after the Russian mafia on U.S. soil," said Calibrisi.

"Hector, you're making a mistake. These killings have the clear markings of a GRU operation," said Jenna.

"Bullshit," said Calibrisi. "The Russian government is not behind everything. I'm sure there are close associations, but this was a Russian mob hit."

"Audra Buczko?"

"I have no doubt the Russian mafia recruits from GRU," said Calibrisi. "That doesn't mean the Russian government is behind it all."

"This new unit—the one I'm not supposed to know about—its charter is the Russian mafia," said Jenna. "Correct?"

"Yes."

"But were it to spill into a larger scenario in which we were potentially exposing Russian government involvement in these crimes, I would bloody well hope you'd give a shit!"

"Of course, I would. Look, we're at a critical juncture in the current mission, and since you've decided to read yourself in, we could really use your help. We need to get someone into a relatively secure area and close to a Russian mafia figure who is both under guard and on alert," said Calibrisi.

Hector explained the situation with Andrei Volkov, giving Jenna all the details Igor had been able to dig up.

"Can you design something for me fast?"

"Of course. I'll call you in hour."

Forty-five minutes later, Calibrisi's cell phone rang. It was Jenna.

"You have a design?" said Calibrisi.

"Yes. I call it 'The Russian,'" said Jenna. "It's straightforward and yet it's not. On one level, we are going after Andrei Volkov. He is the Russian. But what if he was told to do what he did? What if, in fact, it was dictated by someone else? Who is the one who told him to do that? And who is the man who told that man to kill these politicians, and Cosgrove? He, too, is the Russian. We need to see if the GRU was behind all this, and my design will do just that. Audra Buczko was recruited out of GRU. We're going to lure the GRU out—or some other entity—and when we expose them, whoever it is, we should kill them. When I was at MI6, there were vague rumors of just such a man. Frankly, all we had were those few whisper-thin rumors and a name: Kaiser."

"Kaiser?" said Calibrisi, recalling his conversation with Alexei Malnikov.

"You've heard of him?" said Jenna.

"Yes."

"Kaiser might be a myth, or he might actually exist," said Jenna. "The results for them so far would imply a higher architect. O'Flaherty, Blake, Cosgrove. Each killing was brutal and yet very clean. If it hadn't been for Rob showing up at the wrong time, we would've had nothing on Cosgrove's killing. There are clearly rings within rings and so far, we've only been able to attack the outer ones. But I have an idea about how to penetrate the inner circle. The baseline operation achieves the basic function: kill Andrei Volkov. But I believe in so doing we could expose those above him, including, potentially, Kaiser."

"In other words, according to your design, we can choose door one or we can choose door two, still get everything behind door one, but also get something potentially much bigger?" said Calibrisi.

"Precisely," said Jenna. "But with any operation that has different levels of real-time execution, the risk complexity is multiplied. We can simply kill Volkov. That's actually fairly simple. But by doing it in the way I've crafted it, we can potentially get at the hierarchy behind this. Unfortunately, the risk to the operator is multiplied. This is an *extreme*-danger operation dependent on fixed kill ratio over a limited time frame."

"If anyone can do it, Rob can do it," said Calibrisi. "What's the idea?"

"We know Volkov is at the port," said Jenna. "Tacoma is going to go there to kill him and try and find out who he works for, correct?"

"Something like that."

"So he's just going to walk in and start shooting?"

"It wouldn't surprise me. It's his preferred method."

"Well, it's not the ideal method. He might get to Volkov, but he'll die," said Jenna. "He should penetrate the port in a more restrained manner. I have a way to get to Volkov, but it will require a modicum of patience on Rob's part. Use the passport Katie gave him, get a job, and watch. They're searching for him. A day or two of pause will help us. They know we killed Audra Buczko and will assume we're coming for Volkov. The port is where he'll hide. From what I've been able to learn in the past few minutes, he's probably already ensconced there. The first part of the design is simple. Infiltrate the port and wait for the right opportunity. It needs to be organic."

"I'm listening," said Calibrisi. "Before you go into the details, let me try to patch Rob in before he does something rash."

CHAPTER 53

APQA Terminal
Port Boulevard
Dodge Island
Miami, Florida

Tacoma's phone buzzed. He pulled it out—it was a text from Katie. They had found Volkov's location.

Tacoma drove to South Beach and cut across the MacArthur Causeway into downtown Miami. He abandoned the stolen vehicle in a parking lot at Miami-Dade College. It was past midnight when he arrived. He walked down the empty, darkened street until he saw a neon sign outside a Holiday Inn on Biscayne Boulevard. It was a meager-looking motel. He had to wake up the night manager to get a room. The room itself was large but smelled of mold, though he was so tired he didn't care. He climbed onto the bed in his clothing. He lay awake an extra few moments, on the bed. Despite his best efforts to fall asleep, he felt alert. In his exhaustion, he remembered Hell Week. It was the week during SEAL training you didn't get to go to sleep. The instructors allowed one nap per day on the final two days of Hell Week, an hour each. Most of the men who rang the bell in Coronado, dropping out, did so long before that first hour-long nap. If you made it that far, chances were, you were going all the way.

Then, as now, Tacoma hadn't been able to sleep. Given the freedom to do so, he stayed awake, lost in his thoughts. During Hell Week, Tacoma had seen what he was capable of. On the final day of the week, Tacoma had set a record on the Coronado obstacle course. It wasn't the fastest time, not even close—but it was the fastest time ever turned in on the last day of Hell Week.

Tacoma's thoughts were interrupted by his phone. He picked it up to hear Hector's voice.

"Rob. Is everything okay?"

"Yes, everything is fine. What's up?"

"We've got a design that will get you close to Volkov, but we've got to run down some details first. In the meantime, get a job at the port, with Volkov's company. It's called APQA. Once you're in, let's talk about how we're going to get you out in one piece. Okay?"

"Yeah."

Tacoma hung up. He fell quickly asleep.

The next morning, Tacoma awoke to the sound of a siren roaring by the motel.

Tacoma looked at his watch. It was 9 A.M.

He showered and put his clothing back on, packed up, and left all of his belongings in a backpack in the room. A main thoroughfare ran alongside the outer edge of the port. The port was a massive property, covered in warehouses, large tracts of concrete and tar, with gantry cranes, trucks, reach-stackers, and railcars clogging the vista. The port was guarded at its perimeter by a high steel fence, flanged on top with razor wire. He came to the security gate and approached the guard.

"*Ya ishchu rabotu*," said Tacoma.

I'm looking for work.

Tacoma handed the man his Russian passport. The guard inspected it briefly, then nodded. The guard put his cell to his ear and spoke to someone.

"Come back before five o'clock."

At twenty to five, Tacoma returned. He found the same guard, who nodded and waved him over.

"Idite k dveri s nomerom odinnadtsat. Ya ne znayu, priyedut li oni na rabotu."

Go to the door marked number eleven. I don't know if they are hiring.

"Thank you very much," said Tacoma.

"Walk along the fence," advised the guard. "Otherwise you might get run over. The truckers are a bunch of fucking assholes."

Tacoma nodded and walked through the gate, past the guard station, beyond a tall chain-link fence.

The sky was overcast but faintly blue. The temperature was in the fifties and a wind was blowing hard across the concrete and tar expanse of the port.

A lot the size of a football field was filled with brand-new cars, ready to be moved to dealers across the Northeast and mid-Atlantic. Another area was filled with trailers, ready to be used when needed by APQA or one of its customers. The cars, pickup trucks, and motorcycles of workers were scattered about.

APQA owned the port. It was a Swiss corporation with absentee owners, whose revenues ran through the Seychelles then back into the United States. APQA was a corporation owned by the Darré Group—through various phantom legal and financial entities. The letters stood for nothing. It was one of literally thousands of LLCs and corporations the Darré Group owned.

Running down the middle of the huge lot was a two-lane road, demarcated on its outer edge by bright orange paint, as if to make sure the trucks stayed in line.

The Port of Miami was one of the busiest ports in the United States, but like most ports it was a polyglot collection of individually owned and managed terminals, that is, piers capable of bringing in cargo ships and off-loading them. The port was an extended neighborhood of deepwater piers capable of welcoming the largest ships in the world. It was a gateway for the world's products, brought by large ships—container ships, oil tankers, break bulk steamers, LNG ships, and a variety of other specialized cargo-bearing ocean vessels. Like a neighborhood, the port was made of unique individual operations, each pier specializing in certain specific products and services. A container ship coming from Rotterdam had to off-load its containers at a facility capable of handling containers, for example. An oil tanker needed an altogether different set of services.

There were almost thirty thousand employees who went to work every day at the Port of Miami.

There were approximately five hundred people who worked at APQA.

It wasn't an especially well-known operation. APQA handled break bulk cargo only. This was cargo that was not in containers, but was packed in a way that forklifts, cranes, trucks, and men could off-load to some part of the APQA facility, usually inside one of the two massive warehouses APQA owned—both warehouses painted green and sitting near the waterfront, just a few hundred feet away from the pier where the cargo ships tied up.

A typical shipment worked in the following manner: A ship loaded with pallets of paper would arrive and dock up. Then the APQA cranes and forklifts would go to work, moving the eight-ton pallets of paper into one of the warehouses. It was up to the paper company itself to figure out who was going to purchase the paper. Until it was sold by the paper company, it sat in the warehouse. Once the paper was sold, one of the trailers parked alongside the warehouse would be driven to one of the cargo bays on the side of the warehouse. The paper would then be moved into one of the trailers and driven to the customer.

It was the job of the owner of the ship to get the paper to APQA's Miami facility. Hopefully, that same ship, after being emptied, would be reloaded with outbound product to be carried to some other port.

It was APQA's job to handle the logistics of whatever came in and went out as quickly and as smoothly as possible.

Both APQA warehouses were the same, long buildings of corrugated steel, both painted dark green, facing each other across a two-lane road.

Tacoma walked to the warehouse on the right, where a sign said OFFICE next to one of the warehouse's only windows. He opened the door. Inside was a bullpen of desks, copy machines, and people.

A woman was seated inside.

"May I help you?"

"I am inquiring about work," said Tacoma.

The woman turned and nodded to a bald man sitting at a desk, typing into a computer. Tacoma walked to the desk and waited as the man finished and looked up.

"What the fuck do you want?" he said.

"I am inquiring about work," said Tacoma.

The man scanned Tacoma quickly, then stared into his eyes.

"*Otkuda ty?*" the man said in Russian.

Where are you from?

"*Moskva,*" said Tacoma. "I arrived yesterday."

Tacoma continued to talk with him in Russian.

"Why?"

"I am moving to the United States," said Tacoma. "I want opportunity for myself."

The man reached his hand out without saying anything. Tacoma handed him the passport.

The man looked for a few moments at Tacoma's fake passport, then handed it back.

"Did you get questioned by U.S. Customs, yes?" said the man.

Tacoma shook his head, no.

"Save me the time," said the man. "If I research you a little, what will I find, Evgeny? Trust me, you're not the first, nor will you be the last, who committed a crime or two. We're not looking for angels, just hard workers."

"I robbed a bank when I was fifteen," said Tacoma.

The man stared up at Tacoma. His face was blank.

"Did they catch you in the act?"

"No. A few days later."

"How did you get caught?"

"My friend bought a Rolex with some of the money," said Tacoma.

"Are you still friends with this so called friend?" said the man.

"He's dead," said Tacoma. "He died at Romegrant."

"I've heard of it," said the interviewer. "How long were you there, Evgeny?"

"One year, sir," said Tacoma.

The man nodded and reclined back in his seat.

"So you want a job?" he said. "What do you know how to do?"

"I know how to arrive early and to work very, very hard," said Tacoma. "I know how to listen to supervisors. I don't know how to complain, sir. I'm also very strong and can lift a lot of weight."

The man grinned slightly.

"Good answer, Evgeny. So tell me, do you still steal things, Evgeny?"

"No, sir."

"How much did you two idiots steal, if I might ask?"

"A little over a million dollars."

"Okay, fine," said the man. "We can always use more hard workers who don't complain. By the way, my name is Victor."

"Thank you for the opportunity, Victor."

"You'll go to a man named Grigor, on the docks," said Victor. "He'll tell you what to do. The shift starts at seven A.M. sharp. Gates open at six for anyone who wants breakfast. Work starts at seven. If you arrive at 7:01, go look for a job somewhere else. Pay is a few bucks over minimum wage, but we feed everyone two meals a day, and we offer training that lets you learn some higher-paying skills. We offer health insurance. A lot of guys have worked here for more than twenty years."

"I'm grateful, sir."

A loud, piercing horn sounded outside the warehouse. It lasted for ten seconds, then quieted.

"Closing time," said Victor.

He reached into a drawer. He pulled out a thick envelope and removed a small stack of bills.

"There's a store in town that sells clothing. Go buy some better boots and a decent set of gloves," said the man. "They're open until eight. I'll take it out of your first paycheck. See you tomorrow morning, Evgeny."

As Tacoma left the warehouse, a group of workers was moving toward the area between the two warehouses. Soon, a crowd gathered, hundreds of dockworkers, all male, all ripped from years of hard platform work.

The sky was descending into black.

A pair of halogen lights shone down from a crane above. Suddenly, a man emerged from the crowd. It was a very large man. He was at least six foot eight, and wore a dirty T-shirt.

Tacoma looked at Victor, who started walking to the human scrum.

"What is it?" said Tacoma.

Victor nodded.

"Come. See for yourself."

Every worker was gathered in the growing darkness, beneath the halogen lights. Tacoma saw bottles of vodka being passed around. It was a human circle, and the sound of conversation was a rowdy din, inflected with alcohol, the words in Russian or Ukrainian.

Tacoma weaved into the outside of the circle, following Victor, then breaking off to the left, pushing past men much larger than him, trying to be polite, fighting to get to the center of the human scrum. It was loud, with laughter and yelling. A few rows back from the front of the circle, Tacoma encountered resistance. A bearded, thick man turned and swung at Tacoma. Tacoma ducked. As the man's fist crossed above him, he hammered his right knee in a vicious lunge. His knee smashed hard into the man's rib cage. The man dropped to the tar, at least two ribs broken, unable to speak, coughing for air, though amid the chaos no one noticed save for the man and Tacoma.

Tacoma reached the front of the circle. The human ring was at the center of the pavement between the two warehouses. It was drenched in bright halogen. Tacoma stood at the front, along the line, one of many watching the coming attraction—though he alone didn't yet know what that attraction even was.

Shouting began from the other side of the circle as the abnormally large man walked about the ring, swinging his fists in the air, shadowboxing.

The shouting from the circle became louder with each punch in the halogen air.

The big man lumbered with a slow gait. His eyes were set widely apart. He was from the eastern part of Russia, Tacoma guessed, Mongolia or Siberia.

Next to Tacoma, someone threw out a handful of bills. Tacoma watched as others around the circle reached for their pockets. Suddenly, bills began to flutter down on the open lot in the middle of the circle. A ring of green—of cash—enclosed the outer edge of the circle. He saw many one-dollar bills, but then also saw fives and tens.

The yelling and shouting now was loud. It was hard to hear anything other than shouting as the large man walked slowly around the circle, looking at the crowd.

Tacoma looked to his right. He saw Victor at the front.

"What's happening?" yelled Tacoma.

"Just watch," Victor mouthed as he threw down some money.

Victor moved in front of the gathered ruffians, who let him by without a word. They knew not to say or do anything to Victor. He sidled up to Tacoma.

"It's a competition," yelled Victor. "Whoever wins the fight, they get the money. If you pick someone weak, no one puts in money. If you pick someone strong, you can make thousands."

"What do you mean, whoever they pick?"

Victor stared at Tacoma, across the noise.

"The winner from the last night chooses," said Victor, pointing at the giant now pacing the circle, looking for someone to fight. "Tikkar is on his eighteenth night as champion. It's the longest streak in years. He's practically killed all of the bigger men. Nobody knows if he will ever lose. Nobody wants to fight him, but the winner always gives the loser some. Plus, it doesn't matter. If you say no you might as well not show up to work tomorrow."

Suddenly, the huge giant pointed across the crowd.

"You," Tikkar barked in a dull baritone. "Mishka. Prepare to meet your maker."

All eyes shot to an area near Tacoma. The giant—Tikkar—was pointing at a bald, much shorter man, perhaps five foot nine or five ten, but he was thick with muscles and brawny, not the sort of person you wanted to meet in a dark alley. He was standing in the crowd, clutching a beer. He looked to his right and said something to the man next to him. He finished the beer and handed the bottle to someone, then walked into the ring, bowlegged, throwing off a leather coat, and then he started screaming at Tikkar, in Russian.

"Fuck you, Tikkar!" he yelled, loud enough for everyone to hear. He had an angry, devilish grin on his face. "It's about time you had the balls to fight me, faggot!"

The roar from the crowd became a cacophony, and money floated down. Even Tacoma reached for his pocket and tossed down the wad of cash Victor had given him.

Tikkar said nothing as he watched the other man—Mishka—step into the human ring.

The two men, both gorillas but in different ways, squared off as the crowd screamed and shouted.

"Mishka," said Victor, speaking to Tacoma, but pointing at the short, bald man. "He's a rough character. He's like a bear. This is a fight between a lion and a bear. Tikkar will either lose or make a lot of money tonight. This fight has been coming. Mishka is feared. He spent time at Black Dolphin. Perhaps Tikkar desires to lose? Eighteen days in a row is wearing on him, what do you think?"

"What's the record?" said Tacoma.

"Forty-five," said Victor. "By that man."

Victor nodded at the warehouse behind the halogen lights. The second floor had a corner lined with shabby-looking windows, a door, and a fire escape outside. Standing on the fire escape was a man. He was dressed in a button-down shirt and slacks, and held a drink in one hand and a cigar in the other hand. He was bald and large, with arms that bulged out to the sides, showing decades' worth of hard labor, fighting, and lifting. He had a presence. He stood alone, then took a puff on the cigar as he watched the fight from above.

"Who is he?" said Tacoma.

"Andrei Volkov," said Victor. "He's the big boss. The man you work for."

Tacoma studied Volkov, who was obscured somewhat by the fact that he was behind the halogens, buried in the shadows, with a few lines of light cast diffusely over him. He was there to watch the fight.

"Is forty-five nights in a row a lot?" said Tacoma.

Victor turned with an odd grin.

"You really did just get off the boat, didn't you?" said Victor. "Just watch, Evgeny. Then you tell me afterward how many nights in a row you could make it."

Tacoma smiled and turned back to the two fighters, who were now coming closer, shadowboxing in the air between them, which went from yards to feet.

Mishka, the shorter, thicker, brawnier man, led with his left hand, inching closer and closer to Tikkar. Tikkar was nearly a foot taller than Mishka. Tikkar had a strange look on his face, angry, even hungry. Finally, Mishka made the first contact, lurching at Tikkar with his left paw, intentionally missing, stepping back, then lunging with his right fist—his strong arm—striking Tikkar in the chin. It was a fast move, less than a few seconds, and Tikkar, despite knowing it was coming, was exposed. Tikkar's head snapped back as Mishka's fist hit his chin. Tikkar tried to swing in self-defense, but Mishka was on him. Mishka followed the strike to Tikkar's chin—followed his own momentum, chasing Tikkar and diving at his torso, like a football player going for a tackle. Tikkar was a huge man, but Mishka was a ball of hate and fury, and Tikkar went pummeling backward as Mishka was suddenly upon him.

The crowd around the fight was in a pandemonium. Screaming and shouting, with bloodthirst in it.

Mishka was on top of him, all 250 or so pounds of him, straddling Tikkar. Mishka's knees pressed down on Tikkar's arms so that he couldn't fight back. Mishka hammered his fists in a fast, furious windmill, pounding Tikkar's face, and soon blood shot from his mouth. Then Mishka hit Tikkar's nose and red suddenly spurted from one of the nostrils, then both.

It looked like Tikkar would soon be done. Tacoma saw, however, Tikkar's right foot. Lying on his back, as his face was mercilessly beaten to a pulp, Tikkar's leg bent at the knee, his foot moved back toward his hip, as Tikkar looked for the leverage he needed.

Victor looked at Tacoma.

"*He's done!*" yelled Victor over the cacophony. "*I thought Tikkar would last longer!*"

But Tacoma knew the fight was Tikkar's, and that the other man would soon die.

Tikkar's foot pressed against the tar and then he thrust with every ounce of strength he had and sent his knee flying into Mishka's back. It was a brutal hammering. Mishka was abruptly struck at the spine and sent forward, a pained grunt loud enough to be heard above the shouting. As his head catapulted forward, Tikkar met it with a small but precise—and violent—head thrust, butting Mishka squarely in the nose, which shattered.

Tikkar was able to get his hands free and he threw Mishka to the side, standing up as Mishka clutched his shattered nose. Tikkar circled him as the crowd continued to shout. Mishka was helpless, concussed, his back damaged, his nose destroyed, his face drowning in blood. Tikkar wiped his badly beaten face as he circled Mishka, then moved forward and kicked him in the mouth. He jumped down onto him and started swinging—not fast punches like Mishka had delivered, but big, slow sledgehammers from the sky, pounding Mishka's face into a swamp of blood and broken bones. He continued punching until long after Mishka was unconscious.

It was Victor who stepped forward.

"*Enough!*" said Victor. "Tikkar, the fight is over!"

Tikkar stopped beating Mishka's skull and stood up. He walked to to edge of the circle as shouts of "*Tikkar, Tikkar*" filled the air. Tikkar picked up the cash on the ground, moving around the circle, even as some men threw more money down, though the fight was over.

Victor walked back toward Tacoma as the crowd began to disperse.

"Well?" said Victor with a knowing grin. "You think you can go forty-five nights, Evgeny?"

Tacoma's eyes scanned to Volkov, still watching from the fire escape.

"No," said Tacoma.

CHAPTER 54

Signals Intelligence Directorate (SID)
National Security Agency
Fort Meade, Maryland

A knock came at Jim Bruckheimer's door.

Bruckheimer, who ran SID, had put his best cryptologist on the job, trying to find out who had revealed Cosgrove's identity, who was the traitor. Dunn was a twenty-four-year-old BYU graduate gifted at parsing through massive amounts of data and finding patterns. In this case, he found a common "cookie" that ran across various burner cell phones and receipts.

After Dunn presented his findings, Bruckheimer shooed him out of his office and picked up the phone. He called Calibrisi.

"Hi, Jim," said Calibrisi. "How's the family?"

"Great," said Bruckheimer. "Saw them a few years ago."

"I guess you have it easy over there."

"I think we've got your man, chief," said Bruckheimer.

"Who is it?" said Calibrisi.

"Peter Lehigh, senior senator from California. We found the money and traced various receipts and tied them to phone calls.

We were ultimately able to tie him to a geographic history we cobbled together from Uber data and Google Maps."

"Nice work," said Calibrisi. "Can you send me the files?"

"Yeah, no prob. What will you do with him?" said Bruckheimer.

"Not sure," said Calibrisi. "Obviously he's a traitor, but we might be able to play him back in. Who is he selling secrets to?"

"It's not clear, but it's been happening for a while," said Bruckheimer. "He calls on burner phones, but like an idiot, he buys them from the same store every day or two. We tracked him off the buys, then ran the security film. It's Lehigh. Who is he selling to? Hector, let's get real. Lehigh is either selling information to the Russian mafia or he's selling it to the Russian government."

"Who specifically?" said Calibrisi.

"We don't know. Look, we tracked Lehigh, but he played things cleanly. These Korean-made cell phones are near impossible to trace," said Bruckheimer. "A disappearing digital signal replaced by nothingness."

"Got it. Thanks, Jim."

CHAPTER 55

Holiday Inn
Biscayne Boulevard
Miami, Florida

Tacoma went back to his room at the Holiday Inn. He took a shower, rinsing off dirt and sweat, trying to remain focused, though he felt adrift.

The fight earlier had awakened pent-up fury in Tacoma. He'd watched, wanting to enter the fray. Now he was alone in a motel room.

As he dried off, he found the earbud and put it in his ear.

"Katie?" he said.

"I'm here. Are you inside the port?" she said.

"Yes, I'm in, but I need a plan. I've spotted Volkov, but he's protected. I need a way to get to him."

"I'm patching in Hector and Igor. Also, Jenna Hartford. Do you remember her?"

"The architect from London?"

"Yes."

There was a moment of silence, then a few digital beeps. Finally, Katie spoke up again.

"Rob, are you there?"

"I'm here."

"You have me, Hector, Igor, and Jenna," said Katie. "Tell us what you learned today about Volkov and the operation at the port."

"It's a little Darwinian," said Tacoma. "Survival of the fittest."

Tacoma briefed the group on everything he'd learned that day, from the security at the port to the unofficial fight club at the end of each day.

"What's the design?" said Tacoma, cutting to the chase.

"It's pretty simple, despite some potential complexities. It's based on the fact that Volkov works for someone," said Jenna in a precise and firm British accent. "The goal here is supply chain penetration. In order to get at the people behind all of this, you must enter Volkov's inner sanctum. This fight club offers an opportunity. Volkov is a legend. Defeat Tikkar and challenge Volkov, but don't kill him. As hard as it will be to do, Rob, let Volkov win. Allow him to feel pity for you, to feel superior to you, but only after you have nearly killed him. After he defeats you, his ego will be satisfied and he will bring you closer. At this point you will have full access to information leading back to his overseer."

"Got it," said Tacoma. "All I have to do is to beat a six foot eight Ukrainian animal and then fight—and not get killed by— the only guy on the docks who might be tougher than the first guy. You're right. It's simple. Good night, everyone, I need to get some sleep."

CHAPTER 56

APQA Terminal
Miami, Florida

Tacoma arrived at the APQA gates at six thirty the next morning. Semi-trailers were already lined up on the road outside the gates, waiting to bring freight into the APQA facility. He didn't know where to go, but he followed the few men already there into the warehouse on the left, through a door near the corner of the warehouse. Inside was a large room full of lockers. Beyond that was a cafeteria. There were at least a hundred men already gathered, sitting at tables, eating. He could smell coffee and he walked and got into line, picked up a tray, and piled some scrambled eggs, bacon, potatoes, and sausage onto a plastic plate. He filled a Styrofoam cup with coffee and sat down at an empty table.

Tacoma didn't speak to anyone. Instead he kept his eyes focused on his food, though he registered the room around him. The first thing that was noticeable was the sound of Russian words. The conversations at the tables nearby were filled with it. The other thing he picked up was the simple fact of eyes staring at him, checking him out, though no one said hello.

At seven, a siren pealed somewhere outside and those who

hadn't already finished threw their food away. Tacoma followed the crowd into the warehouse, a massive building, brightly lit, already abuzz with activity and noise. Rows and rows of pallets stacked with boxes ran forever, the boxes wrapped in plastic, the rows neatly organized. The warehouse was at least the size of a football field. This was the warehouse for outbound freight. Fork-lifts were moving quickly, picking up pallets and driving toward the pier for loading onto whatever ships were outside. Tacoma walked the length of the warehouse, following others, and walked onto the large concrete pier, where two ships were moored. He found Grigor, a tall man standing next to one of the boats and watching as a mobile crane lowered the bucket and picked up a coiled, drum-shaped roll of steel.

"Victor sent me," said Tacoma to him.

"He told me," said Grigor. He had an impatient, even contemp-tuous look on his face as he assessed Tacoma's frame. "You look strong. You'll work drop crew. Jay will explain. Jay," he barked to one of the men, "put him on the crew. What's your name?"

"Evgeny."

"Do what they say," said Grigor. "When they count down it means get the fuck out from under the load. Understand?"

Tacoma nodded, yes.

"Yes, sir. Thank you for the job."

"I didn't hire you," snapped Grigor. "Get a hard hat, you fuck-ing imbecile."

The team Tacoma was assigned to was responsible for guiding the crane-carried loads down to specific spots on the ground, or on flatbed trailers. The loads came in with momentum, each pal-let loaded with six thousand pounds of cargo. This day, they were off-loading rolls of paper. Tacoma and another man had to guide the pallets down and set them on the ground. If the crane operator took his time, their job was easy, but there was no taking time to do it right. The crane operator—the facility itself—made money by moving things as quickly as possible, and muscle like Tacoma and the others on the drop crew was expendable. The pallets came in swinging, and they had to corral them and get them close before the crane operator let the hook go, sometimes too early.

Whoever the crane operator was, it was clear he didn't give a damn about the men on the ground. Tacoma and the others needed to be careful for the incoming swing of freight. If they were ready for it, he came in sideways, forcing either Tacoma or the man across from him to grab the massive weight and attempt to rein it in. Sometimes, if the operator hadn't adjusted the height, the pallet came in low enough to take off their heads. Tacoma quickly learned to duck and be ready to react.

A loud whistle blew at noon, signaling lunch.

As most of the workers stopped what they were doing and moved toward the warehouse, Tacoma paused next to a pallet of paper. His eyes traced the steel cable still attached to it, up to the arm of the crane and then down the red-painted steel arm, to the cockpit. He watched as the door to the crane cockpit opened and a man climbed out. He descended the ladder three rungs at a time. He was a big man.

Mostly it was curiosity. Tacoma wanted to see the person who'd nearly killed him half a dozen times that day. The man turned at the bottom of the ladder. It was Tikkar. Other than a small white bandage across the bridge of his nose, he appeared unaffected from the fight the night before.

Tikkar was tall, with longish brown hair and a mustache and goatee. He climbed down from the ladder and looked around as if looking for someone to cross him. He wore a white T-shirt and his arms were tattooed and thick with muscle. Tacoma briefly thought about going over and killing him. Instead, he turned and traipsed from the pier toward the warehouse, falling in with dozens of other people, all male. The blond man with the tattoos walked up alongside him.

"Tikkar," said the man in Russian, nodding at the crane operator. "Motherfucker."

Tacoma nodded. *"Da."*

"I'm Zachary," said the blond-haired man.

"Evgeny," said Tacoma.

"Vash pervyy den?" the Russian said.

Your first day?

"Da," said Tacoma.

"Iz Moskvy?"

From Moscow?

"Da," said Tacoma. "Postulov Square."

"Where are you staying?" said Zachary.

"Holiday Inn."

"That's where I stayed when I came. An absolute shithole."

"Yeah," said Tacoma.

"There's an apartment complex. It will cost you about the same for a room. I stay there. I can show you."

"Thank you," said Tacoma. "Perhaps tomorrow I can learn more about this."

Tacoma went to the bathroom and splashed water on his face. By the time he got to the lunch line there was a long, long line of men. Everyone was hungry, including Tacoma, and though the food wasn't great, it was good. After more than ten minutes in line, Tacoma was nearing the front of the line. As he was about to get a tray, the large goon from the fight, Tikkar, came strolling along the line of workers waiting for food and nonchalantly cut in a few people ahead of Tacoma, pushing someone aside and getting into the front of the line without asking and without apologizing.

Tacoma saw his opportunity.

"There's a line," said Tacoma.

Tikkar ignored him.

Tacoma reached out and grabbed the back of Tikkar's shirt, holding tight, stopping Tikkar. Tikkar felt the hand and turned. Tacoma let go as Tikkar turned with an angry look on his face.

"*Otvali!*" said Tikkar.

Fuck off.

"*Yest' liniya,*" said Tacoma.

There's a line.

Tikkar nodded, staring at Tacoma, then whipped his tray at Tacoma's head. Tacoma blocked it, just as Tikkar swung with his other fist. Tacoma ducked, and in the after-wash of Tikkar's whiff Tacoma hammered a hard fist into Tikkar's chin, snapping his head back. Tikkar stepped sideways and paused—surprised more than anything—then, as he started to charge at Tacoma, Tacoma pivoted in a martial 180, slashing his right leg across the air in a blurry, precise movement. Tacoma's foot caught Tikkar in the neck and jerked his head sideways. He let out a deep groan and fell backward, stumbling, then tumbled to the ground.

A group of men quickly stepped into the middle of the fight, stopping it. Tikkar stood up and pointed at Tacoma.

"*Ty pokoynik,*" said Tikkar.

You're a dead man.

Tikkar walked away from the cafeteria.

Tacoma filled his plate with lasagna and green beans and sat alone. The food wasn't bad, though he could've eaten anything at that point. He drank an entire pitcher of water at the table. He ate ravenously. He was still soaked in sweat when the whistle blew twenty minutes later, ending the lunch break. He couldn't remember being so thirsty or hungry, and that included during desert training after he was accepted into the Navy SEALs.

But the afternoon was even worse, as a tramp steamer—scheduled for a noon docking—idled in the channel, waiting as the vessel that was there, a Russian steamer, off-loaded its freight. They were behind schedule and they needed to empty the sitting ship as quickly as possible or else incur penalty fees from both shippers. The pallets came in hot now, and Grigor dispatched another man to help out Tacoma and his partner. He was thin, with long, scraggly hair and arms covered in tattoos, but he handled the incoming pallets with skill, taking charge and quietly directing them.

When the whistle blew at 5 P.M., Tacoma was exhausted. They'd gotten the cargo off with half an hour to spare, then unloaded the second ship.

It was Tacoma's idea to go after the people who killed Cosgrove on his own, but now he questioned his own logic. He could barely lift his arms. All he wanted to do was go to bed, which he realized was a thin mattress in an odd smelling room at the Holiday Inn.

Tacoma followed everyone else out to the open area between the two warehouses. The halogen lights were on, and soon the circle was formed. Bottles of vodka were passed around and the shouting and yelling started.

Tikkar emerged from the warehouse. He looked angry.

The night before, Tikkar had spent time searching around for someone to fight, but not tonight. Tonight, he just needed to find the one who'd embarrassed him. When Tikkar found him, he pointed.

"You," said Tikkar in a thick accent, pointing at Tacoma. "New guy."

Tikkar flicked his finger, calling Tacoma into the center of the human ring.

Tacoma felt the finger pointing at him across the crowd. It made him shiver. He looked to his right, then left, as if perhaps Tikkar was pointing at someone else.

Tacoma stepped forward into the ring at the center of the human scrum.

The shouting and yelling became more subdued as the rest of the workers saw Tacoma enter the middle of the ring. Tacoma, at six foot two, was half a foot shorter than Tikkar. Men abruptly stopped throwing cash down. To a man, they thought Tikkar was selecting a smaller man, a new worker, in order to take a night off.

Only Victor stepped forward, reaching into his pocket and throwing down a wad of twenties.

Tikkar had a dark look, his eyes buried back beneath hawkish sockets that kept his gaze in a gray light at all times, like a phantom. He had thick, dark eyebrows. He came at Tacoma as the yelling from the gathered dockworkers grew louder.

Tikkar bared his fists, a boxing maneuver, bouncing on his feet. He stepped toward Tacoma and swung, but Tacoma ducked and stepped back, though as he did Tikkar's other fist whacked him in the chin out of nowhere. Tacoma was dusted for a moment, blurry and dazed. As he stepped sideways, trying to get equilibrium, Tikkar swung again, this time with his strong arm. Tikkar's fist caught Tacoma in the stomach, a hard, violent strike that caused Tacoma to suddenly groan and bend over in pain.

The crowd went wild.

Tikkar moved in for the kill. Tacoma was doubled over. Tikkar slashed his arm through the air, launching a brutal strike at Tacoma's exposed cheek.

Tacoma saw it, despite the pain. He saw Tikkar and he saw

him swinging and he heard the cheers as Tikkar was about to kill him and he remembered the words.

Never give up.

He ducked quickly back, eluding the fatal blow, then stuck his foot out as Tikkar whiffed. Tikkar's leg hit Tacoma's foot and he spilled sideways, tumbling to the tar.

Tacoma stood, beet red, covered in sweat, and pounded a fist against his breast.

"Get up!" barked Tacoma.

The workers were in a state of pandemonium. The decibel level was rising.

Tikkar stood and charged at Tacoma.

Tacoma timed it. He charted Tikkar's every step, and when he had him, Tacoma abruptly took two steps toward him and then dived to his left, kicking his leg violently through the air in an upward motion. His foot met Tikkar's chin just as Tikkar came within inches of being able to grab Tacoma. A dull snap of bone echoed across a suddenly stunned crowd. Tacoma's strike shattered Tikkar's jaw. Teeth dropped to the tar like Chiclets. Tikkar crumpled to the ground, unconscious, as blood gurgled from his nose, ears, and mouth.

Tacoma got to his feet and stood still, fists bared, waiting for Tikkar to get up, but that wasn't going to happen.

Tacoma cast his eyes around the crowd of dockworkers. A few threw money down, then a few more. Tacoma walked along the edge of the crowd and picked it up. As he did, his eyes cut to the warehouse. Volkov was standing on the fire escape watching everything.

"Not bad," said Victor, who approached Tacoma from across the ring. "When I heard what happened at lunch, I figured you were a dead man."

Victor leaned over and helped Tacoma pick up bills from the ground.

"Thank you," said Tacoma.

"Where did you learn to fight like that?" said Victor.

Tacoma said nothing.

By the time he finished picking up the cash, the crowd had dispersed, except for a few men who were helping Tikkar get into the back of a truck to take him to the hospital. Tacoma walked to the driver, one of Tikkar's friends, and stood in front of the door. Finally, he lowered the window.

"What the fuck do you want?" the driver said.

"*Eto dlya doktora*," said Tacoma quietly, pushing the thick pile of money into his hands.

This is for the doctor.

Tacoma glanced at Tikkar in the back seat, sprawled out and unconscious.

CHAPTER 57

APQA Terminal
Miami, Florida

The next day was easier than the first.

Tikkar, the crane operator, didn't show up for work the next day and a different man operated the crane, someone who was less reckless. It was still brutal work, tiring and constant, but the man operating the crane wasn't a psychopath.

As much as he wanted the work to be done, Tacoma also knew that at the end of the day he would face a decision. Who to fight. He thought about picking an easy opponent and taking a day off, but in fact he had already made up his mind. He would follow Jenna's design.

When the whistle sounded at five, he walked with Zachary to the lockers. Everyone was looking at him as he opened his locker. Finally, it was Zachary who approached.

"It's time," he said.

"I know."

"Who will it be?"

Tacoma ignored the question.

He drank two bottles of water and then walked out to the

parking lot, where a human ring had already started to form. He had to push his way through to the inner ring, and as he did he encountered shoves, kicks. They all wanted to take him on.

Tacoma moved out into the center of the human ring, pulling his T-shirt from over his head and tossing it onto the ground. The crowd of workers started chanting and yelling as bottles of vodka were passed around.

Tacoma scanned the crowd. At least three hundred men were gathered. He saw Andrei Volkov on the fire escape.

CHAPTER 58

Reagan National Airport
Washington, D.C

The plane landed at midnight, a black Gulfstream on an alias flight plan. Kaiser climbed into a waiting Mercedes limousine and was whisked into Washington, a city he was all too familiar with.

His large frame took up the back seat of the limo and, as requested, a chilled bottle of Moskovskaya Osobaya was waiting. When Kaiser drank he took no prisoners. He unscrewed the green cap and opened the window, hurling the cap out as the luxurious Mercedes sped into Washington. He put the window back up, lifted the bottle to his mouth, and started drinking, like a man lost in the desert who suddenly finds a bottle of water. Kaiser drank the entire bottle in less than ten seconds. He opened the window and hurled the bottle out along the freeway.

In Kosovo, at the time of the uprising, Kaiser had been in charge. He made the decision to kill innocent men, women, and children only after drinking a bottle, like tonight. He destroyed lives after drinking like this, but it was only the alcohol that could get him to do what was more important than caring about one individual life.

Kaiser had few personal loyalties or affections. That being said, within the maze that was the Odessa Mafia, he vastly preferred the Bergens over Darré. He didn't like Americans, yet they provided the revenue for everything; America was the engine and Darré was a special earner. There were others, of course, but no one like Darré and his operating partner, Volkov. Darré was more refined than anyone in the broad diaspora of the Odessa clan. Darré had outwitted the Malnikovs along the East Coast of the United States. In addition, Darré controlled 55 percent of all cyber-related crime *in the world*. Darré was an intellectual. He and Darré had once attended the Bolshoi together along with a pair of beautiful women Darré had arranged for the evening. That being said, Darré and his henchman, Volkov, could be just as violent and brutal as the next in line, if not more so. Their crimes might have been less bloody than others, but they were more brutal. Their phishers had no problem taking away someone's life savings, and in the end, the victims of Darré's crimes suffered even more than they would have if they'd simply died.

Bruno Darré had been the logical selection to terminate the two American politicians, Blake and O'Flaherty. Yet, the whole thing was beginning to take on a life of its own. A troubled life. Kaiser knew he needed to end it. It was why he was here, in the United States.

Kaiser was wanted on several warrants—under various identities, none of them his actual identity—inside the U.S. but had long ago figured out how to manipulate the technology governing foreign visitors. He came to America at will, but always remembered that one wrong move could have disasterous consequences. His visits were short but necessary.

The Mercedes limousine pulled up in front of a sleek apartment building in a neighborhood north of the National Mall, a building with stellar views of both the Capitol and the White House.

Kaiser walked around the back of the apartment building and entered through the parking garage. He took the elevator to the fourth floor, then the stairs down to three. He knocked at the door.

After several moments, the door opened. There, standing, was a tall, thin, polished-looking individual.

"Good evening, Senator Lehigh," said Kaiser.

"Who are you?" said Lehigh, trying to close the door.

Kaiser abruptly kicked forward, slamming his foot into the door. The door shot back, ripping the chain lock, and hit Lehigh square across the forehead, sending him back as he screamed and blood suddenly poured from his broken nose.

Kaiser shut the door behind him and walked to the wet bar, returning with a bottle of vodka. He unscrewed the cap and took a large gulp.

"Good evening, Senator Lehigh," said Kaiser.

"Who the hell are you?"

"My identity is irrelevant," said Kaiser. "Now tell me, who is aware of your arrangement with Bruno Darré?"

"Only me," said Lehigh.

Kaiser took another large gulp. He reached into his coat pocket and removed a gun, a Stechkin APS, with a long black alloy silencer jutting from the muzzle.

"What is the name of the other CIA agent assigned to the unit, Senator Lehigh?"

Lehigh paused, his face a picture of abject fear, even terror.

"I don't know. I swear . . ."

Kaiser aimed the gun at Lehigh's head, then swung it to the television and fired a hole into the screen. A flare of cracks spread out from the dime-sized hole.

Kaiser reacquired Lehigh, who was bleeding from a gash across his forehead.

"Tacoma," Lehigh whispered. "Robert Tacoma."

"Why did you not tell us this?"

"He quit," said Lehigh. "After Cosgrove was murdered, he quit. I saw it with my own eyes."

"You saw what they wanted you to see," said Kaiser.

Kaiser set his gun down on the coffee table and sat down on the couch.

Lehigh slowly climbed to his feet, holding his nose and moving gingerly, then he suddenly lurched at Kaiser. He dived forward, across the coffee table, reaching for the weapon. It all occurred in a fraction of a second, and Lehigh grabbed the gun before Kaiser could even move, grabbing it and pivoting the muzzle as he slid across the marble top. He acquired Kaiser and pulled the trigger. There was no sound except for a dull mechanical click of the empty chamber, then a second, and a third.

"This isn't about me, Senator," said Kaiser from the sofa as he swallowed the remainder of the vodka in one large gulp. His Russian accent was sharp, thick, and he made no effort to hide it. "This is about a war. You are a casualty of war, but we must cut off the connection between you and us. You do understand, I hope? I appreciate your courage," said Kaiser, just as he reached out and grabbed Lehigh's arm with his prosthetic hand, snapping the forearm halfway between the elbow and wrist. Lehigh screamed.

"Your wife and daughter will be safe, Mr. Lehigh," added Kaiser matter-of-factly. "Any money that has been given to you by Bruno Darré will not be touched, you have my word. You earned it. Unfortunately, you will not be around to enjoy the fruits of your labor, but your wife and daughter will."

Lehigh moaned and swung wildly, and kicked at Kaiser as Kaiser stood up, absorbing every blow. Kaiser hoisted Lehigh up by the neck, holding him with his prosthetic hand in the air, gripping him tighter and tighter until the skin broke beneath the pressure of the mechanical limb. Lehigh stared back at Kaiser and stopped fighting as his face turned red, and a trickle of blood flowed from his nostrils. Then his eyes rolled back into his head. Kaiser let him fall. He tumbled sideways, taking a chair with him, landing on the carpet in a growing pool of crimson.

CHAPTER 59

Mandarin Hotel
Washington, D.C.

Tacoma.

Once Kaiser had a name, it was a simple matter to get one of his hackers to dig deep and assemble a dossier.

Tacoma.

Kaiser knew he had to be eliminated, for the roots of an American insurrection against the Russian mafia could not be allowed to take hold. They had to snuff it out at its beginnings. Never again would the CIA be able to get such an effort approved. It had to be stopped. Kaiser knew this.

Yet, it was something altogether different that now coursed through Kaiser's brain. He hated this person Tacoma like he'd never hated anyone before.

Kaiser was going to do what everyone else obviously was incapable of doing. He was going to put down the second member of the team, pluck the weed of this special unit before it sprouted.

Kaiser studied the photos of Robert Tacoma. The dossier was building by the minute, after-action reports from places Tacoma had wreaked havoc. Lisbon, Paris, Monaco, Tokyo . . . Moscow.

He stared at photos of Tacoma from his days at UVA, as a Navy SEAL, and fuzzy surveillance photos. A photo from *People* magazine.

Kaiser wanted to kill him. But he knew that more important than who killed Tacoma was that it was done. He had to die.

Kaiser took his phone and tried calling Darré, but it went to voicemail. He tried again, but there was again no answer. Kaiser wasn't going to leave a voicemail. He slammed down the phone as he looked out the window of the Mandarin Hotel over the empty dark waters of the Potomac River.

I'll find you, Tacoma, and when I do I'll kill you.

CHAPTER 60

APQA Terminal
Miami, Florida

Volkov walked to the small window that looked out on the parking area between the two warehouses. Volkov went out onto the steel fire escape, as he did every night. The circle had already formed and Volkov watched as the new champion stepped forward. Evgeny, the newcomer, had protected Volkov's record of continuous victories from Tikkar with his surprising victory last night. Tikkar had underestimated him. Tonight, however, Volkov thought, we'll see what he can really do. The newcomer stepped out into the human ring. The sky was black. The tarmac was illuminated by bright halogen lights on cranes.

Tacoma pulled his shirt off and tossed it to the ground behind him. He looked muscled, even tough, though Tacoma was not as big as many of the men gathered around the increasingly loud scrum. He wasn't massive, but he was covered in chiseled muscle and held himself in a way that projected experience, capability, athleticism, and above all, speed.

Tacoma circled within the ring and, out of the corner of his eye, watched Volkov move along the fire escape to get a better view.

The crowd was getting boisterous, yelling at Tacoma. Many men were taunting him. Alcohol was flowing. Everyone wanted to know who he would choose to fight. The dockworkers were hyped, expressing their heightened sense of anticipation by throwing money down to incentivize him.

Tacoma glanced around the entire circle of men, eyeing the workers, sizing them up. His face was blank and emotionless. Suddenly, he lifted his arm and pointed up at the fire escape—up at Volkov. The crowd went abruptly silent, then turned and looked up at Volkov. They all understood what Tacoma had just done.

Volkov did too.

Volkov was still for several moments. He downed the drink in his hand and flicked his cigarette into the wind. He unbuttoned his shirt as he stepped to the steel stairs that led to the parking lot tossing it to the ground. He stepped into the ring as a cacophony of yelling, roars, and shouting swept through the crowd of men. Dockworkers emptied their wallets. Small arguments flared up at the edge of the human ring as men fought to get closer to the action at the front edge of the fight.

Tacoma stood still as Volkov approached. Volkov's body below his neck was covered in tattoos. His muscles were ripped and he walked with bowlegs. Volkov's thick arms remained a few inches out to his side; his biceps were so large they needed extra space. Volkov had an angry expression on his face as he came closer, entering the human ring amidst a wildfire of shouting and screaming—then he suddenly charged at Tacoma.

The crowd went wild as Volkov ran toward Tacoma and—with both arms out—lunged at him, trying to tackle him. Tacoma met Volkov's outstretched arms with a sudden punch to the head, hammering Volkov, interrupting his momentum. Volkov's head snapped back, though he remained standing.

Tacoma said nothing, weaving slightly back and forth, then he lunged and hammered a right fist into Volkov's nose, moving too fast for Volkov to do anything. Blood shot from both nostrils. Volkov put his hand up to his nose.

Tacoma faked and parried over a half dozen moments, then lurched again, this time two quick punches to Volkov's face and—in the seconds that followed—a straight-on kick to Volkov's chin, snapping his head back hard this time.

Volkov was temporarily taken aback. He reached to his mouth and came back with blood on his fingers. He spat and a tooth went flying to the tar.

The crowd was quiet—perhaps shocked at how quickly Volkov was being destroyed. Every eye was on the two fighters.

Tacoma knew that he couldn't win, not if he wanted to find out who was responsible for it all, who was the man behind Volkov? Who gave Volkov his orders? Who was the person—the people—who had dictated that Audra Buczko and Slokavich assassinate Nick Blake and John Patrick O'Flaherty?

Yet, as much as the rational part of his mind told him to let Volkov win, Tacoma was governed by a more basic set of instincts, and self-defense was one of them. Killing. Already, Tacoma had seen two specific instances of opportunity, moments where Volkov had exposed a core point of vulnerability. He could have killed Volkov twice by now, and the fight had barely begun.

Tacoma understood on some deep level why he needed to lose this fight, but losing would be harder than winning.

Volkov charged again—again with both arms out, trying to

tackle Tacoma. This time, Tacoma hammered a crushing fist into Volkov's chin just as Volkov came within range, but this time Volkov was not going to be stopped. This time Volkov absorbed the hard punch and tackled Tacoma, driving him to the tar, onto his back. Tacoma let out a pained grunt. The crowd went nuts.

Volkov was now on top of Tacoma and started punching, but Tacoma blocked the punches until, finally, Volkov landed a tremendous punch to Tacoma's eye. The back of Tacoma's head slammed into the tar just as Volkov started beating him viciously, punching and punching over and over again. Tacoma tried to block Volkov's punches with his forearms, but it was no use. He endured at least a dozen blows, then, when he sensed Volkov tiring ever so slightly, lunged up at Volkov and hit him squarely in the mouth. Volkov bit through his tongue, and blood spilled from his mouth. From the ground, on his back, Tacoma swung again, catching Volkov in the chin. Volkov was sent sideways and Tacoma used the respite to squirm away and climb to his feet.

Tacoma was drenched in sweat and his eye was bleeding. He breathed heavily. He tried to open his right eye, but it was swollen shut. He understood what to do in a situation in which he only had one working eye. He'd been trained in it. When Tacoma first entered the CIA, it was a small but important thing, learning how to fight with some sort of disability, be it a broken leg, a loss of hearing, severe pain, or loss of vision.

Tacoma knew how to adjust to the element. In fact, Tacoma realized now—as he squared off against Volkov—that killing him would be easy. Volkov was very strong, and moved without fear of consequences, yet Tacoma had long ago recognized the vulnerabilities in such fighters. He knew—based on Volkov's stance now—how his next attack would occur. It would be his right leg coming at him, a surprise, the tackling and punching up until now meant to take Tacoma off course and not expect what was—when delivered properly—the most deadly face-to-face martial strike known to man.

Tacoma knew what Volkov would do next, and the counterstrike was embedded inside him. Block, punch, then, with torque from the block, and the opponent open due to the punch, a 270-degree kick across the diagonal that ended at Volkov's exposed trachea.

But he couldn't do it. He remembered Cosgrove, dangling by a rope. He didn't even know him, but they were brothers. SEALs, Americans, and instead of killing Volkov, Tacoma focused on figuring out how to lose. He already had a black eye. It didn't hurt, much, but he also didn't feel like allowing Volkov to cause any more physical damage. He needed to lose—but could he do it in a way that looked worse than it actually was?

Tacoma caught his breath as he waited for Volkov to stand up. Slowly, the Russian got to his feet. His face was a mess, covered from the nose down in blood. He breathed heavily. A look of intense hatred was on his face.

Volkov charged at Tacoma, then dived forward and, as he became horizontal, slashed his foot across the air at Tacoma's head. Tacoma ducked, but stuck his arm up, punching at Volkov's leg, catching it with a glancing blow. Volkov went sideways in an awkward tumble, landing on his back.

He quickly stood back up as the crowd went from loud to deafening.

The two combatants circled each other.

It was Tacoma who stepped forward this time, holding his fists up, shadowboxing near Volkov. He stepped closer and Volkov stood his ground, facing Tacoma even as blood spilled down his face. Both men were tired, and now Tacoma's eye was bleeding from the seam of the contusion.

"What do you say we split the money?" said Volkov as a bloody grin appeared on his face.

"I would like that," said Tacoma.

Tacoma dropped his fists, as did Volkov—and as they walked toward each other to shake hands, Volkov suddenly swung, punching Tacoma in the chin. Tacoma was knocked back and nearly off his feet, though he remained standing. He put his hand to his mouth and soon his fingers were covered in blood.

"*Eto dolzhno byt' urokom?*" said Tacoma.

Was that supposed to be a lesson?

Volkov paused as Tacoma squared off, then glanced sideways, as if sensing something that was coming. Tacoma followed the direction of his eyes—and it was at this point that Volkov removed a knife from a concealed sheath beneath his armpit and slashed it at Tacoma.

It was a small knife—a punch knife—short, with two finger holes. The workers wouldn't see it. Only Volkov and Tacoma knew it was in his hand. He swung at Tacoma, who blocked Volkov's arm with his forearm. Tacoma realized the stakes had been upped considerably, and that his life was in danger. He hammered a hard strike to Volkov's rib cage, then another, then pivoted and kicked, striking Volkov in the groin. The kick was hard enough to drop Volkov, and he fell to the tar.

Tacoma stepped over him, trying to catch his breath. Then Volkov's leg swung along the pavement, a hard kick that caught Tacoma at the ankle. He fell sideways, and soon Volkov was on his feet. He again dived at Tacoma, hands first, the punch blade still locked on his fingers, and soon had Tacoma in a vise, his arms wrapped around Tacoma's neck. He could break Tacoma's neck at any moment—or simply slash it.

Volkov let go. He knelt, trying to catch his breath, as the crowd started cheering. He stood and extended his hand to Tacoma. Volkov took Tacoma's hand and pulled him back to his feet.

"You have skills," said Volkov.

"I apologize if I should not have done that," said Tacoma.

"Don't ever apologize for standing up for yourself, Evgeny," said Volkov.

"I won't, sir."

Volkov was wet with perspiration and his face was bleeding badly. He looked around the crowd, and showed a wide grin.

Volkov looked at Tacoma.

"Do you like vodka?" he said. "I don't know about you, but I could use a drink."

"It would be an honor," said Tacoma, respectfully, but with a hint of shyness, above all obeisance.

"Come up to my office," said Volkov, waving the crowd away. "Your eye doesn't look very good and my nose hurts. I think we can both use a drink."

As they started to walk to the fire escape, Victor approached.

"Andrei," said Victor. "What about all the money?"

"Collect it and bring it to my office," said Volkov. He nodded at Tacoma. "It's his money anyway."

CHAPTER 61

Mandarin Hotel
Washington, D.C.

Kaiser felt one of his cell phones buzzing. It was one of his right-hand men, the one he had researching Rob Tacoma. Kaiser put the phone to his ear.

"*Dobryy vecher, Dostya,*" said Kaiser. "*Chto vy uznali?*"
Good evening, Dostya. What have you learned?

"They have murdered several people," said Dostya.

"Who has?"

"The CIA. They've killed Ripsulitin in Moscow," said Dostya. "In St. Petersburg, Sverdlov. Dr. Gonz was killed a few hours ago in Bogota."

"Is that all? They are all replaceable. That is weak revenge at best," said Kaiser. "What about the CIA man, Robert Tacoma?"

"He may have been the one who captured Slokavich," said Dostya. "He's undoubtedly the one who killed Volkov's men at the airport. He found Audra and killed her. He's fairly notorious, this Tacoma, and we should be concerned, Kaiser."

"Dostya, thank you as always for your excellent work," said

Kaiser. "Now, let me ask you a question. What information did he get out of Audra?"

"My guess is, the furthest she could take an interrogator is to Andrei," said Dostya. "Audra Buczko didn't know about Darré."

"She gave up Andrei's name, at least we must presume that," said Kaiser.

"So you want to kill Volkov before this Tacoma gets to him?" said Dostya.

"No," said Kaiser. "I'm not worried about Andrei Volkov. He's Russian. I am worried about Bruno Darré. If Tacoma gets to Darré it will all be exposed. Everything."

"I was the one who suggested only killing one of the American politicians," said Dostya.

"Congratulations, Dostya," said Kaiser. "But you're missing the bigger picture. We succeeded in mobilizing the CIA. The killing of Robert Tacoma will be a nail in the coffin of Washington's attempt to tell us what to do and how to behave."

"I found some more information on him. I'm sending you a file I found on I2P," said Dostya. "Some German computer hacker leaked a bunch of BND files."

Kaiser hung up the phone and opened his laptop. The file from Dostya had already arrived. He opened it and started reading.

BND DATEI NR. 453-1

Die Vereinigten Staaten

Tacoma, Robert

US Navy SEALS

CIA Spezialbetriebsgruppe

Riscon-Gruppe

WARNUNG: Tacoma sollte als Stufe 9 betrachtet werden

Extrem gefährlich

A translation was below:

BND FILE NO. 453-1

USA

Tacoma, Robert

U.S. Navy SEALS

CIA Special Operations Group [DDA:6-R}

Riscon Group

WARNING: Tacoma should be considered Level 9

Extremely dangerous

Several photos appeared, all showing Tacoma in very different lights. The first few were more casual shots. Several from a UVA college yearbook; Tacoma standing next to a blond-haired woman at a fraternity party, a photo of the UVA lacrosse team with a red circle around Tacoma's head. In all, he was handsome, boyish looking, even a little shaggy. Other photos suggested his skill at disguise, or at least hinted at a chameleon-like quality. A face pic showed Tacoma the day he was commissioned as a Navy SEAL, looking tanned and sharp in his white combination cover. Another photo was taken by a BND spy in the water off Coronado, an excellent example of HUMINT, or human intelligence, as differentiated from SIGINT, signals intelligence. The intel had been procured by an agent, not a camera or other type of machine.

Even then, Tacoma was being watched by intelligence professionals from other parts of the world. Another photo was from *People* magazine. Tacoma had helped to prevent a nuclear strike—a dirty bomb—in New York Harbor, near the Statue of Liberty. Tacoma was standing in a short-sleeved, midthigh tactical black wet suit, soaking wet. He'd been named one of the Sexiest

Men Alive by the gossip sheet. He looked confident, Kaiser realized, that was for damn sure.

Tacoma's bio came next:

TACOMA, ROBERT THIERIAULT

Citizenship: USA
DOB: 4/12/90
Home:
New York City, NY
Middleburg, VA
Milan, Italy
Washington, D.C.

University of Virginia May 2010   Russian Studies B.A. 2.77
GPA
Varsity Lacrosse [Captain 08–09, 09–10] All-American 06, 07,
08, 09
U.S. Navy: enlistment Jun 09 [Charlottesville, VA]
U.S. Navy SEALs—training Coronado, CA
Rank: 4 in class of 232
U.S. Navy SEAL Team 6 [DEVGRU 1]: Virginia Beach, VA
[Mar 10—Dec 12]
CIA Special Operations Group [Dec 12—Jul 15]
RISCON LLC, Middleburg, VA [Jul 15—present]: private
security firm founded with Katherine "Katie" Foxx,
ex-director, Special Operations Group

MISC:

- Raised in NYC. Youngest of two brothers [Bo Israel Tacoma]

- Bo Tacoma Lt. Cmdr, U.S. Navy SEAL Team 4 [Mar 09—Oct 14]: Bronze Star [Oct 09], Navy Cross [Oct 09]: Both awarded for actions resulting in the rescue and exfiltration of U.S. diplomat and family captured in Sri Lanka and subsequent firefight in which 4 members of SEAL Team 4 were KIA.

- Father, Blake Tacoma [b. Oct 58—d. May 12] U.S. Attorney for Southern District of Manhattan [Jan 07—May 09]. U.S. Attorney General June 09—May 12

- Portland, ME [May 12]: Blake Tacoma assassinated at public restaurant while on vacation with wife (Susan). Murder remains unsolved though FBI believes killing was reprisal for actions taken as D.A. against factions of Russian mafia.

- Severomorsk, RUS (Murmansk Oblast region) [Oct 14]: Bo Tacoma, US Navy SEAL 4 (AD5-I), while on Observation + Assessment operation in the waters near the Port of Severomorsk, headquarters of Russia's Northern Fleet, is lost in winter storm. After two days of reconnaissance efforts, he is declared Missing In Action officially Code 4.1 MIA and presumed drowned. All other members of unit survive.

ADDENDUM:

- RISCON clients (current) include: EXXON/Mobil, Dmitri Sarkov, Altria/Philip Morris, Apple, KKR, The Blackstone Group, The Carlyle Group, Alphabet Inc., Raytheon, Abbott Laboratories, Microsoft Inc., The Gladstone Companies, Ryan Herco, E.A. Davis, Digital Fuel Capital, Anadarko, IBM,

The Disney Companies, and others. GOVERNMENT: United States (CIA), Saudi Arabia, Israel, Jordan, Brazil, Japan, Mexico, England (MI6).

It was time to call Volkov directly. Kaiser removed a cell phone and dialed. After a few moments, Volkov's gruff voice came on the line.

"Hello?" said Volkov.

"Hi, Andrei. It's Kaiser," said Kaiser. "You must listen to me very carefully. You are in imminent danger. We have found the other member of this CIA unit and he probably has your identity. He is coming for you."

Volkov stood in his office, drinking from the bottle of Stolichnaya, sharing it with a man he believed was a newcomer from Moscow named Evgeny. He took a big sip as he listened.

"Say that again, Kaiser," said Volkov.

From across the office, Tacoma registered the word: *Kaiser.*

Volkov took a sip from the bottle and then walked toward the window, away from Tacoma. He listened to Kaiser.

"The man who killed Audra Buczko is a high-end CIA operative," said Kaiser. "You should lock down immediately."

"Don't worry, I'm still at the port."

"You must have your eyes open, Andrei," said Kaiser. "Don't go anywhere on your own. Keep tight security at all times and watch out for anyone new or suspicious. I'm sending you photos right now."

Volkov looked at his phone as he pressed the small towel against his nose. The first photo popped up and Volkov recognized the man immediately. He'd shaved his head, but the man in his office, Evgeny, was the American spy, Rob Tacoma.

He put the phone back up to his ear and hung up, but pretended to continue talking.

"I think dinner next week sounds perfect," he said. He stared out the window but quietly removed the punch knife from his pocket, out of Tacoma's sight. He spoke loudly and enthusiastically. "Leana has been dying to go out for a nice dinner. What sort of food are you two in the mood for?"

Volkov swiveled in a fiery, swift instant—and hurled the razor-sharp blade toward Tacoma. He caught Tacoma by surprise. The blade flew through the air and landed in Tacoma's biceps, slicing an inch in.

Volkov followed the knife blade and charged across the small office just as Tacoma understood he was under attack. The blade hurt, but he needed to avoid the oncoming strike before dealing with the knife. He slashed his leg out and caught Volkov at the side of his head, a ferocious kick. He followed his momentum—and Volkov—to the area near the door, grabbing the punch knife, yanking it from his arm, then slashing in a downward diagonal at Volkov's neck, cutting his throat wide. A chug of blood, deep red, spilled from Volkov's neck. He watched as Volkov cringed, trying to say something, and writhed spasmodically, like a fish.

Then he heard the knock at the door.

Tacoma went to Volkov's desk and started opening drawers. He found a .45 caliber Glock. He slammed in a mag and chambered a bullet, then walked to the door. He paused, then opened the door. Victor was standing in the hallway, alone, holding a large pile of money. Tacoma fired, sending a bullet through Victor's chest, killing him instantly.

The sound of unmuted gunfire ricocheted out into the port.

Tacoma dragged Victor's body inside Volkov's office as shouting began, then a siren was sounded. He heard footsteps.

Tacoma popped his earbud in and tapped it three times.

"Katie? Igor? I've got a problem. Volkov found me out and I had to kill him. I'm trapped here in his office, but I've got an idea."

Without waiting for a reply, or even an acknowledgment that they had heard him, Tacoma pulled the earbud out and dropped it into his pocket. He went to Volkov's corpse and placed the Glock in Volkov's hand. He then grabbed the punch knife and put it into Victor's hand. Both men were dead, and it looked as if they had done it to each other.

Finally, as the drumbeat of footsteps drew closer, Tacoma lay down on the floor, holding his bloody arm. The wound wasn't that serious, all he needed was a few stitches, but he needed to play a part right now.

When a small crew of security men from the port opened the door, Tacoma was on the ground, holding his bloody arm. There were three men, all clutching Uzis. They found Victor on the ground, his chest a riot of blood, and then they found Volkov, his blue eyes staring blankly up at the ceiling.

They looked at Tacoma.

"What happened?"

"I don't know, it was so fast."

"Are you okay?" said one of the gunmen.

Tacoma just nodded, as if in shock.

"Tell us what you saw."

"They argued over some money," said Tacoma.

"And how did you get cut?"

"Victor pulled out a knife and charged Mr. Volkov," said Tacoma. "I tried to defend Mr. Volkov but Victor slashed my arm, then he cut Mr. Volkov's neck."

As if anticipating the man's next question, Tacoma spoke.

"Mr. Volkov grabbed his gun and shot Victor," said Tacoma. "Victor would have killed me next but Mr. Volkov saved my life."

One of the gunmen came closer to Tacoma and knelt. He took his T-shirt and ripped a strip off. He tied it above Tacoma's knife wound, a tourniquet to stem the blood loss. He then went to find a first aid kit.

One of the other security men pulled out a phone.

"I have to call the emergency number and report this."

"You're calling the police?" Tacoma said.

"Not that kind of emergency number," he said. He stepped out into the hallway and began speaking to someone in hushed tones.

Someone returned with a first aid kit. He bandaged Tacoma's arm.

"This will hold you for a while, but you're going to need stitches. We should get you to a doctor."

The other man hung up the phone and turned to the others.

"He needs a doctor," said the man who'd just bandaged him.

"Not yet, I'm afraid. This one is going on a flight," said the gunman.

Tacoma looked startled and pulled back. Even injured, he knew he could take all three of them and get away, but he needed to find out who was on the other end of that emergency phone call.

"What do you mean? I did nothing wrong."

"No one says that you did," said the gunman. "I told the man how heroically you defended the boss. But I do as I am told."

"Where am I going?" said Tacoma.

"Even I don't know the answer to that question."

CHAPTER 62

Commonwealth Tower
1300 Wilson Boulevard
Arlington, Virginia

"I think I have something," said Igor.

Katie, Jenna, and Calibrisi all gathered behind Igor as he put up a video on one of his computer screens.

It showed the port, and the human ring. An orange circle was painted on Tacoma as he walked out into the middle of the ring and removed his shirt.

"Where is this from?" said Katie.

"I sent a drone overhead," said Igor. "Technically, it's against the law, but I figured, why not? Know what I mean?" Igor looked back at Katie. "Impressive, don't you think, gorgeous?"

Katie met eyes with Igor for the briefest of moments, then rolled her eyes backward and shook her head.

"Not to say you aren't also a fetching woman," said Igor, pivoting to Jenna, though Jenna did not return Igor's look. She was focused on the video.

The video showed Tacoma and Volkov engaged in face-to-face combat. They watched in silence as the two men exchanged blows.

"He infiltrated the fight," said Jenna, her English accent crisp and elegant sounding. "The question now is, what does it mean?"

Calibrisi, Katie, Jenna, and Igor watched the fight on Igor's screen, from a perspective high above the fight, and watched as ultimately Tacoma went down and lost to Volkov.

"Rob did what you said," said Calibrisi. "He lost. He could've killed Volkov at several points, three by my count."

"Five," said Katie.

They watched as Volkov extended a hand and the two wounded fighters went up to Volkov's office.

"I'll tell you what it means, it means Tacoma is now on the inside," said Jenna.

"I don't about the rest of you, but after that, I need a drink," Katie said.

Just then, they heard Tacoma's voice come over the speaker.

"Katie? Igor? I've got a problem. Volkov found me out and I had to kill him. I'm trapped here in his office, but I've got an idea."

And then the tone went busy, as if the call had ended.

"Fuck," Katie said. "Rob, are you there? What's going on?"

But there was only silence.

The four looked at one another in shock, until Katie turned to Jenna and said, "Well, what now, Miss Genius Architect?"

CHAPTER 63

Darré Estate
Greenwich, Connecticut

Tacoma was blindfolded and flex-cuffed. He was placed in the back of a black sedan. After an hour of driving, the car stopped and Tacoma was led to a plane. From the stairs, he knew it was a Gulfstream.

He was pushed into a seat in the cabin, a large, luxurious leather seat, but then he felt a steel rope between his hands, and heard the sound of a lock. Someone pulled off the blindfold. Tacoma winced at the pain, as part of the material had stuck to his eye, sopping up the blood but hardening. It was like having a Band-Aid torn off. The steel rope between his flex-cuffed hands was wrapped around the chair itself. He couldn't move. He recognized the cabin of a Gulfstream G650.

The plane soon took off. In addition to the pilots, there were two gunmen, a young, scraggly-looking man who held an Uzi trained on Tacoma, and an older man, in his late thirties or early forties, with a crew cut.

"Where are we going?" said Tacoma.

He repeated the question several times, in both English and Russian, but was not given an answer.

Tacoma shut his eyes, willing himself to go to sleep. Wherever they were flying, it would take time. These two were not going to kill him. They were supposed to transport him. It meant he could sleep without worrying about being killed. Tacoma shut his eyes and thought about his brother, Bo, a random thought—playing checkers in the lodge at Stowe, after a day of skiing. They were just boys then. He fell asleep as he tried to remember the moment.

He awoke as they unlocked him from the steel rope, though he was still flex-cuffed.

Near the stairs leading down from the jet, Tacoma was met by a man in a gray suit. He led Tacoma to an idling BMW limousine. The man rewrapped the blindfold over Tacoma's eyes, then shut the door and hit the roof twice, telling the driver to go.

An hour later, the vehicle came to a set of majestic iron gates in the Greenwich countryside.

After passing through the gates, the driveway went on for nearly half a mile, through manicured fields, lawns, and sweeps of beautiful trees. At the end of the driveway was a four-story mansion, white stucco, slate roof, and surrounded by precisely coiffed boxwoods and flower gardens and lawn.

Tacoma was led inside and down a hallway. He was pushed down into a chair.

"Evgeny," came a man's voice. He wasn't Russian. He sounded friendly, an American accent, even a little southern. "I'm going to have them remove your cuffs and your blindfold. Don't do anything stupid. There are three gunmen with guns aimed at you."

He felt his flex-cuffs loosen. Finally, the blindfold was removed. Again, Tacoma felt the pain as the cloth detached from his injured eye.

Tacoma looked around, assaying the environment. It was a fancy and spacious room. The walls were lined with bookshelves. A large desk was on one side of the room. Behind the desk stood a man with longish blond hair, dressed in white pants and a white button-down shirt. There were three gunmen flanking him.

"My name is Bruno Darré," he said. "You witnessed Andrei Volkov dying earlier?"

Tacoma nodded, yes.

"Yes, I did."

"Who killed him?"

"Victor," said Tacoma. "Mr. Volkov accused him of stealing and they were shouting at each other. Victor cut him with a knife. He then stabbed me." Tacoma looked at his biceps, which had a makeshift bandage and tourniquet over it. "Mr. Volkov shot Victor. Then everyone came. We were merely having a drink. He invited me there."

Darré stared at Tacoma for more than half a minute. He studied Tacoma, as if attempting to find a flaw in his narrative.

"Tell me, Evgeny, do you have any prison tattoos?" said Darré.

"No. I was in prison, yes, but I was young and I made sure to avoid the gangs."

Tacoma felt the outline of the lightning bolt on his shoulder. He didn't react. He recognized that there were three gunmen there.

"I have one tattoo on my shoulder, it's a lightning bolt."

Darré smiled and seemed to visibly relax. He went to the bar and poured himself a bourbon.

Tacoma watched him carefully and pieced it all together. This was the man that Volkov reported to, his boss. Tacoma was now just feet from the man who had ordered it all. The man who orchestrated the assassinations of Blake and O'Flaherty, the man who told Andrei Volkov to kill Billy Cosgrove.

And though he wanted to kill him, this man Darré, Tacoma recognized something in Darré's eyes. He sensed another presence, a shade of outright fear, and he knew that Darré wasn't the one in charge. He couldn't be. Jenna was right, there was someone even bigger, hiding behind him. He saw that in Darré's eyes, in his actions. What it told him was, he needed to keep playing his part.

"Will I be able to still work at the port?" said Tacoma sheepishly. He spoke with a hint of a Russian accent. "I only just arrived in the United States. I like the work. I wish I had not seen the fight. I tried to defend Mr. Volkov. I'm sorry I failed, sir."

Darré stepped over to Tacoma and stood before him.

"You did nothing wrong," said Darré. "We just need to be careful. I need to be careful. Of course you still have a job. But maybe you could work directly for me. Security is an important issue in my life. I heard that you and Andrei fought, that you almost won. I could use someone with that kind of skill."

"Of course, I would work for you. I'm saving up to bring my sister to America," said Tacoma.

Darré grinned and snapped his fingers. An older woman stepped into the room.

"Put Evgeny in the guest cottage," said Darré. "And call the doctor. We need to get our friend's wounds looked after."

CHAPTER 64

Darré Estate
Greenwich, Connecticut

Inside the small guest cottage on Darré's estate, Tacoma didn't sleep. He lay on the bed, thinking.

He needed to act now. Time was working against him. His improvised story would only hold together so long. Eventually they'd learn that his story about Volkov and Victor wasn't true. Something would tip them off. They were still searching for him, and whoever tipped off Volkov would eventually—inevitably—find him.

He couldn't count on backup. He didn't know if Katie had even heard his last message, and she couldn't know where he was. Even he wasn't sure where he was.

It was a race against time. He didn't have a weapon.

Always know where your weapon is.

Tacoma believed his greatest weapon was his fists, followed very closely by his feet. But lying in wait without a gun was not easy.

He thought about something someone said at the Farm one day.

Don't wait. Act immediately. If you think tomorrow night would be a much less risky opportunity to kill, and tonight is fraught with peril for various reasons, choose tonight.

There was somebody larger out there, a man above even Darré and Volkov.

When that man learned of Volkov's death, he would find out where Volkov's killer had gone. The story of Victor and Volkov's fight would be seen as what it was, a charade.

Tacoma needed a weapon. Not for the feeling of security, but because they would be coming. He would be coming. The one behind it all. The fact that Darré didn't know that Evgeny was really Tacoma spoke volumes. It meant the one in charge of it all didn't trust him.

Tacoma had at most a few precious hours.

He glanced at the black sky out one of the windows in the small but pretty cottage. He knew what he was about to do was high risk, but it was necessary. Tacoma climbed out of bed and pulled on jeans and a flannel shirt. He remained barefoot.

He climbed out the window and then waited until his eyes adjusted to the dark. Surprised that Darré didn't have any security walking the grounds, Tacoma walked quickly across the lawn to the back of Darré's mansion. He came to a French door off a rose garden and tried to turn the doorknob, but it was locked. Tacoma pressed his leg against the door and tried to create space between the two doors. He managed to get the tips of his fingers in the small opening, then slammed the door handle up. The door opened and Tacoma moved to the upper right corner of the doorjamb, holding his fingers over the sensor. He waited several seconds. The sensor would register it as an anomaly. He waited, then removed his hand and shut the door.

He moved through the dark mansion, finding Darré's office. He went to Darré's desk and opened drawers. Several were empty.

Others contained business files. In the top drawer was a manila envelope with no writing on it. He opened it and pulled out a sheet of paper.

ORLOV, EVGENY

The sheet had Tacoma's photo from his fake Russian passport. Other than that and his name, it said nothing. So far, Darré didn't know who he was. That was good.

Tacoma went behind Darré's desk and, in the darkness, felt along the floor. He searched for a false spot, possibly indicating a safe or hiding spot. He found a split seam in the hardwood and ran his finger to a small switch, pushing it. A section of floor opened up and Tacoma reached down. He felt the steel of a gun barrel. It was an MP7. A stack of magazines was next to the hidden weapon.

Tacoma took the gun and slammed a mag in, then spent a few seconds feeling over a weapon he already knew well. He pocketed three extra mags and then slung the MP7 over his shoulder, training it in a diagonal direction in front of him.

He crossed the yard and went back to the guest cottage. With no one around to observe him, he went in through the front door, then climbed back in bed, clutching the MP7.

CHAPTER 65

White Plains Airport
White Plains, New York

Kaiser's jet touched down in White Plains and he walked down the stairs, where a pair of helicopters were waiting, lights on, rotors slashing the air. One was a Sikorsky S-76C, and the other was an Airbus H225 Super Puma. Kaiser walked to the Puma and opened the door. He looked inside at four highly-trained, black-clad operators. He focused on one man in particular, a bald man whose face was painted in camouflage.

"You understand the mission?" said Kaiser.

"Yes. Find the American and kill him. Do we know where he is on the property?"

"In the guest cottage. Use extreme prejudice. He must die. If you come across one of Darré's men, kill him. In the meantime, I will be visiting with Darré inside the house. I want all bodies taken away and dropped several miles out in the ocean. Is that understood?"

"Yes, sir."

"You won't see me again," said Kaiser.

He scanned the men. No one said a word, but every man nodded silently, yes.

Kaiser slid the door shut and walked to the waiting S-76C, climbing into a spacious cabin and a comfortable leather seat. He was alone in the cabin. The lights inside the chopper cabin suddenly went out and the chopper took air, just as loud thunder from the Puma rattled everything.

Kaiser leaned forward and watched through the window of the Sikorsky as the dark phantom of the Super Puma cut through a moonlit sky, on its way to the same place Kaiser was headed, though the Puma would get there sooner. The design was simple. Land, then kill him.

Tacoma, then Darré.

The news of Volkov's death didn't surprise Kaiser, and he had no doubt as to who had done it. There was no question. It was Tacoma.

The time to go after Tacoma was now. He would kill two birds with one stone. Kaiser knew that the American agent was now chasing Darré. Presumably, he'd gotten Darré's identity from Volkov before killing him. Rob Tacoma had gift-wrapped it all for Kaiser. He would erase Darré and Tacoma. He would tie off and shut down the entire thing. The objective had been achieved, but even Kaiser felt bad for the loss not only of an important revenue source, but, in Volkov, a youngster who reminded Kaiser of himself and, in Darré, a financial mind unparalleled to anything he'd ever known. He would miss them both, for different reasons. But now it was time to destroy this entire arm of the Odessa Mafia.

The first CIA agent, Cosgrove, had been relatively easy, but his partner was proving to be very difficult. He was backed up by technicians and perhaps even an architect. The American was dealing with complexities in real time, relying upon instinct—

and his raw skills as an assassin were impressive. But Kaiser understood his enemy. He knew his name. His name was Robert Tacoma. He repeated that name to himself several times.

Kaiser grinned and looked at his watch. In a few minutes, the Super Puma would settle down on the lawn at Darré's estate, and the team of men would start their mission.

Darré needed to die tonight. He was the only link still left in the chain back to him.

"How much longer?" said Kaiser.

"Ten minutes, sir."

CHAPTER 66

Darré Estate
Greenwich, Connecticut

Tacoma heard the rotors and sat up in bed. He saw the lights, and then a chopper gunship came over the trees. A black helicopter cut down from a starry sky, its red and green lights illuminating a dark steel skeleton as it descended. It was a Super Puma.

Tacoma went to the window as the chopper descended and landed on Darré's lawn. He watched as a swarm of black-clad operators with submachine guns and rifles emerged from the back.

A minute later, he watched as a smaller, sleeker chopper swooped in from the west. A Sikorsky S-76C.

Then he saw a towering man, very tall, in a suit, as he stepped down from the S-76C onto the lawn and walked toward Darré's house.

Tacoma allowed his eyes to adjust, then scanned. He registered several men, but he couldn't be sure. He caught undulations in movement, bathed in ambient light, and then saw a small green light on a device that should've been shut off or hidden. He sighted another gunman, moving along the perimeter of the carriage house.

He wasn't sure, but it looked like he was surrounded.

They knew who he was. It was the only logical conclusion.

The man—the giant—who'd entered the mansion was the one Jenna spoke of. The one behind it all.

Tacoma had only one option. That option crystallized into a realization as he went to the floor and started crawling along the rug, removing himself from any direct sight lines.

He heard the voice.

There's only one option. Kill.

Tacoma pulled the MP7 he'd stolen from Darré out from between the bed frame and the mattress. He crawled to the French doors which led to a small deck just off the bedroom. He quickly examined the scope atop the submachine gun—it was an ATN Thor 4 384 thermal scope, a great instrument that would enable Tacoma to site whoever was out by sensing body heat in the sight zone of the optic.

Slowly, Tacoma turned the doorknob until it was clear. He let the door open as if drawn by the wind. He knelt and swept the rifle to his chin, tracing the line of the railing with his movement, mechanical, like a machine; anyone watching would think it was something nonhuman, the movement of the stars.

Tacoma reached the corner of the deck with the MP7. He swept the weapon slowly, staring through the scope. He counted three men in all, then saw a fourth, in a loose perimeter. They had some sort of prior intelligence, down to his whereabouts in the cottage.

Tacoma ran his fingers down the smokestack of bullets in the mag, then took aim. But before he fired he ran the sequence through his mind. He could take them down easily—just a line of quick bursts from the silenced MP7, but then he realized that no matter how precisely he could shoot, there was no way to shoot all four without the risk of one of them firing back an unmuted rifle, or shouting, or triggering an alarm. If just killing the operators was his objective, the noise wouldn't matter. But Tacoma's objective was inside the mansion. Tacoma couldn't let the man inside know he'd killed any of them. The element of surprise was essential. In fact, it was the single thing that might keep him alive.

Of all four men, only one was isolated. He was kneeling near a stone wall, clad in black, aiming his rifle at the front door to the cottage.

The other three covered the back perimeter, where Tacoma was. This was because, were Tacoma to try and escape, this was where he would run to. Into the woods on Darré's property.

Tacoma took aim and fired a single shot toward the man kneeling at the stone wall. He could only see what happened through the optic, and he watched as the green digital of the killer fell abruptly right and down. Bull's-eye.

He didn't have a lot of time. If there was commo, he had less than thirty seconds, if he was lucky.

Tacoma skulked back inside and sprinted down the stairs to the first floor of the cottage. He went out through the front door, knowing he'd just gunned down the one killer who was supposed to be guarding it. He went left and came to the corner of the cottage. He scanned the back of the cottage and counted the three other killers, all lined up and looking up at the cottage, preparing to move in.

Again, Tacoma worried about the risks of shooting them from his current position. He couldn't allow any noise to get back to the mansion. He couldn't alert the Russian.

He needed to have the three targets in a proximal area—near the center, so that the killings could be done with a slight tilt of the weapon, versus having to swing the weapon.

Tacoma—well aware that the men had on night optics, undoubtedly also thermal—had to distract them. So far, he'd used the building to hide whatever thermal imprint his body gave off. But in order to get all three men in any sort of proximal kill pattern, he needed to get to the right of the gunman to his right. Behind him.

Tacoma reached into his pocket. He popped in the ear bud and tapped twice.

"Igor?" he whispered.

A moment later:

"Yeah, I'm here."

"The guy I just killed, can you patch into his cell?"

"Yes."

"Call him, but make it ring. Is there a way to make it ring?"

"Yes, give me a few seconds."

"Thanks, brother."

Tacoma waited. Five, ten, fifteen seconds. He shut his eyes as he heard the sound of the killers moving closer to the cottage.

Suddenly, the sound of the dead man's cell chimed somewhere in the distance.

CHAPTER 67

CIA Headquarters
Langley, Virginia

"I just spoke to Rob," said Igor. "He's at Darré's house in Greenwich. Once I was able to pinpoint him on the property, I scanned. He was surrounded by four gunmen. Meanwhile, there are two individuals inside the house. One is Darré. The other must be Kaiser."

"We've got to get someone over there!" said Katie. She looked at Calibrisi. "You sent him on a suicide mission, didn't you?" she shouted emotionally. "So you could find out who was behind it all! *You killed Rob! There's no way out, Hector!*" she sobbed.

Calibrisi turned back to Katie. "I would never send Rob, or anyone, on a mission if I thought it was a suicide mission. This is a high risk job, Katie, but Rob can get through it."

"How? He's trapped!"

"I sent Dewey to Connecticut this afternoon," said Calibrisi.

Katie looked up, her sobs stopped.

"You did?" she asked hopefully. "Oh, thank God."

Calibrisi lifted his phone to his ear, close enough so that Katie could listen.

"Are you ready?" said Calibrisi, putting the phone on speaker. "I've got a chopper on the way."

"Yeah, I'm ready," said Dewey.

CHAPTER 68

Delamar Greenwich Harbor
500 Steamboat Road
Greenwich, Connecticut

Dewey Andreas climbed the fire stairs to the roof of the Delamar. A helipad wouldn't be necessary. He heard the distant roar of the chopper, which soon came into view: a sleek-looking Bell 525 Relentless. The chopper descended until it was just a few feet off the ground. Dewey climbed aboard without the chopper even lowering its wheels. The chopper soared away as Dewey shut the door.

He put an earbud in and tapped.

"Priority?" came a female voice.

"Virgo."

"Peacemaker."

"NOC two two four nine dash A."

"Andreas, provisioned in."

"I need Hector or Bill."

"Hold."

A few seconds later, Calibrisi came on the line.

"So what do we got?" said Dewey as the chopper purred north across Greenwich. "What's the situation?"

"He's surrounded. You're coming into a live environment."
One of them inside we want alive. The tall one. Kaiser."

"Kaiser?" said Dewey. "Good. I hate those fucking Germans."

"We need him alive," said Calibrisi.

"I understand," said Dewey. "I won't kill him, but is it okay to
cripple him?"

"Yes," said Calibrisi. "Dewey, Rob is undercover, but they figured it out. They're there to take him out."

"I get it," said Dewey. He tapped his ear, ending the call.

As the chopper sped across the Greenwich countryside, across
the main part of the town, then over hills dotted with mansions
and tennis courts, sweeping lawns and swimming pools. He
found a long, wide silencer and removed it from the cache. He
screwed it onto the muzzle of his 1911 just as the chopper began a
slow descent into a field a short distance from Darré's home.

Dewey climbed out of the chopper and flashed his hand across
his neck to the chopper pilot. It meant, shut it off and wait.

Kaiser's chopper set down on Darré's lawn, and Kaiser climbed
down. He was dressed in a gray suit, with a blue shirt and a red
tie. The wind from the rotors tousled his hair, but he walked
though the wind toward the back door of Darré's mansion.

He opened the door. He could hear a loud chorus of voices
coming from the other room. There was a dinner party going on
at Darré's mansion.

As Kaiser stepped down onto the beautifully kept lawn, he
suddenly remembered why the CIA agent was bothering him so
much. It suddenly made sense. A long forgotten order, dispatched
to one of the families. Kill the attorney general.

Tacoma. Now Kaiser remembered. He was getting old after
all. The reason the file on Tacoma struck a chord. It was because

Kaiser himself had ordered the murder of the man's father, the attorney general of the United States.

He came to the hallway outside the slightly raucous dining room and waited until a servant came down the hallway, carrying a bottle of red wine from Darré's cellar.

"Tell Mr. Darré he has a visitor. I'll be waiting in his office."

The servant nodded and pointed Kaiser to that office. Kaiser turned and walked back down the hallway. When he saw a large desk, fireplace, and several sofas and comfortable chairs, he entered.

Kaiser looked at the photos on the credenza behind Darré's desk. There were pictures of his family, skiing, on a boat somewhere, standing in front of a Christmas tree.

Kaiser heard the footsteps, even on carpet.

"Hello, Bruno," said Kaiser, still staring at the photographs. "You have a beautiful family."

"What do you want?" said Darré. "How dare you show up unannounced. You have no idea what you could have interrupted! I am in the middle of a goddam dinner party with some very important clients."

"You're actually in the middle of an American plot to destroy the Russian mafia," said Kaiser. "A CIA plot."

"This mess is all your fault. You were the one who ordered us to have O'Flaherty and Blake killed," said Darré.

"Which is exactly why you are in the middle of this," said Kaiser. He took several steps toward Darré, coming within striking range. "I don't give a fuck about your dinner party. Or your very important clients." He pointed to the door. "You have an American agent on this property. Not only did you fail to eliminate him, you actually let him into your home. Really, you are the worst kind of idiot."

CHAPTER 69

Darré Estate
Greenwich, Connecticut

As Igor set off the dead man's cell phone, and the chime rico-cheted across the quiet canopy, Tacoma watched the gunmen through the scope, registering the fact that all three men turned their heads. In that moment, Tacoma started running toward the gunman to his right. Tacoma fired and the bullet struck the side of the man's skull, just above his ear.

The groan was low, and the next killer heard it, and his sudden movement, in turn, caused the third killer to pivot.

Tacoma sprinted toward the man he just shot—moving the fire selector to full auto—just as the remaining killers pivoted toward him. By the time they were about to fire at Tacoma, he pumped the trigger. A spray of metal staccato—hushed by a suppressor—signaled the fusillade Tacoma unleashed. The two men dropped, the loudest sound having been the ringing of the killer's cell phone.

Tacoma walked silently toward the main house. Tacoma felt it now. He knew it. There was a man, and he was an evil man.

He was the one behind it all, the one who'd ordered Cosgrove's hanging.

Now, that person was inside Darré's mansion.

Tacoma crossed the expansive lawn, looking for movement, but seeing nothing. He was soon at the back terrace of the mansion, and could see the two figures talking inside Darré's brightly lit office.

Darré took a step forward, walking directly at Kaiser.

"I'm not an idiot," said Darré, pointing at Kaiser. "You guys blackmailed me. Who did I let onto my property? That's my business. It's my goddam property. How do you know he's even a spy? That kid is just another poorly educated Russian criminal—and they're a dime a dozen."

Kaiser removed a large pistol from inside his coat.

"That dumb Russian kid?" said Kaiser slowly, in a thick Russian accent. "That dumb Russian kid is actually Robert Tacoma, a high-level CIA asset, who killed Andrei Volkov and at least ten of his men. That dumb Russian kid infiltrated his way all the way up to you, Bruno. And he's right here on your estate. You let the fox into the henhouse."

Darré stared at the gun.

"Don't do this, Kaiser," said Darré, shaking his head, imploring Kaiser. "Whatever happened, I'm sorry. If I let someone get close to me, that was a mistake, but you need to take responsibility for your own reckless decisions."

"That's why I'm here," said Kaiser. He chambered a bullet and stepped closer. "I'm cleaning up one of my reckless decisions."

"*So let's go kill him!*" begged Darré.

Kaiser paced slowly through the middle of the room, keeping

Darré trapped to one side. He had no escape. Kaiser took a long, cylindrical suppressor and threaded it into the muzzle of his pistol. He aimed it at Darré.

"Tacoma is already dead," said Kaiser. "I brought men with me, the sort of men who do not get fooled by some American spy."

"We can rebuild this. It's not too late."

"It's not too late, you're right," said Kaiser. "But I'm afraid there must be a scapegoat. Surely you understand this?"

"*What are you saying?*" yelled Darré.

"We'll tie everything back to you," said Kaiser. "The assassinations, the deaths of the two American CIA agents—Cosgrove and Tacoma. We'll tie it around you like a bow."

Darré looked nervously around his office, at photos along the credenza, books lining the shelves, at a pair of tan leather Barcelona chairs. He couldn't believe it. It wasn't possible. How could it all end up like this? Could this really be his last few seconds on earth.

"I did everything you asked," said Darré, a look of anger on his face, no fear, no other emotion, just pure hatred.

"But sometimes this is what we ask," said Kaiser. "Your sacrifice is not unappreciated," said Kaiser as his finger started to pull back on the trigger.

Darré winced at the metallic *thwack* of suppressed gunfire. He reached for his chest, reached to where the bullet should be.

But he felt nothing.

Instead, Kaiser let out a low, deep groan.

Darré looked at his hand—expecting blood—but his hand came back dry.

His eyes found Kaiser. The big Russian was clutching his right hip. He still held the pistol, though it was aimed at the carpet as he struggled to keep from falling.

"So, I hear Tacoma is dead," said Tacoma. "Sorry, I was eavesdropping."

Darré and Kaiser looked to the door. Standing in the door that led to the backyard was Tacoma. He held the MP7 and had it trained on Kaiser.

"Drop your gun," Tacoma said. "Drop it, or this time I'll aim for your fucking head."

Kaiser was hurt, and seemed to struggle. He moved slowly and deliberately, signaling to Tacoma that he was putting the pistol down on the ground. But it happened suddenly. Instead of putting it down, Kaiser lifted his gun and fired. The silenced bullet spat from the pistol—*thwap*—and tore into Darré's forehead, sending his body toppling to the floor, dead.

Kaiser pivoted the weapon at Tacoma.

It was the man he was looking for.

Each stood, in momentary silence, holding the other in the crosshairs.

Tacoma fired—but the mag clicked empty.

There was a momentary lull, then Kaiser spoke, as he raised the suppressed pistol and targeted it at Tacoma's head.

"*U tebya vpechatlyayushchiye navyki, moy drug,*" said Kaiser.

You have impressive skills, my friend.

"You're pretty cute yourself," said Tacoma, dropping the MP7. "I must've miscounted. I swear I thought I had another one. I guess it took a few extra to kill all those guys you brought."

"The problem is," said Kaiser, "we both heard your mag click empty. You are done. I'm almost sorry it had to end this way."

Kaiser held the suppressor up, targeting Tacoma's forehead, and stepped closer to Tacoma, who stared back with a cold, emotionless look. The sound of breaking glass came a second before Kaiser let out a howl, as a bullet from outside the house struck him in the right shoulder, kicking Kaiser sideways and down to the carpet. He didn't move.

Tacoma was frozen for a moment and then looked to the door. Dewey was dark faced with camo. He held Kaiser in the crosshairs of his Colt .45, but Kaiser didn't move. He was dead.

Dewey walked to Tacoma.

"Hector said you needed some adult supervision," said Dewey.

Tacoma grinned, and for a split second felt a deep sense of relief. Then his eyes saw movement on the floor. Kaiser. Tacoma tried to push Dewey out of the way just as a low, brassy *thwap* echoed in the room. Tacoma felt the bullet hit him in the chest, mostly the pressure, because the pain went from acute to surreal quickly. He fell backward. Tacoma looked down at his chest and saw dark blood, gurgling from a hole in his chest.

When he looked up, he saw Dewey with a look of horror on his face. Dewey reached for him. As Tacoma was about to lose consciousness, he looked past Dewey to Kaiser. Kaiser climbed to his feet, dripping blood from his hip and shoulder. He was a monster in size. Kaiser charged out the back door to the terrace just as the wind picked up and the noise level elevated. The Super Puma pivoted down and touched the terrace just outside the room, the skilled pilot leaving mere inches between the ends of the blades and the roof. Kaiser climbed aboard and the helicopter lifted up into the air.

Dewey tapped his earbud, then said: "Hector."

"Yeah."

"Rob's been shot in the chest. We need to get him under a surgeon in the next hour or so. He's bleeding badly."

"Is he still alive?"

"Yes."

"That means they didn't hit his heart," said Calibrisi. "I'll line someone up. Tell the pilot to bring him to Columbia Presbyterian."

"You got it. See you there."

CHAPTER 70

Columbia Presbyterian Hospital
New York, New York

The helicopter soared toward Manhattan, carrying Tacoma, who was unconscious and bleeding badly. Dewey kept his hand over the wound, pressing down to try and keep the blood inside Tacoma.

The chopper landed on the roof of Columbia Presbyterian Hospital, in the middle of the night. A team of medics was waiting, holding a stretcher. They ran Tacoma into a brightly lit operating room, populated by a number of nurses, surgeons, and anaesthesiologists. As soon as they moved Tacoma to the stainless steel operating table, a tall man with blond hair, one of the surgeons, pounced and took control, slashing into Tacoma's chest as various people injected Tacoma with needles and someone else slammed an oxygen mask on his face.

"What do you got, Roger?"

"He's alive."

"How alive?"

"Heartbeat is strong."

"Let's get some designer blood in there, Carol," said Page as his fingers started to dig around inside the cavity he'd just cut. "It's in the lung. Someone get me an XS. Get the sutures ready. We're going to do this quickly, before his heart starts giving up."

CHAPTER 71

Vertag Avenue
Berlin, Germany

By the time Kaiser was driven to the clinic, he appeared pale.

They put him down on the table and two separate surgeons cut in, despite the fact that there was no anaesthesia. One cut a bullet from his shoulder as the other surgeon removed one from Kaiser's hip. Kaiser let out not even a groan, even though he wasn't in shock. After they sutured him up, he climbed off the stainless steel table.

"Vodka," Kaiser panted, sweat dripping from his face. *"Get me a bottle of vodka!"*

CHAPTER 72

Columbia Presbyterian Hospital
New York, New York

Tacoma lay in bed, with a network of wires, IVs, and various other apparatuses meshed around him.

He was awake. He looked around the hospital room. He saw Katie first, reading a magazine. Then Calibrisi, seated on a chair, legs crossed, looking at him. Igor was in a chair in the corner, typing into a laptop. Finally, Tacoma's eyes found Dewey, standing next to the bed. Tacoma realized that Dewey's hand was clutching his arm, shaking it, digging his fingers in. He'd been shaking Tacoma.

"Hey, bud," said Dewey.

Tacoma nodded, barely getting out a whisper.

"Hey."

"I've got some good news and some bad news. What do you want first?"

Tacoma stared back at Dewey with a blank expression, various tubes and IVs sticking into him. He was dazed.

"Okay, I'll make the decision," said Dewey. "Let's start with the good news. The good news is you're alive and—when they were digging around in there—they found out you have a heart. The bad news is, the surgeon left his phone in there and is going to have to go back in. Also, everyone in the Russian mafia wants to kill you."

Tacoma grinned, feeling a sharp pain in his chest.

"You're not supposed to laugh for a few weeks," said Dewey. "They're apparently afraid your padookis might fall off. They had a hard time finding it. They needed a magnifying glass."

Tacoma laughed, then immediately winced again.

"Where am I?" he whispered.

"Columbia Presbyterian," said Calibrisi.

"Did you get him?"

Dewey shook his head, no.

"No, Kaiser got away," said Calibrisi. "But now we know who we're up against. For someone who's been invisible, that can't make him happy."

"Kaiser might not be dead, but he's no longer a ghost," said Katie. "We also avenged O'Flaherty, Blake, and Cosgrove."

"It was a damn good start," said Calibrisi.

Tacoma couldn't hide his disappointment.

The door opened and a tall man with a shock of blond hair stepped in. He was young, in his thirties, and wore light-blue surgical garb and a white surgeon's coat.

"Sorry to interrupt but I heard you were awake, Rob. I'm Fred Page," said the doctor. "I'm the one who operated on you."

Tacoma stared at Page.

"The bullet went through your left lung," said Page. "We were able to repair most of it, but it's going to hurt for a while, mainly because we had to cut through a bunch of muscle to dig out what was left of the bullet."

"How long do I have to be here?"

"A week or two."

"Thanks," said Tacoma.

"I'm going to continue my rounds, but I'll check back on you," said Page, then he turned and left.

The nurse came in with a tray and said, "It's dinnertime."

The tray was piled with orange Jell-O, a scoop of mashed potatoes, and an unappealing, unidentifiable gray meat. The nurse set it down in front of Tacoma and said, "Eat up. You need your strength."

Dewey looked at the tray and shuddered. He turned to Calibrisi and Katie.

"I think Rob needs some rest."

"Yeah, I agree," said Calibrisi.

"I could go for a steak," said Dewey. "A big, juicy ribeye."

Dewey and Calibrisi started laughing as Tacoma stared down at the tray. They stood up and walked to the door.

"New York City has some excellent steak houses," said Calibrisi, rubbing it in. "Though if you don't mind I'd rather not go to Sparks."

"We'll bring you a doggy bag," said Dewey. "A bone. You can chew on it tomorrow while you're watching soap operas."

Tacoma smiled, then winced. Katie, however, remained seated with a serious expression.

"I'm going to stay here and keep Rob company," she said.

"You don't have to, Katie," said Tacoma weakly.

Katie put her hand in the pocket of her blazer. She felt the butt of a pistol.

"I know I don't have to," said Katie. "Maybe I want to."

But Katie did have to. Someone had to.

Katie imagined Kaiser, Volkov, and the men at the airport Rob killed, the men who were trying to kill him. She thought of Audra and Slokavich, of Darré and the small army of corpses left at his estate. Katie knew that though this chapter was over, the war with the Russian mafia was only just beginning. They couldn't rest. As long as Rob Tacoma was on American soil, he was in danger. As long as he was alive, he was in danger. He would always be in danger.

Calibrisi paused near the doorway. He sighed.

"There are four FBI agents posted outside the room," said Calibrisi, as if anticipating her concerns. "Four more in the lobby, not to mention a bunch of NYPD."

"As long as there are men like Kaiser out there, there will be traitors like Peter Lehigh," said Katie.

Calibrisi glanced at Dewey. The odds of someone getting to Tacoma were incredibly small, but they both knew she was right. Suddenly, they lost their enthusiasm for a big steak dinner at a fancy restaurant. They also felt slightly guilty for giving Tacoma flack. They stepped back near Tacoma's bed and sat down.

A small television showed a college football game, though the volume was down. All four sat in silence, watching the game.

Finally, it was Dewey who broke the silence.

"Hey," said Dewey, getting Tacoma's attention. He pointed at the gray pile of meat on the plate. "You gonna eat that?"

Acknowledgments

The Russian is the first book in a new thriller series. As such, it required me to start all over from the beginning. After writing eight books in the Dewey Andreas series, I assumed the ninth would be easy. Instead, it was as hard to write as my first book, *Power Down*, a decade ago. While I'm not complaining, I would be negligent if I were to not adequately thank the people whose encouragement and understanding enabled me to finish this book.

First and foremost, thank you, Nicole Kenealy James and Keith Kahla, my agent and editor, respectively, for your guidance, support, and incredible patience. I couldn't have done it without you, and those aren't just words.

To Sally Richardson, Jen Enderlin, Andrew Martin, George Witte, Martin Quinn, Lisa Senz, Paul Hochman, Jenn Gonzalez, Hector DeJean, Rafal Gibek, Amelie Littell, Mary Beth Roche, Robert Allen, Alice Pfeifer, and everyone at St. Martin's Press and Macmillan Audio, thank you for your continued confidence in me.

Thanks also to Chris George, Rorke Denver, and Ari Fialkos.

To my family: Charlie, who ten years ago carried coffee to me in his pajamas as I wrote and now is in college and a wonderful sounding board for plot ideas. Teddy, who, when I was working on *Power Down*, would come in and demand that I take him to Dunkin' Donuts, and who, as I wrote *The Russian*, would come in and demand that I take him to Dunkin' Donuts. Oscar, who, way back then, would climb onto my lap wearing his sleepers to snuggle and keep warm and who now lets me climb on his lap in my sleepers to snuggle and keep warm. Esmé, who was just a smiling little peanut way back then and is a smiling big peanut now, albeit a peanut with a sailor's vocab and a right hook not to be trifled with. Thank you, guys, I love you.

Finally, to Shannon, my wonderful and beautiful wife, thank you for continuing to be the compass that guides me through it all.

Wellesley, Massachusetts 2019